The Four Winds

DAVID BEATY

THE FOUR WINDS

WILLIAM MORROW AND COMPANY, *New York*

Published in the Dominion of Canada
by George J. McLeod Limited, Toronto
Printed in the United States of America
Library of Congress Catalog Card Number: 54-10300

CONTENTS

The Four Winds

The first sign that an aircraft is overtaking the south-east quadrant of a storm is often a swell on an otherwise calm sea, which may extend over a thousand miles from the seat of the disturbance. Tufts of cirrus form the windswept ends of a thin haze hanging high over the sky, producing haloes or rings around the sun and the moon. Gradually, this cloud thickens into globular alto-cumulus, which in its turn is hammered out into a leaden sheet of alto-stratus. Deeper into the storm, a steep drop in atmospheric pressure accompanies a tremendous increase in the strength of the winds. Ominous clumps of cumulo-nimbus tower out of a low grey base of nimbo-stratus. Visibility is poor in a continuous downpour of heavy rain.

Suddenly, the rain stops and the wind dies down to nothing. Now, in the centre of the storm, there is a tiny circle of quietness, where the sky is usually broken or cloudless.

It is immediately followed by the sharp end of the north-west quadrant, called by mariners "dangerous" because the winds, now gusting in the reverse direction, tend to blow a ship onto the storm's track. From a confused mass of cumulo-nimbus and low stratus, rain falls in torrents onto a furious sea. By degrees, this heavy precipitation dries up to a cold misty drizzle. Then, as the outer edge of the quadrant is reached, the wind slackens and the cloud base rises, giving way to alto-stratus and cirrus. There is a line of light on the horizon that promises a clear sky for the pilot. But for the forecaster, the problem remains: where will the storm move next?

Book One

The Beginning of the South-East Quadrant

October 15

1

A hurricane in the Caribbean Sea, nicknamed Felicity after the whimsical manner of meteorological officers, had made a brief and spectacular appearance as a series of closely packed concentric circles on all the weather charts of the world. For three days it had steamed as leisurely as a paddle-steamer towards Cuba and Miami. There seemed every likelihood that it would follow the well-worn path of its ancestors up the American seaboard, and recurve to the right, south of Newfoundland. But suddenly, it disappeared. For a week, no sign of it was reported. The forecasters said it had decayed, spun itself out, committed suicide. Felicity, however, was very much alive. Instead of moving west, like a big black sheep it had strayed in the opposite direction. In the middle of a deserted Atlantic, far away from the shipping lanes, it had dawdled and sunned itself. Then it had started, stealthily and unseen, to move north-east towards the Azores.

By now, it was middle-aged and had begun to spread. The speed of its terrifying roundabout had dropped from a hundred miles an hour to a little less than eighty. It was half-way through mellowing into a severe storm. But its influence was far greater. Huge areas of sea began to feel its presence, and in the air above them the winds were being dictated by the furious counterclockwise circulation round its quiet heart. And instead of moving at a sedate eight knots, it was shooting across the Atlantic faster than the most modern destroyer at full speed.

Felicity gave little warning. Weather-ship Easy, stationed near the middle of the two-thousand miles separating Bermuda from the Azores, started to pitch and roll in a sudden swell. Before the meteorologists on board could work out the cause, the morning sky darkened, and the north-west corner of the storm was upon them. In a Marlborough aircraft, G-AHEZ, of British Empire Airways, flying at nineteen thousand feet from Bermuda to the Azores, a navigating officer called Bates had just plotted an astro-fix on the chart in front of him. He pencilled in the wind that the position had given him, a little arrow from the north-east. He looked at it, shook his head, and then rubbed it out. He climbed once more into the astro-dome, and taking the sextant in his hands, called up to the cockpit, "Keep her steady again, Skipper, please. I'm taking another. That one was up the pole."

From his place in the left-hand pilot's seat, Mark Kelston turned round. A glimmer of amusement showed only in the deepening of the two little wakes of wrinkles at the corners of his grey eyes.

"What's the matter . . . Mrs. Bates on your mind?"

The navigator grinned good-humouredly back at the captain. Throughout the Mid-Atlantic section of Empire Airways, which ran between Panama and London, with stops at Jamaica, Bermuda, the Azores, Lisbon and Madrid, Number Two, the port inner engine, was known as Mrs. Bates. It was the only one he could see from his desk, and he spent a good deal of his time keeping a watchful eye on it. Already on this trip he had had a difference of opinion with the engineer officer, Hawkins, on what he considered the sickly yellow colour of the flame from its exhaust.

"No, sir," he said, "Mrs. Bates is doing fine."

Hawkins interrupted his vigil over the engine instruments. "Which means, Skipper, Mr. Bates hasn't had the baby . . . yet."

"No, nothing to do with babies. It was only a sun and moon fix . . . and the moon's too low for an accurate shot. Might well be wrong." Bates looked wistfully at the black steel box which hung over the navigation table. The control knob was switched to "Off." "We're out of Loran range—worst luck." That bulky oblong direction finder could give almost pin-point positions to aircraft well over a thousand miles away. But the Loran ground stations were mostly in America, too far away to be of use to him now.

Up at the front, Kelston was looking intently towards the horizon, south-east of Easy Zebra. Suddenly, what appeared to be a big black bruise had darkened the clear blue skin of the sky. Then, as the aircraft approached nearer to it, he saw an immense carpet of cloud formations, stretching towards every point of the compass. There was a pattern about those clouds which was not as careless or haphazard as he might expect from the inconsequential weather that had been forecast for their flight. It was a pattern he saw very rarely. But he knew the design by heart.

The navigator had finished taking his sights now. Kelston called back to him, "What was the matter with your position, Mr. Bates? Did it show a strong north-east wind?"

Bates' eyes showed a child-like surprise.

"That's right, Skipper . . . dead right. Ninety knots from zero four five degrees."

"I've got a feeling you're slandering that last fix. Have you noticed the clouds on the starboard quarter?"

"No, Skipper."

"Well . . . come up and have a look at 'em."

Bates left the navigation compartment and walked up into the cockpit, past Hawkins on the right, making up his hourly log on the readings of the instruments. He saw Draper, the radio officer, busy sending the last position of the aircraft to São Miguel ground station, which had now accepted control of them. The first officer was off watch, asleep. In accordance with Kelston's custom (most other captains believed in two-hour watches) after the take-off he had done the first four hours from Bermuda.

"Careful you don't wake Mr. Shaughnessy." There was the slightest tinge of exasperation in Kelston's voice. Mr. Shaughnessy was very new. He was one of a whole batch of young and very inexperienced first officers that had been lately posted to the line. "Mr. Shaughnessy needs all the sleep he can get."

"These growing boys, Skipper." Bates looked back at the captain and gave a knowing little grunt of amusement. It was odd how someone sleeping seemed always to cut such a comical figure. More so, on an aircraft. Then he looked out of the cockpit windows to the right, and the indulgent smile which had been forming on his face abruptly disappeared. "Christ," he said.

Now only a few miles ahead of the aircraft, a wispy veil of white cirro-stratus hung high above them. Then, towards the south, the cloud rapidly thickened. What Bates saw looked like an X-ray photograph of the skeleton of the sky. Regular alto-cumulus made a neat grey pattern of rib bones, gradually merging into the dirty dark mass of the intestines of a storm. Above everything else, still visible well over a hundred miles from the aircraft, towered massive clumps of jet-black cumulo-nimbus heads.

"Never seen them as high as that, Skipper," Bates said.

"No . . . about thirty thousand feet, I should say. They were the first things I saw."

Easy Zebra seemed to sense the presence of something strange. Very gently, she started to buck and bump. The wings shook, and gave the engines a jerk which disturbed the synchronization of the four propellers. There was a momentary uneven roughness that vibrated the pilots' instrument panel, as Hawkins smoothed them out again on the switches.

The noise was enough to wake Mr. Shaughnessy. He blinked his eyes, squeezing them tight together, as though to wring the sleep out of them. But when they were fully open again, they were still glazed over with sleep-shocked, innocent unawareness of the past or the present or the future.

Then he, too, saw the cloud. "Looks like some bad weather, Skipper." He said the words professionally and pompously, as though he was translating unconcernedly out of a text-book signs that meant bad weather for someone, but never for him.

"Nice work . . . spotting that," Bates said gravely, and gave him a light pat on the back. "They certainly seem to put you through the hoop on meteorology . . . these days."

Kelston saw the boy go red. "Don't mind Mr. Bates," he said. "*He* had to have the stuff pointed out to him." Then he looked up at the fraying cirro-stratus ends that strung out above them. "Better get another astro-fix, while you can. Cloud's thickening. Might not see the sun again for the rest of the trip."

"Shall I work out the other one first?" Bates asked.

"Not the time. Get the shots now. Then we'll have three fixes, fairly close to each other. So we can cross-check."

Bates went back to the astro-dome, and again started to measure the altitude of the sun. It was shining through a layer of cloud, like a round yellow ball surrounded by a halo of blue and red and green. By manipulating the altitude control, he kept that ball within the bubble that served as an artificial horizon for the instrument. The clock-work mechanism whirred on for two minutes, averaging out the readings to compensate for the slight roll and hunt of the aircraft. When it stopped, Bates noted down the mean time of the shot, 13 hours 46 minutes and 15 seconds, and the altitude 39 degrees, 11 minutes. Then he turned his attention to the pale slice of moon, low down on the eastern horizon.

Sitting with his eyes glued to the weather in front of him, Shaughnessy shyly suggested, "Might make us late on flight plan, sir."

"Will do. The winds will change to easterlies pretty soon . . . dead on our nose. Good thing we were able to leave Bermuda well ahead of schedule."

"Not forecast was it, sir?" Shaughnessy's tone implied a righteous indignation with meteorological officers.

"No. But these things have a habit of jumping up from nowhere. Not much Met. data round here. Got to be prepared to meet 'em."

"Any chance of going round it?"

"Looks too big. Anyway . . . I haven't the fuel to try."

The first officer looked out again, and saw the starboard wing was now being bandaged by loose folds of wet woolly cloud. With a faint feeling of surprise, he realized this storm was, after all, going to be part of his future. He shivered slightly. "Could be nasty, sir," he said. "So big . . . and so sudden."

Kelston shrugged his shoulders without concern. "On this job . . . these things happen." He leant forward and scrutinized the minute crystals of opaque frost that were forming on the windscreen. "Mr. Hawkins," he said. "Watch the fuel flows for carburettor ice. And I think we'll have the alcohol on the props." The aircraft started to bump a little more heavily. "Mr. Bates," Kelston called back. "You might tell the steward to warn the passengers we're approaching bumpy weather and see they're all strapped in."

With these few, unhurried preparations, Kelston was fitting out Easy Zebra to face the storm. Tiny fragments of ice might form on the impact tubes inside the carburettor, cutting off the petrol from the engines, and causing them suddenly to cut dead. But before this happened, the instrument recording the fuel flowing to the engine would give a tell-tale drop. If that drop was small, alcohol (a liquid with a freezing point of −130 degrees centigrade) could be sprayed into the tubes. In much the same way, it could also be sent over the propellers to prevent ice getting a grip and spoiling their bite into the air. If the drop on the fuel flows was large and quick, the whole carburettor could be enveloped in a melting blanket of hot air, drawn from the exhausts. There were just two snags to an otherwise admirable arrangement. Easy Zebra carried only twenty gallons of alcohol. And hot air increased her petrol consumption at the same time as it decreased the power on her engines. Both could, therefore, only be used sparingly.

Now and again, Kelston gave a glance at the wings. As yet there was no sign of white on them. That was another hazard —air-frame icing, which would increase the weight of the aircraft, and spoil its aerodynamic performance.

Bates had now worked out both the last sights. The results of his calculations were two little pencilled crosses, not very far from each other, or from the original position, the accuracy of which he had doubted. The wind was strong northeasterly all right. With a mixture of admiration and respect, Bates glanced through the cockpit door at the unmoving broad shoulders of the captain of the aircraft.

If Featherstone, the flight captain, had been the skipper, by now he would have been clucking round the navigation compartment as though it was a barnyard, worrying about their position, harrying the engineer for figures of fuel consumed and fuel available. Another captain on the route, Ferris, would have laughed with almost hyena-like exultation. His orange moustache would have quivered. "Good show, chaps," he would have said. He seemed to have his own private feud with the weather. It was a fight in which Bates had no desire to get involved. Captain Leeming on the other hand, in a similar situation, would have said, "I'll do the navigation now," and would have pushed Bates right out of his own seat. That man never seemed to trust anybody, Bates reflected.

With Kelston, there was just complete calm. The weather might have been a perfect example of an idyllic afternoon for all the difference it seemed to make to him. Among the crews who flew with him, he was nicknamed the Iron Man, partly because no one had ever seen him shaken, partly because he was always pretty sharp with any crew member who made a mistake, and could be ruthlessly hard on anyone who made the same mistake twice. For that reason, some of the aircrew fought shy of flying with him. Not Bates. Always mindful of the safekeeping of that part of his anatomy which he called "the ass that nobody's interested in but me," it was an attitude to the job which had Bates' whole-hearted approval. Only two years ago, he had lost his best friend, Lonsdale, when a Marlborough disappeared completely off Gibraltar on this same route.

On this trip, everyone had been right up to scratch, apart from the new first officer, whom Kelston was obviously nursing. So it was with an unruffled and good-humoured quietness on the flight deck that Easy Zebra nosed into the wicked-looking mass of grey water-vapour that formed the outskirts of Felicity, and submitted suddenly and almost meekly to being pitched and tossed all over the cloud-filled sky.

"Throttle back to twenty inches manifold pressure, Mr. Hawkins," Kelston said.

"Twenty inches, sir," Hawkins echoed, as he eased the power off the engines from the throttles in his position.

The needle on the air-speed indicator crept back, and then fluctuated violently round a mean of 160 knots. If Easy Zebra tried to negotiate those high speed up-currents too fast, there was as much danger of structural damage as if she had hit something far more solid than air; too slow, the lightning changes in her attitude and speed might cause her to stall. Already she was becoming difficult to hold. The rate of climb indicator soared to four thousand feet a minute upwards one minute, then crashed down to a descent so steep that it was beyond the reading of the instrument. Kelston let her ride it out as though she was a wild and untamed colt, frightened by shock. It was useless fighting a force a million times more powerful than he had at his command. Easy Zebra banged up and down with the resilience and persistence of a bouncing rubber ball.

"Any more for the roller coaster?" Hawkins called out. "The Big Dipper. All the thrills in the world . . . at no extra charge."

From the navigation compartment, Bates said wryly, "Fly *above* the weather in a fully pressurized Marlborough of British Empire Airways."

Kelston held the control column tightly. It was jerking up and down now, and from side to side. He kept his eye on the gyro-controlled artificial horizon in front of him. When a wing dropped suddenly and the bar tilted up at a crazy angle, he gently pulled up on the spectacle-shaped aileron control to ease it back level. Without that instrument to help him, Easy Zebra could almost turn on her back and he would be none the wiser, so inefficient is the human sense of position relative to the ground when it cannot check on the yardstick of the horizon.

Illuminated streams of rain rattled down over the windscreen, writing weird neon-lighted hieroglyphics on the glass in front of them.

"Any ice forming your side, Mr. Shaughnessy?" Kelston asked.

"No, sir. None I can see."

Number Two engine coughed slightly. Kelston saw the boost pressure drop off. He looked round at Hawkins, as though to say something, but before he spoke the engineer called out, "Carburettor ice." He moved four levers slowly away from him. "All four in hot air, sir." Then Hawkins smiled at Bates' face, which had suddenly looked up from his chart. "Nearly lost her that time, Ricky."

"If you can't do better than that, Hawkins," Bates said, "I'll have to give up my navigation. And take over your panel."

Hawkins covered his eyes with his hand. "God help us all then."

"God help us all now . . . there'll be no more positions for the rest of the trip, I reckon."

Not that Bates was worried—they would stay up really high until they were nearly on top of the São Miguel Range Station, and then let down. He added, "Here's a new course . . . give it to the skipper. Zero-eight-three degrees." He mouthed the sound of the figures slowly, as though he was tasting them, chewing them over. "We've been blown eighty miles south of track already."

The engineer took the slip of paper, and passed it to the front. "If you'd only stick to your job, Ricky . . . instead of trying to do mine as well . . . things like that wouldn't happen."

"Had the Met. winds been right, Hawkins—"

"If the Met. winds were always right, there'd be no point carrying a navigator."

Bates considered that one for a moment. "For once, Hawkins, I agree with you. But that day will never come."

"For the sake of your bread and butter, Ricky . . . better touch wood."

Bates touched the navigation table. "For many things," he said.

By now, Easy Zebra was well in the grey mass of Felicity's enormous web. For such a frail-looking cockleshell, she was showing an almost impudent unconcern. The storm had the punch of more than four atom bombs, attenuated maybe by the wide area of its structure, but still powerful and still dangerous. Great unseen hands seemed to clutch out of the grey blankness in a grab for the aircraft. But each time, Easy Zebra just shivered in all her thin eighth of an inch plates, soared up or plunged down, squirming out of the storm's grip. Although outside an icy wind roared at over ninety miles an hour, within the aircraft's fuselage there was no other sound but the accustomed steady humming of her motors and the clatter of the rain on her metal skin.

Inside, certainly it was impossible to walk. The lunch the steward had been about to serve was indefinitely postponed. Most of the sixteen passengers on board felt ill. A Mr. Parkinson, a Very Important Person, a member of numerous political boards (Kelston had had a note from the company, requesting him to see that Mr. Parkinson "had a comfortable trip"), strapped and imprisoned in his seat, had been sick in a most undignified way. But these things were very minor. Slowed down considerably by the winds against her, Easy Zebra still managed to slip through the storm at over a hundred and sixty miles an hour. Down in the Atlantic, a little further to the east, a Portuguese tramp steamer called the *Santa Lucinda* was not so fortunate. Her plates were many times as strong as Easy Zebra's. Her weight was two thousand tons compared to the aircraft's forty. But she moved the way the storm pushed her, her engine room flooded by the endless sea. Felicity had, after all, caught something in its web. Something far more substantial than an outsized tin fly.

In his position behind the pilots, Radio Officer Draper was moving up against his straps every time a bounce lifted him off his seat. As a result, his log for the last half-hour was an appalling scrawl, in contrast to the neat clerical hand of the first part of the trip. The earphones were jammed over his head, and he was listening hard. A sad little rhythm of dots and dashes, not unlike a wood-pigeon's call in the evening, was making a badly matched fight against the crackling static of the storm.

He turned to Kelston. "Some poor bastard's sending an S O S, Skipper."

The captain had appeared to be concentrating entirely on the instruments that guided the safekeeping of Easy Zebra. Now, he allowed his mind to take in what Draper had told him, while his hands and his eyes, experienced and well-disciplined, carried on the mechanical motions of flying the aircraft through heavy turbulence.

"Ship?"

"Oh yes, Skipper . . . ship. Name's the *Santa Lucinda.*" In Draper's mind, that was that. A ship in its own element should be well able to take care of herself. He would have expected surface vessels to alter course to go to the help of an aircraft in danger of falling out of the sky. An aeroplane, after all, was a butterfly form of travel, the delicate youngest child of transportation. The distance she could go was severely limited. Special Air-Sea Rescue aircraft certainly might be used for such rescue operations. But an ordinary airliner could only look after herself.

Kelston jolted these thoughts clean out of his mind. "You got the position of her?"

"A position? Yes . . . she did send a position."

"Give it to Mr. Bates to plot on his chart. I want to know how far away she is."

"But a couple of tugs have already left Ponta Delgada, Skipper." Draper's voice implied that this was none of their business.

"All the same . . . do as I tell you."

There was a muffled interchange between Draper and Bates. Then the navigator shouted up, "She's about thirty miles south of our track, Skipper . . . only twenty miles from the harbour of São Miguel. Still over three hours' flying away, if this damned head wind keeps up."

"Thanks, Mr. Bates."

The navigator looked at the captain anxiously. If it had

been Ferris, he thought, any fool thing could happen. But Kelston was steady. Bates had always found him sensible.

However, he saw no harm in pointing out, "We'll be over an hour late, Skipper."

"I'd expected something like that."

"And our own position . . ." Bates made a helpless shrugging gesture at the cocoon of violent air that now smothered them.

"We should get Horta Beacon," Kelston said.

Bates looked doubtful. "If the static isn't too bad."

"Static's terrible, sir," Draper said promptly.

That was another trick Felicity had up its sleeve. The jumbling electrical interference might howl down the signal sent from a beacon, and could pull the needle on the radio compass far away from pointing to the station.

Kelston appeared to take no notice of them. "Work out a fuel state for me, Mr. Hawkins, please," he said. Then he added to Shaughnessy, "They'll have a tough job finding her . . . in weather like this."

The first officer didn't answer. He was gazing in hypnotized fascination at the way the leading edge of the starboard wing was furring up with a deposit of millions of tiny diamond-coloured crystals.

"Ice, Skipper." He tried to keep his voice from sounding excited.

"Bit on the windscreen, too," Kelston said. He put on the windscreen anti-icers, and watched the alcohol seep over the glass, mixing in with the sleet.

He asked Shaughnessy, "How much on your wing?"

"About an inch . . . but it's still building up."

Kelston looked down at the temperature gauge for the outside air. It was very high for the altitude at this time of year—minus fourteen degrees. Hawkins had heard the magic word *ice,* and he struggled out of his seat to look for himself. When the stuff started to form on an aircraft, something had to be done. Fast.

"Going to go up, Skipper?" the engineer asked. "I reckon the old tub'll reach twenty-three thousand. At this weight." He had looked in the maintenance log book and found Easy Zebra was just recently off a Check Four, a thorough overhaul done every twelve hundred hours' flying.

"No, down. Mr. Draper, get me a clearance from Control to descend to eleven thousand feet." Then he noticed that the radio officer was busy sending, and he waited, while Hawkins and Shaughnessy impatiently watched the cloud paint another layer of ice on the wing. As Easy Zebra started to take on this extra frozen cargo, her weight increased. The jagged edges of the formation were spoiling the flying properties of her wings. The needle of the air-speed indicator now fluttered around 150 knots.

"Lost nearly ten knots already," Hawkins muttered to the first officer.

Kelston heard him and smiled. "Still another fifty knots to go before we actually stall, Mr. Hawkins," he said. "Have you got those fuel figures yet?"

"I've nearly finished them, Skipper."

Just then Draper's hand suddenly started to push against Hawkins' substantial body, which was blocking the small space between the two pilots. The engineer edged to one side, and looked down at the radio officer.

"What's the matter . . . what's the rush?" he asked, as he sat down again at his panel.

"Message," Draper shouted. "Urgent. The tugs can't find the ship. Control are asking have we the fuel to help?" It was not, in Draper's opinion, a reasonable request.

"Tell 'em yes." Kelston's words snapped back at him so suddenly, Draper bounced in his seat again. Not this time from the storm. "Ask Control to clear all levels below us."

"No aircraft up, Skipper. Air-Sea Rescue at Lagens is out for weather. Gale force cross wind."

"Tell them . . . we'll be glad to help."

Hawkins turned round with the fuel figures. "Only eight thousand pounds of fuel left, Skipper," he said dubiously. "And we're still in hot air."

"Static's terrible even at this height," Draper put in. "Wouldn't be surprised if we couldn't hear a damn thing near the deck."

Bates came pushing forward from the navigation compartment. "If I can get a word in edgeways, Skipper . . . Looks like we'll be an hour and a half late over the island. The trouble now is . . . the speed."

Shaughnessy and Draper immediately looked at the airspeed indicator. It had crept back to just below 135 knots.

"Fifteen inches," Kelston called out. "Hang on to your hats . . . we're going down to find her."

The motors died down to a slow protesting grumble, as Easy Zebra's nose dipped towards the storm-tossed sea, three and a half miles below her.

2

Kelston knew that the request to search for the *Santa Lucinda* was an unusual one. Several times, aircraft had been asked to keep a look-out for a ship in difficulties near their course, which meant nothing more than a vigilant watch over the water that was almost invariably fruitless. As captain of the aircraft, his first responsibility was to the twenty-three souls on board Easy Zebra. He had already decided that he had an extra margin of safety which would be spent looking for the ship. But what was that margin in hours and minutes? And how could he use it to the best advantage? Used to splitting up his attention, part to flying (which had always to go on), part to an emergency or difficulty that had suddenly arisen, he started, as he always had to, to make his plans well in advance.

He knew it wasn't going to be easy. They were late and he would have to go slow on the petrol consumption. Then there was the question of getting down safely below the base of the storm clouds, which he reckoned would probably be about eight hundred feet. The islands of the Azores were scattered with high volcanic mountains, one of which—Pico—rose up nearly eight thousand feet into the air. And at the time she approached them, the position of Easy Zebra (due to a complete absence of radio or astro-fixes) would be anybody's guess within a circle of probability as much as a hundred miles in diameter.

"Ask Control if they've got the winds at the lower levels," he told Draper. "Should have got some information on this stuff by now."

Draper was still muttering about the static, as he keyed out Control's call-sign. "Wouldn't be surprised if I'm stone-deaf after this," he prophesied gloomily to Hawkins.

Just as they were passing through fourteen thousand feet, the air became smoother. They seemed to have emerged out of a colony of cumulo-nimbus clouds into the dank undergrowth of less violent stratus.

"D'you think you can take over, Mr. Shaughnessy?" Kelston asked.

"I'll try, sir." The boy gingerly gripped the wheel.

"See the speed doesn't go above 170 knots . . . there may be bumps . . . big ones." Kelston watched him. He was not very expert. Easy Zebra was now rolling as much from his movements on the control column as from the air currents of the storm. But even though he was heavily overcorrecting, Kelston saw that he was coping. Shaughnessy doing the flying would allow him a little more time to think. Ice was still forming, rather quicker now the temperature was approaching zero degrees centigrade. But that didn't worry Kelston particularly. The freezing level should be around five thousand feet. Below that height, they'd be able to burn the stuff off pretty fast. He was also certain that the weather over Santa Ana would be poor, but there would not be fog. The high winds would see to that, blowing a gap between the earth and the cloud which would provide reasonable visibility for landing.

He glanced at the altimeter. The needles were nearing ten thousand feet. Mindful of Pico, he told Shaughnessy, "Keep her at this height." Then he noticed that the first officer was getting more used to the sudden movements of the aircraft in the uneven air. "You're doing all right."

Shaughnessy flushed with pleasure.

"Think you can manage on your own for a while?"

"I think so, sir."

"I want a word with Bates. And I suppose the passengers better be told what we're doing."

"Seems a little smoother now, sir."

"Yes . . . but for how long?"

Kelston put his seat back, and hunching himself up to avoid the ignition switches on the roof, clambered out of the front position. There was enough room for his tall, rather lanky body to stretch full length, just behind the engineer. He felt suddenly stiff and cramped after so much heavy flying.

"Engines seem O.K.," he said to Hawkins, looking at the instruments on the panel.

"No worry there, sir."

He walked on to the navigation compartment. Bates was sitting with his arms folded. The only thing he could do now was to keep his eye on the air speed, and occasionally plot their dead-reckoning position.

"I'll tell you what I think we can do," Kelston said to him. "Even with strong easterlies, we estimate Santa Ana in about ninety-five minutes. Right?"

"Right, sir."

"Winds down here should be less. Even so . . . gives us just over an hour to search, with the fuel we've got available."

"Cutting it a bit fine, isn't it, sir?"

"We've *got* to cut it fine. Some men are down there in that sea."

Bates said nothing.

"Now the ship's only twenty miles or so off Ponta Delgada. We've got to avoid the mountains. With this static, the Horta Beacon will be bad. So I plan to go over it at ten thousand feet. Then turn out away from Pico, and make a quick descent to the sea."

"What height d'you reckon the cloud will be?"

"A thousand . . . probably less. But with this wind, it won't be on the deck."

"D'you want me to alter for Horta?"

"Yes. Pass the new course up to Shaughnessy."

"It'll make us a bit later." Bates looked none too happy.

"Number Two all right, isn't she, Mr. Bates?" Kelston asked suddenly.

"Oh yes, sir . . . Number Two's still doing fine."

"Well, then . . . what's there to worry about?"

Bates managed a grin. "Nobody's worried around here, sir."

"Good," Kelston said. "Let's hope the same goes for the passenger compartment."

But he didn't really expect it would—and it didn't. The smell in the place was nauseating. Kelston knew from experience that a quarter of his passengers would be frightened of flying in the best of conditions. In a bad storm, that percentage would increase to well over half. Standing with difficulty, trying to balance himself in the turbulence, he looked at the faces in the rows in front of him. Briefly, he tried to explain to them what he intended to do. He told them about the ship in distress, without available help to find her position. Searching for her would mean another hour or so bouncing around in the storm for them. And already they were late.

A woman with two small sick children asked, "Will it be as rough down below, Captain?"

"Rougher, I'm afraid."

A slight shudder ran through the passenger compartment. Kelston looked at them with understanding. Some of them would consider they were being heroic enough just buying a ticket on an aircraft. This off-schedule quixotism was obviously difficult to swallow.

He said gently, "You would all want us to do everything in our power to help . . . wouldn't you?"

There was a slight pause. Then a man with a well-trimmed pointed beard said, as though he was the spokesman, "Of course, Captain. Do everything you can. We'll be all right."

Mr. Parkinson, the only V.I.P. on board, said nothing. His eyes were closed. He looked very ill. It was even doubtful whether he had heard the things that Kelston had so carefully explained to them all.

Kelston made his way with difficulty back to the crew compartment. The air was again rougher. Bates sat, swinging the tuning knob of the radio compass around 294 kilocycles. "Can't get Horta yet, Skipper," he said.

For another half-hour he went on trying. The cloud was still heavy and turbulent. Then suddenly he heard the voice of the beacon, just audible above the crackling static. Dit dit da dit. Da dit da da. FY.

The navigator tried the compass position, but the needle was still being wrenched in all directions by the electricity of the storm.

"Hopeless," he called up to Kelston. "Hopeless, so far."

But gradually, as Easy Zebra plunged on with no visible reassurance that she was progressing a yard, the Morse sounds grew louder. To Bates, listening hard, it seemed almost unbelievable that there *was* anything beyond these clouds, that the world's laws of physics and motion still held good in this grey, limitless universe. As though some unseen hand was disciplining it, the needle on the radio compass started to hunt only about twenty degrees either side of dead ahead.

Seeing its performance, Bates felt more cheerful. "We're getting nearer, Skipper," he said. "Seems just slightly port. Could you alter five degrees to the left?"

"I'm following the needle now," Kelston replied. "As far as it'll let me."

Ten minutes later, the pointer steadied. Still slightly left. FY was pounding out now with a much more heartening strength. Suddenly, the needle seemed lost. It turned now one way, now the other, as though trying to make up its mind. Then decisively, it toppled over, and pointed behind them.

"Over it, sir," Bates shouted.

"So I see," Kelston said. "I'm turning onto one-three-five degrees . . . out to sea. Throttles right back."

The engines died down to nothing. "I'll have to put gear and half-flap down, Mr. Hawkins. We got to get down fast and I don't want the speed to build up. Not in this turbulence."

The pump whined as it forced the hydraulic fluid into the terrific pressure needed to put the wheels down. When they were locked, Kelston lowered the flaps. Due to their drag effect, only 140 knots showed on the indicator, yet Easy Zebra was approaching the sea at over four thousand feet a minute. Had the aircraft been aerodynamically clean at that rate of descent, the speed would have been a hundred knots more, and the aircraft's fuselage liable to heavy punishment in the inevitable collisions with the up-currents of the storm. The pressure built up uncomfortably fast, as though they were all in a vertical type of Super-Chief, hurtling downwards instead of horizontally. Bates swallowed hard, trying to clear his ears.

Even at that slow speed, Easy Zebra shook and shuddered as though she had suddenly gone mad. The pilots' panel vibrated like a steel and glass jelly, making the erratic readings of the instruments blurred and difficult to follow. The aircraft was plunging deep into the black stomach of the storm; and Felicity retched violently in an effort to dislodge her.

When the altimeter showed three thousand feet, Kelston eased up on the rate of descent, and put some power on the engines. There was one good thing, anyway, that he had noticed. The air temperature was above freezing at last. The ice over the fuselage had started to melt rapidly.

"How far d'you plan to take her down, Skipper?" Shaughnessy asked.

"Till we see something."

Kelston brought the flaps up. Then he raised the gear. Cautiously now, he felt his way slowly down. The altimeter unwound past one thousand feet. The clouds grew straggling and ragged. At six hundred feet on the radio altimeter, he suddenly saw a mass of white that contrasted sharply with the grey nimbo-stratus now breaking up around them. It was the sea.

Easy Zebra shook herself clear of the cloud, while her crew gazed down in awe at the sight below them.

They seemed to be looking down into a cauldron of boiling milk. The wind whipped up the spume and blew it over the frothy surface of the waves like steam. Easy Zebra was flying in a tiny layer of weeping visibility, sandwiched between the clouds and the sea. Rain still washed over her metal body, but it was possible to see a mile or so all round her. The wipers clanked across the pilots' windscreens. The turbulence was still bad. Now and again, an up-current hurled the aircraft five hundred feet up, blindfolding her once more in the torn hem of the cloud, or a down-draught pushed her lower over the surface of the sea.

Kelston put the minimum possible power on the engines. He brought back the revolutions to 1,500 a minute. The motors started to clank like tin cans, but they would save sixty gallons an hour. Now he was contact and could see where he was going, he turned back towards São Miguel island, on a course sent back by Bates of zero-seven-zero degrees.

He said to Draper, "Can you get the ship to transmit, so we can take a bearing?"

"I'll try, Skipper . . . conditions are pretty bad. The tugs can't contact her at all."

For half an hour, they saw nothing but the cloud and the rain and the windswept sea. Kelston's arms were weary, fighting and yielding alternately, as the stick jerked in his hands. Then Bates called up, "This is the area . . . approximately, Skipper."

"What have you got on the radio compass?"

"Santa Ana range."

"Eighty degrees to port. That's about right."

"Do you want a square search?" Bates went on.

"Well . . . as near square as we can make it in this weather. Best way possible of not missing her."

"I thought of using a visibility of a mile for the legs."

"That'll do," Kelston said.

Easy Zebra started flying on a series of short courses, every minute or so altering course at right angles, as though she was cutting a series of box-shaped Chinese puzzles in the air, with each succeeding box slightly larger than the one it contained.

Kelston stared down at the sea. He was used to this sort of work. For six years in the war, he had been a pilot in

Coastal Command, looking for submarines. His trained eyes inspected each huge white mountain of wave, looking for the dark shadow colour of a hull. There was nothing but the grey rain beating endlessly down.

"Haven't you got them to transmit yet, Mr. Draper?"

"I can just hear her now . . . very faint. It's only the bit of height we've got that's letting us get her at all. Any chance of going higher, sir?"

"None at all. We're just under the clouds as it is."

Draper said suddenly, "Try the radio compass on 500 kilocycles now, sir."

Kelston turned the tuning knob on the roof, hunting for the signal. "I can hear her . . . not very clear." He switched to the compass position, and watched the needle. It wavered, hesitated. Then pointed thirty degrees to the left.

"That may not be accurate, Skipper," Draper said. "He seems to have a very weak transmitter."

"Time to turn," Bates called up. "New course two-six-one degrees."

"Less than an hour's fuel left, sir," Hawkins reminded him.

By no visible indication did Kelston show that he was absorbing the information that kept pouring helpfully on him from all sides. But his mind took it in and correlated it all, while his hands eased the aircraft round in a huge quarter circle to the left. He dare not put on too many degrees of bank. The storm was doing its best to turn the Marlborough upside down, without any help from him.

"I suppose they'll be firing rockets, Skipper?" Shaughnessy asked.

"Should be . . . if they've any left."

Feeling ill himself now, and thoroughly wretched, Draper muttered into Hawkins' ear, "If the bloody thing had any sense . . . it'd have gone down by now." Then he shouted, "Transmitting again, Skipper. Forty degrees starboard."

Kelston saw the needle on the compass was steadier. "Seems to have got over its fit of the shakes," he said. He waited to see whether it would alter as the aircraft moved away from it. The pointer went rapidly past ninety degrees right, then slowed up, pointing behind them.

"That looks more like it," the captain said, half to himself. He called back to Bates to find out whether he had obtained a position for the ship from the number of bearings the radio compass had given him.

"Yes, sir," Bates replied. "Should be eight miles north-east of us now."

"I'm turning back towards her."

For a few seconds after Easy Zebra had wheeled round, the needle pointed dead ahead. Then it sagged down to the right.

"Damn them . . . damn them," Draper shouted. "They've stopped transmitting."

Kelston kept on the same course. He was watching the sea keenly. "Must be round here somewhere," he said to Shaughnessy. But he knew that the waves, house-top high, could easily hide a small steamer. The white wash of the sea would be continuously belting over the ship, forcing her, chameleon-like, to assume its own colour.

Hawkins said suddenly, "Isn't that a rocket, Skipper?"

"Where?"

"Thought I saw one out to starboard." Hawkins pointed out of the first officer's side window.

Kelston peered across to the right. The excitement on his face died down. There was only a grey curtain of rain there now.

"See anything, Mr. Shaughnessy?" he asked.

"I wasn't looking that way, sir."

"What colour?" Kelston asked Hawkins.

"Red, sir."

Kelston put Easy Zebra in a slow turn to the right. His

eyes searched the sea on the starboard bow. Suddenly, the folds of the rain clouds parted. The wind seemed to yank at their indefinite edges, as though trying to pull them to pieces. Just underneath the nose of the aircraft, Kelston caught a glimpse of what looked like a huge horseshoe in the sea, before it disappeared below them.

"That was her stern all right," he said, and he banked round to the right to have another look. With difficulty, he made out the outlines of a superstructure being pounded by a torrent of water. Then the whole black hull was laid almost flat, silhouetted against the white fury of the waves.

Bates came up to the front to have a look at her. "Christ," he said, with a mixture of horror and pity in his voice. "They're taking a beating."

Kelston turned to him. "Send her position to Control. Tell them we're circling. And ask them where the tugs are."

"Not much fuel left, Skipper," Hawkins said.

"I've been keeping an eye on the time. Reduce the power on the engines to eighteen inches. I'm going to try and hover just above stalling."

For ten more minutes, Easy Zebra flew slowly round the stricken ship, using less than half the fuel for normal cruising speed. It was difficult to keep her in sight. Kelston kept his eyes steadily on her. Again and again, the *Santa Lucinda* bobbed up, only to be pushed over by another enormous onrush of the sea. It was as though some huge bully was punching the life out of a defenceless, half-drowned child. Kelston felt the irony of not being able to reach out and help her. All he could do was to keep her company.

But the tugs had got her position now. "They're only ten miles north, Skipper . . . so Control say," Draper informed him.

"We'll go and see if we can find them," Kelston said, and he turned Easy Zebra towards the north. A few minutes later, he saw them. They were far easier to see than the tramp steamer. Smoke gushed from their funnels like huge brown markers, pin-pointing them in their grey and white background. They were ocean-going types, stationed in Ponta Delgada in case of emergencies to the large Atlantic liners and merchantmen. In size they were not far short of the *Santa Lucinda* herself. Kelston dived down low over them and headed Easy Zebra towards the stricken ship. Four times he circled them, diving down each time to give them their heading. They plunged forward slowly in the direction he gave them.

The minutes slipped by. In an hour's time it would be night. Already the grey light of the storm was turning darker. Hawkins was fidgetting. "Very short of fuel, sir," he said unhappily. They still, after all, had to land at Santa Ana. Kelston appeared to take no notice. He went over the tugs again, and then, pulling out, he headed the aircraft up towards the north. He looked at his watch. Then reluctantly, he said, "We'll have to go now." The tugs were still about four miles away from the ship. Bound to find her, he reassured himself. And yet, in this visibility, with darkness coming on, she must be easy enough to miss, more than half-hidden by the mountainous waves.

As he moved off, taking a last look at the steamer, he felt that his job was only half-done. He knew that when they found her, the tugs would have a devil's game trying to get her in tow, unless the sea abated. He kept on saying to himself, as Easy Zebra flew under the cloud towards São Miguel, They'll be able anyway to get the men off her.

Just a couple of miles ahead, they suddenly saw a brown cliff, emerging from the cloud and stretching down to the sea. Then a couple of tiny houses. Kelson turned to the left, parallel with the coast and followed it round at a height of eight hundred feet.

"*Not* an orthodox method for approaching an airfield in

bad weather," Kelston said to the first officer. "But in the circumstances . . . the only damn thing we can do."

Shaughnessy contacted the Tower on Channel B of the Very High Frequency voice radio. "Cloud base over the field nine-hundred feet," they told him. "Wind north-easterly sixty knots, gusting seventy. Landing Runway One-Three-Zero magnetic."

Kelston screwed up his face when he heard it. There would be a heavy cross-wind component on the runway. But he said nothing.

Easy Zebra gradually followed the coastline round to the north shore. The radio compass still pointed at Santa Ana range station, now edging round to the right. Kelston saw the large tump of Rabo de Peixe Hill to the left of the runway, its head buried in cloud. He called for the Before Landing Checks to be made. As the first officer droned out the sixteen items, Kelston went through his part of the drills automatically.

"Field Approach and Landing Checks complete, sir," Shaughnessy reported.

Kelston had lined up Easy Zebra pointing in the direction of the hill, on the runway heading of one-three-zero. It was still pelting with rain. Twilight was beginning to drain all the light from the sky. Just over a mile away, they saw the green threshold lights. Very slowly, bumping around in the gusty wind, Easy Zebra approached them, drifting nearly fifteen degrees to starboard.

"Seems to be a bit of cross wind," Shaughnessy said brightly.

Kelston kept the power up until he was flying level with the runway. As the air speed dropped below a hundred knots, he kicked off half the drift with the rudder. Purposely, he had kept the left wing slightly down, to prevent the gale blowing him off the runway. The port wheel crunched down, followed a second later by the starboard, this time a little more heavily.

"Nice work, sir," Hawkins said.

As they taxied over to the ramp, Kelston said, "Better get on with the After Landing Check, I suppose."

Mr. Dudley, manager for British Empire Airways at Santa Ana airfield, was a very keen chess player. He wasn't just enthusiastic; he was good. The Chess Club at Ponta Delgada had already voted him chairman at their elections in July.

Chess was to Dudley such an obsession that it had become inevitably involved in his everyday dealings with other people. Life, he had found, was not unlike a gigantic chess game. And he played it accordingly. His job was to deal with four airline services a week, two outbound and two homebound. On all four there was a night-stop in the Azores of fourteen hours, where the souls on board rested up before proceeding on, the crew at the Carreras Hotel and the passengers at the Castle.

This night-stop was not popular with Dudley. But it wasn't as bad as a slip. At Bermuda, the crew that brought the aircraft in handed it on (like a baton in a relay race) to the crew who had brought the previous aircraft in. The passengers did not stop, but the two slip-crews (for the northbound and the southbound services) were always there, a continual, ever-changing collection of fourteen human beings doing nothing but wait for their aircraft and being a nuisance to the station manager. At least in the Azores there were three nights a week when he was completely free of all responsibilities. It was his first station and he was determined to make a success of it. As soon as he saw an aircraft, therefore, he was anxious to get rid of it. Marlboroughs, passengers, aircrew—they frequently had him playing innumerable and completely different life chess-games at one and the same time. Dudley was perfectly well aware that the less he saw of any of them, the more chance he had of winning through. There was not so much danger of him putting up a black. He hated that word anyway. White, after all, always played first.

After the passengers had disembarked from Easy Zebra, he was immediately presented with an example of these hazards. A Mr. Parkinson almost literally buttonholed him. Dudley, who had a good memory for the position among the passengers of kings and queens and knights, remembered receiving a notice, advising him of Mr. Parkinson's arrival. Obviously not a bishop. Probably a rook.

The man's face, which a few minutes before had been pale green, was now red with rage. Dudley heard the words ". . . utter discomfort . . . endangered . . . reckless flying." They were enough to give him the clue he needed. It wasn't his game at all. Mr. Parkinson had the wrong opponent.

"I'll ask the captain of the aircraft to have a word with you, sir," he said soothingly, and edged over towards Kelston.

When Kelston saw him, he inquired at once, "Have the tugs found her?"

"We haven't heard, Captain . . . but there's one other matter." Dudley pointed. "Mr. Parkinson. A V.I.P. He's very upset, Captain. Very upset."

"Probably shock," Kelston said. "He'll feel better in the morning."

"I thought, perhaps, a word from you . . ."

Kelston went over to Mr. Parkinson. He saw that the man had been frightened out of his wits. This violent self-assertion was just the reaction.

"I'm sorry you had such a rough trip, sir," he said.

But the man wasn't going to let himself be smoothed down. Somewhat more intelligible now, he still seemed just on the edge of a nervous collapse. "I shall write . . . company . . ." he said. "Certainly write chairman . . . old friend. You"—he pointed a finger at Kelston—"not fit . . . aeroplane."

Kelston looked at him in exasperation. Then he saw the man with the pointed beard, who had been the spokesman for the passengers when they were told about the *Santa Lucinda,* was beckoning him to come over to the other side of the ticket counter.

"That's all right, Captain," he said to him behind his hand, "I'll smooth him down."

Kelston said, "Thanks. Looks like a lifetime's work."

"I am a sailor, Captain. A ship's officer." He looked contemptuously at the rest of Easy Zebra's passengers, still half-dazed from their experiences. "They cannot understand."

"Sometimes difficult for them," Kelston said, not without sympathy.

Before he left in the crew transport for the hotel, Kelston shouted out to Dudley, "See the aircraft's put in the hangar. And everything's battened down. There's a hell of a wind."

Dudley said frigidly, "Of course, Captain. Of course."

Someone was trying to move his pieces for him. And *that* wasn't allowed.

3

Kelston walked down the long corridor on the first floor of the Carreras Hotel. A porter followed carrying his shabby leather suitcase. At the far end the pilot waited, while the man fumbled with the key. There was a tinkling jangle for a moment. It seemed to fit the lock badly. Then there was a click and Kelston pushed the door open with the flat palm of his hand.

Immediately the captain's room made him welcome. He

felt soothed by the quietness which contrasted sharply with the bouncing turbulent air and the everlasting noise of the engines. He seemed suddenly to have entered the small isolated stillness in the centre of a storm.

It had originally been the bridal suite. There was a magnificence about it that still managed to preserve a kindly discretion. The high ceiling was supported by Corinthian pilasters wreathed with gold leaf. In the centre a chandelier covered the electric light with a torrent of crystal drops. Though it was dark outside now, when the sun shone it glittered through large windows, crowned at the top with red and blue diamonds of stained glass; but at the pull of a velvet cord, brocade curtains of an understanding thickness would shut the daylight out. A damasked sofa waited beside a marble fireplace. The mahogany desk pined wordlessly for love letters. The painted French wardrobe seemed specially designed to house the silks and satins of a bride's trousseau.

Few brides, however, came to the Azores. Honeymoons these days were more often spent on beaches and bar stools. So the Portuguese gave it to O Capitão, next on the list of their sentimental hierarchy. In the never-ending rotation dictated by the crew roster, eight English captains slept here before flying on to Bermuda on their way out, or back to Lisbon, Madrid—and at last London—on their way home. The wardrobe had to be content with a blue serge uniform. The desk was used mainly for working out fuel figures and endurances. Even the largest captain was a little inadequate for the soft voluptuous prairie of the bed.

Kelston felt tired. His arms ached after their continuous wrestling with the controls. Dried sweat and oil had caked his hands with grime. He turned on the taps in the adjoining bathroom, and then, sitting on the bed, he started undressing slowly and mechanically while he thought about the *Santa Lucinda.*

Now that he was back on the ground, like most other airline pilots, Kelston had a lost look about him which even the kindliness of the room could not quite drive away. Not even his own house, where he spent a week out of every three, could be called his home. The nearest thing to it was the inside of a Marlborough. That noisy, confined little kingdom was where normally he felt happiest. There were so few things he could do. He could check with the navigator, talk to the passengers, study the weather, eat a meal. The only place where he would doze off was his seat, for the crew rest compartment had been converted into a mail locker. But even this sleep on board while the first officer did his watch, was always on the brink of consciousness, as though his mind insisted on waiting up for the unexpected. And like the few things he could do when everything was running smoothly, there were only a few things he could do if anything went wrong. The emergency procedures for coping with fire and failures were always near the tip of his tongue. Applied quickly, they could deal with nearly anything except instantaneous disaster. Apart from an occasional out of the ordinary incident, such as had happened that afternoon, everything was very cut and dried. The places and times of departure and arrival were already ordained in the schedule that he served. So, for better, for worse, life on board was very simple, happily unhampered by the bewildering and endless possibilities that could happen on the ground.

When he was not flying, Kelston tended to feel frustrated, conscious of the many things he had not done with his life. He had gone into his father's export business, which had been one of the first casualties of the war. He had joined the Air Force, learnt to fly, acquired a certain tight-lipped stoniness on his face, which conveniently walled out his thoughts from other people. And afterwards, partly because there was nothing else to do, partly because flying was in his blood, he had joined British Empire Airways. It was a familiar pattern that he shared with many people, but in his heart he was not satisfied with it. As a kind of sop to an active and intelligent brain that largely lay idle since his work was mainly routine, he wrote articles on the technical side of flying for several aviation magazines.

When he was fully undressed and his clothes lay in a heap around him, he padded across the carpet to the bathroom in his bare feet and turned off the hot tap. He waited till he could bear to get into it and then lowered himself down into the steaming water. Looking round for his soap and flannel, he discovered he had left them still packed in his suitcase.

"Damn," he said aloud, and dripped back again into the room to get them. As he splashed back into the water he was still in a daze, lost in the problem of the *Santa Lucinda*. Could he have done more to help her? The thought that he had not been able to wait till the tugs actually reached her gnawed at his mind and would not let it go. He went over the things he might have done. Reducing the engine revolutions would have given him another few minutes. An earlier descent might have meant all the difference. Then there was still nearly half an hour's fuel in his tanks when he landed. He could hear the wind howling round the hotel. They were still in it while he was comfortable, pampered, safe.

Then he noticed the bottle sitting in the corner of a shelf, just above the bath. The sight of it for the moment took his mind away from the tramp steamer. It was the shape of a busby. A label declared it to be the after-shave lotion with the manly tang. Kelston reached up his wet hand and took it down to study it closely. In small print, the proprietors described the mixed smells that in their opinion made a person smell like a man. Each one was an ingredient of their inexpensive elixir: leather, salt sea, horses, brand new books, the air in the early morning. Kelston undid the stopper and smelt the oily liquid inside. Nobody but Ferris, he decided, could possibly own that sort of stuff.

People were always leaving bits of themselves in this room, sometimes a collar or a tie left behind in a rush of packing, sometimes a magazine or a letter. The blue carpet at the foot of the bed was stained with little stars of dried metal polish, souvenirs of last-minute attempts to brighten uniform buttons. Kelston had once found a copy of Ovid's *Art of Love* translated from the Latin. There was no name inside, but partly because it belonged to the Charfield Public Library—where both of them lived—partly because it was an odd book for a pilot to read and he was the most likely of an improbable bunch, he guessed it was Mike Leeming's. Kelston had handed it over the next time he was home. Oddly enough, Leeming had been embarrassed. For a moment he seemed on the point of disowning it.

"How did you know it was mine?" he had asked, almost accusingly.

Kelston told him.

"The title—the title's misleading. It isn't an encyclopaedia of Sex, if that's what you're thinking."

"I'm not," Kelston had replied. "I've read it. Parts of it anyway. At school, years ago, for some exam or other."

"Then you know it's—" Leeming had paused before the word with the capital "L." "Literature."

"Don't bother with the lesson, Mike. Take it back to the library before you go broke in fines. It's well overdue."

Kelston put the bottle back on its shelf. That incident with Leeming had taught him to leave things as he found them. The busby could wait for Ferris' return to the Azores.

After he'd scrubbed himself clean, Kelston relaxed in the warm water, feeling its comfortable touches all over his skin. Then with an effort he got out, dried himself and put on his pyjamas. He would have a couple of hours' sleep till dinnertime.

Normally his body was used to misuse. It had to be prepared for long hours on duty without a rest. Even at home, five hours' sleep at night was enough. Round dawn, he would wake and read until everyone else was ready to get up. But this time the storm had taken more than the usual amount of energy a trip demanded. He was dead tired. He stretched on the bed. Within a few minutes he was asleep.

The room's quiet serenity hung over him as he lay looking strangely defenceless, his long fingers unaware how tightly they gripped the coverlet over him. The old-fashioned furniture in the room seemed to hold its breath lest it disturb him. But nevertheless, he slept restlessly. For three hours he always seemed just on the point of waking. Even in unconsciousness, the *Santa Lucinda* was still weighing on his mind.

It was past ten when he awoke. That meant he had missed dinner, and he swore softly when he looked at his watch. It was still pouring with rain outside. He pushed back the bedclothes and dressed in a grey lounge suit. Going downstairs he saw the dining room was locked. Bates was having a drink at the bar.

"Hello, Skipper. Will you have one?"

"Not yet, thanks. I've missed dinner."

"Have you tried the kitchen?"

"No. They'll probably have gone home by now. It's my own damn fault."

"Overslept?"

"Yes."

He was just about to ask Bates if he had any news of the tramp steamer, when the head waiter came up.

"Captain Kelston. We did not see you at dinner?"

"No."

"This way then, please." The man pointed towards the dining room. He was all smiles.

"Don't bother. I'm very late."

"No trouble. No trouble."

Kelston was escorted to the door of the *Sala de Jantar*. The head waiter unlocked it and the pilot found himself seated at a table, the only guest in the empty dining room. He was not used to such deferential treatment and wondered vaguely at the reason for it. The head waiter himself served him, helped by two others. When roast chicken appeared, he was presented with a bottle of Madeira "with the compliments of the management." Knowing that the Carreras was always on the edge of bankruptcy and therefore practised a not unreasonable parsimoniousness, Kelston wondered still further.

"Mr. Olivarez phoned, asking for you," the head waiter said.

"Olivarez. Who's he?"

"The shipowner. Olivarez owns the *Santa Lucinda.*"

"Have you any news of her then?"

"Of course. The tugs found her. They have her in tow."

Kelston felt an immense relief surge over him. "Then she has a good chance?"

"I think so." Then the head waiter added shyly, "I have a brother on board her. Our youngest. Pedro. And he," pointing to the waiter who was filling up Kelston's glass, "he has a cousin on her."

"Quite a family affair."

"We Portuguese," the head waiter said. "We have large families. Perhaps you know. Nearly everyone in Ponta Delgada has a connection somewhere with the *Santa Lucinda.*"

Kelston drank up the glass of Madeira, not because he wanted it, but to give his hands something to do. The waiters stood in an admiring semicircle around him.

"That was very nice. Thank you for letting me have it so late," he said.

"But a sweet, sir, fruit salad, orange sponge?"

"No, thank you. I'll just have coffee in the lounge."

"You will not forget to telephone Mr. Olivarez, will you, sir?"

"No . . . I won't. They'll have his number at the desk?"

"Yes, sir." All three waiters bowed to him as he walked, a little too fast for proper dignity, out of the dining room into the lobby.

There was the same deference at the hotel desk. The clerk insisted on getting through for him. Then he said, "Mr. Olivarez, this is Panchini . . . Carreras Hotel. Mr. Olivarez . . . here is Captain Kelston."

A tired voice said in careful English, "We owe a lot to you, Captain. You have heard she is in tow?"

"Yes, I heard."

"I was wondering whether you would care to watch her come in, Captain."

"I would very much. When?"

"They are having enough trouble as it is in the open sea with the gale. At present, it is out of the question to try for harbour. These meteorologists . . ." Olivarez lapsed into some ferocious Portuguese. "Anyway, they *think* the storm may pass to the east of the island. Instead of south-east winds, in an hour or so they're forecasting northerlies. Then they're hoping to bring her in under the lee of the high mountains to the north of us. Otherwise . . ."

"Otherwise, I suppose they'll have to wait till the storm is over."

"No, Captain. Otherwise it will be too late. The tugs have signalled."

"She won't stand much more?"

"She has so much water on board already. No steam, you see. No pumps working."

"I see," Kelston said unhappily. He had thought that as soon as the tugs got her in tow it would be all over. "Well, let's hope the Met. men are right."

"Please God. Just this once. The trouble is, they don't know with any certainty which way the storm's moving next. There's even a possibility it may back over the island."

"That's the trouble with these things. I'll come down straight away."

"I would be glad to meet you, Captain. My office is on 'A' wharf. Tell the police I asked you down."

Kelston drank his coffee, looking out of the lounge window. The wind was still tearing at the rhododendron bushes as though to uproot them. A dark overcast hung heavily over the hotel.

Because there was nothing else to do to keep his mind off the steamer, he put on his coat and set off for the harbour earlier than he intended.

As he walked down a steep back street he suddenly noticed that the wind had dropped a little and gone round more to the north. The weather if anything was slightly better. The torrential rain seemed to be drying up into a thin drizzle. With a feeling of immense relief, he said aloud, just to make sure it was true, "Look's like she's going to be in luck, after all."

Near the gates of the harbour, crowds began to materialize. Everyone on the island seemed intent on seeing the home-coming of the *Santa Lucinda.* They jostled good-humouredly against each other, swarming over the cobbles, ignoring the horns of the grumbling cars.

Kelston spoke a little Portuguese, learnt from a year hunting submarines from Lagens during the war. The police at the gates were doubtful. They waved their hands to illustrate their problems. There were so many others who wished to get in.

"But Mr. Olivarez," he said. "He asked me to come down."

They still waved. All the others, too, it appeared, had provided the same plausible invitation. He was not employed by the company? He had no near relative aboard? They were friendly but firm. What could an Englishman want, they seemed to say, coming down at this time of night to watch a Portuguese steamer trying to limp back to port?

Then a voice said in English, "Is that Captain Kelston?" Turning round, the pilot saw a man in a white mackintosh standing beside him, hemmed in all round by dark pushing figures. The arc lights above them shone down on a plump bald skull edged by a down of white hair.

"Yes. Kelston."

"I am so sorry, Captain. I have been at the wireless station. I did not expect you so soon."

"The wind's much more northerly," Kelston said, "and the weather's better."

"Perhaps." The flat voice sounded cautious, unconvinced.

There was a quick burst of fast Portuguese. The police smiled. The steel gates opened. "I am Olivarez," the man said when they were through them. Now that there was room, they could shake hands. "I am the man who is so much in your debt."

"The tugs did the job," Kelston said. "I expect they'd have found her without me."

"I do not think so." The shipowner's tone was quite definite. "Not before darkness. She had been blown well out of position." He seemed determined to pin the credit, like a medal, on Kelston's breast.

They walked along the edge of the quay. A few feet away a ribbon of illuminated water washed against the stone.

"Anyway," the pilot said uncomfortably, "glad they found her. How far away are they now?"

"Two miles. The lighthouse has sighted them."

"And if the storm moves back over the island?"

"Unless there's a northerly wind and they get the protection of the mountains, they haven't a chance to make harbour."

"What's their speed?"

"They are making four knots."

Kelston whistled. "That's damned good. Dunno how they manage to tow her at all in that sea."

"They say it's calmer out there now."

"I think they're going to make it," Kelston said slowly.

The man kept silent, as though wary of predicting anything lest he offend the storm.

"And if the south-east gale catches them again at the harbour mouth?" the pilot asked.

Olivarez shrugged his shoulders. "The tugs could not—how do you say?—manoeuvre. The best would be to tow her out to sea again. The rocks are too near. They'd save the men. That is the main thing—the men."

They walked on past rusting iron chains towards the cranes and the sheds. Kelston saw a little knot of people waiting beside a low building, the only one on the quay that was lighted. There were women with black shawls over their heads. The men doffed their caps to Olivarez. The electric lamps on the wharf struggled to keep the surrounding darkness away from them.

Kelston felt the man's nervous unhappiness suddenly increase.

"The families," Olivarez said, jerking his head towards them. "This waiting is the hardest part." Then he added fiercely, "Until she is safely moored here, I will believe nothing. Nothing."

Then he put his arm round Kelston to guide him. "This way, Captain. Mind the steps. My office is to the left."

It was quite dark inside. "The bulb has gone," Olivarez said. "It is a thing I have been meaning to get fixed. One of so many things. But Karena will have coffee ready. I think a cup of coffee . . ." His voice trailed away as though it could not compete with the sound of their steps on the concrete corridor.

They stopped outside a door framed by a thin gold band of light. Olivarez seemed to hesitate before he opened it. "The telephone," he murmured softly, almost to himself. "Perhaps already . . ."

At the end of the room, a girl in a green coat was standing by a table pouring coffee from an urn. Six cracked cups stood side by side on a tray, sending up their own little clouds of steam. Not looking round, she called in Portuguese, "Carlos, they are so cold outside I am taking coffee down. They know it will be half an hour at least, but they *will* wait outside. They are so anxious to be the first to see her lights."

"Any message?"

"None."

"Karena," Olivarez said, more relaxed now, "this is Captain Kelston."

The girl turned the tap off carefully, and put the cup on the tray beside the others. Then she turned round. Kelston saw an oval shaped face, framed by black hair. She was about twenty-eight. Perhaps younger. It was hard to tell. Her skin looked smooth and young. But those smoke-coloured eyes had seen things of which the rest of her body had been blissfully unconscious.

She came towards them and put out her hand a little shyly. "I too wish to say thank you."

She spoke the English words too correctly, too carefully, with none of the slurring of overfamiliarity. Each one seemed to be a separate, important guest, to be treated with delicate consideration. "And now," she said, holding up the tray. "Coffee. These are all the cups there are. Take this one. It is a little less cracked than the others. And this is Carlos'. Look, because he's manager, he has his name on it."

Kelston took the cup she recommended. Olivarez said, "You see how well she looks after me. Karena is as valuable as one of my ships to me." Then he added, "And far less worry."

"That's only because I don't go to sea."

"Good secretaries sit in offices. You are a good secretary."

Turning to Kelston, the girl said, "He has promised me. One day, he says, I can go to sea."

"Oh yes, Karena. One day soon."

"Three years ago it was one day soon. Today it is no nearer. Some time, I must purposely worry you so much, you will be glad to see me go."

Olivarez smiled across at Kelston. For a moment he had forgotten the *Santa Lucinda.* "I would like to see you try, Karena," he said, almost happily.

They both drank their coffee. Karena went outside to wash their cups, and returned to refill them. "I'll take the tray down to them now."

Kelston said, "Let me take the urn. That would be easier."

He swung it up in his hand and opened the door for her.

"Leave it open, please." She smiled. "Then we can see down the corridor."

She walked lightly and carefully down the beam of light, holding the tray high in her hands. Kelston saw the quiet grace of her slight body, her small, well-shaped head, her short hair glowing softly in the brief light, before she gradually merged into the darkness at the end of the corridor.

She swung the door open. "Four steps," she called back. "Can you see all right?"

"Fine."

He put the urn down on the concrete. The families crowded up, and she called out quickly, "No more news yet. Just some coffee for you."

Kelston filled the cups while she handed them around. The same cups came back and were refilled and refilled. "Not very hygienic, I suppose." She laughed. Her face was close to his, as she held a cup under the tap. "But no one minds. Not tonight."

She mingled among the crowd, sympathizing, encouraging, smiling. She knew all their names, and like them, her eyes wandered continuously to the wide black emptiness beyond the harbour wall.

When she was no longer beside him, he felt like a stranger intruding on a family trouble, and he went back inside.

"Karena is talking to them," he said, as he closed the office door behind him.

Olivarez was staring out of the window that faced south towards the harbour mouth. "I should be there, too," he said. "But I am as fearful as they are. No use at words of comfort. Karena will say them for me."

"Yes."

"You must understand–she is more a daughter to me."

"Portuguese?"

"Oh, no. Czech. She has had a hard life."

"She is very beautiful," Kelston said.

"Yes." He seemed unwilling to talk more about her. The two men waited in silence. Then Olivarez stared hard at Kelston. "Listen," he muttered, "wasn't that the wind on the window?"

"I can't hear anything."

"I thought for a moment the wind had swung round to south." The shipowner looked at his watch. "Just a little more of these merciful northerlies," he said to it, as though begging a favour. His head nodded, counting the seconds. "One seems so powerless."

Everything outside was still quite quiet. The minutes dragged by. Every now and then Olivarez said, "If only they'd hurry!"

Suddenly there was a slight whispering. At first, it sounded so like a change in the wind direction that Olivarez's eyes widened in fear. Then there was a shout. A huge cry of joy.

The invisible mountains round the bay echoed it back, increasing the strength of its gladness. A little group of flimsy human beings were defiantly roaring out in triumph at their victory over Felicity.

Kelston peered over Olivarez's shoulder. Out in the blackness of the harbour mouth a cluster of red, green and white lights glowed together like a little coloured constellation.

"They're in," Olivarez said breathlessly.

A searchlight on the end of the quay picked out the *Santa Lucinda.* Her broken foremast hung down over her bows. She was listing to port as though hunched up in pain. The tugs were gushing great clouds of smoke from their funnels. Now they were so near they seemed to be pulling at her harder. The *Santa Lucinda* bobbed up and down in an effort to do her best for them.

They dashed down the corridor. The crowd had now swarmed to the brink of the water. Karena threw her arms round Olivarez. "See, Carlos. They are all right now." Then she turned to Kelston and smiled. "Safe home again."

"You knew everyone on board?"

"Everyone."

They stood side by side, while Olivarez now chattered with the families, gesticulating and happy. The steamer grew bigger. They could see men on her decks waving their hands above their heads. Ropes were flung out to her from the bollards.

Kelston said, "She's not too badly knocked about."

The girl kept silent. Glancing down at her he saw the tears on her face. A little embarrassed, he turned away. But for a fraction of a second, their eyes had met.

He looked at the muddy pools round their shoes. It was suddenly important that he should let her know that he wasn't being tactful or polite or unfeeling. He reached out into the darkness and took her hand. Her fingers felt icy cold.

There seemed no point in saying anything. He felt he had, after all, made himself understood. The rain had started again. It was beginning to bang at the tin roofs of the warehouses. With their wet hands clasped together, they watched the *Santa Lucinda* bump gently against the rubber tires that were strung along the end of the granite quay.

As though in a fit of temper at losing the *Santa Lucinda,* that same night Felicity blew a squall of wind through a door of the hangar at Santa Ana airport someone had carelessly left open. Caught by the gust, a pair of steel maintenance steps clattered across the floor and rammed the port tail fin of Marlborough Easy Zebra, leaving a jagged hole in her thin plates.

It was very much a last fling. Felicity's strength had now been measured. Warning of its advance had flashed across the world, suddenly spoiling the shape of hundreds of carefully drawn meteorological charts. By nine next morning, most of its rearguard had passed over the Azores. São Miguel came to life again. The neat fields glistened in the sun. Little houses gleamed white as sugar, perched on the top of cliffs too steep to be true. The conical hills looked like so many dunces' hats covered in green marzipan. Everything was just as it should be. The ogre had been driven out of the kingdom on the top of the beanstalk.

As Felicity moved rapidly towards the Bay of Biscay, its strength began to wane. On the B.B.C. one o'clock news, it had degenerated into "a deep depression well south of Ireland." But nevertheless it had begun to dominate the whole pressure system around the British Isles.

Even far in advance of its centre, the wind was still strong. Blowing through the office window of Mr. Veitch, manager of the Mid-Atlantic Line of British Empire Airways, it scattered some papers helter-skelter on the floor. They were reports from people all along the route; from captains, station managers, engineers, sales representatives. He sat at the far end of a business six thousand miles long, being fed these endless pieces of paper. One of them was a signal from Santa Ana for a new tail fin for Easy Zebra. He stared down at them before bending to pick them up. "Damned things," he said.

At the other side of London Airport, halfway down Runway Ten, the heavy cross wind tugged sideways at the tail of Marlborough Easy Dog just taking off for the Azores with Easy Zebra's new tail fin on board, under the command of Captain Peter Ferris. He put on full left rudder to correct for the violent swing to starboard. Rain suddenly flooded over the windscreen. He grinned, first at the second pilot, then at the weather outside. "Here comes that man Ferris," he said, "on his eight thousand horses."

Blowing down a country lane south of London, it caught hold of the scarf round Veronica Kelston's thick fair hair, filling it out like a small gay sail. She was going to visit friends near the golf course. They had a large house with a long drive.

"Darling," she said, as her hostess opened the door, "I *am* a sight. This wind has just *murdered* my hair." Four gold bangles she wore on her left wrist jangled like a tambourine.

The wind snatched at a pair of nylons, the property of Libby Challoner, a new stewardess on the Panama route. They had been put out to dry on the window ledge of the room she rented near Baker Street. She just missed grabbing them as they disappeared downwards. She watched them walking on air over to the garden two doors away. There they impaled themselves on a holly bush. "Au diable," she said aloud. She had a habit of colouring her conversation with little daubs of foreign languages. "Zut. Dash. Botheration."

Sweeping down to Charfield in the late afternoon, it blew on the chrysanthemums belonging to Captain Michael Leeming, and sent him hurrying out into the garden. He struggled to build a wind wall of heavy glass plates to protect them. Already, the petals of two rosy-bronze ones were strewn over the ground, like the feathers of a robin mauled to pieces by a cat. They were prize chrysanthemums and he was proud of them. With infinite care he made the survivors safe against the wind.

"Tea, darling," his wife sang out to him from the front door. "In the drawing room, as usual."

The woollen dress she was wearing was pastel blue, and it suited her quiet prettiness to perfection.

Book Two ~

The Middle of the South-East Quadrant

October 16-October 19

1

To Melanie Leeming teatime was always the sweetest hour of the day. At their house called Fairoaks, it lasted from five to nearly half-past six, when she put the two children to bed. The green china cups clinked. Toast oozed butter. Cakes made a sugar pattern in heavy relief on the silver dish. Through a crack in the chintz curtains she could see the garden getting darker. The winter cabbages by the back fence became odd blots of black before they finally vanished. For a while longer the little crew of apple trees fought the oncoming darkness with their bare bony arms. The many-coloured prize chrysanthemums were slowly dyed a uniform black.

Inside the drawing room a patch of grey air smouldered into a pink haze around the electric fire.

"Shall I put the light on?" her husband asked her.

"Not yet, Michael. D'you mind?"

"No . . . I like it, too."

"Pity about the wind."

"Got to expect it this time of year. Should have given those bigger ones more protection."

He put his feet up on the sofa, and lay full length. "Anyway," he said, "certainly peaceful in here. Nice to think I've still got some leave left."

Tea was always just for the two of them. On that, Melanie insisted. The boys played in the attic or the garden all afternoon, and had their supper in the kitchen. The drawing room belonged to their parents. It was their private territory. Of course, when Michael was out on the route, things were different. Melanie didn't bother with tea then. She had something to eat with the children before tucking them in for the night. Then she read a little, sewed a little and went to bed early. Now, she looked contentedly across at her husband, half a smile curling the corners of her nice-looking lips. Everything pointed to the fact that they were settling down to the eighth tranquil winter of their married life.

"More tea, Michael?"

"Can you see to pour it?"

"Just."

"Then I'd like some."

She went over to the sofa and a shadowy hand held the cup out to her. Almost invisible, the tea still made the same comfortable gurgle as it poured from the pot. "Thanks, Melanie. On the table . . . so I can reach it when I want it."

She ruffled his hair before going to sit down again. "Waited on hand and foot. Utterly spoiled," she said.

"That's your privilege. I like it. *You* like it."

"Oh, I like it," she said. "That's the only reason I do it."

"Now you're in the mood, get the evening paper . . . there's a dear. Should have arrived by now."

"*You* get it, for a change."

"I've just bedded myself down." He pointed to his horizontal legs as though they were twin roots. "And you're nearer the door."

"One of these days, Michael Leeming," she said, as she got up again, "I'll have to take you in hand. Seriously."

"That's my girl." He leant over to give her an affectionate tap on her bottom as she passed him. "Put the light on, would you, as you go out?"

She turned down the switch. The sudden brilliance shut out the dim struggles of the flowers and the trees against the wind. The colours of the room were warm reds and browns. A copy of Van Gogh's "Cornfields in Provence" over the mantelpiece provided an uneasy yellow. The carpet was a dull rust. Nearly everyone said, when they first entered the Leemings' lounge, "What a bright, cheerful place you've made it, Melanie!"

She brought the paper back and put it over his face. "There," she said, "that's the last thing I'll do for you tonight."

While he was reading it, she cleared away the tea things, and took them to the kitchen, across the hall. When she was halfway through the washing up, Michael shouted through the open door, "I say, Melanie . . . that's interesting."

"What?" she called back.

"Something in the paper about Mark Kelston."

There was a little pause. Then, "He's all right, isn't he?"

"Of course he is." Michael sounded slightly irritated with the sudden tremulous note in his wife's voice. She always assumed that when a pilot got into the papers, he'd crashed. She was always reading about incidents to aircraft happening all over the world—Hong Kong, the Arctic, Timbuctoo, all faithfully reported by the daily press. Sometimes she would ask him timidly, "What does it mean when it says a master-rod failed?" or "Michael, where's the main spar and why does it seem to crack so often?" Michael had once asked her point blank whether she was frightened of him flying. And she had replied, "No, no. Only now and again, when you're away on the route . . . I get nervous."

"Well, don't," was his advice. "These papers are just a lot of scaremongers."

Michael read through the paragraph for the second time. Then he shouted out again, "He's made himself a bit of a hero. Something about rescuing a ship off the Azores."

"Sounds exciting, Michael."

"Not very. It was only a tramp steamer. Clot of a captain

got himself caught in a storm. Come on in and read it yourself."

She put the cups and plates back on the shelves, and went into the lounge.

Sitting on the hearthrug with her back against the sofa, she read the paragraph Mark pointed out to her.

"Quite a splash," she said. "Good old Mark."

"I can't see he did much. It all happened not far from Santa Ana. Almost on the circuit."

"Veronica will be pleased."

He grunted. "Yes. Just the sort of thing she likes."

Melanie looked across at the twin red bars of the fire. "Poor Veronica," she said.

"Why poor? You've never liked her."

"No. That's the reason. I feel guilty about people I don't like. So I say 'Poor Veronica.' "

"You're wasting your pity."

"It isn't pity. It's sympathy."

"Same shilling. One's the head. The other's the tail."

"Why d'you think Mark married her in the first place?"

"Don't ask me, Melanie. People meet. Go out together. Sometimes have fun. Then they think they'll have more and better fun if they're always together."

"They're not happy together, would you say, Michael?"

"Oh. I don't know."

"Not like *us,* I mean."

He smiled at her. "No, not like us. But they're not unhappy. That's the main thing."

Melanie considered for a moment, holding her chin in her hand. "He seems awfully gentle with her. Kind. But there's no spark between them, is there? Together, they seem to neutralize each other, if you see what I mean. Almost . . . make each other dead."

Michael took the paper away from her, and glanced through the headlines. "Anyway," he said, "let's not talk about Veronica. Not at one of our teatimes. There's not that many left."

"No," Melanie said, much more quietly.

"This leave's flown by. Let's see—when am I due out again?"

"Five days' time." She said the words promptly and precisely.

Michael glanced over at her. He swung his legs off the sofa. His feet thumped together side by side on the floor. "Only five? I thought I'd got more than that."

"No."

"I suppose everything's ready, Melanie? You got my uniform back from the cleaners? I had two white shirts that needed mending."

"Everything's ready."

"Ah, well." He stretched himself. "It's been pleasant while it lasted."

She said in a soft small voice, "Not that we've done anything special."

He looked at her, surprised. "You said you didn't want to go away."

"Yes," she said. "Yes. I agree. I *did* say that."

"What with the kids . . . hotel rooms . . . uncertain weather. Far better at home."

"But we might have done *something,* Michael . . . gone *somewhere*. Even for a day. All we seemed to do was to potter round the house and the garden."

"We went to Bournemouth," he reminded her. "And the New Forest."

"Yes . . . that was nice," she said flatly.

"What's the matter with you, Melanie?" He looked across at her in concern.

She sighed. "Sometimes . . . oh, well, sometimes, the house gets on top of me. I seem caged in, you know. Chained to the children and the housework."

"The house gets you down, Melanie?" His voice sounded very nearly shocked. "What's the matter with the house?"

"Oh, it's a lovely house. And it cost a lot of money. And you provide everything I ever want. Only, sometimes . . ."

"Sometimes what?"

"Nothing . . . just sometimes."

"Sometimes what?" he persisted.

"Oh, Michael," she said, hunching up her knees to her chin, and putting her arms round them. "It's no use trying to explain."

"I'm sorry you haven't enjoyed my leave." Always easily hurt, he was offended now. He withdrew into a self-righteous little silence.

She said, "I have. I have."

"Just now you said–"

"Oh, Michael . . . sometimes–"

"God, Melanie. That word again–*sometimes.*"

She said sadly, "Don't quarrel with me, Michael."

But he was thoroughly irritated now. "There's nothing to quarrel *about,* as far as I can see. You say you don't want to go away for my leave. Then you say you do. Now you say you enjoyed it all along. I'm not quarrelling, I'm just trying to understand what you mean."

"You shouldn't always have to have things explained in black and white, Michael. You've been living with me for a long time. Can't you sometimes see how I feel, without me saying anything?"

He said heavily, "I wish I hadn't *taken* my leave now."

"Oh, the leave." She shook her head impatiently. "It's nothing to do with how we spent the leave." She sounded very close to tears. "It's just that it's coming to an end before somehow we even realized it had begun. And then . . . you'll be going away again."

"Oh, so that's all it is," he said. He hadn't meant the relief to sound quite so loudly in his voice. He was pleased to find that Melanie's mood had at last been resolved into something he could understand. But there was nothing on earth he could do about it. He knew it all centred round her overflowing love for him—a love that sometimes made him feel uncomfortable. Not very demonstrative, and by nature and upbringing inclined to be a little prudish, he would have preferred a less intense relationship, if it hadn't been for the fact that her love for him was the powerful and plentiful cement on which he had built not only their marriage but their whole way of life.

He saw immediately now that it had been the wrong thing to say. Melanie's quiet eyes had suddenly blazed with anger.

"Yes . . . that's *all* it is."

She got up from the floor and stood with her arms folded, staring at him.

"Come on, Melanie," he said. "Don't go off the deep end. I know how you feel." He tried to loosen one of her hands from their tight grip of her arms.

"No, you don't. A remark like that shows exactly how much you understand me."

"Melanie . . . you're making a lot of fuss about nothing."

"There you go again, you see! Shows how selfish you are. All the love you produce is strictly for home consumption."

He nodded, agreeing with her. "For you and the children."

"For yourself!" She was trembling with a helpless fury now. Her arms hugged her body as though to protect it. Tears streamed down her face.

He looked at her, really worried. Melanie had her moods, of course. All women did. But he had never seen her like this before. The placid peace of teatime lay in shattered little pieces all round him. "You know very well I love you, Melanie," he said wearily.

"I don't. All I know for sure is that I love you. Sometimes I think I love you too much."

"That's ridiculous."

She took no notice of him. "Your love for me I have to take on trust. Everything here revolves around you. This house, the children, myself. All we want in return is the sort of love I have for you."

"You've got it. You can see it in the things I do for you."

"*What* do you do for me, Michael?"

"Well . . . the usual things. Nice house . . . good food . . . clothes." The list seemed suddenly, even to him, inadequate.

"This house is your harbour. You return here. Rest here. Get your clothes washed, your uniforms pressed. Then—off again. For two-thirds of our life you're out on the route. You go off for over a fortnight. And come back for less than a week."

He was angry now. This was plain unreasonableness. "I've got to earn my living. You know that as well as I do." A flush crept up his neck and reddened his round face.

"You don't seem to see that as soon as you go out life in this house seems snuffed out. Dead. We all go into cold storage till you return." She pulled out a handkerchief and started dabbing her eyes. "It's too long away, Michael. There's no horizon for me, and a week's far too short. As soon as you're in, there's the shadow of you going out again."

"But we've got to keep the schedule running!"

"I don't care what's got to be kept running. It's still far too long. Our marriage hasn't a chance, continually under a strain like this. Then there's always the shadow of that awful Gibraltar crash."

"Melanie . . . you're upset. You're exaggerating." He said the words as though he was diagnosing a disease. "The Gibraltar crash was two years ago. Everything's been going perfectly for a long time now."

She said, "The trouble is, I love you too much. For anybody's good."

"That's not love. That's possessiveness."

For a long time they stared at each other without saying anything. The marble clock on the mantelpiece ticked away the seconds placidly. Then, with a jaunty little tune, it struck seven o'clock.

"God knows what you expect me to do," Michael said.

She shrugged her shoulders. "Right now . . . what *I'm* going to do is put the children to bed." And she walked out of the room, carefully picking off imaginary fluff from the fabric of her blue dress.

The violence of their quarrel left Michael in a dazed and angry stupor. They rarely had a row. When they did, it was made up half an hour later. But not this one. That evening they spent apart. Melanie did some baking in the kitchen. Michael read in the lounge. They met in bed. But Melanie immediately rolled over to her corner quickly, after saying a cool "Good night."

All next day, the strained atmosphere hung over the house. Even the children noticed it. They became fractious, which increased the tension. Several times Michael tried to make the first move to break it up. "This is being stupid, Melanie," he said after lunch. "We're supposed to be adults."

"The trouble is . . . *you're* not."

That started it off again. The wretched thing seemed to be like an atom bomb. Self-generating. At half-past five in the evening he went looking for her in the garden. She was picking blackberries for a pie she planned for tomorrow's lunch.

"You can't see properly to do that," he said. "Look . . . you've scratched yourself. It's bleeding."

"It's nothing."

He put his two arms round her neck. "Come on, Melanie," he said softly. "It's past teatime."

She stood as still as stone. "No tea today." Her eyes looked straight beyond his face, as though they saw through him.

"Oh, but there is." He smiled virtuously. "I made it myself. Everything's ready in the drawing room."

"Well, you can eat it by yourself," she said. "I'm . . . busy."

At eight o'clock on the day after Felicity's dramatic reappearance in the world—the same day as the Leemings, over a thousand miles away had their own private little storm—the station manager at Santa Ana played his first move with Kelston: a bare account on the phone of the damage to Easy Zebra. Then he waited.

If the pilot was going to take it philosophically, Dudley intended to be regretful without being deferential, and without admitting he was in any way to blame. In other words, the game would be off. If, on the other hand, Kelston was going to be difficult, Dudley intended to use the classical defence—pawn to queen's bishop three—which, according to all the books, would limit his opponent's opportunity for speculative attack and yield an equality of chances.

Kelston asked, "You saw the hangar door was closed before going home?"

"That happens to be the engineers' job, Captain. They all swear they closed it after their inspection."

"Who left it open, then?"

"Now this has happened . . . of course, nobody."

"Any suspicions?"

"No, Captain. I can't say I have. The maintenance staff are above suspicion."

Kelston considered that reference for a minute. Then he said, "Yes . . . I think they are. They're a good lot here."

"I'm afraid it must have been one of the Portuguese employed by the airport."

"Looks like it."

Dudley decided with a sense of relief (he was rather afraid of Kelston), that the pilot was going to be philosophical. No game after all. "It's a nuisance," he said, "I've already sent off to London for a spare fin, but it'll mean a two-day delay. However . . . there it is. Just one of those things."

Kelston said sharply, "It isn't one of those things at all. It's damned inefficiency."

Too late, Dudley played the classical defence. "Nothing to do with me, Captain Kelston," he said, with offended dignity. *"I* don't control the weather."

"No, but you control the staff down there. You're supposed to know the Portuguese personnel on the airport. If they're liable to do such stupid things as leave a hangar door open during a whole gale, you should have put a guard on the aircraft."

"That's being very wise after the event, Captain," Dudley retorted. Attack with all the major pieces was often the best defence.

"Not at all. Plain common sense."

"I'll put in a report, Captain."

"And I'll put in a report, too. You're responsible for my aircraft, when it's on the ground here."

It looked like check.

Dudley edged his invisible king out of harm's way. "I don't agree, Captain."

"I didn't expect you to," Kelston said as he hung up. Listening to the empty phone, Dudley had an odd feeling that he'd been tricked into fool's mate.

Kelston told his crew over breakfast. He was the only one not in uniform. Hawkins said, "Typical. You'd think a Marlborough was made of china. Soon as these ground characters get hold of one, it comes apart in their hands."

Bates remarked, "Two more days in this place . . . Christ!"

Then, having got it off their chests, they became resigned. The rest of the conversation over their bacon and eggs was about the home-coming of the *Santa Lucinda.*

After breakfast was over, Kelston went back to his room, and wrote out the beginning of the report on the accident to Easy Zebra that would eventually find its way to Mr. Veitch's desk. He would check again with the engineers, of course. But, considering his own last words to the man were a warning to watch out for the gale, unless he could shift the blame onto some known culprit, Dudley was obviously responsible, and Kelston made no bones about saying so in his report. Then he went downstairs and walked over to the verandah.

He knew perfectly well what he intended to do that morning. The accident to Easy Zebra was unfortunate operationally; but now it had happened, and nothing more could be done about it, he felt a glow of anticipation at this unexpected present of a few more days in the Azores. He had thought for a long time of Karena as he lay in bed that night. He had tried to fit her in as a Portuguese shipowner's secretary—puzzled at the strange twist of life that had brought her to Olivarez's office in Ponta Delgada.

He read for an hour on the verandah overlooking the bay —idly turning over the pages of a magazine, glancing at it only, taking little of it in. The only thing that Olivarez had said about her life was that it had been hard. He had seen that, anyway, in her eyes. The glossy pages on his lap suddenly blurred and became meaningless. In his mind, he could see her face perfectly. He remembered her little gentle gestures with the families, the oddly old-fashioned way she said her words, the feel of her cold hand in his.

Just after ten, Dudley phoned him again with a careful politeness in his voice. A reply had come in from London. An aircraft was being sent as soon as possible with a spare fin on board. This Marlborough would collect Kelston's passengers and take them on. Dudley said he had laid on a bus (the usual diversion) to take them on a tour of the island while they waited.

Kelston went out into the sunshine that had now rubbed up to a shining polish the white houses with their red roofs, the blue sea and the bright green backcloth of the pantomime mountains beyond. He walked across the town to the Castle Hotel, where the passengers were accommodated. Most of them were sitting in the lounge. Carefully, he explained about the aircraft and the arrangements that had been made for them. As usual in such circumstances, most of them were reasonable. They had had a comfortable night; the idea of exploring a foreign island was not unattractive. He left word with the hotel that all their drinks would be at the Company's expense—every airline's universal panacea for irritating delays.They were quite cheerful when he left. There was no sign of Mr. Parkinson, but once again, the ship's officer came to his help, volunteering to "break it to him gently"—an offer that Kelston gratefully accepted.

Then he set off for the harbour, oddly excited at the thought of seeing her again. But he was, after all, disappointed. Karena was not in the office. Olivarez welcomed him warmly enough, but it was not the same. The look on his face as he told the story of the damage to the aircraft, Olivarez interpreted as depression at the delay. He sympathized. It seemed so especially unfair, he said, after all the aircraft had done for the *Santa Lucinda.*

"I suppose you've assessed her damage now?" Kelston asked. "How bad is it?"

"It's considerable, of course, Captain. But nothing compared to the cost of a new steamer." For half an hour he elaborated details of the repairs that had to be done. "The insurance company is pleased, nevertheless," he said. "They thought they were in for a total loss. Karena is down at their office, now."

Kelston steered the conversation away from the *Santa Lucinda* and on to Karena. "You were saying last night," he said, "she came from Czechoslovakia. That's a long way from the Azores."

"It was the war, you know. She was on the wrong side in the war."

"But that's all over, long ago."

"Perhaps. In any case, she spent it nursing in Prague. All the same, she was barred entrance to all the victorious countries."

"Whatever for? Was her family Nazi?"

"There was a brother, Joseph. Very high up in the German Army. The British have been looking for him for years."

Kelston said impatiently, "Surely that's finished with now?"

"I suppose it might be." A glimmer of a smile crossed Olivarez's face. "There's a bigger bogey now. But when the Russians brought communism to Prague, she tried to gain entry into England."

"They wouldn't admit her?"

"No."

"But why ever not?" Kelston's voice sounded angry with the injustice of it all. "She couldn't be blamed for what her brother did."

"They were certain she knew where he was. She said she did not. But then, I suppose, so would I. So would you. The terrible thing is, under the circumstances, so would they."

"Portugal was the only country who would have her?"

"Yes, she came to the Azores to get away from Europe. In one of my boats. With practically no money at all. Just her name on a permit—Karena Karantikova. Fortunately for me . . . I was the first person she came to for a job."

"Has she tried to get to England again? I mean . . . things have changed since then."

Olivarez laughed. "Yes. It's wonderful how things change," he said. "Though she lives on her own, I think she's happy here. She wouldn't want to leave. In any case, even now communism is the big enemy, the search for her brother is still nominally on. I suppose in the end they'd let her in. After all the usual official difficulties. But now—there's no point."

Kelston sat in silence.

Olivarez went on, "You see . . . her life hasn't been easy. But it hasn't embittered her. Just seemed to make her more understanding. You've seen her with the people here. You can tell how they love her."

"Yes."

Olivarez looked over at him. There was something in the studied way he said that bald little monosyllable. "You seem interested in Karena, Captain?"

Kelston said defensively, "She's a very striking-looking girl."

Olivarez nodded with a gentle, amused sympathy. "If I were you," he said, "I would ask her these things myself. Not get them second-hand."

Kelston mumbled something about having to go anyway pretty soon, he was keeping Olivarez from his work.

"The odd thing, Captain"—Olivarez was smiling now—"when you'd gone last night, she asked me questions about you." He shrugged his shoulders. "Not that I could tell her much, of course. And now"—Olivarez suddenly became bustling, efficient—"you must excuse me. I have so much work—" He waved his hands over the papers on his desk. "Perhaps you would like to go to the insurance office. It's on the Via Pergale. Number sixty-six. Karena should be finished there now."

Trying to appear casual, Kelston left Olivarez and walked to the main street. He found the office. Yes, they said, she was still with the manager. Would he wait?

Half an hour later, when she came out, she did not seem surprised to see him. All she said was, "I was hoping you'd come sometime soon. But I didn't expect you today." She smiled at him as he explained about the aircraft. She did not pretend to sympathize. "You'll have two more days, then," she said. "Two whole days!" It seemed to be the most natural thing in the world to her that they should spend them together.

She took his hand and they walked back along the quay. He looked at her face, the black hair dancing in the wind over her white forehead, and saw that in some strange way there was a new joy in her eyes where before he had only seen sadness.

He said, "Queer you should have known, too, Karena."

"I knew," she said, "as soon as I saw you, I knew."

Outside the office she said, "Wait here. Just for a minute. I'll go and ask Olivarez if he can do without me."

He waited, watching the muddy little waves in the harbour glitter into gold as the sun caught them. He heard Karena's quick steps. She was hurrying down the corridor as though afraid he would be gone. She looked up at him, smiling and breathless.

"Well?" he asked.

"Olivarez says yes," she said.

2

"Look, Mark," said Karena, putting her hand lightly on his arm. "Over there, just by the woods. Those houses round the church. That's like the country near Orava. We used to go there when we were small."

The bus rattled over the ruts in the road up towards the volcanic lake of Furnas, hidden in the middle of São Miguel's mountains. Mark looked where she pointed, at the tall white candle of a church tower crowned by a triangular roof like a black snuffer, the sun-bleached cottages and the road that wound around them in regular sweeps like a helter-skelter. He smiled. He knew he didn't have to say, "How pretty," or "It looks nice," or "You must miss it all here." She was talking to him exactly as she had been over lunch in the half-empty Carreras, just saying: This is me, that's where I come from, I wasn't always here, away from my home, my background and my friends.

"But there was a river there too. We used to fish, Joseph and I and our cousins. We caught a trout once. It weighed about three pounds, and no one was allowed to eat it. Just admire it. Until in the end, it smelled so strong that Aunt Magda took it out and buried it."

She paused and looked at him, perhaps for encouragement from his face. Then she chattered on, a small smile curving the corners of her mouth, as though this particular part of her memories together with this present combined to make a taste of incomparable sweetness.

"Now the hill. Look, Pereira is getting ready for the big climb!"

The driver was hunching his enormous shoulders over the wheel and almost standing on the accelerator. "At the top, there is a tavern. Pereira can just last out till we get there."

Her voice was warm and husky with laughter. He put his hand over her own and felt a tremendous upsurge of happiness and peace. The events, the characters in his life, no more before than black and white photographs, touched by her nearness became bright and colourful, alive and moving. He was almost shocked when she took her hand from under his and held on tightly to the seat in front. The bus was wobbling from side to side and growling along the road like an ancient aircraft about to take off.

"Is this like flying? A great rush like this? Then suddenly you're in the sky?"

"A little. Not quite so much rattling. No steam coming

out—we hope!" He jerked his head at the white mane of steam fluttering from the radiator cap.

She leaned back in her seat and looked at him. "And will you always fly, Mark? Always?"

He hesitated for a moment. "I expect so. Sometimes I think I'll get another job. Sometimes I know I'll never settle at anything else." He smiled down at her. "It's an occupational disease of flying. Every airline pilot is about to get another job. That's usually as far as it goes."

She tilted her head back and her eyes were dark and shaded by her lashes. "And will you come here? Often?"

"Very often," he said gravely and without thought.

He hardly realized that the bus had stopped. Everyone was getting out, and automatically the two of them moved with the stream.

In the dark overcrowded tavern he bought two Madeiras and looked around for Karena. He went to the doorway and the sunlight broke hard and painfully in his eyes like a shatter of gold glass. Then he saw her, sitting on the wall looking away down the slopes to where the fields ended in the blue line of the Atlantic. He was conscious of the grave beauty of her face, the delicate shapeliness of her small body. Then her grey eyes turned serenely towards him and she smiled.

Embarrassed, he pressed the glass into her hand and said, "Cheers." He felt the idiocy of the word as soon as it was out of his mouth and he added quickly, "I don't know what you say in Czechoslovakia. I know skoal, if that's any better."

"Cheers," she said. There was the faintest clink as their glasses touched, but they drank the wine in silence.

"You'll never go back, Karena?"

"No, never," she said vehemently.

"And Joseph and your cousins and your Aunt Magda, what about them?"

"My aunt and cousins stayed. Joseph escaped, when the Germans were defeated. But—"

"But?" he prompted her.

"But my father was killed."

"Do you want to tell me?" he asked gently.

"Some of it. Not all. Some of it I never want to tell." She waited for a moment. Then she said. "My father was not a Nazi. You must not think that he was. But he was important to them. He was a steel manufacturer. He was a kind employer, and with much influence. He was mayor, and he—" she raised her eyebrows and moved her head deprecatingly—"he was much loved."

She sipped her wine slowly. "The Nazis courted him. They flattered him. They appeared to confide in him. And my father was proud, and a little—a little too believing. There were many evils that threatened our country. This—this co-operation with the Nazis, that seemed the lesser to him. He feared the Communists much more than he feared the Nazis."

"And at the end of the war?" he asked.

She looked down. "Great trouble came to those who had collaborated. They wanted Joseph, but he had gone. My father. They stoned him in the street. Some were people he had known all his life."

"And Joseph?"

She cupped her glass in both her hands and stared down into it as though it were a blood-stained crystal. "Joseph," she said softly, "was a Nazi."

"But it's because of him . . ." he began. "Because you wouldn't say . . ."

"He was also," she said stiffly, "my brother."

She tossed off the rest of the wine with a little final gesture. She slid off the wall and smoothed her skirt. "And now," she said, suddenly bright again, "this is a holiday." She took his hand and squeezed it as though it was he who needed reassurance. "It is," she laughed, "a great honour to be taken on an expedition by a man who is—at the moment anyway—the most popular man on the island."

They walked slowly back to the bus. Pereira had finished his wine and was waving impatiently at the little knot of his passengers who were still laughing and talking in the doorway of the tavern. He hooted his horn and it had no effect except to increase the laughter. Then he started the engine, and they came scurrying for the bus as if blown by a gigantic puff of wind.

The road was much more even now, winding along a slow downslope into a valley. Then, suddenly turning a sharp corner, they saw Furnas Lake, pale yellow in the sunlight and shining like a captive moon among the surrounding spikes of the mountains.

Gradually, the bus descended to a village, and pulled up abruptly outside the main hotel. "This is as far as it goes," Karena said. He followed her out of the bus, listened to a few words of Portuguese she said to Pereira, and then walked beside her along the rough road, bordered on either side by the long green tongues of the rhododendron bushes. The air was as still as the lake beneath it, and the quietness that held the guarded hollow enfolded them. They walked along in silence, finding and knowing and accepting one another.

"There are a few vineyards up the hillsides," Karena said at last, pointing to the terraced slopes. "And in the warm valleys they grow pineapples."

"How many times have you been up here?" he said lightly, drawing her hand through his arm. "And who with?"

"Three times," she said promptly. "And with myself." Then after a moment, "There's a path right down to the lake shore if you want to go. But it will probably be wet and muddy now."

He pointed to his heavy shoes and her own strong brogues. "Let's try it," he said. "If it's wet, I'll lift you over the worst."

For no reason she flushed and started to pick her way competently over the wet patches, but he still kept hold of her hand. They walked along steadily, half-listening to the mushing of the wet leaves under their feet, and the far away crying of a gull. Mark Kelston looked round for the road and found that the isolated trees and bushes they had passed had somehow marched together to screen them from the rest of the world. He tightened his grip on her wrist, but she went on walking. Then she took her hand away from his to hold back the shrubs that were thrusting over the path.

"We're getting near it now," Karena called. "The trees are so thick and I can smell the water."

Then, glistening through the dark leaves they saw the lemon-drop lake. Mark parted the bushes and held the branches high so that Karena could push her way through. The ground was soft and slippery under the trees, heavy with the rain and the half-decayed petals of last month's rhododendron blossoms. Mark took his hands from the branches and let the bushes snap back, cutting the two of them off in a little green hut of leaves and twigs. There was no sound except the almost imperceptible whispering of the lake. A tranquillity that was of her and the place and of him surrounded Karena. She made a little gesture with her hand towards him and drew him in. His hands felt the thin bones of her shoulders, her lips were warm, her face cool and soft against his own. His senses absorbed the feel of her body, the soft slithering of the ground under their feet, the swords of pale yellow light that the sun struck from the lake which darted through the leaves and onto their faces, the faint perfume that came from her neck and hair mixed with the heavy loamy smell of the ground and the pungent sulphur from the hot springs. But beneath it all was a sense of peace, of fulfilment, of homecoming. Then suddenly he dropped his arms from her shoulders and pushed her gently away.

Her hair was rumpled and she swept it back absentmindedly from her face. She turned away from him and started to follow the trail of sorts which skirted the water's edge. Gradually the bushes thinned out and the ground became more broken and rocky. A small stream no more than two feet wide was twisting and jumping its way over the impeding stones to the lake below. Karena looked into it for a moment, pushing the tip of her brogue to the edge of the stream and watching the little gold bubbles spark and spit over the toe of her shoe. Then she saw the lilac bush.

"Look," she said, breaking off two of the leaves that still held to its branches. "One each."

He raised his eyebrows and looked from her to the tree and back to the crumpled leaf she had thrust into his hand. She laughed at the half-puzzled, half-mocking look on his face. She reached up on tip-toe and smoothed her hand over his brow. "Don't look so bewildered! Your eyebrows! You almost lost them. And your forehead looks like the corrugated iron roof on Olivarez' new warehouse. This," she said seriously, pressing the leaf between the palms of her hands, "is an old Czech belief. The lilac is a kind of magic tree. It can tell your fortune, choose your lover, oh"—she flicked her hand in a queer little gesture she had—"do *anything.*"

"And what," Mark grinned, opening his palm and thrusting it, with its treasure of a half-crumpled leaf, under her nose, "is this little thing going to do for me?"

"It's going to sail down the stream, and so is mine. And—" Her voice trembled a little. Then she laughed, but not quite convincingly. "They will tell us as they sail, if we shall meet again, and if our fates are bound together."

Kelston frowned. He stood there, saying nothing and watching her.

"We must do it together," she went on, bending down to place hers carefully in the stream. But she had seen his face and there was no more laughter.

"I expect," she said with an attempt at gaiety, "that they'll founder on the first little stone."

"If they move at all." Kelston tossed his in carelessly beside hers. "I have an idea mine's not going to move."

But a small wave as perverse as the rest of the crooked stream, lifted the two leaves and dropped them down a minute waterfall to a pool no bigger than a teacup. First Karena's wriggled its way out and then Mark's. For a time they went together, then they were stuck on a small reef, then a marsh, then a sandbank. Then a large rhododendron leaf nearly sank them.

"They're getting near the lake." Karena clapped her hands. "That's good, Mark. And yours is forging ahead. It's doing splendidly. Mine is stuck," she said wistfully. "But yours is pushing on and on."

Then Mark's leaf drifted into a quiet backwater and Karena's moved up. It twisted round madly in a whirlpool, and caught hold of Mark's. Joined by their two stems the two leaves bobbed up and down leisurely on tiny waves in the last short stretch of stream. Mark and Karena walked right up to the edge of the lake to catch the last glimpse of the two locked leaves drifting quietly away over the lake's smooth water.

Mark lit his pipe while Karena chattered on in a voice that was now high and brittle and lifeless. "We used to break twigs from the lilac bush, and count them," she said breathlessly, not looking at him. "If the pieces were even, it was good luck."

"And were they?"

"Oh, sometimes." She swung her scarf gaily in her hand. "Sometimes not."

Then after a moment, "The view up the hills is pretty." She spoke like a hostess, polite but unsure.

"Let's go then," he said abruptly.

They climbed in silence until the grass gave way to dark

yellow stone, and the path was strewn with rocks and boulders. There was only room for one person and Karena led the way. Kelston looked down at the sun-filled valley, the yellow and green and gold of the fertile land and the square white boxes of the houses. The sun was warm on his head and shoulders and the cool clear air beat back into his lungs like miniature salt-water waves. It was as exhilarating as swimming in the early morning in a sea not yet warmed by the promising sun. Ahead of him, Karena moved with a quiet unconscious rhythm of hips and thighs and ankles, as powerful to his senses as the sun and the air and the mountainside.

Within sight of the top, the path levelled out into a narrow platform filled with jumbled stones. She stopped and waited for him, looking out across the valley. The wind whipped her skirt tightly around her legs, tangled the dark curls and flicked the colour into her cheeks.

Mark pointed to a large boulder. "Sit down, Karena," he said almost sternly. Then he stood with his arms folded and his back to the valley looking down at her questioning face.

"There's something that I want to tell you. Now. Before we go any further. I should have told you before."

She waited in perfect stillness. He pushed his hands in the pockets of his trousers, and gripped the bunch of keys and the loose change. He looked away from her face and down at the weather-smoothed rock at his feet. When he drew a breath to speak, the wind seemed to have scoured out his mouth and left it as dry as the mountain stone.

"I can't," he began, "I mean, we can't—"

"You mean," said Karena, gently prompting, "that we can't go on. That you're married."

"So you knew?"

"Not till now. Not till you said there was something. Though I knew," she said sadly, "down by the lake, by the lilac tree—" Her voice trailed away.

"And what made you guess it was that?"

For some time Karena hesitated. Her eyes were thoughtful. Then she said simply, "Because I could think of no other reason. For us."

"But there's something else, too," he went on grimly. He watched her face closely as though the sight of her obvious distress by that much diminished his own. "I have a son."

Her eyes were hidden by her lashes, but her mouth was wistful. "A son, Mark," she repeated, mingling with the obvious love and pride in his own voice, a tenderness of hers for his child.

"So there it is, Karena. Now you understand." He spoke the words slowly and finally. She said nothing. Only her eyes changed. She looked beyond him at the fields and the mountainside, and when her eyes came back to him again they seemed to have travelled like twin grey winds, to have drawn up all the wetness from the valley and the hills, and to be that much heavier because no tears fell.

She looked down at her own quiet hands, her body quite still. The wind fluttered her hair across her forehead and swept it back again. Then she said, "You're right, Mark. If you can go back"–she frowned in concentration, picking her words carefully–"to–to what you were before–" She looked up at him to help her to express the feeling that she knew he shared, but his face gave her a blank refusal. "If," she struggled on, "you can be happy to forget this, then you should go back."

"There's no going back," he said coldly. "I haven't left anyone."

"Not in that way," she said flatly.

He shrugged his shoulders, and she went on quickly as though anxious to finish with it all. "Anyway, it's your decision to make."

"It's made," he said and reached out a hand to help her.

But by herself she stood up, and started to walk along the path that led down the other side of the hill.

Kelston swung down the track behind her. She walked a pace in front of him, her head high, her feet finding their way surely over the rough stones. He whistled softly, scuffing his feet against the loose pebbles, sending them noisily down the path ahead of them.

He was glad that it was over before it had begun, glad that she was hurt and withdrawn from him. He kept his eyes fixed on the huddle of white houses at the bottom of the path, telling himself that he did not want to see her face, to watch her graceful swinging walk, to touch her. He wanted to get to the bus and back to the hotel and on that aeroplane, just as soon as it was serviceable. Then the strange feeling that he had for her, the oneness, the drawing of him to herself would go. As tenuous as the mist now rising above the lake, as colourful and as beautiful while it had lasted, it would break and disperse in the high wind of his reason.

The sunlight was leaving the white houses. Only a brightly coloured fragment remained over the western mountain, and the valley was filling up with a soft luminous light. He had been concentrating on their whiteness as if they were the only visible light on which to go home on for a dark and difficult landing. Now, they merged with the fields and the trees, and the terraced slopes of the vineyards. Far away, at the other end of the quiet valley, he could hear the sound of the bus from Ponta Delgada.

He drew his hand out of his pocket to look at his watch. Instead, he took hold of her arm, and suddenly twisted her round. He held her tightly as though now she was all he had left in the world. Her mouth was surprised and sweet and joyful, and round her eyes was salty wet. She gave a little murmur of pain as his lips tried to bruise away the troubles and the complications that separated them. But she did not draw away.

He tilted up her chin and looked into her face for a moment. Then he said softly, "That decision. You were wrong, weren't you? There never was one. Not for me to make. Nor for you."

A golden sun, suddenly released from two days' imprisonment behind the immense grey walls of the storm, shone out for a moment into the cockpit of Easy Dog. By now Felicity was heading off towards Norway, and the weather over England was improving rapidly. Ferris was bringing home the passengers who had been stranded in the Azores. He was not in the best of tempers. Instead of spending just one night in Ponta Delgada he had been forced by a mechanical delay to wait there two. Easy Dog had developed a leak in one of the many hydraulic pipelines that ran through the aircraft like veins. Inflammable hydraulic fluid had dripped out of the system which actuated the flaps, the brakes, the undercarriage and the nose-wheel steering. On top of it all, he had a white-faced, self-confident little first officer called Cockcroft who had been getting on his nerves.

"London has just cleared us down," Cockcroft said, in his pompous little voice.

"I heard them. I heard them," Ferris said irritably. "I've got my ear phones on as well, you know."

"Down to seven thousand."

"I know. I know."

Ferris put the nose of the Marlborough gently down. Below them the white edges of the Channel made an irregular fret-saw pattern around the French coast.

"Perfect evening to fly," Cockcroft said.

"Too perfect," Ferris grumbled. "Visibility unlimited. No wind. Old woman's weather." He sniffed as though he was smelling the orange coloured moustache just under his nose.

The training captain who had given Ferris his command

course on Marlborough after the war had said to him, "My job is to turn gallant young gentlemen into fussy old women." Then he had looked at Ferris' long row of war decorations. Ferris laughed. It was not the thing to do, and the training captain was not pleased. The course had not improved their friendship. Ferris had picked up civil flying remarkably quickly. He soon proved that he was a good deal better than the man who was instructing him. At the end of the course, the training captain had said to him, "I don't say you're not an excellent pilot. All the same I can't help feeling you'd have done better to stay in the Air Force." In its own way it was an admission of failure. Ferris, after all, had *not* turned into an old woman.

Now, almost irritated that he was matched against such a weak opponent, Ferris stared out at the clear air without appreciating the immense view it gave him. He saw London Airport forty miles away. Slowing down the Marlborough he called for Field Approach Check. Cockcroft droned out the fifteen items, while Ferris and the engineer checked each one. "Shall I put sixty per cent flap down now?"

"Yes."

The speed steadied around 150 knots. Gently and gracefully Easy Dog descended in the still air.

"You can cancel Instrument Flight Rules," Ferris said. "Tell 'em we can see the whole works."

Cockcroft got into the Tower. "Cleared straight in. Runway Two-Eight Left."

"I heard," Ferris snapped. "I heard. Gear down. Landing Check."

The wheels rattled down. The hydraulic pump whirred at full pressure, putting the gear into position and locking it down. The speed dropped to 125 knots.

Ferris lined up the aircraft with the runway. "Twenty inches," he called to the engineer. The engine noise died down to a steady hum. A mile and a half out Ferris called

"Eighty per cent flap," and the speed dropped another ten knots. Just over the hedge he asked for fifteen inches manifold pressure, and full flap. Then he pulled back on the stick slightly for the flare-out.

Easy Dog was running just level with the runway now, a few feet up. As the speed dropped off past 100, Ferris eased the stick further and further back. "Power off," he called.

Imperceptibly the wheels touched.

"Nice landing," the first officer observed.

"Oh, I dunno," Ferris said. "Any fool can land a Marlborough in conditions like this. Even you."

They taxied up the ramp in silence. The crew went through Customs. Afterwards, Ferris signed up the innumerable documents required by the Landing Office. He went over to the captain's room to finish off the paper work that he called *bumpf*. A voyage report had to be filled in for the round trip. He wrote: "Delayed twenty-four hours due excessive maintenance on a small hydraulic leak." There didn't seem anything else to add. He looked at the Crew Confidential Reports he was supposed to fill in. The thought crossed his mind that somebody should take Cockcroft down a peg or two. But in his opinion there was more chance of that happening on the line than back in the training section. Ferris never bothered with Confidential Reports anyway; he prided himself on telling a man to his face, and letting that be that. And at least on this last trip he'd lost no opportunity of deflating Cockcroft. So he just, as usual, sent his Voyage Report, such as it was, to be added to the other bits of paper on the line manager's desk. Then he went along to the harassed individual who made up the crew roster, to see when he was out again, exploded because it wasn't soon enough, and went along to collect his mail from his cubby-hole. Through the window of the Operations Room he saw a Marlborough come in to land. That would be Kelston in Easy Zebra flying empty from São Miguel direct to

London. He knew they'd pretty well finished the repairs on the tail fin when he left. But he hadn't realized how close Kelston was behind him. Then he saw Leeming, also looking for his letters.

"Hello, Mike," he said, slapping him on the back. "Thought you were on leave."

"I am."

Ferris looked closely at him. The man seemed a bit down in the mouth.

"What's the matter? Champing to get back on the route?"

"Oh, no. We're having a very good leave. Quiet you know."

"I know." Ferris pulled a long face. "Anyway, let's look at my mail. Ah," he said, opening up an envelope, "P. Ferris, aged thirty-one. Gone, maybe, but not forgotten." He had once more resumed his position on the top of the world. He waved a scented, violet-coloured note under Leeming's nose. "Proof, you see. I'm to make my entrance at—" He looked down at the page again. "Nine o'clock. A considerate girl, this one. Theatres practically over. Too late for dinner. Just time for a drink or two, and then—*business*."

"Ferris," Leeming said, "about time you got married. Calm you down a bit."

Ferris held up his hands. "No sale," he said. "I don't like your samples. Not in this racket."

They walked out of the annex to the Operations Room. "Got your car?" Ferris asked.

"No, I came by bus. The car's having a two-thousand-mile overhaul."

Ferris said, "You *must* have been keen to get your mail. Or was it just to get away from the kids?"

"I've been expecting a letter."

"So you get them to write to the company address, too, eh?"

Leeming said irritably, "Don't you think of anything else but women?"

"And aeroplanes. Somehow they go together in my mind, Mike. Like bacon and eggs, and knife and fork. Anyway, like a lift? I'm going your way."

Leeming accepted. They got into Ferris' low fast sports car, and shot off into the mist that was already beginning to mix with London's evening smoke. Driving at well over forty, the tires screeched round the frequent bends on the road to Charfield. Ferris chatted gaily on.

A large neon sign glittered a couple of hundred yards in front of them. "Feel like a noggin, Mike?"

"Well . . . I think I've got time for the odd one."

They stopped outside the Lamb and Dragon.

"What'll you have?" Ferris asked, when they were in the private bar. "Bitter?"

"This one's mine. I'll have a half of Home Brew."

"If you don't mind, Mike, I think I'll make mine whisky."

They sat on stools by the counter. "Heard you were a day late," Leeming said. "Hydraulic leak, wasn't it?"

"More like finger trouble, if you ask me."

"How's Mark? He came in just behind you, didn't he? Bet he was wild with Dudley over the tail fin business. Featherstone told me about it."

The smile on Ferris' face widened. "I dunno about wild." He seemed suddenly lost in thought, peering down into his glass. "Come to think of it—wild isn't a bad word at that."

"What on earth are you getting at, Peter?"

"Old Mark's beaten me to it."

"Beaten you to what?"

"I never *could* line myself up something in the Azores. I'll bet he was sorry he had to leave so soon."

"You're not trying to tell me Mark's found a woman in São Miguel. It's not possible."

"Didn't believe it possible myself. Otherwise—"

Leeming interrupted. "God, Ferris," he said with sudden venom. "You've got a mind like a sewer. Mark's not like that. Just because you're a–"

"Bastard," Ferris supplied placidly. "Oh, I know. I never thought the Iron Man was that way either. But it's true." He said the words almost with satisfaction. "Nice bit of stuff–I saw her." Then he added the final recommendation. "White, too."

"Ferris, you're dreaming things."

"It's old men who dream dreams, old chap. Young men see visions. And, brother, what visions!"

"You're making it up."

"Never did have much imagination, old chap. I'll tell you exactly what I saw. I spent the last two nights of course in the Carreras. Mark had the captain's room. So they gave me another one, two doors down. Not in the same class at all. But it had what was necessary. I didn't see Mark all evening. Then, towards midnight I was sitting by the bar, when he came into the lobby. He had a girl with him. 'Hello there, Mark,' I said. He wasn't embarrassed. In fact, he seemed quite pleased to see me. 'Hello, Peter,' he called back. I strolled towards them to have a good look at the girl. He introduced me. Karena, her name was. Foreign, but don't let that fool you. I asked them to have a drink. Mark said, 'It's getting late, thanks all the same.' Then the two of them started to walk upstairs hand in hand to the captain's room." Ferris looked across at Leeming. "Now what d'you make of that?"

There was an expression of mistrust on Leeming's face. He knew Ferris of old. Yet the story had the cold stamp of truth on it. Ferris couldn't possibly have thought it out himself. "They were probably going to dump some things in his room," he said at last. "Then she'd go home."

"I was at the bar till two. No one came down. Didn't see

them at all yesterday morning and afternoon. Then damn me if the same thing doesn't happen last night."

"Looks queer, certainly," Leeming said. "All the same, I think you're reading a lot in. If they'd been doing what you think, they wouldn't have been so open about it."

"Enough evidence there for me. Human nature being what it is. Though I'll admit it was a shock to me."

"Mark's the last person–"

"Next to last, anyway," Ferris said. "You're the last person, Mike. Can't imagine you up to any fun and games." He paused to say, "Same again, barman," then he added, "Ah, well, another aviation marriage on the rocks. Let me see . . . how many's that?" He started to count on his fingers. "Seven . . . eight . . . nine." He whistled. "Ten I can think of straight away. One of Ferris' few commandments 'thou shalt not mix flying with marriage.' Either gives the men ideas. Or the wives can't stand it."

Leeming sat silent, drinking his beer and saying nothing. Ferris noticed he seemed lost in thought. "I'll make an exception in your case, Mike," he said kindly. "You and Melanie are the exception that proves the rule."

They finished off their drinks. Ferris was keen to have a few more. "Nowhere near nine o'clock yet," he pointed out. But Leeming insisted that he had to get home. "The eternal cry of the married man," Ferris said regretfully, as they left the bar.

There was another five miles to go before they reached Charfield. Leeming didn't say a word.

"You look as though you've had a bad day at the races," Ferris said to him. "Snap out of it, old chap. After all, it's Mark's little problem, not yours."

Leeming was not, however, thinking about Mark. At least, not directly, though the extraordinary incident in the Carreras had some bearing on his thoughts. He was pondering the immense difficulties of making an airline pilot's marriage happy and contented. "Another aviation marriage on the rocks," Ferris had said. The rocks, he had discovered conclusively, were not only in one direction.

Michael Leeming was very proud of the tranquil happiness of his home. It was an important ingredient in his life. And now, for the last two days, it had been shattered. The pieces lay all around him, jagged-edged, dangerous. Melanie was still barely on speaking terms with him. An atmosphere hung over the house that unsettled and dismayed him. He had gone to the airport that day, purely to get away from a place that previously he had never dreamt of leaving willingly, except to go out on the route. Suddenly he said, "How long would you say you could go on flying for, Peter? How many hours without a rest?"

Ferris said immediately, "Ol' Man River . . . that's me, old chap. Ferris keeps on rollin'."

"But how long d'you think would be reasonable on a schedule?"

Ferris considered for a minute. "Twenty-five . . . twenty-six hours, I suppose. More if there's a rest compartment."

"The Americans have a law limiting the hours at a stretch to–"

"But we haven't," Ferris said. "If we have to come under American laws, I want American rates of pay."

"I thought twenty-two hours on duty, including three refuelling stops, wouldn't be too bad."

"Good Lord, no. An old woman could do that. With both hands tied behind her back."

"Twenty-two seems all right to me."

"But we haven't a schedule anywhere near twenty-two," Ferris said. "What's on your mind?"

Leeming was offhand. "Oh, nothing . . . I was just thinking."

They drove up to the gates of Fairoaks. "Thank you,

Peter," Leeming said. He was still lost in thought as Ferris roared away down the road.

All Melanie said when he came in was, "Your supper's in the oven." He ate it alone, and spent the evening poring over the operational schedules of different routes on Empire Airways and a number of other airlines. He was scribbling down figures and doing small sums. He gave little grunts of satisfaction. All the answers seemed to please him.

When they were in bed he said to Melanie, "I'm going to see Mr. Veitch tomorrow afternoon," and he looked expectantly at his wife's face. "You know," he added, "the line manager." He meant to imply that there was something important in his mind, something that vitally affected them both.

Melanie turned round and clicked the switch of the bedside lamp. The pink light went out behind the shade that was made like a ballerina's skirt. "You can do whatever you like," she said coldly into the darkness. "Makes not the slightest difference to me."

Veronica Brownlow had achieved everything she most wanted out of life when she became the wife of Captain Kelston. Not because she had married Mark, but because she had now obtained a husband. That was what every attractive girl should have, and when she was younger, Veronica had been pretty in a pink and milk sort of way. Even now, she was striking to look at. Tall and rather thin, she kept herself beautifully groomed. There was never a hair of her head out of place. Her clothes were expensive, and she wore them well. She could say the right thing at the right time, and at parties she was in great demand as a person who totally lacked shyness, one who could be relied on for a swift flow of chatter among strangers and for the juiciest cuts of the local gossip among friends.

For herself, their marriage had been a success. Mark could

afford a comparatively high standard of living, which had automatically opened a good many doors in Charfield for cocktail parties and bridge evenings. It was the sort of life she liked, and even the coming of the baby had made little difference, since she had found a village girl to look after him most of the time. Her one disappointment had been that Mark made little effort to get to know her friends, and disliked entertaining. But he was, in any case, rarely at home. She had all the advantages of married life with few of its difficulties. She was perfectly content, and assumed Mark was, too, until she gradually realized they were growing further and further apart. It did not trouble her greatly. In the end, they led their own lives, each going their own way, but still living in the same house. When they were together, they treated each other usually with a careful politeness—the easiest way of what Veronica called "jogging along together."

She had once told a woman friend that Mark was really "married to aeroplanes." It was such a plausible reason for their present relationship, so common (she had read) among sailors and airmen, who spent most of their lives away from home, that she had accepted it herself without question. Seeing the beautiful, glittering silver things in the sky, she had thought, without any tinge of jealousy, how well she could understand it. As she grew older—she was now thirty-five—she acquired a certain hard-faced look, not unlike the successful business-woman, which (in a sense) she was. Her voice inclined sometimes to shrillness, and her habit of wearing a lot of jewellery, long pendulous earrings, rows of bangles jumping round her wrists, together with the gay scarf, that she invariably wore (the easiest way, she had found, of keeping her hair in place) at all the more informal gatherings, had given her the nickname among her friends of "the white-faced gipsy."

She had read about Mark and the *Santa Lucinda* in the

papers and had been pleased. It gave her a certain added position. It was something to talk about. The night Mark came home, an hour or so after Leeming had returned to Fairoaks, she opened the door of the flat they rented in Charfield, and said—the remark was second-hand; she had already used it at a cocktail party two days previously—"I *never* expected to read about you in the *News of the World,* Mark. In amongst the vicars and the choirboys. And all the naughty girls."

He had smiled automatically. It was past seven and the child was in bed. They went into the lounge and Veronica produced the sherry. She chatted on and on, unaware of the strained tenseness on Mark's face. Just before eight she stopped talking for a moment and walked over to the window, to pull the chintz curtains across the darkness outside. The clang of her bangles and the rattle of the wooden curtain rings combined in a queer little duet. From the sofa, Mark said quietly, "Veronica . . . I want a divorce."

Because of the sudden complete silence, he knew she was standing quite still. Knowing what he must see, he had to force himself to turn his head, and look at the horrified self-pity glistening in her eyes.

"Mark, whatever d'you mean?"

He said wearily, "A divorce. I'm sorry, Veronica."

"But why? Why, suddenly, like this?"

"Well . . . our marriage was never exactly a success."

"You've never said it wasn't before."

"There was no point. There is now."

"I know we went our own way. I thought you liked it that way."

"I liked it that way because it was the only way. Our marriage was a bit of a shell." He spoke gently to her. Even so, the words sounded harsh. He had not meant them to. All he felt now was an urgent, pressing need to get away from this place, from Veronica and the dry emptiness of his life with her.

Now that the first shock was over, only cold calculating anger showed on her face. She came over and sat on the sofa, away from him, frigid and furious.

"It's another woman," she said. "I can tell it's another woman."

Knowing that she could never understand, he nevertheless explained it all to her. He knew he could hardly expect her to, anyway, but he had hoped, perhaps, that she might realize the futility of their marriage. On her own terms, he thought, she might possibly be swung round to a settlement.

"I never expected this sort of happiness. The sort Karena and I have together."

"But you've never said you were unhappy."

"I wasn't unhappy. I don't think I was alive enough to feel any emotion at all. Not a very satisfactory way of living."

"This talk about happiness!" She snapped the word out at him. "Just like a child reaching for the moon. What's happened is that you've become infatuated with some female or other. It's common enough. Don't bother to gild the . . . well, lily must be the wrong word. I can think of a better one."

"It isn't an infatuation–"

"No . . . no. It never is. Not to the man. But it is to me. I can tell you one thing. You'd better get over it."

He said grimly, "Look, Veronica. There's nothing to get over. Except our marriage. I've told you, I want a divorce."

"Why d'you want to make it so respectable? There are other ways."

He cut her short. "In this case, there aren't. I wouldn't care a damn for respectability as you call it, unless I had to."

She laughed. A shrill, grating, triumphant little noise. "So she's putting the screws on. She wants a ring on her finger. Well, you can tell her straight . . . she won't get one." She waved her own gold band in front of his eyes. "Not this one. Not one *you* can give her."

"I wish to God, Veronica—"

"Now stick up for her. That's what you should do now, Mark. Is she too innocent to understand? Perhaps her family—"

"It happens," he said slowly, "that she's been barred entry into this country, for political reasons."

"So she's an undesirable alien into the bargain?"

"Her brother was a Nazi. She wasn't."

"Of course not."

He took no notice of the sneer in her voice.

"There's one way, Veronica. If I could marry her—"

"You happen to be married to me."

He said wearily, "That's why I want a divorce."

"If you think I'm going to give you one so you can marry her and make her a British citizen, you must be off your head."

He said that he would see she wouldn't lose financially. There would be no question of just the usual alimony. She could have just about everything he had, if she would only agree to it.

"And the child?" she asked. "What about John?"

"You know how much he means to me. If you'd let me I'd like to keep him."

She grinned at him. Her mouth went wide with a sharp white mirthlessness. "You want everything, don't you?"

He said to her, "It's your right to keep him. All the same—"

"All the same, you're *not* going to get a divorce. And you're *not* going to get the child. I know you, Mark. You know you're in the wrong. That must make you feel pretty powerless just for a change!"

"No. Just hopeless. I know I'm in the wrong as far as society goes."

She yawned. "Please don't talk ethics now, Mark. We've already had politics and economics tonight. And this happiness idea could almost be called religion. If you really want to interest me, let's talk about what it really is. Sex." She peered across at his face. "I suppose that's what you've been doing, all this time in the Azores?"

For three hours, well into the night, they went on discussing it. Veronica alternated between fury and contempt. Knowing the weakness of his position in the eyes of British law, Mark tried every way he knew how to make her understand how futile their own marriage was. With an urgent pleading in his voice, he told her she could have anything she wanted in return. "You'll live the same way as you live now," he said. "Probably better. The only difference would be that I won't be there."

He did not see what an important difference that was to her. Their marriage might be a shell, as he called it, but he *was* her husband. A woman whose husband had left her was an object of a certain amount of ridicule among her friends. She would lose face. She might, as he had promised, live up to the same level as she always did, but it would not be the same as being a free agent within a framework of marriage.

"It's no good going on talking, Mark," she said. "You're wasting your breath. You're my husband. And I'll tell you right now, you'll never be anyone else's."

3

Mr. Veitch was a heavy-jowled, stout little man. When he was standing up, with the circle of his head perched on his plump round body, he looked like an odd little hour-glass, considerably overblown at the bottom. Every morning he started the day off with a smile, but by degrees, as though it was sand, his cheerfulness disappeared. By six o'clock there was usually none apparent on his face at all. It was thought that somebody (perhaps his wife) must turn him upside down during the night, so the sand could run back up again. For in the morning, the smile had invariably returned.

Now he sat at his desk, pleased with life. It was only nine-thirty. The day had just begun. And then the phone rang. A cool, efficient female voice asked for the manager, Mid-Atlantic.

"Speaking," he said.

"Hang on please."

Like a flurry of little trumpeters preceding a procession, other female voices joined in, talking to each other, checking back to see if Veitch was still on the end of the line. Then the first voice said, "The chairman will be speaking to you in one minute's time."

He waited. The sand grains had already begun their daily descent, rather more quickly than usual. Now the chairman, naturally enough, was most anxious to secure a profit for this large airline which he controlled. That could be done by cutting down expenses and boosting up contracts. He attacked the job with an enthusiasm that was not so infectious as he seemed to think.

Suddenly, a rich voice that was all bounce and jollity boomed into Veitch's ear. "A very good morning to you, Veitch. I've got a bit of news for you today that's really going to bring a smile to that overworked face of yours."

"Good." With the greatest difficulty, Veitch stifled the word "God." "And what's that, sir?"

"I know you'll be pleased." The words dripped with satisfaction. "It's about that night-stop of yours in the Azores."

Veitch looked across at the map of the route painted on the wall opposite his desk. With its huge daubs of dazzling colours, the thing could be palmed off as an assortment of tropical fruit in any native market place. On it was all the information he was supposed to need for immediate reference. The whereabouts of his eight captains and his four aircraft was most clearly indicated. Rafferty and Crichton were the two slip-captains in Bermuda, northbound and southbound respectively. Brookdale was airborne, two hours out of Nassau in Easy Fox. Easy Uncle had taken off on schedule to Madrid with Captain Featherstone, the flight captain, in command. Easy Dog had just gone into the hangar for a Check Four—a thorough inspection of the engines and the air frame done after twelve hundred hours' flying. Easy Zebra was the stand-by. Ferris and Kelston were on stand-off. Leeming was still on leave. And Willoughby was sick.

Veitch had studied it all carefully as soon as he came in that morning. Now his eyes lingered on the blob of green that represented São Miguel Island, a quarter the way across an Atlantic Ocean that was six feet wide. The sand was simply pouring away now. Jumping Jupiter, he thought to himself, he's going to mess around with the route.

"Now that night-stop is rather expensive, Veitch."

"We pay about nine thousand pounds a year to the hotels for accommodating the passengers and crews."

"*Very* expensive." His voice sounded shocked at the cost. "Now if I were to say that we could save that money *and* gain a fat contract into the bargain, I can just imagine how you'd feel."

"That sounds wonderful, sir," Veitch said unhappily. "What had you in mind?"

"The Panama Government have been angling for an express air service with Europe for some time. Especially with Madrid. After a good deal of political lobbying (which wasn't easy, mind) and a straight fight with the Americans, who have the contract now via New York, I think it's coming our way. At present, your service does the distance from Madrid to Panama, counting all the stops, in about forty-two hours. Cut out that night-stop in the Azores, and we can do it in twenty-nine. Quite a difference, Veitch. When I told them, they were most impressed."

"Do you mean to put in a slip-crew in the Azores, sir?"

"That would be expensive, wouldn't it?"

"With only two services a week, like we're running at present, it would cost almost as much as a night-stop. We've already got two slip-crews in Bermuda. What with the wait at Panama before they come home, the crews are fourteen days away on the Tuesday service; seventeen on the Thursday one. With slips both ways in the Azores, too, they wouldn't get much time at home. Unless we're going to have some new crews, sir?"

"No, no, Veitch, we've pushed enough as it is."

"Well, sir, I don't see how we can put in a slip-crew, then."

"Quite, quite," the chairman said genially. "We've quickly disposed of that one. No slip-crew."

"If there's to be no night-stop, and no slip-crew, sir," Veitch asked, "what's there to be?"

"Why, nothing of course, Veitch. The same crew will operate from London to Bermuda."

"It's a long way, sir," Veitch said evenly. "Nearly twenty-four hours on duty. You remember we made the crew rest position into a mail compartment on your suggestion. There's nowhere the pilots can lie down for a while."

"They've got adjustable seats. Very comfortable ones. Been right off to sleep in one myself. No trouble at all."

"If you have to spend a whole day and night there, it's not quite so nice."

"We're wasting our time on small details," the chairman said. "Things I can safely leave to you. This is a big contract. Might be the making of the Mid-Atlantic line." There was a pause. "After all," he said deliberately, "the Marlboroughs haven't been exactly pulling their weight."

Veitch said stiffly, "I know we've been losing money, sir, for a long time, but we've had our difficulties. We had to build up public confidence after that Gibraltar crash. That takes time."

"That was two years ago, Veitch. The public's memory isn't as long as you seem to think. After all, at the inquiry, no blame was attached to the company."

All the same, Veitch thought to himself, it cost Macclesfield the job that was now his. And it happened to be one he intended to hang on to. The Marlborough had disappeared near Gibraltar. There was no evidence of the cause. It might have been two years ago. But it had happened on the same route, on the same type of aeroplane.

At least, in the chairman's proposal, Veitch saw an opportunity to do something that was long overdue. "Anyway, sir, I could have a trip along the line and talk it over with people." His main difficulty was to find out just what *did* go on down the route. He was stuck at his desk, trying to operate a business six thousand miles long by remote control.

"You've *been* down the route."

"Well over a year ago now, sir."

"There's no need to trouble yourself. It only concerns the pilots. You can take it easy. It'll take us six weeks to work out the contract. You'll have plenty of time to get their views while they're in England." He clinched it by saying, "I'll be doing a trip myself, fairly soon."

"Oh, well, if *you're* going, sir . . ." He would come back crammed with compliments and cocktail parties. Very well pleased.

The chairman seemed to change the subject completely. "The Astroliners on the North Atlantic are doing extremely well. Packed out. We've even had to charter aircraft from other companies."

But Veitch saw the connection immediately. A profit from

the Marlboroughs please, or they'd be transferred to cope with the rush of business on the North Atlantic.

That would mean no Mid-Atlantic route. And no manager either.

"I'm certain the pilots will object on the grounds of crew fatigue, sir," Veitch said, "but I'll do what I can."

"You'll be able to fix it, Veitch. You always fix everything."

Veitch managed to grind out the next words through the skin of his teeth.

"It certainly seems an opportunity not to be missed, sir."

The chairman chuckled. His good humour was back again now. "I knew you'd be delighted, Veitch," he said. And he rang off.

With a gesture of impatient weariness, Veitch put down the receiver. The smile on his face had now completely drained away. And it was only ten o'clock.

He knew that this one was going to be tough. He could imagine what the pilots were going to say, faced with a twenty-four hour duty and no rest compartment. He was not a pilot himself. He had reached his position through long and efficient service on the Traffic and Sales sides of the company. All that morning, while he attended to various reports that were sent to him about what happened down the line, most of his mind was engaged on the problem of the night-stop in the Azores. At lunchtime, he was so certain that there just wasn't a solution that would please both the pilots and the management, that he ate practically nothing. And there was some excellent roast beef that looked done to a turn.

If only, he said to himself over and over again that afternoon, the chairman would let him go down the route. Then he could get everyone's opinions by direct contact. He could sit in the second pilot's position on the Marlborough all the time, and watch the effect of long hours' flying on himself and the pilots. Flying fatigue was a thing people knew so little about. He'd never had to worry over it before, the route was so well equipped with night-stops and slip-crews. Some people said that after flying a long way, the crew did things automatically, exactly as they were trained to fly, forgetting all their complexes and their worries, becoming what all airlines most wanted—mechanical airline pilots. Veitch could see that might be the case in normal flying. But what if an emergency arose? Wouldn't their reactions be slower at the very time when immediate action was required? Some people had hinted that Bassingbourne, captain of the aircraft that disappeared off Gibraltar, had been in the air too long without a rest. He had been on duty only eighteen hours. Where on earth did one draw the line and say with confidence—this is too long?

The only way to deal with it, he decided that afternoon, was to tackle the pilots squarely and see what they thought. They *should* know the answer. Though it wasn't the same as finding out for himself. Veitch sometimes felt like a judge—hearing all the evidence, seeing practically nothing of the action. He had to rely completely on his knowledge of human nature. Nearly everyone seemed to have a personal motive, he had found, behind every opinion or suggestion that they made, which inevitably coloured up the true story. He had to get to know those he could trust, and those he couldn't. He had to watch for the little warnings or assurances that he got from men's faces, and the way they said their words.

At the same time as she brought in his tea, his secretary said to him, "There's Captain Leeming outside, sir. Asking to see you."

"Bring him in," Veitch said. He was always pleased to see his captains. They might be able sometimes to provide a bit of information about what was going on down the route.

"Come in, Michael," Veitch said, as Leeming entered. "Glad to see you. How's the leave going?"

"Fine, sir, thanks."

He was glad of any relaxation from this problem that now so perplexed his mind. Leeming was a likeable man. His information was usually accurate, and his opinions and advice were valuable. He was happily not equipped with the axe most pilots had as a tool of their trade, and which they produced for grinding at the most inconvenient and inopportune moments. If it hadn't been for the lines round his eyes and the long streaks of grey in his tufty brown hair, his rosy face could easily have belonged to a boy. Leeming took the seat Veitch offered him. "Now, Michael, what can I do for you?"

"It's about my last trip, sir. I've been meaning to come earlier. But you know what it is on leave—"

"I know," Veitch said. "Of course."

"The flight wasn't a bad one, if you see what I mean. Good weather and so on." He leaned forward and looked at Veitch almost in dismay. "But the loads, sir . . . the loads! Only half full most of the time." He leant back again in the chair, and added with an air of finality, "We've go to do something about those empty seats."

That was another thing in Leeming's favour. He was always dead keen on making the Mid-Atlantic the most successful route in the company. In Veitch's opinion, he was a company's man in the nicest sort of sense. He didn't go browning around the managerial foundations of the chairman and the Board. He was out for good results as part of his pride in being a first-class airline captain.

As Veitch looked at him, he thought the blue eyes looked tired. Maybe a little dispirited. "I know, Michael," Veitch said sympathetically. "We're still losing money. But what can we do?"

"There's one thing that stands out a mile. The night-stop in the Azores. Cutting that out will save quite a bit. Apart from providing a far faster service to Panama. After all, the thing we're supposed to be selling is speed."

The line manager blinked as though he was squeezing the disbelief out of his eyes. He must, he decided, have heard him wrong. His mind, which had done nothing but worry over that particular problem all day, had superimposed a sound track of the chairman's words on the film now running on the real-life screen in front of him.

"The night-stop in the Azores," he said blankly. "Are you suggesting we do without the night-stop in the Azores?"

Leeming noticed the stupefied vagueness on the manager's face. "I'd hoped you'd like the idea." He sounded disappointed. "If you think it's impractical of course—"

Veitch's words fairly streamed out in a mad dash to catch up with a subject that seemed to be running away from him. "Wait a bit, wait a bit." He was nearly shouting now. "I certainly don't think it's impractical. I like the idea. I like it very much indeed." Almost breathless with effort and excitement, he panted, "But how on earth can we do it?"

"Simply by the same crew taking the aircraft all the way to Bermuda."

"No slip-crew at São Miguel?"

"I see no need."

"It'll mean nearly twenty-four hours on duty. Without a rest compartment. D'you really think the pilots would wear it?"

"I don't see why not, sir."

Steady, Veitch said to himself, let's look at this thing fairly and squarely. Pilots did not, as a general rule, come into his office with a disinterested scheme for benefiting this airline for which they all worked. If it had been one of the others, he'd have been sceptical. But Leeming was different. Leeming he had learnt to trust.

"Well, it's good of you to come with this excellent suggestion, Michael," he said at last. "I'll certainly take it up with the Powers That Be."

"D'you think you can talk them into it, sir?" His voice was full of anxiety. Veitch thought how keen the man was on his job.

"I'll try, Michael. I'll try," he said. "You know what they are. But I think they'll see the sense in this one."

"It'll save them a lot of money. I've always had the impression that saving money was a bit of a thing with them."

"Yes . . . money . . . expense. Certainly a tricky subject with the chairman," Veitch said vaguely. Then he added, in a much more definite tone, "You think it's all right, Michael? You wouldn't get too tired?"

"I know it's all right."

"Perfectly safe?"

"Of course."

"What about the other pilots?"

"I've talked it over with Ferris. He seems to think twenty-two hours would be perfectly all right. I'm certain most of the others would, too."

It was difficult to control the satisfaction on Veitch's face. So very rarely did the orders of the management and the wishes of the pilots run in two parallel lines. Leeming had obviously considered the thing carefully. Now, he went into details, brushing aside the idea of fatigue, and pointing out that the aerodromes at the end of the leg, when the pilots would be most tired, were Bermuda, with its good weather record, on the way out, and London Airport, with its excellent aids for landing under poor conditions, coming home. He also showed Veitch schedules of other lines and other companies, some calling for even more hours on duty.

There were other considerations, too. Due to the fact that at present the aircraft arrived in Panama in the morning, and had to leave in the evening to connect with the South American companies, it stayed at the airport there over twelve hours. If the night-stop in the Azores came out, it would arrive in the late afternoon, and could be turned round in less than three. That time added to the saving achieved by only refuelling at São Miguel would mean that the aircraft would be home nearly two days earlier, allowing a much more efficient utilization.

They talked it over earnestly for two hours, examining the idea from every angle—except two. Veitch saw no need to mention the secret of the Panama contract. It would only complicate the issue. He had found out from experience that if the pilots were going to benefit the management over doing a particular thing, they tended out of sheer habit to dig their toes in, and say they wouldn't hear of it, having always at the back of their minds the idea that their acquiescence might easily form the basis of a new salary agreement. And Leeming saw no need to say that as well as the aircraft, the crews would arrive home two days earlier which would be added to their stand-off to give a more equitable ratio between time-in and time-away.

When at last Leeming left, Veitch suddenly felt like a man newly released from hard labour. He had obviously been making a mountain out of a molehill. After all his fears that he wouldn't be able to budge it a yard, the night-stop in the Azores looked like being a pushover.

He walked over to the window and stared out at the evening settling down on the hangars and the parked aircraft, the rubble and the half-finished buildings that together made up London Airport. His little hour-glass figure was silhouetted against the dying sun.

Defying the laws of gravity, the sand of his good humour flowed back into his face.

After a silent lunch that day, Melanie had watched her husband make his little preparations to go to the airport with a feeling of helpless love and anger inextricably intertwined in her heart. She disliked having rows with Michael, and this one was a real storm. She knew that she spoiled him far too much, waited on him hand and foot. Her boundless affection for him seemed automatically to flood in those directions. The fact that the object of all this love was only present to receive these attentions for a third of the year filled her with a deep resentment. She mistrusted flying—"I can't understand," she had once said to Michael, "what makes it possible for the things to stay up in the air"—and it seemed unnecessarily tempting the fates to allow part of her life (for that was how she regarded Michael) to be suspended so entirely without support for longer than was utterly necessary. Over a fortnight away she considered far too long, and she could always see the abominable skyline that bounded his week at home with an aridly accurate clarity.

Before he left to catch the bus, he said cheerfully, "Well, I'm off."

"So I see," she said. Part of her wanted to hug him and make it all up. But her pride had been wounded far too much to allow it. She was certain he was going to the airport, as the day before, just to get out of the house. He needn't have looked so glad to be leaving.

He came over to kiss her. She turned towards him a pale, cold cheek. He looked depressed again when he went out.

All that afternoon, she thought, Should I make it up or shouldn't I? It had been going on for nearly three days. But Michael seemed to take so much for granted. Certainly he couldn't help being away. She knew he was only trained for the job of flying.

He came back just after the children were put to bed, obviously pleased about something. He told Hugh a bedtime story, and tucked them both in for the night. The best of spirits seemed suddenly to have come over him.

She said to him reproachfully, "You're very full of beans tonight." They were eating a hitherto silent supper.

"I've got something to tell you, that's why."

For all her efforts to prevent it, interest crept into her eyes. "What about?"

"You know I saw the line manager this afternoon. About the route. Your favourite subject in fact. The time we spend away from home."

"I didn't think anything could be done about it." She sounded disappointed.

"Well, it can," he said triumphantly. "It may not sound much. But it'll show you that I've tried."

"You haven't told me anything yet." She kept herself purposely away from the hands that sought hers.

"I saw Veitch about the length of the trips. Fourteen days on the Tuesday service. Seventeen on the Thursday trip. I agree with you. They're far too long. And the stand-offs are ridiculous. Nothing can be done about the Bermuda slip. But the Azores night-stop—" He paused and looked for the effect of his words on her.

"Well . . . what about it?"

"It can come out. I'm certain he agreed with me. It'll save the company a lot of money, besides providing a faster service. And it'll cut nearly two days off our time away. So we'll have two days longer stand-off." His eyes seemed to plead with her. "I told you it might not sound much, Melanie, but you're pleased, aren't you?"

The little offering might certainly not look very wonderful, but to Melanie it was worth far more than the most magnificent diamond brooch. She was being presented, perhaps, with nearly another two days every three weeks. Suddenly, her stunted dwarf of a year, only a third as big as most people's, had another month in it. Not only that, Michael had done this on his own. Thought it all out and presented the case. Because he had realized at last how she must feel.

She was filled with an immediate, joyful delight. She put both her hands in his now. "Michael," she said. "Oh, Michael

. . . you've made me feel such a bitch. This silly row." Tears of happiness glistened in her eyes, now it was over. "And all the time you understood, and you were trying to do something about it. While I thought you were just sulking. Michael . . . it's wonderful."

He was pleased. "I'd hoped you'd feel this way," he said.

Then she drew away and looked doubtful. "But it's a long way to fly. All the way to Bermuda without a rest."

"Other people do it every day. And I've often done longer."

"But will the other pilots agree?"

"I don't see why they shouldn't. Ferris is flat out for it."

"Michael . . . it's too good to be true. There must be a snag in it somewhere."

"Not one," he said in a voice full of such calm confidence that she felt lulled and convinced. She trusted Michael entirely on things she knew little about. She knew he was a professional, experienced and skilful. She trusted him in his job, just as she had trusted him (before the row) with their life together. And now that life looked like being enlarged —fractionally, some people would think, until they, too, had to wait for someone they loved to come home, only to fly off far away again almost as soon as they were back.

"Can't think for the life of me why it didn't dawn on me before," Michael said.

As a kind of celebration for the end of what Melanie described as "the row to end all rows," they shared a bottle of Bristol Cream Sherry. They talked and laughed and chatted together. There seemed so much (after a three day fast of silence) to get off their chests. It was past midnight when they went to bed. They went off into a deep sleep immediately, clasped in each other's arms. Fairoaks stood firm again.

But in a house a half mile down the road, the Kelstons' family life was being rapidly broken up. That same morning, Veronica had said to Mark, "It's no good talking any more about it. If it was a passing affair, it wouldn't have mattered. So long as you finished it off."

"It's not a passing affair."

"I'm beginning to believe you. She seems to have bitten you pretty badly."

"You can call it what you like. So long as I've made you understand I'm in love with her."

"I never said anything about love. But if you think I'm going to stay here with you, while you carry on—"

"I'm not suggesting you do."

She had thought it all out. People would be bound to hear. People would talk. The only choice open to her was to leave him first. There was always some respect felt for a woman who wouldn't stand for her husband's monkey-tricks. The other way round would be unbearable.

"You won't get a divorce, I promise you that," she said. "But I'm not going to stay here. Nor is John. Not for a minute longer than we can help."

In the afternoon, she made her preparations to take herself and the child off to her parents' flat in London. During the evening, she got down to how they were to be supported. To the last, she maintained her strict business sense of marriage. She knew Mark's salary, and in a shrewd bargaining way, she began to talk of how much they would need. To her surprise, she found that there was, after all, no argument. She was, in fact, staggered by the amount he proposed to give her. He intended to live on a couple of hundred pounds a year. The rest was for herself and the child.

All she said was, "I suppose that way you can keep your conscience quiet. You know damned well you're in the wrong."

"Nothing to do with conscience. It's all I'll need. You might as well have the rest. But I'm putting a third in trust for John. And then there's my insurance policies to keep up before any of it is divided."

She did a rough quick sum in her head. "So there won't be very much after all."

"It's all I can give you," he said. "I've got to live in order to *make* my salary."

Before she left for the station next morning, she said, putting on her gloves with an air of knowing the immense power she held in those long, injured-party hands, "When you come to your senses, you'll know where to find me."

She wore a black, flowered hat. It was, after all, a formal occasion. Mark kissed the child good-bye with real sadness. But he saw Veronica go on her way out of his life with immense relief. He had begun to realize these last few days the strain that there had been on him, just living in the same house with her, playing out appearances with their sham marriage as the easiest way out of an apparently hopeless situation. He heard the clang of her bangles die away as the taxi door shut behind her. He watched the stiff ramrod back sitting straight up in the seat. The hair behind her hat and her golden earrings competed with each other to outglitter the weak autumn sunshine. Then everything about Veronica disappeared together round the corner of the road on the way to the station.

Before he went out in command of the next Tuesday service, he had vacated the flat and put their furniture into store. He went up to London to find a room to live in, happy anyway that some decisive action had been taken to alter the course of his life, that had seemed to be aimlessly and sluggishly just drifting away. As for the divorce, he couldn't help thinking that Veronica would change her mind. She had, in the past, changed it so many times.

He also went to the Foreign Office, to discuss the chances of Karena coming to England. There was the usual trouble seeing anyone. The usual politeness. They agreed that things had changed. But there would still be many difficulties and a long delay while inquiries were being made. These things, they said with a smile, couldn't be hurried. But the thought of seeing her again so soon kept his spirits high. For the next few months anyway, the pattern of his life would be very simple. As soon as he was back in England, he would ask the man in charge of the rosters to get him off on service again. A couple of days' rest would be all he would need. It was the only way of being with her more often. The peace he had known with her was already having its tranquil effect on his mind. He looked forward to the future, as a gift to be eagerly awaited. Happiness (even his own little bits of it) was so well worth waiting for.

Book Three

The End of the South-East Quadrant

October 20-November 26

1

Like an inefficient laundry, the roster collected a pair of pilots, one navigator, one engineer, one radio officer, one steward and a stewardess every Tuesday and Thursday, sent them through the long washing machine of the route, and delivered them back half a month later every Tuesday and Sunday. Leeming was collected. Featherstone went slowly onwards. Crichton was delivered. Day by day the names changed on the map in front of Mr. Veitch's desk. With an inevitable slowness he managed to see the pilots as they came back, discussed the question of the Azores night-stop with them, and then ticked them off the list he had so carefully drawn up.

To the first few he said, "It's Captain Leeming's idea, of course. Not the management's. I was just wondering what you felt personally about it."

Later, he changed his approach very slightly. Now he said, "It's a long time on duty, of course. But Captain Rafferty and Captain Crichton both say they can do it. I was wondering whether you felt up to managing it, too?"

He was delighted with the results he was getting. Ferris had breezed in with, "Amount of time we spend on the ground on a trip, it's a sheer fluke some of us haven't grown roots and sprouted."

To Crichton, the line manager had said, "It's Captain Leeming's idea, of course. Not the management's. I was just wondering what you felt personally about it?" Crichton had been a shipping clerk before the war had given him this job at well over a thousand a year. Unlike the others, he could remember the day when he didn't travel first-class on the gravy train. His answer was, "If it helps the company that much, I guess we can manage it."

Amongst the pilots on the line, Ferris was admired for the way he could put a Marlborough through her paces, Leeming was respected for his attitude to the job, and Crichton was liked for his good sound horse-sense. Now Veitch said, "It's Captain Leeming's idea. Captain Ferris is flat out for it. And Captain Crichton is in complete agreement." Rafferty and Brookdale listened carefully to the names of the sponsors, watching at the same time the eager determination on the line manager's face. Then both of them said, "Jolly good idea!" Willoughby, now fit again, was the only one who was doubtful. "It's a long time on duty." To which Mr. Veitch said immediately, "If you feel you're not up to managing it, of course, there are other routes—"

Willoughby hadn't realized how far down the lonely plank those six words of his could carry him. He had only been an airline captain six months. Back he scuttled into the ship with, "I can manage it all right, sir."

As for the first officers, the older ones quickly mastered the equation: a quicker service equals a likelihood of more captains equals a certainty of overdue promotion. The batch of brand-new ones on the line opened their young eyes wide in astonishment at the courtesy of even being asked for their opinion.

By the time it came to the flight captain's turn to be delivered, Veitch had seen most of the other pilots. And now Featherstone leaned back in the managerial chair of the flight captain's office and said to the line manager, "In my day I've done longer. Very much longer."

Veitch studied the grey tufts of hair around Featherstone's

balding skull, the eyes that looked like acorns in their little cups of shrivelled flesh, and thought if he can do twenty-two hours at a stretch, there's no reason why the others, all at least seven years his junior, can't do it, too.

Disregarding the fact that most of the swinging had already been done, Featherstone went on, "If I tell them it's all right, the pilots will do it. Don't worry. I'll swing it your way."

"I'd be grateful if you could use your influence," Veitch said. If the flight captain wanted the credit, he should have it. All he wanted was the result.

And that, to his surprised relief, was exactly what he was getting. One after the other they all agreed to Leeming's proposal with a most unusual unanimity. After only three weeks, he had seen everyone except Kelston. And as Kelston always seemed to be away on the route, he was proving difficult to get hold of.

Veitch was particularly anxious to obtain Kelston's final stamp of approval on the whole idea, as a man well worth listening to. True, so were some of the others, especially Leeming and Featherstone. But the articles that Kelston contributed to the aviation journals had impressed the line manager. They seemed to have a foundation of good common sense to them. And there was no doubt that he was more technical than most other pilots, particularly on aerodynamics and stresses.

Because there seemed no other way of seeing him, Veitch came to the airport deliberately early on the Thursday that Kelston was taking out the service. He inquired for him at the Operations Room. Surprised to see the line manager appear at eight o'clock on a cold November morning, they told him there that Kelston was out on the tarmac. Veitch found him disconsolately looking up at two ground engineers who were working on the starboard inner engine of Easy Fox.

Trying to make it appear that their meeting (even at that time) was casual and unexpected, Veitch said, "Ah, Captain Kelston. Just the man I want to see. Can you spare me a minute?"

Kelston looked at his watch. "I can spare you six hours," he said.

"Aren't you supposed to be off at nine?"

The pilot nodded. "Delayed. Magneto change, Number Three engine. And a rough Number Two."

Veitch remarked sympathetically, "Irritating."

"That makes it sound like a flea-bite, which it isn't," Kelston said shortly. "Maintenance should never have passed an engine in that condition."

"I'll look into it," Veitch said hastily. Most aircrew had learnt to take delays almost as routine. But Kelston was obviously annoyed about this one.

"This delay will cost me nearly half of my night-stop in the Azores," the pilot went on.

"You think that night-stop important then?" As soon as the words were out of his mouth Veitch knew he could have started the subject off more tactfully.

Kelston raised his eyebrows. "Very important."

Jumping Jupiter, Veitch thought to himself, he should have realized things had been going too easily. He'd never known the pilots agree unanimously on any subject yet.

He did his best to give a short, rueful laugh, but the effort nearly choked him. "Pity," he said. "All the other pilots seem to think it unnecessary."

"So I've heard."

"I was hoping we could do away with it. The expense angle, you know."

"I'd heard that, too. As I see it there are two reasons why that night-stop is necessary. First—it's far too much to expect the pilots to cope with nearly twenty-four hours on duty. Azores-Bermuda is a nasty leg. Two thousand miles of nothing but water. And you yourself know what London weather's like. Especially in the winter."

"The other pilots think they can do it."

"If they'd been Americans they wouldn't have been allowed to try. Over the other side they have some sensible legislation on the subject. But I will agree that pilots can do it normally. It's if anything went wrong that they'd be slow to react."

"There's two of them," Veitch pointed out. "And the rest of the crew as well."

"Most of these new second pilots are more a liability than an asset. And anyway, it still doesn't alter the fact that people need a break between long flights. Not necessarily sleep. The amount of sleep required depends on the individual. But a change from the sound of the engines, the cooped-up feeling, the stuffy rarefied atmosphere on these pressurized aircraft."

"And the other reason?" Veitch asked.

"These Marlboroughs are old. They need a thorough looking over somewhere on the route. As well as at the base terminals. The Azores is ideal. A night-stop gives the engineers a chance to give them a good inspection. And as far as I can gather from talking to other pilots, you're thinking of turning them round in three hours at Panama . . . into the bargain. Once out of London, they'll hardly be looked at for nearly sixty flying hours."

"The Marlboroughs have been giving particularly good service," Veitch said stiffly.

Kelston said nothing. He just gave a meaningful glance at the men working on his aircraft.

"They have their delays, of course," Veitch added hastily. "Like all other aircraft."

To the line manager, Kelston gave the rather condescending impression that the interview was over. "I've got to go to the Met. Office now, Mr. Veitch," he said, "to tell them to make out another folder." He moved a few steps away from Veitch. Then over his shoulder he added suddenly, "All the same, my advice to you is, don't expect too much from your crews. And keep an eye on the Marlboroughs. We don't want another Gibraltar."

Veitch coloured up. "I don't see how the Gibraltar business comes into this, Captain Kelston."

"It was either the aircraft . . . or the crew. One or the other," the pilot said, as he walked away from Easy Fox in the direction of the Meteorological Offices.

The line manager went on to the deserted administrative buildings, thinking he'd never been more depressed in his life. His mind was far away in the Azores. Although he had asked all the pilots and Kelston was the only one against the removal of the night-stop, Veitch felt uneasy. He seemed to be almost back where he started. All his fears about crew fatigue, his worries about the aircraft returned to garnish his already overloaded plate.

For the next day or two he became moody and irritable, even in the mornings. At one stage he was on the point of ringing up the chairman and telling him the removal of the Azores night-stop was a complete impossibility.

Then, just after lunch on the Tuesday, he received a note from the company Public Relations Office, enclosing a letter received from Mr. Parkinson, the well-known politician. It complained that Kelston, in his efforts to help a Portuguese tramp-steamer, had placed all his passengers in a position of considerable jeopardy. He had risked his aircraft in a bad storm. It was Mr. Parkinson's opinion that he was not fit for the responsible job of an aircraft commander.

Veitch remembered the incident of the *Santa Lucinda*. The company's attitude had outwardly been approving, but as the chairman had been quick to point out, it was undesirable to have their aircraft associated with any form of near-disaster, since the public's memory being what it was, the next thing people would be saying among themselves was that the ship had gone to the help of the aircraft. Which wasn't good for business. Not only that, the incident had given Kelston a certain amount of publicity. It was hard enough having to deal with pilots at the best of times without having under him a man who for the present was news value, and might, therefore, be tempted to air in some irresponsible publications views that were not in accordance with company policy. Such as this Azores night-stop, for instance. An article on crew-fatigue right now would be inconvenient and ill-timed.

Veitch had dealt with passenger complaints before. Sometimes they knew what they were talking about, more often they didn't. But Mr. Parkinson was an influential man. It was a serious accusation. He would certainly have to get the training captain to investigate it. Inevitably, Kelston slipped a notch downwards in Mr. Veitch's estimation.

As soon as he'd finished digesting the contents of this letter, he was called upon to deal with an engineer called Crayfield. The Saracen Hotel in Bermuda had written to say that while he was accommodated there as a member of the northbound slip-crew, he had been found by the house detective with a woman in his room at four in the morning. They added that if this was the sort of behaviour they could expect from the aircrew, for the sake of the other guests it might be a regretful necessity to ask the company to seek accommodation elsewhere.

Veitch had the man's personal file sent in before he saw him. Not a very brilliant career in the company. He saw that Kelston had reported him for inefficiency on duty only a couple of months previously. Presumably the training section had dealt with him on that one.

When Crayfield came in through the office door, Veitch saw at a glance that he was the typical gigolo type—brown gipsy skin and frizzy hair dripping with grease. The manager began guardedly. Sometimes there was a different side to these stories. But the man presented no defence. He admitted it was true. There was nothing left but to tear into him.

Halfway through a scathing lecture on the company's good name and private morality, he saw, with a mixture of surprise and irritation, that Crayfield stood in front of his desk with a bland smile of complete indifference on his face.

He interrupted himself. "What's so funny, Mr. Crayfield?" he said quietly. "Tell me the joke. I'd like to hear it."

The man just went on smiling.

Veitch repeated his question, much more loudly.

With an impudent up-and-down lilt to his voice, Crayfield at last deigned to talk. "I suggest I'm rather small fry, sir. Why don't you deal with the really big fish?"

Veitch looked at him blankly. "What on earth d'you mean by that?"

"I mean . . . Captain Kelston's affair in the Azores."

For a minute Veitch said nothing. Used to the petty backbitings of human beings, his mind went immediately back to the fact he had only just read. Kelston had reported this man for inefficiency. He might be in danger of losing his job on that account. Anything he said against Kelston must, therefore, be treated with a margin of reserve.

Then he cupped his chubby face in his hands and glared at the engineer. "You must realize," he said icily, "that what you're saying is tantamount to slander."

"The Iron Man." The words were meant to sound as a jeer. "There isn't such a thing."

'You're going to explain this to my satisfaction, Crayfield, or you're out on your neck."

The man kept on smiling. "There's not much to explain, sir. Captain Kelston disappears into the captain's room with a girl as soon as he gets in to the Carreras Hotel. He even has his meals sent up. I was on his crew on my last trip. I saw it all myself."

Veitch stared at him in disbelief. "A most unlikely story, Crayfield."

The engineer shrugged his shoulders. "Happens to be true . . . all the same."

Still unconvinced Veitch said, "I shall verify this, of course. You might as well know I don't believe you. If your story isn't confirmed one hundred per cent, God help you. In any case, two wrongs don't make a right. If I have any more complaints about you, the company will be glad to dispense with your services. And now—get out."

Immediately the engineer had left, Veitch went along to the flight captain's office. He didn't give any credence to Crayfield's accusation, and he was thinking of a few choice words to say to the man when he fired him. But when, incredulously and indignantly, he had told Featherstone about it all, the flight captain didn't look in the least surprised. All he said was, "I expected you'd hear of it one day."

"You know then?"

"Oh, yes. The crews are talking—"

"So it's all true?"

"Much the same story as Ferris told me. Seems to be true."

"How long's it been going on?"

"Only since that Portuguese tramp-steamer business. About a month ago. Kelston was three days in the Azores. You'll remember Easy Zebra's tail fin?"

Veitch said grimly, "Difficult to forget."

Featherstone laughed. "Even more difficult now."

"Why didn't you tell me?"

"Not my pigeon."

"I'm always the last to hear anything." Veitch's voice was full of resigned irritation. "I can't understand why the hotel hasn't complained."

"Ferris says Kelston has the management exactly where he wants them. He became quite the local hero, you know."

"But he's got a wife and a child—"

"I know. Shocking business. If he wants to do that sort of thing, why the hell doesn't he keep it decently dark?"

Veitch went back to his office to think it all out. The interruptions that day, added to his absorption with the Azores night-stop, had made him way behind with his paper work. He struggled with the endless reports that lay on his desk. It was past nine o'clock when he finally finished for the day. He went over to the Operations Room, as he always did before he went home, to check on the latest signals that had come in from the Route. There he saw Leeming in uniform, collecting the Journey Log Book of Marlborough Easy Zebra. He said to him, "Delayed, Michael?"

The pilot grimaced. "Over twelve hours, sir. Hydraulic leak and an engine change."

Veitch was not particularly worried. Bad serviceability seemed to go in spasms. The Marlboroughs ran like sewing machines for three months. Then there was a bad spot. Then back to the sewing machines again. He said, "Kelston was delayed, too. On the Thursday service. Still, I suppose we can't complain. Things haven't been too bad up till now."

"First long delay I've had for nearly a year," Leeming said.

"The Marlboroughs are running all right?"

"Perfectly. You couldn't want a better aircraft."

Veitch hesitated. It might be a good thing, he thought to himself, to get further verification on the Kelston affair. In a quiet corner of the Operations Room he discussed it with Leeming. Reluctantly the pilot confirmed the story. "It'll blow over," he said. "These things always do."

"I hope so," Veitch said. "For everybody's sake, I certainly hope so."

The crew car was waiting for Leeming to take him to his aircraft. "Have a good trip, Michael," Veitch said absently. On his own now, he studied a movement signal that had come in—Easy Fox had left Jamaica for Panama, Captain

Crichton in command. The little slip of paper did not really interest Veitch. He was thinking about Kelston. The puzzle of the odd man out in the question of the Azores night-stop was beginning to take definite shape. So that was why he was so dead against its removal. That was why he had been so annoyed by the delay to the Thursday service. All the time there was a woman behind it.

The whole imposing façade that had been Kelston crashed to pieces in the line manager's mind. The thought of a man putting up a front like that in order to do dirty little things behind it sickened and infuriated him. The pilots often had their own personal motives for suggesting things. He had been a fool not to have suspected they might also have their own egoistic schemes for opposing them. All this red-herring stuff about crew fatigue and the Gibraltar crash! Kelston had just been playing a particularly unpleasant game of blindman's buff with him.

But there *were* compensations. The Kelston affair clarified the problem of the Azores night-stop. Like a high-powered searchlight, it probed into all the unknown corners, making everything as plain as daylight. Veitch was now perfectly satisfied that it could be removed. All the pilots agreed with him. Kelston couldn't be counted. Kelston had his own little reasons. He would phone the chairman in the morning. The Azores night-stop could come out at the end of the month, at the same time as the Panama contract became final.

That at least was a load off his mind. And yet somehow . . . He couldn't explain it, but he still felt a little uneasy. Not so bad as before, of course, but his worries were still there. In his car on the way home, he saw the arc lights around the tarmac glittering on the fuselage of Marlborough Easy Zebra. The chocks had been pulled away, and Leeming was slowly taxiing forward, his two landing lights probing the darkness in front of them like twin antennae. Veitch stopped for petrol at the all-night garage opposite the airport gates and then went on down the Bath road, cutting off to the left towards the Staines' reservoirs.

He saw the lights of Runway Two-Eight stretching out into the misty blackness. Between their double row moved the red and green navigation lights of an aircraft taking off. He stopped. A dark field separated him from the end of the runway. He looked down the centre of that long straight string of illuminated pearls, watching Easy Zebra start on her long journey to Panama.

The aircraft moved so slowly, she stayed on the ground so long, it seemed impossible that she would ever get airborne. It was too much to expect that she could leap over even the small hurdle of Veitch's car, dead in her path.

The noise increased. Now much more quickly, the Marlborough became clearer and larger, till she covered momentarily the sky above him. The red and green lights blinked. The exhausts sent a number of yellow comet-tailed fireworks into the night sky.

But it was the noise that was so heartening. It shouted away the last remnants of all his uneasy fears. The huge healthy roar of those four engines suddenly deafened him with their powerful reassurance.

2

Sitting in the back seat of Easy Zebra, Miss Libby Challoner spent the twenty-six seconds of the take-off from London Airport studying her shoes. This was her fourth trip as a stewardess, and the initial period when she had sat glued to the glass counting the runway lights as they flashed one by one past the porthole was over. The shoes were new. They had very high heels. And the steward, Mr. Atkins, had already commented on their utter unsuitability for walking about in an aircraft.

"They'll break your ankles," he prophesied with a certain gloomy satisfaction. He had taken one look at her, and decided this trip he'd have to work hard.

Stewardesses in his experience fell into three categories: square-figured homely types, coldly lean efficient types, and glamour-pusses. The first two tried to make themselves useful. The last tried to fit in with the décor of the inside of a Marlborough.

By the very fact of choosing shoes like that, this one had typed herself with an unmistakable clarity.

As Easy Zebra set course for Madrid, the passengers started to grumble to each other about the delay, then allowed themselves to be soothed by the free drinks the catering crew were handing round.

When Michael Leeming appeared to have his usual few words with them, they had been lulled, partly by the engines, partly by the alcohol, into a comfortable anticipation of a few hours' sleep.

Leeming was feeling particularly pleased with life.

Melanie had said good-bye to him in her usual affectionate way. Fairoaks was in excellent shape, and even this delay was not really unwelcome. It provided a convenient challenge that he had every intention of accepting.

He would show Mr. Veitch that he meant what he said when he told him that London-Bermuda would be done without a rest.

The passengers asked him the usual questions. It had always amazed him how little they knew about flying.

The well-worn sentences tumbled out of his mouth, one after the other:

"No sir, the engines aren't on fire. Those are the exhaust flames you can see."

"We're flying at eighteen thousand feet, madam, but we're pressurized down to eight. If we weren't, everyone would have to wear oxygen masks."

"No, the wing isn't broken. That's the aileron, the control that allows us to turn, that you see moving up and down."

"We're moving at two hundred and fifty miles an hour in the air. But as we have a head wind against us, our speed relative to the ground is two hundred and ten."

They were all especially pleased when he told them that he did not intend to stay longer than an hour, just to refuel at the Azores. They might with luck catch the schedule up at Bermuda.

He worked down the left-hand row methodically.

When he got to the back, he noticed the stewardess for the first time. She was dispensing drinks from the table near the door. A fair-haired girl of about twenty-four, with large blue eyes, her neat figure accentuated by the little uniform waistcoat she wore over her white blouse.

"You're new, aren't you?" he asked. He remembered her name on the crew manifest. Miss Challoner.

"Yes, sir."

Then he noticed the shoes. He pointed at them.

"Not very sensible, are they?"

"So the steward said." She gave a gay little laugh. "I rather like them, sir."

Leeming looked at her again. For a new stewardess, she showed a remarkable lack of shyness.

"All the same," he said, "I think you'll hate the sight of them by the time we've finished this leg. We're going right through to Bermuda."

"But what about the night-stop in the Azores?"

"We've got to try and catch up on schedule."

She sighed. "Pity."

"There'd be no point in stopping anyway. It'll be lunchtime when we arrive there. Anyway the passengers will be settling down soon. You can curl up at the back."

"Oh, I'll be all right." Jauntily, she shrugged her shoulders accepting the situation.

But up at the front, the rest of the crew, in Leeming's absence, were discussing it without the same resignation.

The crew roster had given him Bates as navigator, a new first officer called Timperley, Draper as radio officer, and a hard-bitten old engineer called Drewitt.

Leeming had said to them, "I'm all for trying to catch up with the schedule. How about everyone else?"

Everyone else had kept quiet, which Leeming had interpreted as unanimous consent. As soon as the crew compartment door closed behind him, Bates said to Draper, "How d'you feel about it?"

Draper was cautious. "Well . . . they say we'll be doing it pretty soon anyway."

"I know. But starting off at this time of night . . . it's damned ridiculous."

Drewitt chipped in from the engineer's panel. "All you've got to do is to say so. Go crew-fatigue. Nothing to stop you."

Bates considered this for a minute. "I'll do it if someone else does."

He looked round them. "What about you, Draper?"

"I dunno, Ricky." Draper turned to Drewitt. "What d'you think?"

Drewitt said, "What the hell d'you think I am? A schoolgirl? Trouble with you people . . . you're too pampered."

"Christ," Bates said. "If you're going to tell us how hard you worked before the war, Drewitt, kindly close the door to the navigation cabin."

"I will with pleasure," Drewitt snapped back. "Stop you getting fidgety over the engine instruments. I'll tell you straight, Bates, if you start pointing out low oil pressures to me on this trip, so help me I'll—"

Draper interrupted quickly with, "What does the first officer think?"

"Oh, Junior . . ." Drewitt said impatiently.

From their careful watch over the automatic pilot, First Officer Timperley allowed his shy eyes to turn back towards the crew. He was second in command of this aircraft. He had been feeling uncomfortable about the trend of the conversation ever since it started. Leeming had already told him that he was responsible for crew discipline. Vaguely, he had wondered what that meant. He had two hundred hours' flying experience in the R.A.F. But there they had called it "crew spirit." It was all rather difficult. Drewitt was old enough to be his father.

"I'm certain," he said at last, "that Captain Leeming knows best."

"I'll give you this, Mr. Timperley," Bates said with some heat. "He certainly thinks he does."

"One of these days, Junior," Drewitt said, "you'll learn that most people you fly with in this racket are only interested in themselves. Not the company."

Draper suggested, "Let's get back to the subject. Does anyone else except Bates want to go crew-fatigue in the Azores?"

"Not me," said Drewitt.

"The captain and I, of course—" began First Officer Timperley.

"Of course," Bates said shortly. "What about it, Draper?"

Draper hesitated. "Not enough of us, Ricky . . . I'm sorry. If the company are going to do without the night-stop anyway . . . they might think . . . if only two of us—"

"All right, all right," Bates said. "Leeming mightn't be pleased. You've got to look after your position in the company. All the same—"

But he didn't finish the sentence. Captain Leeming had opened the door to the crew compartment.

"Well," he said, with a smile all over his face. "The passengers are as pleased as punch that we're catching up on the schedule."

As Easy Zebra flew over the Bay of Biscay, French fishermen working at their nets saw the purposeful cross of coloured lights move steadily across the sky. She looked very determined, very certain of where she was going, as though from her great height she was unhampered by any mortal horizon.

But Easy Zebra's brain was her flight deck, where five people contributed uneven shares into the common pool, and it was not as single-minded as the outside of the aeroplane suggested.

Leeming, who controlled it, sat looking contentedly out at the stars, and talking to the first officer. He spoke of endurances, blind landings, cross-wind take-offs.

"The main thing on this job," he said, "is not so much to do things quickly as to do them correctly. When you get an order from me, take your time, think about it, and for everyone's sake, get it right." Remembrance of a previous incident crossed Leeming's mind. "I once told a first officer to raise the gear, just after take-off. The clot raised the flaps on me. That one was too close. You see what I mean by getting things right now?"

First Officer Timperley said he did. Conscientiously, he was noting these pieces of advice in a pocket-sized notebook he had bought for just such a purpose.

If they had cared to, Draper and Drewitt could have listened quite easily to the two pilots' conversation. But they were not interested. Draper was already thinking about bed. He looked at his watch. Only two hours gone. Nearly another twenty to go.

Drewitt watched the needles on the engine instruments. All normal—except Number Four oil temperature was higher than the others. He opened the oil cooler's gills a fraction.

As he absorbed the mass of information that the eighty dials fed to him, he remembered the old times, when there had only been three. In those days, you weren't spoon-fed. You had to do it all on your wits, guts and intuition.

Bates sat glowering at his navigation log, irritated with everybody, including himself. He was thinking if he had any real courage of his convictions, he'd go crew-fatigue off his own bat—and the rest of them would have to wait until he said he was fit to go on.

Of all the crew, apart from the pilots, the only person who was quite happy was Libby Challoner.

The men, she had found out, were quite right about those shoes. As she came back from serving an elderly woman with Ovaltine, the steward with shocked horror noticed that she was padding around in her stockinged feet.

He told her about it as though she might be forgetful, unaware.

"But, Mr. Atkins," she said gaily. "My feet are now très confortable. I'm just taking your advice."

As Easy Zebra crossed the Spanish coast, and began to span the foothills of the Cantabrian Mountains, Atkins was considering the immense injustice of a life that had given him a good-looking half-wit to serve in the galley, when for once, there was a full load of forty-two passengers on board.

News of Easy Zebra's progress flashed far ahead of her. All the six stations along her route had been notified of her late departure. Heavy winds were delaying her even further.

Dudley in the Azores said to his senior traffic officer, "I can't understand it. These Marlboroughs are always late these days. Captain Kelston was six hours late. Now it's over sixteen!"

When he received Leeming's signal that he would be

proceeding through the Azores without a crew rest, the station manager's mood improved.

"That's what I call real company spirit," he said. "Only wish some of the others had it."

He was thinking specifically of Kelston. Despite Dudley's careful report on the damaged tail fin of Easy Zebra, putting forward a mysterious Portuguese as the guilty party, Mr. Veitch had preferred someone with flesh and blood arms on him to carry the can. It was certainly Kelston's own report that had put him up to selecting Dudley for a sharp reprimand as being the person responsible.

The station manager hated losing. And Kelston was up to more mischief in this Carreras Hotel business. From what had been hinted to him darkly, the Azores' stop-over looked like it was turning into something out of the Arabian Nights.

With Leeming, when he landed, Dudley was all affability. "Going on will save nearly two hundred pounds in hotel expenses alone," he said to him.

"The main thing is getting back somewhere near the schedule," Leeming pointed out. "In any case, I expect you've heard the rumours that the night-stop is coming out?"

Dudley had. In fact he had written to Mr. Veitch, saying that it was an excellent idea, "on the grounds of economy." He was anxious to show publicly how much he had the company's interests at heart. Privately he was even more anxious than ever (the accident to Easy Zebra had given him a nasty jar) to get aircraft, passengers and crew off on their way as soon as he set eyes on them.

"Well . . . let's get off pronto," Leeming said.

"I'll go and hurry the passengers up over their meal, Captain."

Dudley felt even better in the restaurant, where the atmosphere was bright and cheerful. Everyone had slept.

Everyone was glad that, after all, they were only going to be an hour or two late on the other side of the Atlantic.

Easy Zebra gleamed bravely in the sunshine as she took off that afternoon on the two-thousand-mile ocean crossing to Bermuda. Leeming whistled cheerfully as he guided the Marlborough up into the clear sky. Behind his back, the little tune quickly died away into a gloomy silence.

Draper was doing his best to keep his eyes open. Bates had had an acrimonious argument with Drewitt when he had helpfully pointed out to the engineer Number Four's high oil temperature. The navigator now sat with his elbows on the table, chewing a pencil and glaring at his chart. He was tired and irritated.

And in any case, he had always disliked the Azores-Bermuda leg. Unlike any other route in the company, no alternative aerodrome was named on the flight plan to which they could proceed if the terminal closed in—partly because fog was pretty well unknown over Bermuda, and partly because the nearest landing ground was over three hours' flying time away and it was not economical to provide the reserve petrol to reach it.

This trip they had a full load of passengers.

"Good for business," Leeming had said to him in the Azores.

"Not so good for the petroleum company," was Bates' comment back.

The head winds against them had made the flight plan nearly twelve hours, and they had nowhere near full tanks. Due to the restricted take-off weight of every civil aircraft, it was passengers or fuel. But not both. The petrol that Easy Zebra carried would be sufficient to reach Bermuda, with a little extra in case the winds were more adverse than forecast, plus an island reserve, sufficient to hold overhead for nearly two hours.

As Easy Zebra droned comfortably onwards at 18,000 feet,

Bates forced his weary mind into the alert watchfulness he knew was necessary. Bermuda was a small island to hit after so long over the ocean. Equipped as they were with every navigation device such as Loran and the radio compasses, it wasn't a difficult job if everything went well. Always a bit of a pessimist through previous experiences, Bates had a habit of looking at it from the black side. Unlikely things could happen. It was just as well to be ready for them.

But the hours drifted slowly by with the aircraft riding the air with the gracious ease of a Cadillac on a parkway.

Draper called through from the flight deck.

"You're half an hour late with the position report, Ricky."

"I know, I know," Bates said irritably. "I'll give it to you to send in a minute."

"How're we doing?" Draper asked hopefully. "Early?"

"Late," Bates said. "Twenty minutes late. Westerly winds. More on the nose."

Draper groaned. "My head. Seems as though it weighs a ton." He paused. "Bed," he said. Even the sound of the word gave him satisfaction.

When Leeming came back, the navigator pointed out to him that they were already late.

"When was your last fix?"

"An hour ago."

"Was it a good one?"

"We're not in Loran range yet, sir. Sun and moon shot."

"Not much moon," Leeming commented. He had seen the thin slice of waxing moon from the cockpit. There was doubt in his mind as to the accuracy of the navigator's position.

"Here, I'll take a couple of shots myself."

He climbed into the astro-dome, and took the altitudes of the moon and the sun. Then meticulously, he worked the readings out from the *Air Almanac* and the astro-navigation tables. Finally, he plotted it himself on the chart.

Bates watched him with increasing irritation. Leeming never seemed to believe anybody.

"There," Leeming said with evident pride. "Let's check up on that one."

He took the dividers and measured out the distances over the chart. With a certain satisfaction, Bates saw that Leeming's position put them twenty-five minutes behind. They had lost another five minutes.

Leeming grunted. "Could be worse," he said. "I think the winds'll die down when we get as far as Weather-Ship Easy."

"Do you?" Bates said.

Leeming looked at him suddenly. "What's the matter, Mr. Bates? Tired?"

"Very." The effort of being diplomatic was too much. Bates felt he had no energy to spare.

Leeming said, "Well . . . not long now before you get Loran."

"Yes. Loran." Bates looked at the dials round the desk, the mechanical faces of the navigator's best friends.

"What's your estimate for the halfway mark?" the captain asked.

"Forty-five west in an hour with these winds."

"You'll be able to get Loran then. Be easier for you," Leeming said. A little silence fell between them. "Well," he added, "I'll just see how the passengers are getting on."

When he had left, Bates called to Draper, "What weather are they forecasting for Bermuda?"

"Four miles in rain. Two thousand feet ceiling."

"Not bad," Bates said. "Anyway, thank Christ for that."

Twenty minutes later he climbed into the astro-dome for what he hoped would be the final astro-fix. The sun was slowly going down in the west, behind an enormous barrier of heavy clouds. That would be the front that had been forecast running along their track nearly all the rest of the way to Bermuda. They were reaching it earlier than Bates had expected. The stars were just getting visible in the east. He took a shot on Saturn and the moon, and he was clambering down when he noticed the smell.

He called up to Drewitt, "Hey . . . can you smell something?"

Drewitt glowered at him from the panel. "What's the matter now?"

"I thought there was something."

Drewitt sniffed heavily. "Nothing," he said. "Nothing up here. What sort of a smell?"

"Odd kind. Like bacon and eggs."

"Hell, Bates," Drewitt exploded. "The galley's next door to you. And you start getting wound up about the smell of cooking! Talk about an old woman . . ."

Bates glared back at him. Now he came to think of it, the smell was just like food being fried. But he wasn't going to let Drewitt know how right he was.

He worked out the sights, and drew the position on the chart. Still twenty-five minutes behind. They were losing no more time. That was something.

Then he smelled the bacon and eggs again. Far stronger this time. And they weren't just cooking. They were being burned to a cinder.

He thought to himself, That damned steward's left something in the oven. He banged down his pencil, and walked into the galley. It was empty. He opened one of the oven doors and was just putting his head inside, when he felt his eyes suddenly smart. Then he couldn't see a thing. The whole place was full of acrid blue smoke. He rushed for the door and reached the flight deck just in time to hear the clanging of the fire bell. A fire warning light glittered like a malignant red sore on the engineer's panel.

"Fire in the forward baggage compartment," Drewitt was

shouting hoarsely. "And there's smoke. I can't see for the smoke. For God's sake get the skipper."

Bates dashed to the passenger compartment, then with a supreme effort walked apparently unconcernedly towards Leeming, now talking to an old couple at the back of the aircraft. He whispered into Leeming's ear. By now, smoke was leaking into the passenger compartment. There was no further need to disguise the fact that something was wrong.

The two of them raced to the front, and Leeming leapt into the left-hand seat.

"Emergency descent," he shouted. "Throttles right back!"

There was a horrible silence as the noise of the engines died completely away. Easy Zebra seemed to stand on her nose.

Bates watched the engineer's panel as though his eyes were glued to the warning light. The whole flight deck was filled with smoke.

"Oxygen masks . . . everyone," Leeming said. His voice was still unsteady from the shock. "Drewitt . . . select the fire extinguishers on the forward baggage compartment."

Drewitt looked at the red handle lovingly. But until they were fully depressurized, releasing the carbon dioxide over the fire would mean that everyone on board not wearing oxygen masks would be immediately asphyxiated.

Leeming continued with his fire drill, turning off the hydraulic pumps and all unnecessary electrical circuits, including the one that fed the flight deck lights. The crew produced torches to continue with their own drills.

Bates went back to his desk. The altimeter was unwinding itself like an alarm clock gone mad. By the fish-tail light of his pocket-torch, he wrote in his log "Fire on board. Emergency descent." Then he noticed the air speed. 260 knots. At least, he thought to himself grimly, wherever we're going, we're going there bloody fast.

Just past nine thousand feet, they became fully depressurized. Drewitt leapt for the red handle on the bulkhead wall, and nearly pulled the thing out by its roots.

"One bottle gone," he called up to the captain.

"Draper, send out an emergency signal. Get our position from Bates," Leeming yelled back through the smoke. "I'm taking her down to the sea. If this thing spreads . . . may have to ditch immediately."

But half an hour later, they were still flying just above the dark sea. The inevitable confusion that results from all sudden emergencies on an aircraft was beginning to sort itself out. The fire warning light no longer glowed, and Drewitt had gone below to investigate with a hand fire extinguisher.

The smoke had begun to thin. Draper was asking Leeming for the third time—could he have some electrical power on, so he could send off his emergency signal, and the position of the aircraft.

Bates waited for Drewitt to come back. He seemed to be staying a long time down there. One thing, if it had been bad, he'd have come back straight away and pulled the second bottle.

Just as he was thinking the engineer might be in trouble and he had better go down himself, Drewitt reappeared, his powerful torch flood-lighting the whole flight deck.

"Fire's out, Skipper," he said.

Bates pulled his oxygen mask off. He saw Draper was smiling.

"Can we have the main circuits on *now?*" he asked.

But Leeming appeared not to have heard him. "Thank Christ for that." The captain pulled the aircraft up to four thousand feet. "What was it?" he asked.

"Been a fire in the wiring, Skipper . . . down where the hydraulic pipes run alongside the main electricity supply.

I reckon the hydraulic fluid caught alight. Good thing you turned the pumps off."

"How bad?"

"Not good. Both batteries gone."

The relief that had spread over Leeming's face vanished immediately. "Surely we can get one battery to work?"

"Both burned out."

"But that means no services at all!"

"I know, sir . . . but there's not a thing I can do about it."

Leeming looked round the dark flight deck, and realized with a shock that he was tackling the most difficult navigational leg in the world without one of the modern scientific aids. Petrol was the life blood of Easy Zebra and everyone in her. But electricity was nearly as vital.

All the engine instruments would be completely useless. The fuel gauges would give the cheerful impression that they were using no petrol at all. All Draper's radio equipment would be out. And they hadn't even sent their emergency signal. The navigation aids—the radio compass, the radar altimeter, and the Loran—would be so much tin and glass.

He swore loudly, and ran his fingers through his hair. They had all been on duty nearly twenty hours, and even he was finding it difficult to think.

Weariness weighted down his mind. And now—this had to happen. All the aids he had come to expect automatically and without thinking about had left him. Apart from his suction-driven horizon and his directional gyro, he was left with the simple instruments with which aeroplanes were first born—an air-speed indicator and an ordinary magnetic compass.

Then he saw the high overcast above them and suddenly the whole danger of the situation flooded his tired mind. It was too late to go back. In order to hit the tiny island of Bermuda, it was essential to see the stars. With all that cloud, it meant climbing high, using climb power thirty-five inches, twenty-two fifty revolutions.

At present, the engines were at their cruising revolutions of eighteen hundred r.p.m. Though he could increase the boost, those revolutions were now with him to the end of the trip. The propellers were controlled electrically.

He turned quickly to the engineer. "How high do you think we can get?"

"Can't use too much boost with these low revs. A pot would go."

"Well, how high? How high?" Leeming asked irritably.

"Can't say exactly . . . depends whether we get any ice. I reckon thirteen thousand. If we're lucky."

The young first officer said, "What would you say the cloud base was, Skipper?" He was making up the hourly weather observations, scrupulous as ever.

Leeming looked up at the sky. "Nineteen . . . twenty thousand," he said. There was a lonely despair in his voice. "One thing's certain. With these revs, we'll never get anywhere near them."

Finding Bermuda at night, nearly a thousand miles without a position, and with no radio aids and no visible stars, was like looking for a needle in a hay stack. Within a time limit of less than two hours.

Bates, standing in the astro-dome with the sextant, had realized the danger at exactly the same time. In his ten years' flying, he had had his troubles, but none to be compared with this.

As the navigator he was responsible for the safe arrival of the aircraft. But with nothing to help him except inaccurately forecast winds, it would be a miracle if he could do it.

With the fire, at least there was something the crew could do. Now, as though in a quicksand, they could only helplessly watch themselves being slowly sucked under as the engines consumed their hourly ration of three hundred gallons of fuel.

Leeming came back to have a word with him. "How long ago was your last position?" he asked.

"Nearly an hour."

There was a long pause. Then Leeming came out into the open with his feelings. "I'm afraid of missing the island. Could you see any whitecaps when we were down low? Might give some indication which way we're drifting."

"Not a thing. Too dark."

"Then it's up to astro, I suppose." Leeming said. "If only the damned cloud would clear!"

"Anyway, Skipper"—Bates had seen the unsureness increasing in the captain's eyes—"the longer we stay down here the better. Less wind. Won't use so much fuel. And we'll climb higher when we're lighter."

"Seems the only thing we can do." Leeming noticed the stewardess was standing beside them in the dark navigation compartment.

"The passengers, sir . . ." she said. "What'll I tell the passengers?"

In the trials of the last hour, Leeming had forgotten the forty-two people who so silently relied upon him.

He said irritably, "Oh, tell them the usual. Pressurization failure. Had to get down quickly. Everything's all right now."

The girl moved soundlessly back to the cabin. Despite the steward, Libby Challoner was still in her stockinged feet.

"I'll keep up the dead reckoning, Skipper," Bates said. "And keep an eye on the sky. There may be a break."

But for over an hour, as Bates alternately kept up his log in the light of his torch, and stared out into the dark sky, he saw nothing except raindrops clattering noisily on the perspex roof. The cloud gradually enveloped them. Easy Zebra churned through a clammy black mass of air.

"Not a sign of anything, Skipper," he said, when Leeming

reappeared. "This cloud looks like going on all the way to Bermuda."

"I know," Leeming said drearily. His face in the torch-light looked worn and strained.

Bates pointed out their dead-reckoning position.

"With no fix for the last two hours," he said, "we could be anywhere thirty miles north or south of track."

"And when we reach our estimate Bermuda?"

Bates shrugged his shoulders. "If we're within seventy miles of track, we'll be lucky. With these unforecast head winds, our new estimate is in three hours' time. Then, according to the engineer, we'll have ninety minutes' fuel left."

Leeming said nothing. He stared blankly at the pencilled lines on the chart as though somehow they would tell him the answer.

"We'll have to climb, Skipper," Bates said. "We've *got* to get to those stars somehow."

The words made Leeming suddenly come into action. Climbing was, after all, doing something.

"All right," he said with some of his old briskness. He called to Drewitt, "Richen up a bit. And let's have some more boost. We'll see how high we can get."

The engines roared louder, and Easy Zebra started slowly to climb through dense cloud. Drewitt was grumbling about using too much boost for the low revolutions.

"Nothing else for it," Leeming said curtly.

Up and up the aircraft went, but there was still no break. At seven thousand feet ice started forming in small crystal gobbets on the windscreen and the white disease spread to the wings. Not very much, just an inch or so, but enough to bring the speed down.

At nine thousand feet, they were still in the stuff. And there was no sign of a star.

"She's eating fuel," Drewitt muttered, as the long, slow underpowered climb went on.

Easy Zebra took thirty minutes to make the next four thousand feet. By this time the ice on the wings had increased, and she was mushing badly.

"Can't get any higher," Leeming said hopelessly. "Better lean off the mixture here. While we've got some fuel left."

Easy Zebra flew on at thirteen thousand feet. Bates peered out from the astro-dome into inky blackness. At least it was smoother up here. If a star appeared, he could get an accurate shot of it. But the minutes went by, and nothing appeared.

And then he saw it. Turning his head, hopelessly scanning the sky, he was looking towards the starboard quarter when he noticed a thin blur of light. At first, it was so faint, just a little spark in the sky, that he thought it was some touch of his imagination. Or something in his tired eyes. He blinked twice, and he looked again. It was still there.

He called up to the front, "I can see something, Skipper. Shining through the cloud. Looks like it might be that bit of moon we had earlier."

In a flash Leeming was beside him. "Let's have a look," he said.

He stared out for a full minute. Then he asked, "Are you sure it's the moon?"

"Can't be anything else."

"Not a planet?"

"Nothing near it. It's obviously shining through a high overcast."

"Practically no light. D'you reckon you can get a shot of it?"

Bates shrugged his shoulders. "I'll try," he said. "It's something anyway."

Leeming had another look. "I don't think it's the moon at all." A doubtful uncertainty flickered over the captain's face. In his own mind, he wouldn't have been surprised if he and Bates were looking at some weird will-o'-the-wisp, leading them on into the unending marshiness of the cloud.

"Well, all I can say," Bates said cautiously, "that's where the moon should be."

Bates adjusted the altitude control, and moved the sextant up and down and sideways, hunting for the tiny light. Then, with a leap in his heart, he saw it.

With a grim determination, he held the sextant steadily in his hands, with difficulty keeping the tiny light in the centre of the illuminated bubble that acted as the instrument's horizon. Altitude 25 degrees 10 minutes. Time 23 hours 17 minutes and 1 second. G.M.T.

He climbed down and worked out the shot by the tables. It gave him a position line. It was too great an angle to check his ground speed or his track accurately, since it was nearly forty-five degrees to both. But it was something. They were somewhere along the long thin line he drew on his chart.

He shouted to Leeming triumphantly, "I got one. It works out O.K."

The captain was still inclined to be sceptical. He was worried sick now. The air speed had dropped another five knots, and chunks of ice were being slung off the propellers by their rotation. He knew he had still enough fuel to reach Bermuda. But not very much over to search for the island. When Bates had taken his third shot of the light that he swore was the moon, Leeming went back to pore over the navigation chart again.

"All three position lines agree pretty well," Bates pointed out.

"I suppose you're right . . . I hope to God you are. But what's one position line anyway? A fix is what we need. If we could only see a star to get another position line . . ." He lapsed into silence. Then he said a second time, "I'm afraid of missing the island."

Bates said, "I think we should make dead certain we don't."

"But how the hell can we? With all this bloody cloud?"

"If we alter course thirty degrees starboard, we'll make sure which side of the island we'll be. We'll be north of it —whatever the wind is."

"That means more flying time. Dog leg instead of a straight line. We're getting damned short of fuel."

All the same, Leeming was listening hard, forcing his tired mind to concentrate, trying to find a way out of a situation suddenly grown desperate.

"It's better than having to search for the place. Not knowing which way to turn."

"And when we *are* north?"

"If the moon stays with us, I've calculated that about an hour before E.T.A., the position line from it should run straight through Bermuda, up north-east. If we steer a course so as to be somewhere near that position line, knowing we're north, we can turn south-west towards the island."

Leeming knew that running down a single position line, using it as a course to steer to a destination through which the line transited, was difficult enough under ideal conditions.

"And if cloud obscures the moon still further?" he said.

Bates shrugged his shoulders. "Then that'll be that. But it's the only hope. Once we're on that position line, and I can take further shots, we'll be able to alter course for drift."

Leeming stared out at the unending cloud. As far as he could see they were flying in a thin layer, sandwiched between two enormous sheets of stratus.

"I suppose it's the only thing we can do," he said dubiously. "Hope to hell it works."

He called up to the first officer to alter course thirty degrees to the right. He stayed at the desk with the *Air Almanac,* while the navigator in the astro-dome took shot after shot on the dim, woolly-edged light.

Bates felt the immense weight of responsibility that he and

his sextant carried between them. It seemed as though it was too much to ask that a combination of his readings and Leeming's calculations would lead them to safety.

As time went on, Drewitt and Draper looked anxiously into the navigation compartment where the two men worked. Timperley was a hundred per cent occupied with his instrument flying. Half an hour went by. There was still nothing in the sky but the faint light from the moon.

But gradually, the series of position lines, their direction altering slightly with the movement of the moon in the sky, crept nearer and nearer the one that went right through Bermuda.

Bates held his breath, waiting. Another ten minutes would make all the difference. With infinite care, at their expected arrival time somewhere along that position line through Bermuda, he steadied the sextant in the astro-dome. He shouted up to Timperley, "For God's sake, keep level." Then, knowing that this was the most important shot of all, the one on which so many lives depended, he put every ounce of skill and experience into getting an accurate sight.

He called down the reading to Leeming. There was four minutes' suspense, while the pilot worked it out.

Then Bates heard him shout, "You're sure of that shot?"

"Best I've taken."

"Puts us within fifteen miles of *the* position line." He looked at his watch. "That was five minutes ago. If we turn south-west now, that should be it."

He called up to Timperley to alter onto two-four-zero degrees magnetic. That bearing, now they had made certain of being north-east of the island, was as good as a course to steer sent by a ground radio station.

There remained the problem of allowing for the drift effect of an unknown wind along the unknown number of miles they would have to travel along that course. There was also the danger of sailing over the place without seeing it, since there was continuous cloud below them.

"We'll have to go down," Leeming said to the navigator. "Cloud's pretty thick below us."

"O.K.," Bates said. "I'll let you know if the moon disappears."

Easy Zebra started descending once more. They went through some rough tops of cumulus at eight thousand feet.

Leeming shouted up, "Moon still with us?"

"Still with us. This stuff's well broken up."

At six thousand feet, Leeming told Timperley to level out so that Bates could take another sight.

When he had worked it out, it showed they were drifting to port. He shouted up to the first officer to alter course seven degrees starboard to allow for it. Then he stared for a moment out of the window.

"There's still cloud below. Let's hope to God we haven't gone over the place. Take her down further, Timperley."

Easy Zebra obediently crept down, more slowly now. At two thousand feet, Draper called back, "It's difficult to tell of course . . . but I think we're clear of all cloud now."

"Moon's gone," Bates said, "but I got a shot just before it went." He gave Leeming the figures. "Not a good one," he added.

When Leeming had worked it out, he said, "Shows we're still drifting to port." He told Timperley to alter another five degrees to the right.

Then he asked Bates anxiously, "Moon back?"

"Not a sign."

"Damn thing . . . damn thing." The pilot banged his fists fiercely and impotently on the shadowy navigation table. "Would disappear . . . just when we wanted it most."

With an inopportune, odd sense of justice to that faint partner of his in the sky, Bates said quietly, "I think it's done us proud, Skipper."

Leeming glared morosely back at him. "Well . . . it's *your* moon. What d'you want to do now? Shall we climb so we can see it? We've *got* to have another shot somehow."

"If we get above the cloud, we'll go right over the top without seeing Bermuda. Only thing to do is to stay down here."

It had started to rain again. "May only be a shower," Bates said.

"See anything yet?" Leeming called up to the front.

"Not a damned thing," Draper replied. "Nothing. Visibility's too bad."

It was too late to panic. Leeming now sat in a state of hopeless resignation. Within a few minutes now, he would have to be thinking about ditching drills. He would have to go in to the passenger compartment and tell those forty-two blissfully ignorant passengers the sudden news that they were coming down in the sea. And they were a thousand miles away from their last position report.

The list of figures and calculations stared back at him from the desk. It seemed impossible that all that adding and subtracting could lead them anywhere.

Then from the astro-dome, Bates shouted, "Moon's back." It was just visible, as a damp blob of light. The navigator took a quick shot of it.

"Ten degrees one minute," he called down. "Not a brilliant one. Getting too low for accuracy."

But Leeming never worked that one out. There was a tremendous shout from the front, which came from the combined throats of Drewitt, Draper and Timperley.

"Lights!"

Leeming and Bates rushed up to the front. The five bodies of the crew were wedged tight against each other, their faces pressed hard against the cockpit windows.

Over on the port side, blurred and muzzy through the rain, but utterly unmistakable, was the huge sickle-shaped curve made up of the lights of Hamilton Harbour.

3

The main consequence of the incident to Easy Zebra was another report for Mr. Veitch's desk. Drewitt had been quite right. As far as the Bermuda ground engineers could tell, the fire had started by a short in the main electrical wiring. Unfortunately, the hydraulic leak which had caused the delay in London had been a very large and obvious one around the tail-cone of the Marlborough; once that had been repaired, everything was assumed to be satisfactory. There must, however, have also been a small crack in the system near the position where the short had occurred, and drops of hydraulic fluid (having a flash point of only ninety degrees centigrade) had ignited immediately they fell on the smouldering wires. Leeming had turned off the hydraulic pumps as a necessary part of his drill, and luckily the fire had not spread.

The chances of it ever happening again were considered to be in the region of a million to one. The hydraulic leak had to be exactly over the short in the wiring in order to drip on to it. The possibility of the two being coincident again, without being discovered on inspections, was just about nil. All the same, the Bermuda engineers recommended a rerouting of all electrical lines on the Marlboroughs, away from the hydraulic pipes, as an additional safety measure. The law of averages wasn't always as consistent as the law of gravity, and they had no desire to have another vanished Marlborough laid near their door. The risk was not considered sufficient to ground the aircraft immediately, but they advised the modification "at the very earliest opportunity."

The aircraft was delayed in Bermuda thirty-six hours while

the damage was repaired. Kelston, who was taking it on to Panama, saw Leeming at the hotel and listened to a long and detailed account of the story.

Kelston said, "I've never liked those hydraulic pipes so near the main electricity supply. Must have been a shaky do."

"I don't mind telling you, Mark," Leeming said, "I thought—this is the end. Still haven't got over it yet."

"I hear they've recommended a rerouting of the wiring."

Leeming snorted. "I should damn well think so."

"Long job. At a guess, I'd say it's over a week's work on each aircraft. I suppose after the inquiry they'll ground the fleet till all four Marlboroughs are done."

Leeming brightened a little. "Mean a buckshee week at home anyway," he said.

There was a short pause. Then Kelston said, "Pity you didn't night-stop in the Azores. I've always thought the engineers there give the aircraft a damned thorough inspection."

"Doubt if they'd have found anything."

"You never know. They might have done. Whatever possessed you to come right through?"

Leeming's large eyes filled with surprise at so elementary a question. "Why, the schedule, Mark, of course! I was trying to catch up on the schedule."

But like most pilots, Leeming had his philosophy about such occurrences. It was not so much the emergency that worried him. After all, he had done fourteen years of flying, half of them in the R.A.F. in wartime. He accepted such rare events fatalistically for himself. If something happened he could do nothing about . . . well, that would be that. But if through his own incompetence or lack of knowledge he had lost the aircraft, that would have been in his mind the unforgivable thing. An idea kept revolving round his head that if it hadn't been for Bates, they might never have reached

Bermuda. It was that uncomfortable thought that now kept haunting him.

Out of the five other members of his crew, the only person who appeared completely unmoved by the incident to Easy Zebra was Libby Challoner. The three days they were in Bermuda at the Saracen Hotel, she might have been mistaken for one of the many girls on holiday, except that she sat for meals at the crew table with six men.

She would come tripping through the hotel dining room, as though on tip-toe, invariably late, invariably smiling. For lunch, she used normally to wear a brown tweed costume, but at dinner she would spread herself in a number of quite exotic gowns, most of them black, and most of them with ultra-wide spread skirts, especially designed perhaps to emphasize her tiny waist.

Leeming watched her with an amused interest. She provided a relaxation from the worries that still remained in his mind and from the heavy atmosphere that had descended on the rest of the crew. Bates was convinced that none of their trouble would have arisen if they had night-stopped in the Azores, for which he blamed Leeming, and made no effort to hide it. He had already had a heated argument with Drewitt over why the engineer hadn't acted, immediately the smell of bacon and eggs had been reported. First Officer Timperley sat silent most of the time, very shy with Libby and with Leeming, and only managing to say "Yes, sir," and "No, sir," whenever he thought it advisable that his voice should be heard.

Libby, on the other hand, was so very light and airy in everything she did. Even her "cher amis," her "mis amigos," her "señors" and her "Lieblings," strung as they were on to outlandish English words like "dullish," "blissmaking," "dreamy" and "dashingest," managed to avoid sounding affected and just seemed dainty and very feminine.

Towards Leeming, her manner remained most correct,

with a wide-eyed courtesy coupled with an exaggerated respect, which would have been irritating if she hadn't managed it so charmingly.

"Good evening, everyone," she would say, as she sailed into her seat at dinner. She would take her napkin, spread it with infinite care on her dress, look towards Leeming, take the menu, pause for a few seconds, and then say, "Good evening, Captain."

The conversation when Leeming was not present alternated between their own emergency, and the strange affair that Kelston was having in the Azores.

On the second day at dinner, Drewitt said, "I'm damned if I want to fly with the man. Not now."

Bates was just finishing his soup. "Why ever not?" he asked.

"I was talking to Appleby, his navigator, before they went off. He gets on the aircraft tired. Makes the first officer do the first four hours' watch."

"He always did. That was his normal routine. Even before this business started."

Drewitt snorted, "Well, I just don't like it. That's my view."

Bates looked at him contemptuously. "And you know what you can do with it, Drewitt. I was with Kelston when we found the *Santa Lucinda.* That trip and ours the day before yesterday had their similarities, operationally. You've never seen such weather as we had. But the difference between the captains . . ."

Drewitt reiterated stolidly, "I don't like it . . . somehow makes you have no trust in him."

"God!" Bates' eyes blazed. "You people! I don't mind what the hell Kelston does. I'd still rather fly with him than any other pilot on the line. As for this man we've got now . . ."

Libby Challoner suddenly appeared in her seat, once more

a vision in black. Her perfume fell like balm on the strained air. "Good evening, everyone," she said sweetly.

There was a dinner dance on that night. A Calypso band played softly. Every table was lit by a single candle, standing in a little saucer filled with passion flowers. Libby was in great demand as a dance partner, mainly between Draper and Drewitt.

Leeming arrived late. He watched the others dance with the stewardess. Then he said, just before she started on roast chicken with her usual appetite, "Everybody else seems to have danced with you, Libby. What about giving me a trial?"

Immediately she said meekly, "Of course, Captain."

Once they were close together on the floor, her attitude changed with remarkable suddenness.

"I was hoping you were going to ask me, Michael," she said. She danced well and very lightly, nestling up to him almost as though to warm herself. She chattered gaily the whole time. It amused Leeming to hear her. Certainly this girl took him out of himself.

"For a new girl on the line, Libby," he said, "you show a most disarming lack of shyness."

She smiled at him. "All the better for getting to know people."

The music stopped. Couples walked back to their tables. "Pity," Libby sighed. "Much too soon."

When she was once more sitting at the crew table, she turned to Leeming and said gravely, "Thank you, Captain."

She took up her knife and fork. "You can put them down again, Libby," Drewitt said, as the music started again. "Come on, it's my turn now."

Though the Marlborough was late arriving at Bermuda, their trip down to Panama was easy and smooth. There was hardly a cloud in the sky, and they saw the huge bulk of Jamaica's Blue Mountains well over a hundred miles away.

Tocumen Airport at Panama was free from its usual ration of heavy thunderstorms, and they landed in the evening twilight, just under twelve hours after leaving Bermuda.

The company had a rest house in the hills to the north of the town, where the crew were accommodated before starting the long trip back to England. It was a double-storey white house, surrounded by a garden filled with cannas and banana plants.

On the first two nights that Leeming's crew spent there, everyone seemed too tired to do anything except lounge around reading. On the third, Drewitt had arranged to meet some friends of his in the American sector. They had rung up in the morning to ask whether the crew would like to come along to a party that evening.

At lunch that day, Drewitt broached the subject to Leeming, but he didn't appear keen to go and the invitation wasn't pressed. Obviously, most of the others had been contacted already. The steward nodded his head when Drewitt turned to him. Timperley murmured something about it being "rather fun." Draper said so long as there was free liquor he should be included. Bates forgot his feud with Drewitt, and said after all it was something to do in this dump.

"You'll come, of course, Libby?" Drewitt's little green eyes shone out at her from their wrinkled lids. "There'll be other girls there. We'll be able to dance."

Libby, who'd been chatting away to Leeming while this was going on, had to have it all repeated to her, and then said, "No, I'm sorry, Tom. I'd rather stay in the rest house."

"Oh, come on, Libby," Drewitt said, reddening a little. "Don't be so ridiculous. You know you love a party."

Libby was obviously not a person to be railroaded into anything. Despite her flippancy, the line of her mouth was hard and determined. "No . . . thank you very much, all the same. I'm going to take things quietly."

Drewitt's face turned a bright beetroot. "For Christ's sake,

Libby, don't be *difficult*. I've told them you'll be coming. It's part of your job to fit in with the crew's arrangements."

Leeming heard Libby draw in her breath sharply and heavily. He saw there was about to be an explosion unless he did something quickly.

"It's *not* part of her job. Let's get that one straight. She can do just as she pleases. But all the same, Libby, I think you'd enjoy yourself."

Libby looked down at the tablecloth, rather demurely. There was going to be no storm, after all. "If you think I should, Captain," she said, "then I'll go."

"At last." Drewitt heaved a sigh of relief. "Everything's settled. There'll be a car calling for us at six."

Leeming went into the town that afternoon, and came back to the rest house just in time to see a light blue station waggon start driving away, presumably with his crew. But half an hour later, Libby in white shirt and blue shorts appeared in the lounge, where he was reading. He looked up from his book, surprised. "I thought you'd gone," he said.

"I've been hiding at the back of the garden," she said calmly. "I only said I'd go because you wanted me to say so. You did, didn't you?"

"I did," he said.

"To preserve the peace?"

"To preserve the peace," he repeated.

"Funny how people don't seem to think a girl should ever want a quiet night."

Leeming laughed at the kind of gamin impudence she had, her legs apart now and a look of defiant self-righteousness on her face. Then she suddenly smiled back at him and turned towards the door. "Well, I'm off to have a bath and change."

"See you at dinner." Leeming settled down to his book again.

The blue eyes peeped at him through a froth of fair hair that hung over her forehead. "Enchantée," she said.

The dinner gong went when Leeming was reading, still in flannels and a shirt. He dashed up to his room, put on a tie and sports coat, and came down to find the long table set just for two. At the far end, Libby had already started her soup.

He sat beside her at the head of the table and said, "Punctual tonight, aren't you, Libby?" Then he noticed that she'd effected a transformation since he'd seen her less than an hour ago. There was no sign now of the urchin child. She was wearing a glittering cocktail dress of black and gold lamé. Her nails shone crimson with paint, and around her hung the heavy-sweet smell of jasmine. If she'd been going to a Mayfair party with the most eligible bachelor in town, she could hardly have done him prouder.

He was very conscious of his shabby grey flannels. "Sorry I forgot the time," he said. "Otherwise I'd have changed into my lounge suit. Didn't realize we were dining at the Ritz tonight."

"Oh, this old thing, you mean? Didn't know I'd brought it." Elaborate unconcern showed on her face.

"I'm glad you did. Black and gold suits you."

All the little compliments, which were shared out for the crew to say when the girl was obviously wearing a new dress, he would have to politely deal out on his own.

She wrinkled her nose at him. "Thank you kindly, sir! Even though with *you,* I'm certain it comes under the heading of duty-towards-stewardesses-on-the-ground."

He could see that tonight anyway, while they were alone, Libby and he were to be equals. There was no sign of that exaggerated shy respect with which she treated him in front of the crew. She might be a stewardess on her fourth trip, and he might have eight thousand hours in command of four-engined aircraft, but right now he was a man in a scruffy sports coat, and she was a sparkling ballroom beauty. Leeming might have felt irritated, but he didn't. There wasn't any of the heavy languid glamour-puss about Libby.

He looked at her, domestically and delicately eating her soup, and the intimacy of the two of them being on their own here in this large house, waited on by two white-coated servants, rather pleased him.

Something of the same thought must have struck her. "This is nice, isn't it? Just as though, for tonight anyway, the Lord and Lady of the Manor are dining quietly at home."

"Soup's good, too," he said.

She laughed. "You sound just like a husband! Oughtn't we to be talking about the Stock Exchange, or the losses on the home farm?"

"Sorry to be so dull. We'll have a bottle of wine, anyway. That's about the only romantic gesture I can offer, but you can have it with my compliments."

As they drank the wine, and ate the steak, and afterwards fresh strawberries buried in ice-cream, Libby chattered away inconsequentially, and Leeming felt more mellow and more at peace with the world than he had done since the scare on the Azores-Bermuda leg.

They had their coffee in the ante-room. Aztec masks scowled down from the white painted walls. Someone had left the radio on, rather quietly, and there was a background of Cuban rumbas. Through the open windows came the smell of the fruit trees and the grass in the orchard that someone had cut that day.

"D'you take sugar in your coffee?"

"Two lumps, Libby," he said.

He saw her pale arms and shoulders against the black clinging dress that subtly underlined every curve of her body and every movement that she made. The skirt flared out below her hips, and as she brought the coffee over to him, her thin legs made the fabric rustle and swing and catch the light.

"Isn't this blissful?" she said, as she sat beside him on the sofa. "If this is flying, why on earth didn't I think of it earlier?"

He laughed and asked her, "Didn't you find it rather hard work? You have to be on your feet a lot."

"Don't tell anyone," she said, "but I slept a good deal of the way on the long leg."

There was a little pause. "What about nearly having to land in the middle of the Atlantic?"

She looked up at him and smiled. "I wondered rather sleepily what it was all about. But I knew you'd be doing the right thing. So I wasn't worried in the least."

Such a complete trust rather touched him. Maybe there was more in this girl than he'd reckoned. He'd realized that she was pretty and pleasant and fun, but suddenly he felt quite tender towards her. They were drinking Pisco, a South American spirit distilled from grape skins. It seemed very natural to start talking life histories.

He told her about his life in the Air Force. Melanie was part of him not meant for anyone else to hear. And she told him the usual sort of story he'd have expected a new stewardess to have. Her father was a doctor; she was the only child; her mother didn't want her to fly, but her secretarial job was dull; she had, when she was only eighteen, been engaged to an R.A.F. fighter pilot who'd been killed. She told it quite simply and rather sweetly, cupping her face in her hands. She had taken off her shoes and her painted toes curled up and down inside her nylons as if to punctuate her sentences.

"This Pisco is pretty potent, isn't it?" she said. "I'm beginning to feel I've known you all my life. And that's bad." As she turned her head suddenly to look out on the quiet clear night, her cheek lightly brushed over Leeming's. It was cool and soft. He was surprised how the slight contact excited him.

The silence between them went on for minutes. Then she said she felt cold. She went upstairs to fetch a cardigan, while he closed the windows. When she came down again with a pink wool creation now over the black and gold frills, she looked like a wife home again after the ball. She came back over to the sofa and smiled down at him.

"You're rather peculiar, aren't you, Michael?" she said softly.

Leeming was aware that those words were dangerous. An intimacy seemed to have grown up rapidly between them out of which he could have easily retreated into flippancy. There was a silence while he tried to make up his mind what to do. Then he said, "Why?"

"Because you treat me with such elaborate casualness."

"I don't see that's anything peculiar."

"It is to me. It's so elaborate. Makes everything far plainer."

"Makes what plainer?" he asked her.

"That you're attracted to me," she said.

Now that the words were out and he had neither laughed it off nor denied it, Leeming felt almost relieved. The sweet light worthless femininity that haloed her whole body he had noticed as soon as he talked to her on the aeroplane, just out of London. It was so very much of no consequence that for an inexplicable reason it was interesting. Her little effusive gay gestures had amused him in Bermuda. And the only thing that was really surprising was the fact that, given the first favourable opportunity, she had brought things to a head like this, as though it had been obvious to her for years. He looked at the blue eyes, ordered by her instincts now to be solemn, and said rather lamely and without much conviction, "Any man's attracted to a girl when he's far from home and on his own with her. Especially in a place like this."

"Not you," she said definitely. "Don't pretend to be like that, because you're not. There's something. God knows what it is. But it's there all right."

"I didn't realize you studied men so intensely, Libby."

"Oh yes," she said and smiled. "It's the only thing I know anything about. I can't talk to you about books or politics or religion. But I know my men when I see them."

Leeming searched his mind trying to find a reason for all this, as they sat looking at each other. He had left Melanie perfectly happy. Everything was exactly as it should be at Fairoaks. To talk to any girl like this had never entered his head before. And yet already, to the little tempting tune that she had been playing all evening, he was beginning to dance the first accompanying steps. Surprised and half-suspicious, he wondered if she was deliberately leading him on out of a spirit of pure devilry.

"You look worried," she said at last. "There's no need to be. You attract me, too. I liked you the minute I saw you on the aircraft."

"It was as simple as that, was it, Libby?"

"These things are always simple." She put out her hand to cover his. He felt the coldness of the soft thin-boned fingers. He smiled at her uncertainly. "Are you like this with all the men you meet, Libby?"

"Not unless I have to," she answered promptly. "With you, there's all your captain's dignity and your husband's scruples to be got around. I knew you'd say nothing at all. Not this whole evening, while we're alone together. Not throughout the entire trip. Not *any* time. So I took my pride in my hands, and did your work for you."

She put her arm over his, and as her face drew near and he saw the redness of her mouth open slightly just before they kissed, she asked softly, "Don't you think I've done it well?"

Later, when the house was quiet, she went into his room, dawdling, letting her big skirt swing to and fro with a rustle, her heels hammering the stone floor with little clicks till they were muffled by the rug round his bed. With elaborate concern, she tended her dress lest it be crushed as she sat down on the coverlet. It was such a feminine, futile action, as though to preserve a bubble from bursting or a meringue from crumbling, that he took a large handful of the net and the lace of the frock and crumpled it deliberately shapeless.

He looked at the creased fabric in his hand, surprised at the senseless gesture—one that was alien to his whole character. The ebb and flow of his desires had never risen beyond the efficient breakwaters that a strict moral upbringing and a faint natural distaste for overindulgence had provided. But now, a powerful urgency swept over him, engulfing every barrier of scruple or of fear, like the dangerous high water of a swollen spring tide.

He felt no tenderness for Libby now. It was a hot battle and one that he had to win. Somehow all his troubles and irritations which had been put to sleep so comfortably just before he came out on this trip woke up and bawled their heads off for attention, like a crèche full of hungry children. The uncertainty of his job, the bleak future when he was too old or not fit enough to fly, money troubles, family troubles, difficulties with Melanie and trying to keep the peace at Fairoaks, the tremendous effort to control his fears during the fire on Easy Zebra, they were all in some strange way represented by Libby's body. Conquer it, and he conquered them all.

Her perfume filled the little space where they were locked together with tropical wild flowers. The bed was a darkened jungle, and Libby herself a white animal that threatened his life. Her small arms twisted round his neck with a strength that bit into his skin. The wriggling, slippery insistence of her body, now moving itself from him as though to escape, now boring back lest he free himself from her, taunted and inflamed him. Like a white-hot torch it touched off desires that had remained invisible inside him, which now leapt up, alight and alive.

And afterwards, when he lay back quietly in a brief illusionary peace, not yet ready to look square in the face the consequences of this stupid reversal of everything he had been before, he could notice the rubble round him with a cool detachment. The girl with her eyes closed and her body not moving, the rumpled bed, her clothes in untidy puddles all round the room. One of her high-heeled shoes still stood straight, as though it had been stopped dead on its way to the window. But the other had keeled over and lay drunkenly on its side by the door.

Then gradually it grew on him that he owned this scene. This was now part of his life, a coloured slide for the magic lantern of his memory to hold for ever. Now that the short sweet satisfaction was over, the swift recession of the tide uncovered once more the bare barrier of his fears and scruples which rose in huge conventional accusation above a bleak and empty waste.

Libby stirred and sat up. "Give me a cigarette, Liebling," she said. He fished around in his coat to produce one for this now smiling, contented, conscienceless creature.

"I'd no idea you could be so brutal, darling." She stroked his face affectionately with the tips of her fingers. Before he could think of something to say that would suggest, not too ungraciously, that she go back to her own room, the sound of gravel crumbling under big rubber wheels came in through the open window. Twin headlamps made a zebra pattern across the black ceiling, the light being chased by the darkness till it disappeared into the corners.

"They're back," Libby said. "Must have a look at them." She jumped out of bed, collected her shoes and walked across the cold stone floor to the window. She looked like a white shadow against the dark wall. As she peeped through the curtains, a little of the light outside crept on to her as she stood there, her nudity emphasized so especially by being propped up on those huge high heels.

She giggled softly as she looked. "They're getting out now. Rather raucous good-byes. It must have been quite a party."

"Come away from the window, for God's sake, Libby. They'll see you."

In answer, she seemed to pull the curtains further open.

"Or hear you," he said.

"Don't worry so. Of course they won't. It's fun to watch them like this."

"They'll be up here in a minute."

"They won't come into your room. They may knock on my door, I suppose. But I doubt it. Not at this time. It's past one o'clock."

They listened together to the noises in the corridor, the opening and shutting of doors, the good nights, water running, teeth being cleaned, the little sounds of five men in five different rooms moving around, undressing and folding their clothes and getting into bed. Libby stood by the window still, leaning against the wall, occasionally looking out at the stars and the shadowy landscape of the hills. They stayed as they were, like figures suddenly made into stone, for about ten minutes, and then all was quite quiet again.

"Come over here, Libby," Leeming whispered. "And don't make too much noise. Drewitt's next door. The walls aren't very thick."

She glided over soundlessly and sat beside him, stroking his hair and smiling. Grudgingly he admired and envied this airy insouciance. She was just the same flippant, inconsequential girl as she had been when he first saw her.

"You do worry, don't you?" she whispered. "You're feeling you want to be a good boy again now, aren't you?"

Somewhere behind the wall, Drewitt's snore started up, gentle but insistent. Libby started to laugh quietly. "Funny to hear a lot of men going to bed at the same time," she said. "It's all very quick, isn't it? Women would have chattered for hours. And now, in no time at all, all the crew are asleep, quite oblivious of the fact that I'm sitting on your bed with nothing on at all. Except my shoes, of course. But you can't count those."

Next morning, Libby sailed in to breakfast, late as ever. She wore a bright cotton frock of girlish pink. She said,

"Good morning, everyone," picked up her napkin and spread it like a little white apron over her neat lap. Then she looked at Leeming. She smiled. "Good morning, Captain." The words carried with them the same little aura of breathless respect.

Everything was just as it had always been throughout that trip. The crew went on finishing their toast and marmalade. Libby started on her grapefruit.

"Certainly missed something last night, Libby," Draper said.

Remembering now through the headache that hung over his forehead like a too tight helmet, Drewitt glared at her. "Where the hell were you? We waited—"

She smiled sweetly. "Down in the town. I forgot the time. Silly of me!"

Mollified by her apparent penitence, Drewitt said, "It was some party." Then he added as a free piece of kindly advice, "The trouble with you, Libby—you've got no sense of time. Always late, always late."

"I know," she said, "I'm sorry. Je suis impossible."

But to Leeming's gratified surprise, she wasn't so impossible as she made herself out to be. For the remaining two days of their stay in Panama, her behaviour towards him was above reproach. She had a drink or two with him in the evenings. Once, they went a walk together into the hot, tin-roofed town. But she talked always of casual things, gazed at shop windows, admired the dry flowers in the park, and damned the heat. She never mentioned a word about her brand-new relationship with him.

Neither did Leeming.

He took the home-bound service out of Tocumen Airport on Thursday. Twelve hours later he handed it over to Kelston in Bermuda. The aircraft was Easy Zebra. In the Operations Office he saw Mark supervising his flight plan to the

Azores. "Any snags on the aircraft, Mike?" Kelston asked him.

"None. She's going well." Leeming was feeling tired. Partly from the trip, partly from the thought of two days in Bermuda with Libby close beside him.

Mark, on the other hand, looked pleased. He was humming a catchy little tune, as bright as the daylight outside.

Listening to him, Leeming said with aggrieved disapproval, "What's the happy little song?"

"It's a Czech folk song. I rather like it. Gets into your head."

"Anyway . . . you seem on top of the world."

Kelston smiled. "Sure. Look at that." He pointed to his flight plan. "Forty knot wind behind us all the way at nineteen thousand. Less than an eight hour flight."

Leeming glanced at the Met. folder with its pictorial drawings of the forecast weather from Bermuda to the Azores. "Pretty big build-ups round forty west," he said. "That front looks like being a nasty one."

Kelston shrugged his shoulders. "Not too bad."

Leeming said thinly, "Of course . . . I'd forgotten. Must all seem a bit tin-pot after *your* hurricane."

Kelston seemed not to have heard him. He just went on humming, tapping the time of the tune on the desk with his long fingers.

As the crew car wound slowly round the frequent bends in the road to Hamilton, Leeming was thinking to himself that everything you ever heard these days had to be seasoned with more than a pinch of salt. Here was Kelston, for instance, trying to make out that the reason for his obviously ecstatic good humour was a short trip across the Atlantic. When all along, the real reason was a girl who taught him Czech folk songs, picnicked with him in the captain's room at the Carreras, and led him a gay old dance through hell and high water.

Book Four ~

The Centre of the Storm

November 26-November 27

1

Like a massive dog coming out of the water, Easy Zebra nosed out of the wet black cloud into the clear night, and shook herself all over before settling down steadily to an unaccustomed smoothness. Ahead of her, São Miguel's conical hills stood out against the paler pattern of the sky. Kelston watched the little scatter of lights all over them gradually thickening till they merged into the one huge glow of Ponta Delgada.

He was thinking that this sudden view of the island was like the coming of Karena into his life. Up to a few weeks ago everything about him had been conventional and expected. The constant movement from one part of the world to another quietened the vague dissatisfactions, and concealed from his conscious mind the emptiness of his existence. He had not gone too deeply, perhaps on purpose, into the supposed rocks on which his life was built—the theologians too hoarse from shouting each other down, too busy stretching their shrinking creeds to meet the demands of scientific discovery to preach the simplicity of Christ; the state caught up in a whirlpool of circles of expediency, winning a war that lost the reason for their first entering it, now changing allies and enemies as though politics was a children's game of cowboys and Indians; morals, laws, the structure of society largely dependent on the position of the sun over the various lands of the earth—how much of what grew where and at what time.

On this same day in November, ten years ago, he had been

providing a radar air-escort for a small task-force off the enemy-occupied north Norwegian coast, when one of the destroyers had been caught and crippled in a minefield. It was a pitch black night, with an icy sea running before a gale-force wind. A second destroyer had plunged to her help, only to hit three mines and immediately sink beside her. A cruiser with the senior naval officer on board repeatedly tried to reach the survivor, but was badly damaged by a mine under her bows. Only just seaworthy, she steamed out of the danger area to join the rest of the task-force. While Kelston circled, he read the last message from the retreating cruiser to the destroyer below him. The light flashed out to spell in the seaman's crisp biblical English, "I clearly cannot help you. May your God stand fast beside you." Just after dawn, he watched the stricken solitary ship turn her guns as though they were eyes up into the sky, and sink with all hands.

Not God—but *your* God. That was the touchstone to judge every decision and incident in a man's life. For in the end, there was no help to be expected, except from the individual God that made up the inward strength of the man. That was the only ground to build a life on, a foundation that was separately made by each person, for the structure and safety of which he was responsible only to himself. After that truth was recognized came the peace of emerging finally from uncertainty and doubt.

And now, after they had landed, the calm of the night was everywhere in the island like a physical manifestation of his own present tranquillity. Already he could feel a consciousness of Karena's presence, as he waited for the crew transport to close the six mile gap that lay between them.

When the car eventually grunted through the gates, she was waiting as she always did, just outside the glare of the hotel entrance. None of the excitement showed in the composed gravity of her face. Blinded by the lights, she peered a little, watching the dark silhouettes extricate themselves from the crowded crew car. When she had seen him, she walked slowly down the steps and quietly put her hand in his.

As he followed her through the lighted doorway, he knew that she had heard the little, not-quite-well-enough-suppressed murmur of interest from the crew. Her back was straighter, she held her head higher, and her spiky heels dug slowly and deliberately into the thick pile of the carpet as she walked over to the reception office.

Pancini was on duty in the office, and Kelston could see Mr. Agostino, the manager of the Carreras, at the back of the room, poring over a ledger. Before the key of the captain's room had been handed over, Mr. Agostino suddenly snapped the ledger closed and came beaming up to the desk. "But, Captain Kelston." He bowed. "Captain, this is a pleasure. Always a pleasure." His eyes flickered from Kelston's face, over to Karena, and back again. "And dinner? You will be tired." The large liquid brown eyes became solemn with a little act of pretended persuasion. "Dinner in the captain's room? Pedro will bring it. In an hour? Two?" He waited expectantly for Kelston to take up his cue.

"That would be nice. In about an hour." Kelston nodded gravely. There were more bows, more smiles. Again the high heels moved deliberately across the carpet, but this time more lightly and happily, for at the desk behind them there were friends. Mark and Karena climbed slowly up the wide shallow staircase, turned automatically down the long corridor and stopped outside the captain's room. Their eyes met, clung for a moment and slid away again.

He watched her as she walked into the room, waited for her to turn so that he could hold a picture in his mind of that first look. He knew it well, but each time just as at present it came to him with a fresh clarity, a new appreciation of its beauty, its tenderness and its love. Then he followed her and quietly closed the door behind them.

Mr. Agostino's dinner had, as usual, been enough to feed the whole crew—the chicken, the fresh local pineapple, the wine. Karena ate sparingly and daintily, but the meal lasted so long because they hardly stopped talking. Whenever he was with her, their thoughts touched off one another in a powder trail of talk and little puffs of laughter.

Karena stirred her coffee slowly and deliberately, and then looking across the table at him, she asked, "What is it, Mark? Tell me. What's the matter?" Her voice was as quiet and gentle as usual, but underlining it was a firm insistence as though she spoke from real knowledge.

"Tell you what, Karena?" He hedged, unwilling to break the brief magic spell of happiness, to talk of separation, to admit the bitter sea. Her mouth was still grave, but a faint deepening of the little laughter lines round her eyes acknowledged his evasion, smiled at it tenderly and dismissed it.

"Tell me what's troubling you." Her voice lilted up and down sadly and gladly at the same time. He felt the nearness of her, her knowledge of him, her strength and her pitiful vulnerability. He stumbled, trying to sound more hopeful than he felt.

"There's some talk." He paused, and shot her a steady look to emphasize his point. "Only talk. Nothing more. It's not decided. In fact—"

"Yes. Go on." Her hands rose and fell before him like two white birds.

"That they may—"

"May not let you stay here?" She finished the sentence slowly for him. Only her quick half-hopeful look that begged denial revealed her thoughts. Then as he nodded, she said, "I understand."

She lit a cigarette, absorbed in the small action, before asking him, "Just you? Do the others still stay?"

"Oh, Lord, no." He laughed. "It's not that. Not because of us. Just speeding up the service. Cutting down costs."

"Will it happen, do you think? Isn't it too far to fly? With no sleep?"

"I don't think it'll happen. It *is* too far. I've told them that."

She grinned at him, half-laughing, half-serious. "Then it won't happen. Not if you've told them. They'll listen."

"Oh, they listen all right." He smiled wryly at her. "But there's no evidence that they actually hear."

She lay back among the cushions of the sofa. Her face was shadowed, and though he could feel her eyes, their expression was hidden under the half-closed lids. "If they did . . . when would they stop it? Soon? In a few weeks? Or a few months?"

He thought for a moment. "It would take a bit of time, I should think."

"So it wouldn't be next trip? Or the one after?"

"My dear," he said gently, "I'm only guessing. I can't guarantee anything. But I don't think it would be."

"Then," she said, looking into the fire, the light from the uneven flames showing the little smile around her full mouth, high-lighting the delicate planes of her cheeks, "I won't worry very much. Not if it doesn't happen too soon."

The smile deepened and spread. She peeped at him out of the corners of her eyes. "I, too, have something to tell you. But mine—" She broke off, and fumbled in the rather shabby handbag. "Mine," she repeated, dragging out an envelope and waving it in front of him, "is good." Then she sighed. "At least I think it is."

He looked from her face to the paper with the official Foreign Office heading. In the stilted language of officialdom it acknowledged her application for a visa. It enclosed a form to be completed.

He could hear her quick breathing. "Don't you see, Mark,

last time it was no. Just that. And now . . . well, now . . . oh, anything might happen. They might let me have it straight away. I could get a job. We'd be together. Not just for a few hours. But for days and days. Years. A whole lifetime, Mark."

"Don't build too much on it, darling," he said soberly. "It's not very definite. You're not there yet."

"I know." She still smiled. "But when it's been 'No, No, No' . . . all the way along . . . well, just one 'Not no,' one 'I'm considering' seems like a royal welcome. And now, especially now."

She held out her hand for the letter and stowed it carefully in her bag. She patted it lovingly. "I have a feeling, Mark, that very soon we'll be together. Not just for these few hours snatched in passing. But really together. Always."

She pulled his hand over and kissed it and rubbed it up and down her cheek. He watched the firelight flicker on her black hair, momentarily filling it with little golden sparks. She looked at his face, pondering the things that had gone to make up this individual so inexpressibly dear. A separate person, yet so much a part of her own being.

For the brief time that remained of the evening, she went on imagining aloud a picture of their life together. Her plans were so vivid and so longed for that they merged with her dreams as she lay asleep beside him. They were the first things she thought of when she opened her eyes next morning. And then she saw the blue and gilt clock on the mantelpiece, its two hands merged into one at half-past six. As she watched them, they separated. Each tick drew them further apart till they formed a sharp arrowhead pointing upwards. When they were stretched wide open he would be called. Then they would once more draw tantalizingly closer to each other. But before they joined together again, he would be gone.

Careful not to wake him, she got up and dressed. She put

on his bath. She started packing the brown case that now she knew so well. All the time, above her, the clock ticked away. She was conscious of every second that it struck, aware of the almost indistinguishable sweep of the arms away from each other. Though she did not once look up into its face, she knew when they were furthest apart. There was no need for the knock on the door, the loud "Past seven o'clock, sir!" the hotel porter called out.

Mark stirred. He sat up in bed and shouted at the man, "All right, thank you. I'm awake."

Then he put out his arms for her. She walked across the room to him. Her body bent over his, her face pressed hard against his cheek. It seemed so simple. She held him so tightly no one could ever take him away from her.

"You should have wakened me, Karena."

"There was no need. Nearly everything's ready now."

Together as they lay there, she felt his heart beating against her own and she said to herself, My true love has my heart, and I have his. But aloud to him she said, "Your bath is ready. Hurry up, Mark. Or the water will be cold."

And she took her arms away from him. It was she herself, after all, who had let him go.

"Oh, well." He stretched and turned his legs over the side of the bed. "Here we go again," he said ruefully. "Seems I've only just arrived."

He collected his clothes and walked across the carpet to the bathroom in his bare feet. Karena was putting away the last of his things into the bag when she heard the scrunch of tires on the drive outside. Looking out of the window, she saw the crew car's thick blue back poking out of the hotel portico. It's not there, she said to herself. It's not there. She closed her eyes and looked again. "The transport is waiting," she called out to him. "Mark, do hurry. Please hurry."

"I *am* hurrying," he shouted back. Five minutes later, he came back into the room, washed and shaved, wearing his uniform. His brown hair, tousled such a short time ago, was now neatly brushed and parted.

"Better be going, I suppose," he said. It was the little casual words that were so difficult to say. "You won't be too lonely?"

"Of course not."

"And it won't be long. Three days . . . four days."

For a few minutes more, with everything packed and ready for leaving, they stayed close to each other, not moving or saying anything, letting the peace of the room flood over them. Then a porter arrived to collect the bags. They followed him along the corridor, back down the stairs out to the transport. The whole crew had been waiting. They watched Mark put his arms round Karena and hold her close to him.

" 'Bye, Karena."

"Good-bye, Mark. I'll see you soon."

"Soon."

His shoes clattered on the steel steps. He signalled to the driver. The engine caught. The transport moved away. He waved through the window, a brief movement of his hand—disappearing, it seemed, almost as soon as it started.

Karena felt her face ache with the effort of keeping up her smile. Once through the hotel gates, the crew car turned onto the road, out of her sight. She could still hear the sound of its engine. Then that too faded away. All she had left were the deep tire marks in the muddy pool by her feet to tell her that it was ever there at all.

She walked back to the captain's room. Already the maid had dusted and tidied it. The bed was made up, its coverlet neatly spread over it. The furniture now looked a little more faded, a little too stilted. She collected her few things and tucked them away in her bright coloured Lisbon basket.

For some time after she was ready to go, she stood by the window, looking out at the glitter of the empty daylight. She was still standing there when there was a knock at the door. A porter opened it. Looking round, she saw a blue uniform. Momentarily she imagined he had somehow returned, and she caught her breath with excitement. Then two hot-brown eyes looked at her from a plump pale face. The southbound captain had arrived.

The porter said apologetically, "This is Captain Featherstone's room, Miss Karena."

"Of course. I'm sorry. I didn't think you'd be here so soon."

"This is a special service. Just to Bermuda and back. We're having a rest before going on tonight."

"I see."

The two of them came inside. The pilot gave the porter a five escudo piece. Left alone with the girl, Featherstone said stiffly, "I'm sorry if I disturbed you."

"But you didn't. I was just going."

She collected her basket and went out into the corridor. The door closed behind her.

As she walked slowly away, she could hear little movements: the opening of a suitcase, the squeak of a cupboard door, the sound of two taps filling a bath. The man inside was making his preparations for the next fourteen hours that would be his share of life in the captain's room.

Book Five

The End of the North-West Quadrant

November 27-December 20

1

After a surprisingly quiet two days in Bermuda, Leeming followed Kelston back home to England. Things were by no means as bad as he had expected. That's what comes, he thought to himself, of having too much imagination.

Libby exercised a most gratifying discretion when he was with her. Now and then, at meals, she touched his hand as though by accident, and at the São Miguel night-stop, she kissed him good night (but quite primly), on the landing where her room was. But in public, he was still (breathlessly) "Captain Leeming." And though in private he was "Liebling, chéri and Michael darling," it was all theory and no practice.

By the time he touched down at London Airport, his mind was lulled into believing the incident in Panama was just an isolated emotional storm that had now disappeared completely from the map of his make-up. One of those odd, out-of-character, unexpected occurrences that could not possibly ever happen again.

After clearing Customs, the rest of the crew went to their homes. It was then that Libby said, flicking her cigarette ash on to the Operations Room linoleum with a deft wiggle on the long black holder, "I'll work the roster so I'm out with you next time, chéri."

She smiled. Before he had time to continue the discussion, she moved away from him behind the unassailable moat of being in earshot of other people.

Dully, he watched her meet a friend, cadge a lift to London and disappear abruptly with a gay wave of the hand and a "Thank you for a very nice trip, Captain Leeming."

Mr. Veitch found him by the alphabetical cubby-holes of the line's mailbox, looking in a dazed way at an instruction that his new uniform was ready for a fitting at the tailor's.

"Hello, Michael," he said very affably. "Heard you had a bit of trouble."

"Yes," Leeming said. "Yes."

"Not pleasant. In fact, damned unpleasant. But you certainly seem to have put up a good show . . . getting the thing out." He lowered his voice to a whisper, "Don't tell anyone, but I've recommended you for a commendation from the company."

Leeming's face brightened a little.

"Seems to have been one of those million to one chances," Veitch went on. "What d'you think?" The anxious lines on his face were well hidden behind the cheerful chubby smile.

"Well . . . we've never had anything like it before."

"No. All the same, it's worrying. The engineers have recommended a complete rerouting of the electrical wiring away from the hydraulic pipelines."

"So I heard."

"Quite a job, Michael . . . over a week's work on each aircraft. I've discussed it with the company chief engineer. We're going to do it, of course. But we can't do the lot at the same time. After all, no other Marlborough we know of has had the same trouble."

Leeming was still trying to make up his mind whether or not he wanted to see Libby Challoner on his next trip. Most of him shuddered at the thought. And yet—

"What we're going to do, Michael," Mr. Veitch was saying, "is to get the job done on each aircraft at its next Check Four. Kill two birds with one stone, so to speak. They're doing Easy Dog now."

"Seems reasonable," Leeming said. The incident with Easy Zebra seemed far away now, over and done with, unlike this new spectre, rising on his horizon. It was evident that in Libby's mind, anyway, their relationship had by no means terminated. She obviously did not regard the incident in Panama as a solitary flight of madness.

"And yet, Michael"—Mr. Veitch leaned towards him confidentially—"when I told Kelston a couple of days ago, he went up into the air. Though he's never had any trouble like it. Said all the aircraft should be done immediately."

"Yes," said Leeming absently. "At Bermuda, I rather got the idea he expected something of the sort."

"But that would mean closing down the line!" Mr. Veitch pointed out.

The extra week at home which that implied suddenly seemed unimportant. All Leeming said was, "Not very good for business."

"Exactly. And at a time like this, too. Of all times."

Veitch hesitated. Only that morning he had had final details of the contract with the Panama Government for the express Mid-Atlantic service. The necessary papers now lay signed, sealed and delivered in the chairman's safe. Then he added, "When we're doing so well."

"Quite," Leeming said. "Certainly getting better loads."

Veitch became much more confidential. "Between you and me, Michael," he went on, "I think Kelston's a bit upset. You see, I took your advice. The night-stop in the Azores comes out at the end of the week. The chairman's very pleased. In fact everyone's pleased . . . except Kelston."

Veitch looked at the pilot's face. He was searching for some reassuring sign that he'd done the right thing.

All he saw was polite but preoccupied woodenness. He sighed to himself. It was always the same. He was coming to the conclusion that pilots had their chain of thought severed every time they elevated themselves above the earth. It took some time before they could link it up again.

"But you can understand why Kelston's not pleased," he suggested.

All he got in return from Leeming was an indistinct little nod.

"You went right through last trip." Veitch's voice sounded a little irritable. After all, the whole idea of no night-stop in the Azores had come from this unenthusiastic man standing beside him. "You didn't feel tired?" With an exasperated attempt at a lead, he added, "Or did you?"

"Well . . . we started at night instead of the morning. That makes a lot of difference."

"Yes, yes. I agree with you. But you *had* an emergency. And in spite of such long hours on duty, you did the right thing." He was trying very hard to prove his point. Especially to himself.

"We *got* there," Leeming said. "That's the main thing. Getting there."

Mr. Veitch asked again, "Did you feel tired?"

"I was a bit tired," Leeming said vaguely, "not much."

Not a great deal of help, Mr. Veitch reflected. Still the man had flown all the way from the Azores that day. You had to make allowances.

"You found it all right though?"

Leeming seemed to stir himself up a little. "Oh, yes," he said. "I've told you before. It's the sensible thing."

A short silence fell between them while the line manager thanked God for a definite answer. Then he said suddenly, "Sad business." There was no need to identify the particular business to which he was specifically referring.

Leeming's eyes gave a brand-new flicker of interest.

"Yes," he said. "I hear his wife's left him."

Veitch nodded. "Can't blame her."

"No . . . still seems rather a pity. Might have worked out all right in the end."

"I doubt it. I very much doubt it." Veitch moved his head rapidly from side to side as though he was trying to shake the whole sad business right out of it. "All the same . . . wish we could do something about it."

That sentiment of Veitch's stuck fast in Leeming's consciousness, as he took the bus back to Fairoaks. Somebody *ought* to do something about it. Somebody should point out to Kelston how much he was ruining his life. He and Veronica should be helped to a reconciliation. But people were too busy with their own affairs, too selfish. With a wry smile, he remembered that selfish was the adjective that Melanie had used on *him*. He'd shown her how wrong she was once. This second time, he'd show her he could think of others, well outside the family circle. As the bus jogged down the country lanes, his mind, which had been filled to the brim with the Libby business, became suddenly and blessedly preoccupied instead with Kelston's affair in the Azores.

After Melanie's ecstatic welcome home, he suddenly fell thoughtful.

"What's the matter, darling?" she asked him. "Tired?"

"Not specially . . . just thinking."

"What about, Michael?" She had immediately jumped to the conclusion that something had happened on the aeroplane. Michael never told her anything except that every trip was a good trip. It would as soon occur to him to mention anything about the fire to Melanie as tell her about his hectic night in Panama with Libby Challoner.

He said to her, "D'you remember you told me I only thought about myself? Never about other people?"

She came over to him and gave a cheerful hug. "Oh, *that*. Don't take any notice of *that*. I was just in a state."

"No . . . not altogether. You were quite right."

"Come to that, everybody's selfish."

He nodded. "That's what I've been thinking. Look at this Kelston affair, for instance. Nobody's lifted a finger to help Mark and Veronica try to sort the thing out. Make up their differences."

"But what could anybody do? They wouldn't know where to start."

He looked across at her gravely. "They can try. The least they can do is try."

"*Who's* going to try, Michael?"

Suddenly his eyes became so solemn, they looked as though they had just perceived the whole horrifying confusions and mistakes that make up the world's case history.

"I am," he said simply. "*I'm* going to try."

Normally, the day after a trip Michael Leeming had his breakfast in bed, as a warm little gesture on Melanie's part to tell him how glad she was to have him home. But this time, he was up at half-past six. He gave the children their breakfast. Melanie's he brought in to her on the best visitor's tray.

She stretched out a cosy, affectionate hand to grasp his. "What's got into you, Michael?"

"Oh, I dunno. About time I did more in the house. I want to be off early, too."

"Off?" A puzzled frown settled on her white forehead. "Off where?"

"I told you last night, Melanie. I'm going to see Mark Kelston."

"But, this is the first day of your stand-off! And you've only got a week in, anyway, Michael."

"I know, I know. But I think he'll work the roster to get out straightaway. The night-stop comes out at the end of the week. He'll be able to see her outbound. Probably for the last time."

"What on earth d'you expect to do?"

"Nobody's actually told him what a mess he's making. I don't think he realizes."

"Realizes what?"

Michael hesitated. "How much the crews talk," he said.

"If I know Mark, I don't suppose he cares."

But Michael refused to take any notice of her. "There's his career. The management know all about it now. He doesn't even bother to keep the thing quiet."

"Now Veronica's left him, it's too late to start patching."

"I don't agree. Veronica may have left him, but she won't give him a divorce. Shows she still wants him."

"You think it does?"

He nodded vigorously. "Certainly I do. Now the night-stop's coming out, it's the best time to do something. He'll hardly be able to see anything of this Karena woman."

"Have you got his address?"

"I'll get it from the company."

Melanie started to toy with bacon and fried tomatoes, saying nothing.

"You don't seem pleased," he said.

"It's your first day at home. I'd been hoping—"

"But, Melanie, it's always *you* who says more should be done for other people."

She looked at the boyish anxiety on his face, and wrinkled up her nose in a smile at him. "I'm just a bit surprised, that's all. And I think it's no good interfering."

"Who said anything about interfering? I'm just giving an outside opinion. I dare say he'd be glad to have it."

Michael had not, as a matter of a fact, considered Kelston's reactions to his helping hand. In some odd and inexplicable way, he had identified what he called to himself "this Libby nonsense" with Mark's affair with Karena in the Azores. He had a strait-laced conscience himself. He could tell a sin when he saw one. It was impossible at present to do anything about Libby; naturally, it followed that he should do his best to straighten Kelston out on a few points that he might have missed. He would have welcomed a detached view on his own trouble (but that was impossible, since it would involve letting someone in on the secret), and he assumed Kelston would take a similar attitude. He set off one minute before his eight o'clock schedule, filled with an almost evangelical enthusiasm.

Melanie had expected him to fail, but she wasn't prepared for him to take it quite so much to heart. It was past three when he came back. He started to eat the cold lunch she had ready for him in the lounge, staring at the fire, hardly saying a word.

She said to him, "Come on, Michael. Tell me what happened."

"Nothing."

"You saw him, didn't you?"

"Oh, yes . . . I saw him. Lives in one room. Practically no furniture."

"Michael, it sounds awfully lonely for him."

"Doesn't seem to mind. There's a photograph of the girl. He can't bring her to England, you know."

"Yes, you told me." Her pretty shoulders gave a shrug of impatience. "You're so bad at telling me things. So vague. Was he pleased to see you?"

"Couldn't tell. You know Mark. Didn't seem displeased."

She said, "Well, what did you say to him?"

"The usual things. That the crews gossiped. He was losing his good name. Ruining his career."

"How did he take it?"

"He just laughed." With a sudden vehemence, Michael added, "The man's off his head. That's the trouble. No shame. No sense of wrong-doing. Nothing but slap-happiness."

"If he's happy," she said, "that's the main thing."

He looked at her doubtfully. "That's what he said. Something about being in love with the girl. She had the same sort of mind. The same ideas. He felt complete with her. Unexpectedly, he'd found happiness, and he intended to hang onto it."

"He seems to have tried to explain it to you, Michael."

"If you call that an explanation. I said—what about your family? He wasn't quite so glib then. All he could think of was the fact he'd provided well for them. That nobody could understand his relationship with Veronica, except himself. So I thought I might as well tell him straight."

"What about?"

"These excuses." Michael rubbed his thumb and forefinger together contemptuously. "This happiness idea. I told him he'd made it up for the express purpose of going to bed with someone."

Melanie drew her breath in sharply. "Michael . . . you didn't!"

He was almost as shocked at himself as she was, but he went bravely on. "Oh, yes, I did. Only way of dealing with these things is to get down to brass tacks."

"That made him angry?" she asked quietly.

"Didn't seem to. That's the terrible thing. You don't seem to be able to make any impression on him. One way or another. But I could see he wasn't particularly pleased."

Melanie laughed. Her amusement seemed to break the strained tension that had crept into the conversation. He grinned at her, as she started piling the plates one on top of the other.

As she wheeled out the trolley, she said affectionately, "You're the soul of tact, chéri."

He made a sudden turn towards her. "That's an odd word for you to use, Melanie."

"What is?"

"Chéri. It isn't your sort of word at all."

"Michael . . ." She suddenly caught sight of the look in

his eyes. "Why, whatever's the matter? Chéri's only the French word for darling."

"If you want to say darling," he said irritably, "for God's sake, say it in English."

2

"Good morning, Captain." The same respectful words said with the same slight overemphasis.

Leeming, on his way up to the front of the aircraft, turned his head and looked behind him.

She was putting the crew's raincoats on hangers and hanging them up in the vestibule.

"Morning, Libby," he said, purposely casual. So she had managed to work the roster after all. For twelve days, she would live under the same roof as he did. Eat with him. Work with him.

"Shall I take your coat, Captain?"

"Thank you."

The steward came bustling forward, anxious to make his presence known.

"Morning, Mr. Pollinger."

"Morning, sir. Passengers will be aboard in five minutes time, sir. Log book, ship's papers and catering all present and correct, sir."

He sounded like a regimental sergeant major on the parade ground.

Leeming looked at his watch. "Might get off on time."

Mr. Pollinger said, "Well, I *hope* there's not going to be any hanging round, sir. Going right through to Bermuda, aren't we?"

"We are. The night-stop's out now."

"Nearly a full load, sir."

"Yes . . . excellent, isn't it? Things are looking up. Mind you, one of the reasons is this new express contract with the Panama Government we've got. Mr. Veitch was only telling me about it this morning. Rather a good break for the line."

The steward did not look so pleased as Leeming.

"Dunno what's doing it, sir. But I *do* know with all that many passengers it means serving a hundred and fifty meals. Never mind light refreshments."

"You'll be able to manage," Leeming reassured him. "Between the two of you, you'll do it all right."

Mr. Pollinger looked at Libby. Then he said doubtfully, "Yes, sir."

In the right-hand seat, the first officer was already halfway through the Before Starting Engines Check List with the engineer. Leeming waited in the navigation compartment, sorting papers in his briefcase, till the check was completed.

Then he went forward, said "Hello" to the rest of the crew and adjusted the captain's seat. He liked to be well back, away from the instruments, so his arms and legs were not bunched over the controls.

Before he sat down, he had a look at the first officer. He seemed older than the average of this new batch of second pilots. Much less shy.

Leeming said, "I don't think we've flown together before?"

The first officer turned towards him. "The name's Cockcroft, sir."

"New?" Leeming asked.

He saw the corners of the self-confident little mouth turn down in a deprecating, twisted smile.

"Hardly say that, sir. Done a couple of trips. With Captain Ferris, sir."

"I see."

"I had a command of my own for the last year."

Leeming looked surprised. "In this company?"

"Oh no, sir. Private firm."

"What on?"

"Ansons. Blackpool to the Isle of Man."

"Nice small aeroplane on a nice short route," was Leeming's comment.

The first officer shook his head from side to side in violent disagreement.

"They may only be fifty miles apart, sir . . . but you can still get some nasty weather." The words strutted out like a sentry's challenge, a warning to Leeming not to get the wrong idea.

All Leeming said was, "I dare say."

In the air, between London and Madrid, he conscientiously went through with the first officer the little tricks of his trade, information he had picked up, pieces of advice, things to watch.

For nearly an hour, he passed on facts that he had learnt from his own mistakes, from the mistakes of other people, what he had noticed and procedures that had indelibly stamped themselves on his mind.

He finished up with his warning on carrying out orders correctly, rather than being too smart and too quick.

"Later," he said, "when you've more experience, you'll be able to carry them out both correctly and quickly. But now, all I ask is you carry them out correctly."

Unlike most of the other new first officers, Mr. Cockcroft did not take notes. He asked no questions.

Leeming had the vague impression that, if he let him, Cockcroft could give the lecture himself in considerably more graphic and clarified detail.

The same half-smile had appeared round his lips.

Easy Fox droned on, no matter what anyone said in the cockpit. Leeming noticed the brown, burnt hills of Spain below them. Their estimate at Madrid was in forty-five minutes' time. Normally speaking, at five hundred feet a minute descent, which was comfortable for the passengers, it took thirty-six minutes to come down.

Leeming turned back and asked the radio officer to get a descent clearance for him from Madrid Control.

Then he said suddenly to the first officer, "How old are you, Mr. Cockcroft?"

"Twenty-four, sir."

"Like the line?"

"Well . . . you can guess what it feels like when you lose a command, sir. This job—" He pointed to the right-hand seat and wrinkled his nose.

Leeming went on as though he hadn't heard him.

"What d'you think of the Marlborough?"

"Just like a great big Anson, sir."

Leeming looked at the huge metal wings of Easy Fox, the four enormous engines even now, at reduced power, roaring out their strength. Each one of them had three times as much power as the two engines on the Anson combined—the safe, small, virtuous Anson, on which he had been first trained to fly something heavier than a Tiger Moth, over fourteen years before.

He said, "On this job, the more you fly, the less you find you know about it." He looked across at Cockcroft with a special emphasis. "Teaches you to be wary."

As the trip progressed towards the Azores, Leeming was turning over in his mind the whole question of Libby Challoner, and trying to make up his mind whether or not he was glad she was on board. When he went back to talk to the passengers, she seemed as respectful as ever. Nobody would have dreamed that there was anything between them.

He was feeling not dissatisfied. Despite the fact that she had wangled the roster, the thing looked as though it might have blown completely over.

And then, just as Cockcroft was once more reading out the

check list before the engines were started in the Azores, up she came, shimmying into the cockpit, slap in between "Superchargers—low and locked," and "rich mixture, auxiliary fuel pumps on."

"Any gum, chum?" she asked Leeming. "Peanuts, Ices. Chocolates, Cigarettes. Service with a smile."

He looked in horrified amazement at this complete reversal of her former behaviour. In front of the whole crew. On duty, too.

She pushed at him her little brown basket of chewing gum, barley sugar and boiled sweets.

"Have one, Herr Kapitan," she said.

He could have killed her.

Instead, the muscles of his face pulled up into a sickly smile. It saved him, at least, from the difficulty of finding something to say.

Cockcroft, as though he hadn't seen her, went on reading out the check list. "Tank to engine. Fire extinguisher on Number Three. Fireguard posted."

Leeming took a small boiled sweet. Libby still stood there.

"Thank you, sir," she said, and bobbed down in a mock curtsey.

"Engines clear?" the first officer asked.

"Engines clear," the engineer said, and then, "O.K. to start Three and Four?"

"O.K.," Cockcroft said.

"Accelerate Three."

A few seconds later, the engineer called out, "Mesh Three."

Cockcroft watched the propeller blades going slowly round, counting them aloud. Then he called, "Contact Three," and switched on the magnetos.

His efficient little gesture implied that the captain was too busy. It was really Leeming's job to attend to the switches on the starboard engines. Number Three burst into life with a loud sustained guffaw. Libby still waited.

Then just before Number Four added to the growing noise, she took herself off to the back.

As Easy Fox dug into the two thousand miles separating the Azores from Bermuda, Leeming looked out at the fragile, frosty appearance of the night sky above them, and the indistinct cobbles of good weather cumulus below.

He wondered miserably what the hell he should do.

Four hours went by, and he still kept himself on watch. Somehow, the actual studying of the instruments, the flying of the aircraft in the smooth air, helped him to concentrate on the difficulties in his mind.

"Shall I take over now, sir?" Cockcroft said.

Leeming looked at him suspiciously. His eyes searched the man's bland face, trying to find out if he guessed anything from the stewardess' suddenly boisterous performance. But there was nothing there except the self-satisfaction that had been apparent as soon as the trip started.

"Oh, all right . . . if you want to."

"Aren't you tired, sir?"

"Not particularly." All the same, he put back his seat, and lay back, closing his eyes.

One thing was perfectly evident. Libby had not worked the roster without certain intentions. The incident in Panama was, after all, not over. And something would certainly have to be done about it. Before, side by side with Kelston's affair in the Azores, it ripened into a scandalously outsize fruit on the company's grapevine.

When they reached Bermuda, after an outwardly quiet trip, Leeming had at least made up his mind when he went to bed, desperately tired after twenty-two hours' work, on the action he was going to take with Libby Challoner in the morning.

Leeming slept in so late, he missed lunch. He strolled down into Hamilton for a sandwich and some coffee. While he was coming back through the gardens of the Saracen

Hotel, he saw Libby lazing back in a deck chair. All on her own.

She called out to him, "Isn't it heavenly, Michael? The sun . . . and all this, too." And she pointed out the little white houses dotting the blue curve of the bay.

He walked over towards her and looked at the cool fair hair sweeping carelessly over her white forehead.

"Libby," he said quietly, "I want to talk to you."

She shot a quick glance at him. Then she said, "Oh dear. Oh dear," and whipped her eyes off his face just as though they'd been burnt.

He stood in front of her, "Look, Libby. While you're in my crew, you'll behave like any other crew member."

She looked puzzled. "I don't know what you mean."

"I haven't the least intention of accepting any familiar behaviour from anyone on the aircraft. You included."

"My," she said flippantly, "we *are* being masterful this afternoon. I'd adore it normally, of course, Liebling. But just now—"

"Just now," Leeming said grimly, "the stewardess will listen to some good advice from the captain of her aircraft."

She smiled airily, quizzically. "Odd," she remarked, "I didn't realize this sadistic streak in you before, Michael. You love having a chérie to bring your food and say 'Yes, sir' and 'No, sir.' Rather like making love to the maid, isn't it?"

Leeming ached to get hold of that primped-up little body and shake some sense into it. Violent physical action seemed to be the only way of getting her to understand anything. He glared at the blue, unperturbed eyes.

"It's hopeless trying to talk to you, Libby."

"Then why try?"

He hesitated. "God knows. That incident in Panama, I suppose. I admit I was attracted to you. Most men would have been . . . under the same circumstances. I'm sorry. It won't happen again."

She started to giggle. "Sweetness," she said, "that must be the most moving little love speech of all time. No wonder you're so irresistible, Michael. You think of things to say that all the girls just *love* to hear."

"Now that's said and done with," Leeming went on, ignoring her, "this coming up to the front at the Azores with your wretched boiled sweets. Acting as though you owned the flight deck. Me included."

She said, "Oh, *that*. D'you mean to say this lecture's been about *that?*"

"Don't let anything like it ever happen again."

To his surprise, Leeming saw her suddenly flush up. If he hadn't been certain that she was so hard-boiled, he would have been sure she was on the edge of tears.

"Oh, Michael," she said, "didn't you see? Don't you ever notice things?"

He asked truculently, "What, for instance?"

"That I was just about dead on my feet in the Azores. We'd had an awful lot to do. And then to face another eleven hours without a rest—" She hid her face in her hands. "I was just trying to show I had some spirit left. A little fight. That was all."

He felt uncomfortable, now that she was crying.

"I'm sorry, Libby," he said awkwardly. "I wasn't meaning to be unkind. These things have to be said. Crew discipline . . . that sort of thing." He stopped. "Here . . . take my handkerchief."

She sniffed into it. "I thought I'd been doing rather well. I didn't realize you expected such reverence. Not *all* the time."

It was difficult to know what to say next. He hadn't expected tears. A silence fell between them, punctuated by tiny gulps from Libby. He decided he had to go doggedly on with his plan now. He was, after all, more than halfway through it.

"Anyway," he said, indistinctly, "it's an impossible situation."

But she heard him perfectly well. "What's an impossible situation, Michael?"

"You . . . me."

"His Highness and Her Lowness. Is that what you mean?"

"You know I don't mean that at all."

"The Prince isn't so keen on Cinderella, after all?" she persisted. As quickly as they came, the tears had disappeared. The pretty little features of her face all combined to put on instead a woebegone charade. "Poor Cinderella!"

"It's nothing to do with you. Or with me. It's just . . . circumstances."

"Well, if you feel like that about it . . ." She shrugged her shoulders. "You better not let me get away with your handkerchief, too." She tossed it over to him. "'Georgy Porgy, pudding and pie, Kissed the girls and made them cry.' Fits you in more ways than one, doesn't it, Michael?" She was actually laughing now.

He said heavily, "What I want to get into your head is that it's all finished. I've behaved quite crazily and—"

She promptly finished the sentence for him. "You're not going to behave crazily again. That's quite plain. Even to me, chéri. Finished. Kaput. All over."

He looked out to sea, over the view she had pointed out to him when first he had found her. "I've said all this very ungraciously, Libby," he said lamely.

"I wouldn't say that, sir."

"Now you're being childish."

"No, sir. Just obeying orders, sir."

He gave a long sigh of pure exasperation. "If this is the way you're going to take it, Libby . . . there's nothing more to be said." He stood beside her, waiting.

She said nothing. She had just closed her eyes. The sun highlighted the contented drowsiness on her face.

"Well?" he said.

She opened her eyes again. "I'm sorry, Captain," she said, "I thought the lecture was over."

"Libby," he growled at her angrily, "you're impossible."

"Me and the situation, both," she said. "Snap."

He left her abruptly, and walked over to the hotel. A fury of anger boiled up inside his mind. The stupid, irritating little idiot! If he'd stayed another minute, he'd have put her over his knee and walloped her. Which would have made things even worse.

There was some satisfaction, anyway, in the fact that he'd got it off his chest. The whole thing was rubbed out now. His character was back where it had started, wholesome and untarnished.

Before he reached the screen of oleanders and magnolia bushes in front of the verandah, a little bubbling-over sound sprinkled the drowsy air around him.

The girl was giggling again.

Now it was all over, he felt rather pleased with himself. The little scene in the garden of the hotel might have been undignified, but it had certainly done the trick. His quiet, well-ordered life was no longer threatened. He'd had the courage to recognize the danger and stamp on it.

A pity, he thought to himself, that Mark hadn't seen fit to take his advice. Rather anxiously, he awaited Libby's behaviour towards himself during the remaining day of their slip in Bermuda. Surprisingly, it was above reproach. She didn't sulk. In public, she treated him exactly the same as she'd always treated him.

Cockcroft was now taking a deep interest in her; Leeming heard vaguely of a bathing party being arranged between them. They went off on Thursday evening, chattering and laughing in a taxi to a Hamilton night club.

He noticed that Cockcroft handled the situation of taking a girl out with the same assurance as he flew a Marlborough.

With sense of relief, he found he was allowed to be on his own to do exactly as he pleased. Ferris, the northbound slip captain, said to him, "You're looking very cheerful these days, Mike! Glad to be away from home, sweet home, eh? Or are you just damned pleased to see me?"

Leeming said, "Well, at least you're someone to have a drink with, Peter."

"No need to twist my arm, old chap."

They went down to the bar in the basement. Leeming ordered a Tom Collins each.

"Heard you had a fire on board the other day," Ferris said.

"Yes. Rather a nasty one. Lost all my electrical power."

"Oh, well . . . that sort of thing. Might happen to any one, I suppose."

"Still damned unpleasant while it lasted."

"Sure, sure . . . but you coped." Ferris' voice sounded very casual. "What we're all paid to do."

Leeming was rather annoyed that he should take it so calmly. "They're remodifying the wiring, all the same, as every aircraft goes in for a Check Four."

"Gives the engineers something to do for the next few months, I suppose."

"Doesn't seem to worry you much, Peter," Leeming grumbled. "That might have been worse. And it might have been *you*."

Ferris shrugged his long lean shoulders. "You know me, old chap. Enjoy today. Forget about yesterday. And to hell with tomorrow."

"You can damned well buy me a drink before you forget today," Leeming said. "It's your turn."

"Ah, yes." Ferris turned to the Negro barman and said, "Another Tom Collins."

"Aren't you going to join me?"

"I know you'll excuse me, Michael." Ferris gave him a brilliant, flashing smile. "I have—what would *you* call it?—an assignation. And time marches on."

He slapped Leeming on the shoulder as he left him alone at the bar. "Be good, Michael," he advised him. "And if you can't be good . . . be careful!"

Everyone had so much their own little circle that Leeming began to feel out of things. He found himself rather bored. Bermuda he had explored many times in the past four years. There was nothing to do but mooch around in the hotel.

He welcomed the arrival of his aircraft, Easy Zebra, out from England. For a full twelve hours, he was happily occupied flying another full load of passengers and mail down to Panama, via Nassau and Jamaica.

It was one of those trips without a cloud in the sky, and he finished up with a honey-soft landing at Tocumen Airport. He was in an extremely agreeable mood when he reached his room in the rest house. He was happy. He was hungry. And he was tired. All that added up to what he most looked forward to—a good, solid, ten hours' sleep.

He had two beers after his meal, and said good night to the crew. Within a few minutes of getting into bed, as he had expected, he was fast asleep.

But he woke up in time for breakfast next morning, feeling not as cheerful as he should do. He went down to the dining room, and ate chilled and sugared paw-paw, listening to the crew's plans for spending their day.

Libby was making elaborate preparations with Cockcroft for taking the train up to Colon, at the other end of the Canal. And tomorrow, they were going to spend the morning on the beaches of Taboga Island.

Alone, after breakfast was over, he rattled around in the big house, wondering what to do. He went for a walk into the town, but it was really much too hot to go far. He came back and sat in the shade of a palm tree beside the rest house. This heat, he said to himself again and again. He produced a handkerchief, mopping the sweat from his forehead. The heat, that's what was getting him down.

Everyone else was out to lunch. He was halfway through a plate of cold ham, when it suddenly struck him what the trouble was. It wasn't the heat at all.

He was jealous. Jealous of that ridiculous, self-important boy of a first officer, now laughing and talking with Libby in Colon.

He could hardly believe it. In the afternoon, he went back to his room to lie down for a rest, and there everything flowed back into his memory. The rug she had stood on. The curtains she had pulled aside to look at the crew on their return from the party. The coverlet she had tossed carelessly onto the floor when she slipped into the bed. Vivid images of her little gestures, the movements of her body, the little wrinkles in her dress as she sat down so demurely, the strong sweet smell of her perfume, all now poured back into his mind and captured his imagination. Desire for her started to sweep every other thought clean out of his head.

For the remaining four days they were at Panama, before the long haul back to England, all the communication he had with Libby was her respectful "Good morning, Captain," at breakfast, and her "Good evening, Captain," at night.

An hour out from Panama, on the way home, the Jamaica weather suddenly started to go sour. Leeming looked out of Easy Uncle's cockpit windows, and saw mare's tail cirrus high in the darkening sky above them, followed later by a thick white coating of cirro-stratus.

The weather forecast he had received before leaving Tocumen had given a trace of cloud and twenty miles visibility at Kingston. Now, the amended forecast lay on the steel throttle pedestal between Cockcroft and himself: continuous rain, six hundred feet cloud base, visibility two miles, wind–south, thirty knots, gusting fifty.

It was a weather situation he particularly hated.

It was above company limits, which meant he would have to try and land. There were ten passengers for Jamaica. But the only let-down he could do was on a radio beacon, affected by the mountains and probably by the static in the clouds, four miles from the aerodrome and nowhere near in line for landing. And the wind was well off the direction of the runway, blowing towards the steep mountains that lined the harbour.

While he was thinking about the inadequate let-down procedure, Easy Uncle nosed into cloud and heavy rain. A blinding flash of lightning lit up the shivering wet wing.

Cockcroft said, "Reminds me of the time I hit a thunderstorm over Blackpool. I had to . . ."

But Leeming took no notice of him and he lapsed into silence.

Approaching the island, the pilot let down to eleven thousand feet, still well above the height of the mountains. He could hear the call-sign of the beacon on the radio compass. The needle wavered, and gradually steadied, pointing dead ahead. Then it wheeled right over and pointed behind him.

"Tell 'em we're over the beacon," he called to Cockcroft. "I'll let down to the south. Over the sea."

As carefully as he could, in the bumping, blind cloud, he turned back on the beacon. When once more he was over it, he turned south and punched the stop watch on the clock.

"Eighteen inches," he called to the engineer. With her engines throttled back, Easy Uncle started to descend, while Leeming concentrated on holding an accurate track on a southerly course. That in itself needed all his skill and experience. The wind strength and direction changed continuously as his altitude altered.

At four thousand feet, eight minutes out, he was still in

cloud. He made a procedure turn back onto a northerly heading towards the beacon. Now he was running dead in the direction of the mountains with the wind behind him. He turned and twisted Easy Uncle to force her onto the right track.

The Marlborough wallowed and jerked in the violent air. At a thousand feet, they were still in cloud.

Rain lashed down over the windscreens, while the wipers clanked uselessly to and fro across the glass.

Leeming explained to Cockcroft carefully, "Don't let me get below six hundred feet. Pull back on the stick if I do. I'll be on instruments all the time. Once we leave the beacon and head in the direction of the airport, we're on our own. The wind'll blow us to hell . . . so when you see the runway lights, point them out to me immediately."

"Will you do the timing, sir?" Cockcroft asked in a brisk, efficient voice.

"You bet I will," Leeming said grimly. "One minute . . . one minute only. If we can't see anything then, we'll turn back out to sea."

Easy Uncle was now down to circuit speed. Leeming approached the beacon at six hundred feet, still in thick black cloud and streaming rain. When the needle whipped over, Leeming wrenched the Marlborough round eighty degrees to starboard, and punched the stop watch once more.

The landing gear and sixty per cent flap were down, and the Landing Check completed. The speed fluctuated unsteadily between 100 and 130 knots. He was timing carefully. Fifteen seconds went by. Easy Uncle was still at six hundred feet. Then wisps of cloud scudded past them and out of the corner of his eye he saw lights.

"Runway," Cockcroft shouted. "Turn fifteen degrees to port. We're nearly on top of it, sir."

Even as he turned to the left, cutting off all the power on the engines, the small unoccupied part of Leeming's brain thought, This is strange. If anything, the runway should be to the right. But then . . . the wind was strong. It was fluctuating wildly. Their drift must be terrific. *Could* be to port.

In any case, all his reflexes had been highly trained to obey an instruction immediately. Easy Uncle swung obediently round Cockcroft's fifteen degrees to port.

Leeming took his eyes away from the ghostly glow of the instruments, and peered through the windscreen.

He saw a long, long row of orange lights, far too bright for an electric flare-path. The altimeter flickered at two hundred feet. He saw car lights moving over a glossy surface. A brilliant neon sign flashed out in damp red and blue. *BEVERLEY'S for EVERYTHING.* The shop windows glittered onto Constitution Street, Kingston's main thoroughfare.

Leeming shouted, "Gear up. Rated power."

The engines roared up to forty-five inches manifold pressure immediately. The whole aircraft shuddered at the sudden powerful thrust from the airscrews. He knew now that they were pointing towards the high mountains that started not more than a mile away.

He pulled the stick hard over to the right, tilting the Marlborough up into a vertical turn, trying to pivot round on his wing tip. All the time, he kept the aircraft just below cloud at six hundred feet. That at least gave him some idea of where he was going. The sweat ran down his hands, making the controls wet and slippery.

"You clot!" he yelled at Cockcroft, his whole body shaking with fury. "You goddamned, bloody, stupid little clot."

Somehow or other, he had to get on a southerly course, back out to sea. In the few seconds of the turn, as the heavy aircraft banged up and down in the streaming wet air, Easy Uncle was being blown by a gale force beam wind nearer and nearer to the invisible mountains.

Leeming saw quite clearly the trees below him, the lights flaming out from the little bungalows.

With an agonizing slowness, the gyro in front of him moved round from an easterly heading. Just for a moment, he saw a man's black face glistening in a street lamp, so close that it seemed to be stuck, like an extra navigation light, on the end of his now vertical starboard wing.

And then suddenly, the gyro read south again.

Leeming hauled back on the control column, and Easy Uncle leapt up into the cloud once more.

When they were at eight thousand feet, he said to the radio officer, "Tell Control . . . weather too bad at Kingston. Proceeding to my alternate aero-drome, Nassau."

The rest of the one and a half hour flight to the Bahamas passed in utter silence in the flight deck of the Marlborough. Just beyond Cuba, they edged out of bad weather into a clear night. Leeming saw Nassau Island gleaming in the moonlight, over fifty miles away.

When the engines had stopped at the ramp on Oakes Field, Cockcroft said in a low voice, "I'm very sorry, sir. Very sorry indeed."

Leeming couldn't bring himself to speak to the man just then. He got out of his seat, and climbed down the front steps into the hot Nassau night.

When they were all in the Operations Office, making up the flight plan to Bermuda, Leeming for the first time appeared to notice his first officer's presence by his side.

He turned towards him, and said very slowly, "You didn't tell me, Mr. Cockcroft. What exactly *did* you do in the Anson . . . that time you hit the thunderstorm over Blackpool?"

3

In the Voyage Report that would eventually find its way to the line manager's desk, Leeming wrote, "Attempted a let down at Kingston. Weather unsuitable for landing. Continued to Nassau, where Jamaica passengers were off-loaded."

As far as Cockcroft's attempt at getting him to land in the main street at Kingston was concerned, that could wait till he made up his Confidential Crew Reports on his return to London. Then, he intended to spread himself. A thorough going over, back in the training school, would knock the self-confidence right out of the man, and teach him to think before he opened his big mouth. Leeming had already made up his mind to write him down as "completely unfit at this stage to operate on the line." There had been some grumbling among the captains over this new batch of inexperienced first officers, but this was the first time he himself had flown with any but the shy ones, obedient and anxious to learn. He had no desire to see Mr. Cockcroft out on a trip with him again. Not for a long, long time.

To give the first officer some inkling of what was in his mind, he flew the five hour leg from Nassau to Bermuda without once letting Cockcroft touch the controls. The man sat like a dummy, uselessly staring out of the window, and saying every now and then, "Are you sure you don't want a rest, sir?"

While they circled Kindley Field, Leeming did the Before Landing Checks (most of which were normally done by the first officer) completely by himself. He obtained his own clearance to land from the Tower. When they were on the ground, and Cockcroft started to read out the After Landing Check List, he took it away from him and started calling it out himself, starting again at the beginning, while his own hands dealt with all the levers and the switches.

He handed Easy Uncle over to Kelston. Since their talk together, Leeming had rather gone out of his way to avoid him.

This time, Mark met him as he clambered down from the aircraft.

"Saw on the notice-board you went on to Nassau, Mike," Kelston said.

"Kingston weather was out."

"Did you make a let-down?"

"Yes . . . but you know what the beacon's like there. Terrible wind, too. Raining like hell."

"Forecast?"

Leeming snorted, "What do *you* think?"

They walked together over to the Operations Room.

Mark said, "Anyway, it's made you half an hour ahead of schedule. Which I shall promptly lose on the next leg."

"Bad winds?"

"Dead on the nose. Twelve and a half hours."

Leeming whistled. "Bit unusual . . . this time of year."

"There's a low sitting south of track. Too big to get round."

"Strong easterlies all the way?"

"Just about," Kelston sighed. Then he added angrily, "And no night-stop in the Azores, either."

Leeming prudently said nothing.

"I never really expected they'd do it," Kelston went on. "Damned stupid. Asking for trouble."

Leeming felt bound to say, "Not as bad as all that, Mark."

Kelston looked at him curiously. "Veitch had some fantastic story it was you who started the whole thing."

"Well . . . I did make a suggestion along those lines."

"Bloody silly suggestion," Kelston said decisively.

Leeming maintained an offended silence. How this man had the nerve to criticize—when all along everyone knew about his little reason in the Azores.

They stopped before they got to the airport buildings, and watched the dawn sunshine pour down on the huge hulk of the Castle Harbour Hotel, the other side of the Bay.

Mark said suddenly, "What's your first officer like?"

Leeming hesitated. He had no intention of telling another captain the details of the botched let-down at Kingston. A mistake like that reflected on himself. He, after all, was fully responsible for what went on in his aircraft.

Then he allowed the opinion, "Overconfident."

Kelston laughed. "I've got the other extreme. Underconfident. Hardly likes to touch anything."

"I suppose pilots are hard to get these days."

"Trouble is you've got to watch them all the time. They're doing most of their training on the line. And now there's no Azores night-stop—"

Leeming cut him short. "I better sign up at Customs, Mark." He started to move away. Kelston was still grumbling about first officers, night-stops, aircraft.

"Oh, well," Leeming said vaguely, as he walked off, "these things are sent to try us. Have a good trip."

"Dunno about a good one," Kelston grunted. "It'll certainly be a long one."

Flying against the path of the sun, from west to east, the daylight passed quickly for Kelston. Within eight hours, it was beginning to get dark. But those hours had dragged.

Timperley was his first officer. Shy and a little scared at the best of times, his experience with the fire on Easy Zebra had made him a model of ultracautiousness. As usual, Kelston had put him on watch for the first four hours. But it was no use. He had just put his seat back and closed his eyes and settled down, when there was a gentle shake on his knee, and Timperley pointed out that the airspeed had dropped three knots.

"Probably a couple of passengers gone to the back," Kelston said, doing his best to control his impatience. He tried to doze off again, to recover a bit of the sleep that he had lost when he was woken for service at three-thirty that morning. He had fifteen minutes' rest, the largest uninterrupted slice of peace he had during those first four hours. There was always Timperley saying, "This cloud, sir, shall I alter course to go round it?" or "Sir, there's some ice on the windscreen!" or "Sir," pointing to the fortified battlements of bad weather ahead of them, "shall I go up, or down, or stay where I am?" or "Sir, my artificial horizon seems to be packing up," or "Sir! Number Four engine is very rough. I can feel it on the stick. Look at the instrument panel shaking!"

In the end, Kelston said to him sharply, "Can't you do anything at all on your own initiative?"

In return, Timperley had given him a look full of hurt surprise. "Sir, I've got it down here." He waved the ninepenny notebook he used for jottings on his job. "Anything I'm not sure of, I must ask the captain. Captain Leeming's told me. Captain Ferris has told me. You've told me so yourself!"

Kelston put his seat back up again and said wearily, "I'll take over now."

Timperley stayed quiet as a shadow, resting in the right-hand seat. The automatic pilot started to wander badly and the pressure dropped off. The aircraft began to wallow. Now the Marlborough was being bumped around in cumulonimbus, the instrument no longer made any effort to control her. Kelston said, "Damn" under his breath as he disengaged it. He felt tired enough as it was, without being forced to make the extra effort necessary to hand-fly through turbulent cloud.

At the end of his long watch, he said to Timperley, "Here, take over, will you? I'm going to talk to the passengers."

Kelston saw Timperley's eyes register the fact that the auto-pilot was disengaged. He said, "George is unserviceable. You'll have to hand-fly."

Timperley peered uncertainly out of the cockpit windows. "Looks like we're in for a wet night, Captain." He seemed not at all keen to be left on his own. Kelston hadn't been back with the passengers more than a few minutes, when the steward came up with a message, said in a low, anxious voice, "You're wanted up at the front, Captain."

Kelston stumped furiously back to the cockpit. Timperley thought the compasses had gone "haywire."

"What's the matter with them?"

"They're turning this way and that, sir. And we can't check by astro because of the overcast."

"Both the magnetic and the gyro compasses?"

"Well, I couldn't watch them both at once, sir."

Kelston got back in his seat. He watched the compasses for half an hour. Beyond the swinging of the magnetic needle that could be expected in the combination of bumpy weather and Timperley's erratic instrument flying, there was no evidence that there was anything the matter with them at all.

"They seem better," Timperley was careful to explain to him, "now you've come back, sir."

Kelston gave up all hope of doing anything else but hand-fly the aircraft himself.

The winds, if anything, were slightly worse than forecast. Certainly the weather was. After an uncomfortable ride of nearly thirteen hours, Kelston taxiied up to the ramp at Santa Ana in a cold blustering easterly gale. He had already sent a signal ahead of them: "Night-stopping crew-fatigue, thirty-eight passengers seven crew."

When Kelston met him at the bottom of the crew steps, Dudley could hardly keep still, he was so excited. His first words were "But why here, Captain? Surely you could manage the four-hour flight to Lisbon?"

Kelston was dog tired. He started to walk to the Operations Room, taking no notice of the station manager tagging on beside him. Dudley kept on saying, "You'd have been much more comfortable at Lisbon, Captain."

The pilot suddenly stopped dead in his tracks. "What's the local time here now, Mr. Dudley?"

The station manager looked surprised. "Why, ten o'clock."

"Quite. By the time we got to Lisbon it would be around four in the morning. If we're going to have a delay, we might as well all get a night's sleep at the proper time. You've rung the Carreras and the Castle?"

Dudley admitted sulkily that all arrangements had been made. "Not that we can't cancel them now," he said in a final appeal. When he saw it was going to be dismissed, he added, "It's all very irregular, Captain. All very expensive."

Kelston gave no indication that he had heard him. All he said was, "We'll take off at eight local tomorrow." Then he walked out to the reception hall where Karena was waiting for him.

When he told her about the delay, she smiled up at him and said, "That's a wonderful surprise, Mark." Then she saw the eyelids were heavy over his bloodshot eyes. "Mark, you're tired out!"

It was Karena who quietly organized the taxi for them. In the leather-smelling darkness at the back of the car, purposely she kept up a continuous flow of light-hearted chatter, to which all he needed to do was to listen if he wanted to, or doze off if he was too tired. He kept her hand tightly in his, as though he was hanging onto it for dear life. Twice in the ride to the Carreras, his head dropped and he slumped against her, dead asleep. He stumbled like a blind man as she helped him up the steps to the hotel.

He said to her, "Dunno what's the matter with me. Can't control my own feet."

Left together in the captain's room, he stood up straight and said he felt better and put out his arms for her.

For a few brief moments she rested her face against his rough chin.

"Need a shave," he said to her apologetically. "Had to get up pretty early this morning."

"Was it a bad trip, Mark?"

"Weather wasn't all that good. Neither was the first officer."

"And they expect you to go on to London!"

He managed a smile for her. "Other people, maybe. Not me."

Sitting on the rug by the fire, he started to talk to her about the fourteen days that had separated them, since he'd seen her on his way out. Not that there was much to say about them. He was running his words together, slurring them badly.

But he still held her tightly. "I love you, Karena," he said. "Can't seem to think of anything else but that. And that's all that matters. I love you."

In front of his blurred eyes, the room seemed to swim in the air. Only her face stood out sharp and clear and tender.

"This particular trip," he said, "for some reason, it's knocked me out more than usual."

He heard her say, "You rest on the bed, Mark. I want you to lie down. Just for a little while."

Mark argued, but in the end he allowed himself to be persuaded. He took off his jacket and his collar and tie. As he lay down, he said to her, "You'll wake me in a quarter of an hour, won't you?"

She kissed him on the forehead and said, "Of course I will."

He could feel her stretch out beside him. He could hear her humming the Czech folk song that he loved. Like a blessing, the notes fell down over him.

He forced his eyes open to look once more at her and said, "Karena." His lips went on moving as though he was still talking to her, but no sound came out of them. Then suddenly his face went quite still and calm in a heavy sleep.

He slept like that, on his left side, without moving all night long. Dinner came in on a trolley, but stayed untouched by the fireplace. Karena lay beside him, her arm imprisoned under his body, not moving lest she wake him.

Gradually, as the hours went by, her arm went numb and cold and finally lost all feeling, as though it no longer belonged to her. She watched the dear outlines of his face, so close in the darkness. She listened to the steady rhythmic sounds of his breathing.

Then, an hour before the hotel porter banged on the door and shouted, "Pick-up in half an hour, sir!" the lids dropped down over her own eyes and she slept.

After seven hours' deep sleep, Leeming sat in the garden of the Saracen Hotel, fresh and rested up. The warm evening air reeked with the sweet smell of the dying cedars. Once again, he was finding time lay heavily on his hands. The incident at Kingston seemed far longer than sixteen hours ago. And there was another two days before he went back to England. Some people, he supposed, would give their eyeteeth for a chance of these regular brief holidays in places such as Bermuda and Panama. And here he was, glad enough to talk to his navigator, Appleby, whose thin whining voice had always before jarred and irritated him.

Appleby remarked, "Reckon young Cockcroft'll find himself engaged if he goes on at this rate."

"He *does* seem to be seeing a lot of the stewardess," Leeming said.

"Queer sort of girl," Appleby ruminated, searching his mind for the final verdict. "Likeable. Amusing. Bit too restless for me."

Leeming turned the conversation around to aeroplanes. It was a safer subject. But all the time, he was only half-listening to the whine that went on and on. His mouth said the appropriate responses mechanically, while his whole consciousness was absorbed with Libby Challoner.

Of all the damned things to feel, he was actually missing her. He missed her inconsequential chatter, her irresponsible gaiety. No sooner had he got himself rid of her than he was regretting it. Worst of all, he was missing her physically. He longed to touch her face, run his hands over her smooth, soft body.

Next day, he kept himself in check with difficulty, as he listened to Cockcroft and Libby making their hilarious plans together at breakfast and lunch. He was now distant with both of them. Cockcroft was obviously frightened of what he was officially going to say about him. And Libby . . . well, Libby was just being her infuriating feminine self.

That afternoon, he saw Libby set off on her own into Hamilton. He heard her say she had some things to buy to take back to England. Fifty yards behind the swaying yellow skirt, he followed her into the town. Just before she went into a dress shop, he caught up with her and took her arm.

"Here, Libby," he said. "I want to talk to you."

She turned her big blue eyes innocently on to him.

"Not *again,* Captain? Surely not again? What have I done this time?"

"Nothing," he said. "Just . . . I don't want to quarrel with you."

"I'm not quarrelling."

"I don't think you realize. I've got a lot of responsibilities. Sometimes . . . they get on top of me."

"Well, they're *your* responsibilities. Nobody else's."

He led her to the door of a café. "Here," he said unhappily. "Let's go in here."

Over coffee, he tried once more. "You know what a hell of a mess Kelston is making for himself in the Azores."

"What's that got to do with me?"

"Nothing. Of course, nothing. Except–"

Her face seemed to soften. "Go on. Except what?"

"Well, I didn't want to get you into the same sort of trouble. Wouldn't be fair."

"What you really mean is you were scared people would find out."

He saw she was going to exact her full pound of flesh. He was not to be allowed the private privilege of having things glossed over. But at least she was listening to him now. The look in the blue eyes was far less hostile.

"I suppose so," he admitted. Then he qualified it. "Not altogether."

"They're not going to find out now. It's all over. Nobody had a chance to find out."

"Yes, I know." He hesitated. "All the same, I want us to be . . . friends."

She said gently, "What are you trying to tell me, Michael?"

"Just that I like you."

"Well, I like *you,* too. Funnily enough, I've really tried hard to please you. And all I get is a good ticking off."

"I know, I know. Let's forget about that, shall we?"

She leaned towards him, suddenly confidential and affectionate. "You mean . . . rub it out so it never really happened?"

"Yes," he said. "Let's do that." He tried his best to smile at her.

She gave him an immediate bright smile in return, and put her cool fingers across the table to take his hand.

"I told you the truth in Panama," she said. "You really *do* attract me. Somehow, even when you're being solemn and pompous and all Big Captain."

Then she took her bag and stood up. "Better get some shopping done, I suppose. Early closing day tomorrow." And she tripped out of the café, the yellow skirt still swinging gaily to and fro.

He didn't see her again, except at dinner. She had on the same black dress as she had worn that night in Panama. Leeming thought she seemed friendlier. But still most of her attention was given to Cockcroft. Immediately after their meal, they went out together for the evening.

He had a couple of beers by himself at the bar. He supposed that Libby and Cockcroft, being much the same age, shared the same outlook and the same animal energy. He felt rather old and unwanted. Going over in his mind what had happened that afternoon, he wondered whether Libby had really understood what he had tried to say. With a certain tingling pride, he remembered anyway that she said he attracted her.

Leeming went to bed early. Hours later, when he'd dropped off to sleep, he felt the sheet being pulled away. In a half-conscious state, he put his hand out to pull it up once again. He felt thin silk and cold soft flesh.

Libby's voice said, "You *are* an old sleepy-head, aren't you?"

He opened his eyes to see her fair head glowing in the darkness beside him. She was sitting on the bed in a red dressing gown. Lightly resting herself against him, she ran her fingers through his brown hair.

"I thought I'd let you know, Michael . . . that I understood."

He sat up in bed and put his arms round her shoulders.

"Yet you run off with Cockcroft all evening."

"Oh, *him.* He's sometimes quite amusing. You're not jealous, are you?"

"Of that man?"

She sighed. "Pity."

He sat looking at the white face so near his own.

"Well, now I've come here, aren't you going to kiss me?"

He pulled her closer, as she nestled down beside him on the bed.

"That's better," she said. "Kiss and make up. That's what they always say." She clung to him hard. The dressing gown fell apart, and he felt the thin silk nightdress warmed by her body.

"You're an odd person, Liebling," she whispered. "When I'm with you, I get the feeling I'm flirting with one of the apostles."

He made a wry face. "Can't be much fun."

"Oh, but you're wrong!" she said. "These days . . . it's so unusual."

She left just before dawn. Tying the red dressing gown tightly around her, she kissed him on the forehead, and tip-toed out through the door.

Two minutes later, she was back. She flung herself on the bed, almost helpless with laughter.

"What's the matter, Libby?" He took her by the shoulders. "For God's sake, don't make so much noise."

"It was Cockcroft." She was still laughing. "Just as I was closing your door, I ran into Cockcroft. And the look on his face, Liebling . . . the look on his face!"

On the trip home, in the aircraft Easy Zebra, Leeming let Cockcroft do rather more of the flying than he did himself. He intended to watch him. It would be grossly unfair jumping to a hasty conclusion after just one mistake.

During the long flight to the Azores, as they sat together up at the front, with the bright sun above them and the clouds and the sea below, they talked about flying and planes and people.

He wasn't such a bad sort of boy, Leeming thought, once you got through that self-important skin. His instrument flying was a bit rough. Certainly he alternated between a clumsy slowness, and a breath-taking, alarming speed. But you had to take into consideration the fact that he wasn't very experienced. Competence could only come with practice.

At Santa Ana, the station manager, Dudley, told him with great indignation that Kelston on the previous flight had called a night-stop, "for crew-fatigue." He looked anxiously at Leeming, wondering whether he was going to make the same move.

Leeming, however, said brusquely, "Well, *we'll* be going on."

Relief spread across Dudley's face. "Yet you've had just about the same length of trip, Captain," he pointed out, now he knew he was safe.

Leeming smiled a little sardonically to himself, but said nothing. So this was how Mark was going to continue seeing the girl.

"Very costly," Dudley went on. "No contract now with the hotels, you see. No cut rate."

"As soon as the refuelling's over," Leeming said, "we'll get mobile."

At Madrid he let Cockcroft land the Marlborough from the left-hand seat. It was a perfect night. No wind. Excellent visibility.

They came down with a bump.

Cockcroft said, "Not the sort of landing you do, I'm afraid, sir."

Leeming smiled indulgently, "You're out of practice. That's all it is."

He did the ship's paper work as they approached the December fog that had settled over England. He wrote in his Voyage Report, "On Schedule. Smooth trip." When he came to the Crew Confidential Reports, he thought for a minute. He looked at Cockcroft, taking the Marlborough down slowly over the coast.

Then he put them away. He wouldn't bother to write Confidential Reports. Not this time. Not on this trip.

After all, Ferris never did.

Mr. Veitch read the Voyage Report of Flight 569, service number 271, Bermuda-Azores-Lisbon-Madrid-London, written by Captain Kelston. What he saw displeased him so much he read it again. Finally, feeling he must talk to someone about it, he hustled along to the flight captain's office, and waved the report like a furious white rag under Featherstone's nose.

"Read it," he said. "Read it slowly. Then tell me what you think about it."

It was a long report. In it, Kelston gave the details which led him to call a night-stop in the Azores.

"So he arrived ten hours late." Veitch in his excitement banged the flight captain's desk.

"I agree," Featherstone said. "I agree. Enough to make you tear your hair out."

"As if we're not having enough delays as it is."

Featherstone nodded. "Seem to be in a bit of a slump with mechanical trouble right now. But it'll brighten up in a month or so. It always does."

"Oh, the engineers do their best." Veitch shrugged his shoulders. "I'm not really grumbling about them. But this sort of thing—" And he slapped the paper hard.

Featherstone said nothing. The line manager moodily looked at the flight captain's face. If there was an answer there, it was well covered over with folds of flesh.

Veitch sometimes got the impression that Featherstone was after a ground job. After all, for a pilot he was getting on. He always seemed to agree with what the management said. And that large body, too, looked as though it was expressly designed to slump over a desk.

He sighed. It was a little gesture of resigned exasperation, not connected solely with the problem on hand. Featherstone, however, thought that it was.

"Difficult thing to deal with," he said.

"If you were in my shoes, how would you deal with it?" It was a heartfelt plea for advice.

"Well," Featherstone said cautiously, "depends which way you interpret it."

"What, I'm asking, Captain Featherstone, is *your* interpretation?"

Featherstone hesitated. "I suppose it's the woman."

"What I want to know is, *is* it the woman?"

The flight captain raised two large surprised eyebrows at the harassed irritation in Veitch's voice.

"No need to get so worked up about it, Mr. Veitch."

"Look, Captain Featherstone. Kelston objects to the night-stop coming out. Both for fatigue reasons and so the ground crew can look over the aircraft. After the fire in Easy Zebra, Kelston comes in here and says all the aircraft should be grounded, while the electrical wires are rerouted, even though we're doing that gradually on the Check Fours. Now Kelston says the first officers are inexperienced and they have to be watched all the time. Are the things he says true or aren't they? That's all I want to know."

Featherstone was taking his time digesting all that.

"After all," Veitch added, "you're a pilot. You fly on the route. You should know."

"Well, the engineers certainly have a better clue than Kelston on the modification set-up."

"Trouble is . . . the engineers have pressure from above. Grounding aircraft is expensive."

"Even so, they'll know better than Kelston. He isn't an engineering oracle. As for the first officers . . . well, nobody can say they're brilliant."

"They were the only pilots we could get. If they're bad, we'll push the whole lot back into the school."

"But nobody has definitely said any of them are dangerous," Featherstone pointed out. "They'll learn. They'll settle down."

"Do the captains want more stops for rest *while* they settle down?"

"Oh, no. Nothing like that. Kelston's exaggerating. Just to prove my point"—The flight captain waved a ponderous finger at Veitch—"Leeming arrived yesterday. In Easy Zebra. Haven't you got *his* report yet?"

"Hasn't arrived," the line manager said.

"Well . . . must be in that bottle-neck, Operations. Let's go and pick it up. See how *he* found it."

The two of them walked over to the Operations Room. Together they read the words "On Schedule. Smooth Trip."

"There you are, you see," Featherstone said. "And look at his flying times. Eleven and a half hours to the Azores. Pretty long."

"Kelston took an hour longer."

"What's an hour?" Featherstone fished further into the large envelope. "No crew reports. They must have been all satisfactory."

In Veitch's office, they compared the records of Kelston's first officer with Cockcroft's. Both of them had the approximate same experience. Both of them had done three trips on the line. Kelston had peremptorily sent Timperley back to the training section. But there was nothing at all listed against Cockcroft.

"Yet Leeming," Featherstone said triumphantly, "sees nothing to complain about at all." Then he added placidly, "It's the woman. It all boils down to the woman."

All the same, when the flight captain had left him, Veitch decided he'd go carefully. He stared out of the window, watching Easy Zebra being towed to the hangar for the usual Check Three Inspection before going off on the route again.

All these Marlboroughs looked exactly the same. From the outside, they glittered with a handsome silver beauty. But what was going on slowly inside them, only a Check Four would reveal. And as for people (and especially pilots), it wasn't even possible to give them a Check Four.

On the map opposite his desk, Veitch looked at the names of his aircrew, each on their own little ticket. Then at his four aircraft, Easy Dog, Easy Fox, Easy Uncle and Easy Zebra.

Look after your crews and your aeroplanes, Kelston had said. Well, wasn't that what he was doing?

As for this unofficial night-stop of Kelston's, he would take no notice of it, even though it had been so expensive. The man had listed a number of reasons. They were probably not the real ones, but Veitch's mind worked this way: if it really was the woman, Kelston would do it again.

Book Six

The Middle of the North-West Quadrant

December 20-January 10

1

Veronica Kelston sat in front of the tiny mirror in her bedroom, doing up her hair carefully into a sleek shining cap. She had been living with her parents in their London flat for two months now. It was cramped. The child was inclined to be noisy. Her father sometimes complained. But there *were* compensations. She had a job with a fashion designer which she liked far better than housework. And Mark had certainly been generous as far as money was concerned. Not, mind you, that it in any way excused him for what he had done to her.

Her mother always whispered her story to friends before they met her. When there was somebody coming to lunch or tea, she would wait in her bedroom, hearing the hushed voices. Then, collecting the boy, she would make an appearance at the door of the lounge and stand there, white-faced, while they came over to be introduced. 'This is my son," she would say. The brave clanging of the bangles would echo round the box-shaped lounge. "I'm sorry . . . but I can't introduce my husband to you."

And then there would be a pregnant pause.

Everyone said they could see how much it had hurt her. Everyone agreed she was taking it "marvellously." She had already explained to her mother's best friends that she wouldn't give Mark a divorce "on account of the child."

It was on the subject of a divorce that she was thinking now, the pins in her thin lips, her hands busy with her hair.

There was a man. He was coming to tea that afternoon. This time, on *her* invitation. He was in the fashion business himself. Already he had explained to her his plans for setting up a house of his own. His ideas were fresh, original, brilliantly striking. Veronica could see exactly what he meant when he described his designs. There was one trouble—and here the fluttering little fantasies melted back into the thin air of which they were made. Capital.

Today would be tête-à-tête. Her mother had taken the boy to a children's Christmas party. Veronica was too much of a woman of the world to think that at her age, with a child, just herself would be enough for a man to want for his very own. A husband meant security—not only in the financial sense, but also in the sense of a protective wall against all the troubles in the world. Mark had provided everything for her, except . . . well (she was used to being frank with herself), another husband. She knew she could make a go of it (her own words) with this fashion designer, Ivor Gillett. A business between them would certainly prosper. But if she got a divorce (with Mark as the guilty party) and married again, his generosity would presumably stop. She knew by heart the laws by which society protected her.

Everything seemed to hinge on that horrible little five letter word—money.

She was just carefully outlining her mouth with lipstick when the door bell rang. That would be Gillett. He could wait for a couple of moments. There was no point in rushing to the door. Then the bell rang again.

At the same time as she opened the door, Veronica said, "Why, hel-*lo*."

A man stood in the dark corridor, with the collar of his overcoat turned up, half-hiding his face. He looked slighter than she remembered. Somehow younger.

"Hello, Veronica!"

It wasn't Gillett at all. It was Michael Leeming. She

brushed the disappointment off her face as though it was powder. "Why, Michael," she said, "how nice! Are you coming in?" Then she added, "I'm expecting someone to tea."

"I'll only be a minute, Veronica. I'd like to talk to you."

She said reluctantly, "Well, do come in and sit down. This *is* a surprise."

She led the way to the lounge. He sat down on the sofa, and looked around him. "This your parents' flat, Veronica?"

"That's right."

"Must be rather small for you all."

"We manage, Michael. Somehow . . . we manage."

He hesitated. "Does it still hurt to talk about it? Especially with Christmas only five days away!"

"Well . . . it's not easy." She lowered her eyes to the ground. In a still, small voice she said, "Not a very merry Christmas for us this year."

"You know how sorry Melanie and I were." There was a little pause. "About the whole sad business."

"Sweet of you both. You always were so . . . understanding."

Leeming said gravely, "We were also surprised."

"So was everyone. So was I." She produced a small handkerchief and held it near her nose.

"Not that way. Surprised at *you*."

"At me? Why ever at me?"

"At giving in so easily. At not fighting back."

Veronica looked suddenly as though she was going to be angry. The bangles gave a warning clang.

Leeming looked concerned. "Don't take it that way, Veronica," he said, hastily. "I'm only trying my best to help you."

She relaxed a little. She didn't want to have a scene just at the time Gillett was arriving. "I don't see what you mean —fighting back."

"You didn't really face up to it. You ran away here as fast as your feet could carry you."

She said, to defend herself, "I wouldn't let Mark have a divorce."

"That was something, certainly. But why didn't you stay and beat this woman at her own game? You've got the child. The house. Mark for a third of the year. All the trumps are in *your* hand."

"I was too shocked, Michael . . . hurt . . . dazed."

He said with gentle understanding, "Now surely, you see it in the right perspective. You're not the only person with worries. Everyone's got them. Look at it from Mark's angle. He's not young. A pilot's life is pretty unsettling. He's away from home a long time. On the route, there are . . . women."

"But he says that he loves her!"

Leeming shook his head. "That's half opportunity and half because you just accepted him too much. And now—" He stopped to emphasize what he had to say. He wanted her whole attention. She appeared distraite, looking out of the window, back at the door, glancing at the clock. "And now, the opportunity's been taken away."

"What d'you mean?"

"They've taken out the night-stop. He won't be able to see her any more. At least," he corrected himself, "he saw her on his last trip. Called a delay for crew-fatigue. But he won't be able to do that often. Not if he wants to stay with the company."

He had her whole attention now. "So they won't be able to meet?"

"No. That's just it. There's every indication that Mark's seeing sense. I think he realizes he's ruining his career. Now he can't see her any more, the thing'll die a natural death."

"I see, Michael," she said thoughtfully, "I see." She looked over to him and gave a misty smile. "It was good of you to come and explain it all to me."

"I wanted you to know, Veronica." He was quite excited all of a sudden. "Now's the time to *fight*. Don't give him up without a struggle. Make him see you still care."

"Thank you, Michael," she said. "I do see what you mean."

"Then you will," he asked her eagerly.

She went over to the window, gazing out of it, saying nothing. "I'll have to think about it, Michael. . . . I'll have to think about it."

It was past five o'clock and there was still no sign of Gillett. She'd said definitely four-fifteen. Leeming got up from the sofa and came across to her. "Well," he said, "I better be going, Veronica. I've stayed too long already. Your friend . . . she'll be arriving here any minute."

She turned round. "Anyway, Michael, thank you for coming."

"You've taken what I had to say awfully well, Veronica." Awkwardly he took her hand and held it. "I'll be seeing you, Veronica. One of these days . . . you'll be back at Charfield. With Mark."

"I hope so, Michael."

She saw him to the door. "Here," she said, "let me put the corridor light on. So you can see."

She watched his stocky figure walk over to the lift. He pressed the call-button. The lift came up, but no one got out. He waved to her as he disappeared through the gates.

She went back to the lounge. Twenty past five. It was odd. No phone call. No explanation. She wandered restlessly round the room, straightening the pictures, rearranging the porcelain figures on the mantelpiece, plumping out the cushions. She walked into the kitchen. The tea was still there, waiting. The iced cakes. The little sandwiches were already curling at the corners. She returned to the lounge and sat on the sofa, reading a magazine. But her eyes could not take in the words.

Whatever could have happened to him?

Then the bell rang. It did not enter her head this time to keep him waiting. Joyfully she rushed to the door. Her mother was there, and the child. "I'm sorry, Veronica," she said. "My key . . . I left my key in the other bag."

Her mother saw the tea, uneaten in the kitchen. "So your friend didn't come?"

"He phoned. At the last minute, he was called away. Business."

"What a pity!"

When the child was in bed, as she sat with her mother by the parental domestic hearth, she was thinking to herself that Michael Leeming's suggestion mightn't be such a bad idea, at that.

On the second day of his stand-off, this time arranged with elaborate care so that he could have Christmas at home, they were having one of their quiet teas by the fire in the drawing room when Melanie said to Michael, "You know, darling, I think you've got a touch of flu."

He had been moodily staring at the flames licking round the black coal, turning it slowly into ash. "Me, Melanie? I don't think so. What makes you think that?"

She came over and sat beside him. "You're not looking very well."

"I'm feeling all right."

"You haven't your usual colour. I'm *certain* you're in for something."

"Didn't sleep too well last night. That's all it is."

She put her arm gently around him. "You're not worrying about anything, are you?"

"Course I'm not."

"You'd tell me if you were?"

He gave a shrugging gesture of impatience, as though her arm was irritating his back. "For God's sake, Melanie—" The arm trailed off, down into the depths of the sofa, away from him.

"You've been moody lately, honey." Her voice sounded patient, unbearably understanding.

"Have I?" he said. "I'm sorry. Hadn't noticed it myself. At Christmas time, too!"

"You know what I think it is, Michael?"

"There isn't anything. Nothing at all."

"You've been working too hard in the garden. Then as soon as you get back from a trip, you rush up to the airport. That's not good for you. You should take things more easily."

Yesterday afternoon, when he'd seen Veronica, he had told her he had to go to the airport—that huge vague place where it was easy to make people understand that a pilot on his stand-off would have a million things to do, and where, as a matter of fact, he had practically nothing to do at all. Melanie would not have understood about Veronica. She hadn't been exactly understanding when he'd been to see Mark.

He had also seen Libby. That was what he had been thinking about all day. Perhaps it had made him seem silent, absent-minded.

"You're going to take it easy now," Melanie said. "Here's your book. Put your feet up. I'll get the children to bed. And, afterwards, we'll have supper by the fire." She paused. Then she added with a wistful love in her voice, "It's *so* nice to have you at home for Christmas, for a change."

He heard the bath water splashing. The children were rushing round the house, calling to each other. Melanie was saying, "Not in the lounge, boys. Not in the lounge."

He drank the final cup of tea left in the pot. It was very nearly cold. He didn't want it, but it gave him something to do. Still staring at the fire, his mind turned back once more to that room near Baker Street.

Libby had been difficult. She had started off by saying she was glad Cockcroft knew. Everything had been sort of hole-in-the-corner, hadn't it? It was so different, somehow, from Kelston's affair in the Azores. And yet, in some ways, so alike.

The comparison had darkened his mind. Revolted him. He had turned on her furiously. Cockcroft, he said, would say nothing.

"How are you so sure?" she asked him, with a curious smile.

He was certain. That's all there was to it. Men didn't talk. Not like women.

"Oh, but they do, Liebling. I've heard them. About poor Mark—"

But in the end, she believed him. She had heard that a conspiracy of silence among men sometimes *did* exist. And he seemed so sure.

"Then, there's me, Michael darling."

"I don't think you'll say anything, Libby."

"Michael, these days you're so *certain*. So marvellously certain."

"The company doesn't like employing stewardesses who've attracted the attention of their married aircrew. If this business of ours ever comes to their notice, what d'you think would happen?"

"Chéri, *you're* the one who can look into the future."

"One of us would have to go. Stewardesses are two a penny. Pilots . . . these days, pilots are pure gold."

She had treated him to one of her giggling fits. "Liebling," she said, "you think of the *quaintest* things to say."

All the same, she listened. He had the impression she understood the situation perfectly. "And no more working the roster," he said. "If we're out together too many times, people will get the wrong idea."

She said, "I think you believe if nobody knows about our affair, it hasn't really happened at all. But if that's the way you want it—" The sentence stayed unfinished, but before he left, she became quite loving. At the door she kissed him. "Auf Wiedersehen," she said.

He would have to do something, of course. It would have to be stopped. That affair of Kelston's was at the root of the whole thing. All this glib talk of happiness. It had worried and unsettled him. Octopus-like, it had reached into the tranquillity of his own home.

The only bright spot on the horizon was Veronica. She had taken his suggestion very well. Much better than Mark. She might very likely do something about it.

Melanie came in with supper on a tray. "Liver and bacon," she said. "The tinned peaches you brought back from Panama to follow. Nice?"

He agreed that it was "just right, just what I want."

She noticed he toyed with the food, leaving most of it.

"Now tomorrow, Michael," she said, "if it's fine tomorrow, let's take the car out into the country. For the whole day. Fresh air'll do you the world of good."

Kelston said to the girl in the outer office, "Could I see Mr. Veitch?"

Eyes that had looked at letters and confidential files, classified and pigeon-holed the man now standing before them.

"I'll see, Captain Kelston." The hazel-coloured mercury behind her spectacles, twin barometers of company favour, did not stand high. She went into the line manager's office, closing the door carefully behind her. A duet droned unintelligibly through the glass panel for five minutes. Back again, she gave him a smile that was rather too good to be true.

"So sorry," she said. "Mr. Veitch is very busy."

"When can I see him, then?"

"Not for an hour or so."

Kelston said impatiently, "Well . . . give me a time. And I'll call back."

She looked at him doubtfully. Then she said, "I'll ask him."

Kelston finally left with the information that Mr. Veitch would see him at four-thirty. He was out on service next day, after a four-day stand-off that had already been too long for him. But Ferris had refused to change on the Tuesday trip. He read up a few new orders in the Operations Office, went over to the hangars to have a discussion about the rerouting of the wiring with the engineers, and showed up dead on time. Even so, he was kept waiting.

"Captain Kelston," Veitch said evenly to him, when he was at last admitted. "Sit down, won't you?" The outstretched fingers on Veitch's right hand started to tap their opposite numbers on his left. "Now what can I do for you?"

"I thought I'd like to explain personally. The night-stop I called—"

"Crew-fatigue, wasn't it? You explained it quite fully."

Kelston took no notice. "I came to see you as soon as I got in about it. You were too busy. The day before yesterday when I called, you were away. I'm sorry I couldn't get to see you before." He paused and looked at Veitch full between the eyes. "But it seems rather difficult."

"Busy," Veitch said swiftly. "Very busy. I'm sorry. You know how it is."

Kelston said, "Anyway, I don't know whether you quite realize how inexperienced these new first officers are."

"All we can get. You know what the pilot situation's like. They'll settle down."

"Sure they'll settle down. But while they *are* settling down, the captain is, in effect, training them as well as doing his own job."

Something about the urgency in the man's voice made Veitch hesitate. Suddenly he began to feel unsure again. "Well . . ." He groped for words. "I don't know what else we can do."

Kelston said, "But don't you see? Things are combining too much. All at the same time. New first officers. The curious fire Leeming had. The fatigue angle of flying four thousand miles with three intermediate stops."

"There's nothing there that time won't take care of. The aircraft are being modified–"

"Too slowly."

Veitch proceeded as though Kelston had said nothing. "The first officers are gaining experience every day. And all the other pilots think they can cope with the long leg. If you feel you can't–"

With a hopeless, weary fury, Kelston said, "It's got nothing to do with what I feel I can cope with. It's what I told you earlier. Keep an eye on the aircraft. And on the crews. It's plain common sense."

"There have been no more complaints about the aircraft. You know we have black weeks, and then serviceability suddenly improves. Last three days, we haven't had one mechanical delay. Anywhere on the route. And as for the first officers, you've only flown with two or three of them. And as far as I remember you didn't actually say they were useless."

"All the same," Kelston grunted, "the ones I flew with have had more training. I went personally to see the training captain about that. You can't say a man's useless when he just hasn't the necessary experience."

"Well, nobody else seems to think they need more training."

"But it's the combination that's so dangerous!" Kelston clenched his fists up like hammers, especially to drive his point home into Mr. Veitch's skull. "This express service we're now running to Panama has already increased business. I see there's two extra flights going out this week as specials. I don't say anything against the engineers. They do their best under difficulties. But working the aircraft and the crews the way you're trying to do–"

Veitch said coldly, "Well, Captain Kelston, what d'you suggest as an alternative?"

"You know as well as I do what I suggest," he said steadily. "Put back the Azores night-stop. Anyway for the next few months. Give the crews a rest. And let the engineers have an adequate time for their inspections. Especially on the wiring and the hydraulic pipelines of the unmodified aircraft."

"And what about our express service to Panama?"

Kelston shrugged his shoulders. "In this business you can't have everything. Not all at the same time."

"Sometimes," Veitch said slowly, "people seem to forget this is not a benevolent institution. To be always run at a loss!"

"And sometimes," Kelston countered fiercely, "people forget what a thin dividing line there is between a safe operation and a disaster."

The normally kindly lines round Veitch's mouth immediately hardened. These pilots had not the remotest idea of the complicated ins and outs of an enormous company. And here was a man with an unsavoury reputation almost banging his desk, telling him what he should do, all because of a girl stuck on an island, miles out in the Atlantic.

Both men faced each other angrily. "Your business, Captain Kelston," Veitch said, "is to fly the company's aircraft on the company's routes to the company's schedules."

Kelston smiled bitterly. "In other words . . . go back to your cubby-hole. That's the trouble with this vast organization. Far too departmentalized. Everyone can't see further than the walls of his own office. Or the fuselage of his own aircraft."

"If you dislike being employed by the company—"

"I can go. Anyway, as far as talking to you is concerned, Mr. Veitch, I might just as well." He got to his feet. Towering high above the line manager, all his anger now seemingly dissolved, he added, "As I see it, things are accumulating dangerously. I may be wrong. Let's hope to God I am."

Before he went out of the door, he turned back to look at Veitch's apparently impassive face. "Don't seem to have been able to achieve much," he said, "but there it is."

Veitch sat at his desk, trying to concentrate on other matters. But Kelston had disturbed him. His mind simply would not do as it was told. The walls of his own office, Kelston had said. He felt sometimes that *his* office walls were closing relentlessly in on him. That big wall which carried the door with his name on it—that was certainly the chairman. The wall behind his desk was the aircrew. The wall with the window, giving a gloomy view of the winter wastes of the airport, was certainly Kelston. And the wall with the map, the little bits of colour representing that unknown six thousand miles he so often read about and hardly ever saw—in some odd way he had always associated that wall with the Gibraltar crash, perhaps because each of them always remained so much of a mystery.

He struggled gamely to pull himself out of the mood that was settling down on him. On his desk, there were three pieces of paper that painted a much more cheerful picture than Kelston's troublesome trinity. One was a chart showing the receipts of the route for the last three weeks. The thin red line had shot up, just as though it recorded the temperature of a man suddenly struck with a fever. Well above the profit mark. Another was a programme showing the progress of the modifications to the electrical wiring on the aircraft. Easy Dog was already modified—at a cost, he noticed, of over four thousand pounds. That would show clearly enough they weren't afraid of spending money. Easy Fox was halfway through her Check Four. They were speeding things up specially. By the beginning of February Easy Uncle and Easy Zebra would be finished, too.

By the beginning of February. Just under six weeks' time.

The last piece of paper was a calendar. He looked at it, putting his finger on each day, as though by his touch he brought them to life. Thirty-nine of them. That was all. Then all the aircraft would be modified. And the new first officers would each have a couple more trips under his belt.

It wasn't, after all, very long. It was wonderful how everything eventually could be cured by time.

Just before he went home, he saw Macmillan, manager of the North Atlantic route. Veitch knew they were suffering their usual winter recession. "By the way, Mac," he said, beaming all over his face, "one day soon we'll have to borrow some of those out-of-work Astroliners of yours. We simply can't cope with the rush."

2

Before going back to his room in Earl's Court after his interview with Veitch, Kelston had a meal at one of the cheap Indian restaurants along the Fulham Road. He felt tired and dispirited. These days, no one seemed willing to listen to him. He had talked with the pilots he saw along the route without success. And now the line manager obviously thought he was imagining things. There were days when he himself thought so, too. And yet somehow, in his mind the events of the last four weeks were forming into a pattern, in much the same way as a storm makes well-known designs in the sky, hundreds of miles from its centre.

He ate curry and rice slowly. Anyway, tomorrow he would see Karena. Even though it would only be for an hour, while his aircraft was refuelled, at least he would be able to talk to her, once more suddenly become truly alive and happy.

He went home, thinking about her, recovering from Veitch's cold reception.

There was no mail for him on the table by the telephone. He walked up the two flights of stairs and opened the door of his room.

Veronica was sitting by the gas fire, bolt upright in the only armchair.

Kelston hung his coat on the hook behind the door. Then he said, "Hello, Veronica."

"You don't seem particularly pleased to see me, Mark."

"I was thinking . . . something at the airport . . . nothing to do with you."

He looked at her thin mouth, apparently compressing with difficulty the emotion behind it, the white face, the big unhappy eyes. Veronica was being convincing as the conventional tragic wife.

"I've come back, Mark. Back to stay."

He pulled up a wooden chair. With infinite weariness, he said, "You don't mean what you say, of course."

First Veitch. Now this.

"But I do. You're still my husband. As soon as we get a bigger place, the child can come and—"

"Veronica, we've been into all this before."

"I know. But I've been thinking since then. And, Mark . . . it's Christmas time!"

"I've already explained. I want a divorce."

She leaned towards him, and put her hand on top of his. "Mark . . . you've never given me a chance. Truly, we would be happy together. Somehow . . . I understand things better now."

"I doubt it, Veronica. You wouldn't be here if you did."

"Now you're being cruel. Bitter."

"No, just sad. You . . . John . . . Karena. I've got you all into this. Inadequate thing to say—but I'm sorry. Now I'm trying to sort things out the best way I can. That's why I want the divorce."

"The best way for you, you mean." The hardness was beginning to creep back into Veronica's voice.

"In the end the best way for all of us. Our marriage wasn't a success. I think we both tried to make it one."

"Well . . . *I* did."

"We weren't suited. It was a mistake. But I thought I might just as well stay with you as anywhere else. Then unexpectedly, I found happiness. Real happiness."

"Or thought you did. Anyway, you wanted to grab it, just for yourself."

"Yes."

"I'll tell you one thing. I won't divorce you."

She took her hand away from him suddenly. The bangles on her wrist played a quick little tambourine tune.

Mark looked down at the rug. From the mantelpiece, the photograph of Karena gazed down on them both. Even made up of shadow and light on supersensitive paper, her gentle mouth, closed and compassionate, seemed still to express her understanding.

"So you've told me before," he said at last.

"Now you know that," she said irritably. "What's the reason for going on with all—" Her waving hand took in and condemned the whole shabby room—"this."

"The same reason."

"But you'll never be able to see her anyway. Now they've taken out the night-stop."

He looked up quickly. "Who told you that?"

She turned her face away from the hard glare in his eyes. "Well . . . Michael Leeming. He came to see me."

"Why?"

"To help."

"In what way—to help?"

"He said you're not seeing her so much now. He thought it a good time for us to make things up."

He said furiously, "What damned business is it of his?"

With a prim self-righteousness, she explained, "He did it out of kindness. He said you'd learnt your lesson. And when I heard you couldn't see her any more—"

He cut her short. "We still go through there. She will come to the airport. We'll still have a short time together every month."

She sniffed disdainfully. "An hour or two! You're willing to live on this sort of basis for an hour or two a month?"

He said quietly, "Even if I couldn't see her again, it would be the same."

"You're mad! Leeming was wrong. You're as crazy as a coot!" She got up abruptly. "I'm sorry," she said, brushing down her coat. "I've been acting on wrong information."

"I wish to God Leeming would keep out of this. What the hell he thinks he's trying to do—"

"You wouldn't recognize a helping hand if you saw one." She put on her gloves. "One thing I'd like to say before I go, Mark." Her eyes glittered vindictively. "Don't get any ideas about throwing up your job and living idyllically and pennilessly in the Azores, will you? You've still got a family to support, whether you like it or not. You may not care about me. But I know damned well you feel guilty about John."

Holding his head in his hands, he listened to the furious clacking of her high heels on the worn carpet that trailed down the two flights of stairs to the hall of the house.

He saw Leeming in the morning. He had just signed the flight plan, and was getting into the transport to go out to his aircraft, Easy Dog.

"Hold on a minute, driver," he said, and walked over to the uniformed figure striding towards the Operations Room, carrying a bulky briefcase.

Before he could say anything, Leeming had burst out with, "They've got me on this special, Mark. Leaves an hour after you."

"So I saw."

"But I only just got in on Sunday! I was supposed to be getting Christmas in. They promised me! Fancy having to go out the day before Christmas Eve! Last night they phoned. It's ridiculous." He was panting with indignation.

" 'These things are sent to try us,' " Kelston said. But Leeming was unaware he was being quoted, that these were the last words he had said to Kelston in Bermuda.

"It's not good enough, Mark. Naturally, Melanie was upset. We'd planned things—"

"You might have had a short stand-off. But you still had time to go and see Veronica," Kelston said steadily.

Leeming hesitated. "Veronica?"

"Don't try and pretend you don't know. As far as I can gather you told her the time was ripe for a reconciliation between us. Now the Azores night-stop is out."

"I was only trying to help," Leeming said indignantly. "You know how much this breaking up of your marriage has worried Melanie and me."

"I don't. All I know is . . . you're interfering."

Leeming's blue eyes looked suddenly hostile.

"You've seen me," Kelston went on. "You've seen Veronica. It's no damn good. Now for Christ's sake, will you please keep out of my hair?"

"Don't talk to me like that." Leeming snapped the words out as though the office boy had been rude to him. An air of injured innocence mixed with the anger on his face.

With a sigh of exasperation, Kelston said, "It's difficult managing your own life. Managing someone else's instead—that's child's play in comparison."

Leeming flushed scarlet. "What the hell d'you mean by that?"

"Just what I say."

A girl in a blue raincoat passed them, a smart forage cap tilted at a becoming angle on her fair hair.

"Good morning, Captain Leeming . . . Captain Kelston," Libby Challoner said.

Leeming immediately looked into the crew car. Kelston's stewardess was sitting there at the back, patiently waiting.

For the moment, he was nonplussed. His fury hesitated, uncertain whether it should pour over Kelston or this demure disobedient creature, now tripping into the Operations Room to report her arrival on duty.

The damned girl had done it again!

Just over an hour later, when the weak sun was mixing a watery yellow into the greyness of the sky, Leeming took off in Easy Uncle. As he climbed away from the ghostly English coast below him, the thoughts jostled in his mind, one against the other, for pride of place in his attention. Mechanically, he kept the Marlborough flying upwards on the first course to Madrid, one-nine-five degrees magnetic.

Before he left for the airport, Melanie had said bitterly, "So this is our Christmas, is it? This is the eight day stand-off you promised me? Three days of mooning around the house like a big gloomy bear!"

He had tried to explain to her, as best he could, that there was no one else to go. He had checked on that. Apart from Crichton, who had arrived only the day before, and could hardly be expected to go out again so soon, there just wasn't anybody else but him. Not that Melanie would understand. She still went on saying, "I can't understand why Featherstone or Ferris can't go!" She seemed unable to grasp that both Ferris and Featherstone were now in Bermuda—the flight captain on the extra slip-crew would deal with this special service.

Things hadn't been exactly the way he liked them when

he left home for this trip. And then to have first Kelston and then Libby piled on his plate was really too much. And the Thursday service was the long five-day slip at Bermuda both southbound and home-bound.

Libby, he noticed grimly when he went back to talk to the passengers, seemed anxious to keep out of his way. She was making herself ostentatiously useful in the galley when he passed, and he didn't speak to her. As for Kelston, for sheer ingratitude at the trouble he'd taken, that man took the biscuit. He really deserved everything that was coming to him.

As the trip progressed through Lisbon, with its heavily scented airport buildings, Leeming felt depressed, let down. Kelston had been useless, Veronica worse than useless.

And there remained, after all, Karena. The more he thought about her, the more he was convinced he should have gone to see her first. From her photograph, she looked as though she might be intelligent. If he explained everything to her carefully, from an outside point of view, she might well be able to understand.

Mark was obviously too confused. He certainly felt guilty about it—he seemed quite angry at the airport, and people, Leeming had found, were rarely angry unless they knew they were in the wrong. Veronica was just ineffective and bungling. By the time he reached the Azores, he had high hopes of Karena being the most sensible of the whole damned trinity.

He hadn't expected to see her at Santa Ana. He had planned to phone her up. But there she was, just leaving the restaurant. Immediately he recognized her from the photograph in Mark's room—the long white forehead, the black hair, the curious sad look about her eyes. Obviously now, she'd come over to see Kelston, who, still keeping an hour ahead of him, had taken off for Bermuda a few minutes before Leeming had landed.

Leeming acted on an immediate impulse. It seemed too good an opportunity to miss. While the navigator went off to make up the flight plan, he went up to her and said, "My name's Leeming. I'm a friend of Mark's."

Immediately she put out her hand. "And I'm Karena. But, of course, you know." She smiled shyly.

"Yes, I did know," he said awkwardly. "I was wondering whether you'd care to have coffee with me. I've got half an hour or so."

It seemed a perfectly normal kindly suggestion. He followed her back into the restaurant. Over coffee and thick ham sandwiches, he said, "So you saw Mark, then?"

"Yes." Her eyes lit up. "I saw him. He's just taken off. I watched him go, and then I came in here."

"You wouldn't see him for very long, then?" He injected a generous amount of sympathy into his voice.

"An hour."

"Hardly seems worth it," he said judicially, but still sympathetically.

"Oh, but it is," she said very firmly. He felt she had withdrawn from him a little.

He wanted to feel his way carefully, but he was so pressed for time. He said, "But what's the point of it all? Just an hour or so every month like this?" Then he added, "That's no life for you, Karena."

"*I* think it is. That's *our* life. Nobody else's."

He ignored her warning and said heavily, "I hope you don't mind if I speak to you bluntly. It's ruining Mark's career. The management knows. The crews talk."

She made a little hopeless gesture with her hands. "The talk doesn't matter. People always talk—about something. If it wasn't me, it would be you . . . or someone else."

He looked at her suspiciously. Then he went on, "But his home. You're destroying his home, his—"

"I'm destroying *nothing*," she said vehemently. "They

didn't love each other. Without love, his home was already destroyed."

He shook his head. "I'm sorry you feel like this about it. I wanted to help, but–"

"But you *can't*. No one can. You can't think my thoughts. Feel my feelings. Come into my life. No one ever can. Each one of us is apart. Isolated. Unless–"

"Unless they're in love," he finished for her with heavy sarcasm.

"Yes."

He sighed. "But what difference does it make if you are? His wife won't divorce him. You can't come to England. For a few hours a month. It doesn't make sense. What's the point of it all?"

"If you don't understand," she said at last, "I can't explain it to you. And you don't. Otherwise you wouldn't ask."

Exasperated now, he said, "That's an easy excuse. 'Wouldn't understand.' Of course, I wouldn't, if you don't tell me."

She looked at him steadily for a few seconds. Then she said softly, "We love each other." She turned her face away, and looked out of the window. Reluctantly he admired her almost perfect profile, the full red lips, the poise of her dark shapely head. She said, as though to the night outside, almost like a litany, "We're not separate any more. Somehow we're one. No one can separate us."

She turned back to him. "The short time we have together, that's when we really live. And after he's gone, there's a sort of afterglow, that lasts until he comes again."

Her eyes searched his face to see if he understood.

"Well," he said, "you're right about one thing. I *don't* understand." He shook his head and curled the corners of his mouth down. "Not one bit of it. I've got another name for it."

He saw that he had hurt her deeply. The defences were up against him, around her mouth and jaw, but she could not guard her eyes, which were now enlarged dark vulnerable holes in the well-defended face. Quickly, he pressed home his advantage, "And his wife, his child? They don't matter of course?"

"They matter very much," she said huskily. "That's the reverse of the coin. Thinking of them."

"Doesn't seem to stop you, though. Doesn't seem to cast a blight on the captain's room."

"But how can *you* say? How can *you* judge?" Her voice was low and angry.

He drew a deep breath, and said pompously, even in his own ears, "I can judge, all right. I know what's right and what's wrong."

"But not what's right or wrong for me . . . for Mark."

"But as his friend, I can—"

Her slight body tautened. "You are *not* his friend," she interrupted hotly, "nobody's. Not even your own."

Then she stood up. "I'm sorry," she said sadly. Her anger had gone now, her face once more a pale mask. "Thank you for the coffee."

He walked out of the restaurant with her. He put out his hand, and she took it. "I hoped you'd understand," he said.

"And I hoped you would," she said wistfully. "We're both trying to say different things. In the same words."

As he watched her walk towards the road, he was aware he had failed. He had struck home so many times, it should have been a victory. It was odd that he should feel just the humiliation of defeat.

Before he went to sign the flight plan, he saw Libby in the corridor, standing by herself, waiting for the catering stores from the restaurant.

"Saw you talking to Mark's Karena," she said, and giggled.

"What are you trying to do, Michael? Get off with all the girls the whole way down the route?"

He was thinking of a suitable crushing retort, when Dudley came up and said efficiently, "Load sheet's ready for your signature, sir. And I'll get the passengers aboard in five minutes' time."

In Dudley's opinion, Leeming looked tired. He had half-expected Kelston to call a night-stop. In his subsequent relief, he was particularly anxious to get Leeming airborne before the words "crew-fatigue" had time to crystallize in his mind.

Leeming saw Libby twice during the next quiet eleven hours, while Easy Uncle transported them, with a majestic and trouble-free momentum, over the long Atlantic to Bermuda. Once, during the night, she came up to the front with some tea for him. All he said was, "Thank you." Then he saw her at the back, when he went for a shave before the passengers woke up and crowded out the toilet.

He asked her, "Get any sleep?"

She smiled brightly and said, "Yes, thank you, sir."

But the day after they arrived at Bermuda, she said to him when they were on their own in the lounge of the hotel, "I know what you're thinking. This time you're wrong. I didn't work the roster. They just told me I had to come. Nobody else."

"All the same," he said, "looks a bit suspicious. Three trips in a row."

She laughed. "You do love to cover up the clues, Michael darling. At least we haven't got Cockcroft with us this time. I saw him in London. He's on leave."

He said solemnly, "No, that's something."

She gave his face a quick, shrewd scrutiny. "Michael, are you trying to tell me it's all off again? Because if so, do try and be a bit more explicit."

He hesitated. "No . . . nothing like that. Only we have

to be careful—" He was thinking that he and Kelston would be going round the route together. It was impossible that Mark could suspect. All the same, those words about managing someone else's life instead of your own were rather curious ones to use under the circumstances. Libby said suddenly, "You've given me a very full book about it. Code of Etiquette for use by Stewardesses having an affair with Captains. I'll try not to break the rules."

"No need to take it that way, Libby."

"If I didn't find that double-headed penny character of yours so damned amusing—"

He said icily, "I don't know what you mean."

"That's what makes it even *more* amusing."

He put his hands in his pockets and abruptly walked away from her.

For the four days of the slip that remained, he avoided Kelston, since there seemed no more to say to him. Anyway, the man always seemed to be on his own. Libby was perfectly friendly with him at meals. The little brush in the lounge appeared to have been forgotten. But she did not attempt to seek out his company. Either by day or by night. Which was just as well, as the hotel was full of extra crews, sent out to cope with the new influx of extra services that the express service to Panama had produced.

Kelston and Leeming eventually went on, still only about an hour apart, through Nassau and Jamaica to Panama. Apart from the odd word, when they saw each other after landing at the refuelling stops, they hardly spoke. They had rooms next to each other at the rest house, but when Leeming arrived, Kelston had already gone to bed.

Next morning they chatted desultorily to each other at breakfast. And then after lunch, Kelston went on his long tirade, preaching about the aircraft, the night-stop in the Azores and the first officers.

He said to Leeming, "Don't you see the danger? The aircraft have got to be looked after. So have the crews."

Leeming smiled and said, "Off on your old hobby-horse, Mark?"

Patiently, Kelston explained there were four things that could cause an aircraft accident: a foreign body hitting it, which was a rare act of God, and nothing much could be done about it; weather, which these days could be largely discounted, except as an additional aggravation to the two main causes—a major fault in the aircraft or a bad mistake on the crew's part.

"You're not telling me anything I don't already know," Leeming said.

Kelston said angrily, "That's the terrible part about it all. Everybody knows these things. Yet nobody does anything."

Leeming said comfortingly, "These things are being watched, Mark."

"Who by?"

"Oh . . . someone in the company."

"Only wish I knew his name," Kelston retorted. "So I could buy him the spectacles he so badly needs."

He didn't seem disposed to talk any more. He wandered off to read in his room. Leeming thought to himself, The man's certainly got it badly.

For the rest of the day, Kelston gave the impression he hardly noticed Leeming was round. He kept himself strictly to himself. So there was, as usual, nothing to do at Panama, except wander round the town and sit under the hot sun in the garden.

That night, Leeming woke at two in the morning. The whole rest house was quiet. He looked out and saw the palm trees quite still in the moonlit, windless air. He tried to go to sleep. But he wasn't tired. He read for an hour. It was still no good.

He knew perfectly well what the trouble was. In his imagination, as though it was a fresh and vivid film, he went through the details of that night he had spent here with Libby.

He lay on his back for a while, staring at the ceiling above him. But his mind insisted on making a moving mural even of that rectangular black screen.

He put on his slippers and his dressing gown, and carefully tip-toed down the corridor to her room. She was awake when he came in. But she said nothing. He closed the door and sat on the rug beside her bed.

She propped up her head with an arm that came out of a little tunnel of white nylon sleeve.

Then at last she whispered, "I didn't know when or how, Liebling. But I knew damned well you'd come."

3

Still almost side by side, a week later, Kelston in Easy Uncle and Leeming in Easy Fox closed rapidly on the Azores. All the way from Bermuda a tail wind had increased their speed to two hundred and eighty miles an hour. On the other side of the island, Ferris in Easy Zebra was letting down to Santa Ana on the normal southbound Thursday schedule.

Ferris was on the ground first. "Looks like you're getting just about the whole fleet in," he said to Dudley and grinned. They got on well together. There was never any difficulty getting Ferris airborne. "Well, I'll pop along to Met. before the rush sets in."

The Portuguese meteorological officer spoke poor English. His sleek black hair reeked of some oriental pomade. For

Ferris' benefit he put a fat finger on the weather chart in front of them. Stretching all the way from Iceland, a thick blue line trailed right down the Atlantic, approached the Azores and then curved to the left, out towards Bermuda. With a good deal of spluttering, the meteorological officer defined it as "a quasi-stationary cold front."

Ferris' eyes immediately riveted themselves upon it. "Nice bit of blue crayon you've got there," he said appreciatively.

The Met. man assured him it wasn't as bad as it looked. He pointed. "Still to der north, Captain. Eet hardly moves." Then he moved his pencil round and round, trying to draw rain and cloud on the air between them. He smiled. "Not till mornin'."

He had his back to the window. Ferris faced him. On his radio-range approach to the field the pilot had been in solid overcast all the way down from eighteen thousand to fifteen hundred feet. Now he noticed the glisten of drizzle on the darkness. Just as Kelston and Leeming landed, one after the other, it started to rain very slightly.

The Met. man droned on. There was a low over Lisbon. See—there it was on the map, the tight little rings looking like an archery target with Lisbon as the bull's eye. Up his arms went, as though in supplication. He was preaching an almost unintelligible sermon. This chart before him was the text.

Ferris asked, "What about conditions for take-off from here?" He was watching a grey blanket of mist and thin water drops being weaved before his eyes on the air outside.

At first the Met. man did not understand. Then, as the light dawned, the pencil pointed all over the place. The high to the south, the "vairy slow fro-nt," the low over Lisbon. He seemed to be doing an adding sum. At last, the answer came out: Santa Ana would remain not bad, not good. Then he pronounced perfectly the international meteorological words: so so.

Ferris said, "Visibility and cloud base, that's what I want."

The Met. man saw that the customer appeared unsatisfied. He was unhappy at being pinned down to cold figures. The hands waved. The shoulders shrugged. He looked at Ferris as though he was trying to sum him up, like a salesman who's been asked the price of a second-hand piece of furniture he's never been sure of selling. Finally, he came down to brass tacks: "Fife mile veezibility. Cloud twelf hunderd feet."

Ferris whistled. "Fine. Now what about a return alternate?" On the flight plan it was necessary to name an aerodrome to return that was above company limits, in case trouble developed or the destination fogged in.

"Lagens." The Met. man cut the air in front of him. "No goot. Santa Maria, no goot. Santa Ana—" He hesitated. Then he said there would be no great change till morning. Same weather as for take-off.

"Good." The pilot rubbed his hands together. "Ferris back once more on the gravy train."

The Met. man was all smiles. In Ferris' experience, meteorological officers fell into two distinct categories. They either liked to please, or they liked to frighten. This one was a real one hundred per cent pleasing merchant.

Then Ferris asked casually, "And what's the weather at present over the airport?"

The Met. man did what Ferris knew he would do. Rooted round among his litter to find a slip of paper that had the observations of nearly an hour before. "Fife mile veezibility. Cloud base, fifteen hunderd feet."

Ferris said suddenly and very genially, "Let's look out of the window, shall we? Just for a change—the window. Not at little bits of paper."

The Met. man turned his head as quickly as an animal alerted of danger. Together they looked out at the fog outside. They could just see half a wing of Kelston's Easy Uncle jutting out of the dirty night, one of her navigation lights making a woolly red smudge on the grey air. The rest of the Marlborough was utterly swallowed up. That triangular piece of dark fuzzy metal hung all on its own, like a ghost wing made of ectoplasm hovering alone above a medium's séance.

There was an immediate and noisy waterfall of Portuguese. The hands went up and down as though they were semaphoring the Met. man's distress. For a moment Ferris thought he was going to burst into tears.

"Obrigado," he said, in an effort to calm him. It was the only Portuguese he knew. It meant "thank you."

Just at the crescendo, Kelston came in. Surprised at the sight of a Met. man beside himself with rage, he looked across at Ferris.

"He's suddenly gone off the deep end, Mark."

The Met. man shifted his attention to Kelston. He listened to the Portuguese, answering him slowly in his own language. They palavered back and forth. The waterfall gradually lost its power. The torrent dried up. The Met. man departed to the inner office.

Kelston said, "He thought you were making fun of him, Peter."

"Only pulling his leg. Getting a rise out of a Met. man—only damned rise a British pilot's ever likely to see."

The Met. man came back, all smiles, with both forecast folders in his hands. He had altered the visibility at Santa Ana to three hundred yards. When Leeming arrived a few minutes later, everything was once more as calm as a mill-pond. Ferris waited in the background, while the other two captains listened to much the same briefing as he had. Only this time it was "Lagens and Santa Maria, no goot. Santa Ana, no goot either."

Kelston spent twenty minutes poring over the conditions reported at various times from the weather stations in the

Azores. Then he said, "There's not a damned place in the Azores fit for landing. Lucky we got in when we did."

"Anyway," Leeming pointed out, "Lisbon's all right."

"Except that it's over eight hundred miles away."

Before the three of them went out, Kelston said to the Met. man, "Not today, thank you."

Outside in the corridor, Ferris asked, with a smile lurking under the corners of his moustache, "Night-stopping, Mark?"

"Yes, this stuff's going to stick. Won't clear before to-morrow."

Ferris pointed out, "You can still see a couple of hundred yards. Good enough to take-off."

Kelston said, "Company limits in Line Standing Orders are a thousand yards for this place."

"Quoting the Bible to me now, eh?"

The three of them stood together in the corridor, away from the station personnel and their own crews purposely, so that no one would hear them about their sometimes un-happy business of reaching a decision.

Leeming said, "Well, you certainly seem to have made your mind up pretty smartly on that one, Mark."

"What are *you* going to do, Michael?" Ferris asked.

"You've taken the words right out of my mouth, Peter."

"Well . . . I know damn well I can get off."

"It's Runway One-Three," Leeming said doubtfully. "Into the hills. I'll be pretty heavy."

"Oh, Christ, Michael," Ferris retorted. "I'll be at maxi-mum all-up weight. Three tons heavier than you can pos-sibly be." He paused. Then he added, "If you can't take off in this, you should damn well knit socks, not fly Marl-boroughs."

Kelston said, "There's no question of anyone not being able to take off—so long as everything goes all right. I happen to think there's an added risk if you can't land immediately if anything goes wrong."

"As far as the Book's concerned," Ferris remarked. "Those rules are meant to be *interpreted*. They're not rigid. I got that from Veitch himself. If you can do it safely, then do it. After all, we've each done about fourteen years' flying. Should be able to make up our minds by now. Without the help of the Book."

"Sure," Kelston said. "And I have done."

"There'll be a lot of people to get hotel rooms for," Leeming put in. "I doubt if Dudley can do it."

"And I can tell you," Ferris said, "they're screaming for your two Marlboroughs at London. There's another special going off tomorrow. Supposed to be Easy Uncle."

"Well, that's just hard luck." Kelston shrugged his shoulders nonchalantly. "Because Easy Uncle is staying right here."

"You've made up *your* mind, Mark," Ferris said. "So have I. I'm going."

"And if something goes wrong? There's nowhere in the Azores you can land."

"Nothing *will* go wrong, Mark."

Kelston said, "Nice to be so certain." Then he walked away from them, back to the office.

It was only Leeming now who was sitting on the fence. He looked gloomily at the wet fog outside. "Doesn't look brilliant."

"Some people want to see beyond the damned horizon before they take off," Ferris snorted. "Hell, man, you can see a few feet in front of your nose, can't you? What more d'you want?"

"Mark's not going."

"And we all know why!" Ferris leaned over confidentially towards the other pilot. "If you ask me . . . I think he's losing his nerve. Does nothing but chatter about the aircraft, the crews and flying fatigue these days." He smiled cryptically. "That girl's turned the Iron Man into a regular old woman."

Leeming took one more long look out of the window. "I think it's getting a bit better, anyway," he said.

They started walking down to the Operations Room. Dudley was inside on the phone, alternately cursing the weather and the Carreras Hotel at the other end of the line. Trying to play his form of life-chess with three aircraft and three crews, and so many passengers all at the same time was really too much for a man. He raised his eyebrows when he saw them come in. When he heard that both of them were going, he put down the receiver in order to give them his fervent congratulations. "That's excellent, Captain Ferris . . . Captain Leeming. I really don't know how we'd have managed. Captain Kelston's given us enough of a headache as it is." He looked up towards the roof. "Fifty people to accommodate at a moment's notice."

"Well, you can thank your lucky stars it's not a hundred and fifty."

"Oh, I do, Captain Ferris, I do. And it isn't only that. It's the *expense*."

Suddenly the loud-speaker announced, first in Portuguese, then in English: "Empire Airways regret to announce the delay of its 569 service to London, due to weather. Will passengers please check at the booking office, where night-stop accommodation is being arranged."

Ferris said, "Two go. One stays. Same aircraft. Same weather. There's going to be some mighty puzzled passengers."

Bates was Leeming's navigator again on this trip. He looked up from the desk, and then said, just audibly, "Not only passengers." Then he added more loudly, "Flight plan finished, Captain Leeming. If you'd sign it."

As Ferris and Leeming walked over to their aircraft, Ferris said, "I saw the girl . . . waiting for him. I must say, Mark did a pretty quick disappearing act."

They parted on the tarmac. Ferris climbed up the steps to Easy Zebra's crew door. As he had expected, on the flight deck all his crew were talking about the weather. Whenever captains differed, he had found, they got a bit jumpy.

"Come on, chaps," he said with a wide grin, "let's get off before Easy Fox."

They were all tired. There was not much enthusiasm. The first officer, Parker, started to read out the endless items of the Before Starting Engine Check with maddening slowness. He was one of the new ones. Listening to him, Ferris irritably pulled at his moustache.

Then there was a traffic delay. Five of the passengers had lost themselves on the way to the aircraft. Dudley could be heard calling to them, like a shepherd to his lost sheep. Eventually, the steward announced forty-three passengers on board, cabin secure. Five minutes later, all four engines were turning, and Ferris moved Easy Zebra cautiously forward in the fog.

Now that the other passengers had left the terminal to board their two aircraft, the remaining bodies belonging to Easy Uncle took on a forgotten, rather ship-wrecked appearance, dotted around a lounge that had suddenly gone quiet. Kelston had already spoken to each one of them, explaining the delay. They were a good lot. Most of them looked out at the fog and said they saw his point. But all the same, he knew it was difficult for them, watching other people going on.

Kelston saw Dudley about transport and hotel accommodation, and arranged a provisional take-off time for eight next morning. He walked off to the Reception Hall, ignoring the thin knowing smile on the manager's face.

He found Karena waiting for him by the ticket office. He

said to her, "Well, the weather's on our side," and watched the delight spread across her face when she realized he wasn't going till morning.

In the taxi to the Carreras, she started to talk gaily. Then she said, "What was the trip like this time, Mark?"

"Good one. No complaints."

"Not tired?"

"This time, not particularly."

She fell silent, looking from Mark's set face to the opaque square of window and back to Mark again. The taxi was nosing its way slowly, respectful of the thick mist that twisted itself in streamers and clumps like black seaweed in the air outside. He felt her eyes on his face and turned. He smiled very slowly and squeezed her hand. His eyes reassured her by their familiar effortless look of love. Nevertheless, because her tongue had already formed the words, now she said, "The other two went. Will they say *you* should have gone?"

"They won't say so. And what they think doesn't matter."

The taxi lumbered into a pocket of dense fog. At first far away and then louder, came the sound of the first aeroplane taking off. Karena shivered. "Things aren't easy for you, Mark, are they?"

He raised his eyebrows gently and quizzically.

"I mean . . . decisions are difficult. And the company, they must know about us. It's bad for your job. It—"

He interrupted her quietly, "It, as you call it, is the joy of my life."

For a long while she sat there saying nothing. Then she lifted the large thin hand in both of hers and kissed the fingers one by one.

Outside, the whole sky seemed to be leaning on the island and every dark bubble of mist shouted the swelling triumphant noise of an aircraft's initial climb. Automatically, Mark listened. It had scarcely died away before the second aircraft's run-up started behind them with an angry, muffled roar.

Karena wanted to get back to talking lightly and happily. To drown the noise of the aeroplanes in the sound of their laughter, to shut out the mist by the curtain of their love.

"Karena," Mark said suddenly. "I didn't cancel for you. Nor for me. But because it was the right decision." He tilted up her chin and kissed her. "Have you got that straight?"

He kissed her again. With his finger, he tried to draw up the corners of her mouth. "Smile," he said.

But she didn't. Instead she said wistfully, "Sometimes the mountains seem to move in on Ponta Delgada, and sometimes," she waved her hand at the thick night outside, "the clouds and the fog seem to come in. And it's like that with us, I think. Circumstances, people, close in and squeeze us out. There seems to be no room for us."

"I know what you mean, Karena. No visa for England yet, no night-stop here, no future to look forward to together."

"And," she went on, "I'm so afraid that anything we do or say will make someone else join the ranks against us. And our time together will get shorter still. Until in the end, there isn't any left at all."

He brushed his lips gently over her forehead. "But I don't feel that at all. You see, the mountains only *seem* to move in. The clouds and the fog come down all right, but by the morning they're gone. And that's the feeling I have, Karena, that all these *seeming* difficulties will vanish, and everything will be all right in the end."

"Like the fairy story?"

"Just like that."

He drew her head down to his shoulder. "It's the fog, Karena. It's making you see giants and goblins and ogres."

Feeling the warmth and strength of his body beside her, she closed her eyes and kept them tight shut, counting the twists and turns along the road. Even this route, she thought, could never have so many. Then the driver braked and swerved, scraping his mudguard on one of the pillars of the Carreras' gates.

Opening her eyes, she saw the hotel loom up, misshapen and blurred. The beams of light from the long windows were wet and smudged like a child's painting.

But inside, there were warmth and light and voices murmuring and shouting and laughing in a reassuring stream of welcome. The glass door snapped shut behind them, like an armoured hand halting the clamminess outside. The thought of those threatening circumstances, of hostile faces—the goblins as Mark called them—faded in her mind, erased by the smiles and flesh-and-blood gestures that had taken the place of the trailing damp arms of the fog.

Already, ten paces before they reached the captain's room, Karena's face was flushed and happy. The small sound of the key scraping in the lock, the feel of the carpet under her feet, the sight of Mark opening the door were of supreme significance. In the taxi, while she had been brooding, whole minutes had been wasted. From this second onwards, she must hold to every moment.

She walked through the door slowly. She let her hand touch his. As though the room had been waiting, allowing her to taste in the foyer only a weak dilution of its own strong essence, the walls, the ceiling and the furniture seemed to draw them in, and surround them with perpetual echoes of their own acknowledged love.

When the door closed behind them, Mark turned her round suddenly towards him and said again, "Smile, Karena."

This time, it was easy.

As Easy Zebra went down the dip along the taxi-way at Santa Ana towards Runway One-Three, Parker said,

"Doesn't look like three hundred yards to me. More like fifty."

They heard Leeming run up his engines. Ferris commented acidly, "He came down well after us. Now he's off first. If people didn't talk so much—"

Easy Fox's engines interrupted him, roaring at take-off power into the fog.

"Can't even see his navigation lights," the first officer said.

"Ask the Tower permission to run-up in the take-off position on the runway," Ferris ordered.

They received a doubtful assent. Ferris had found what he was looking for—the thick white line in the centre of the mile long runway. He could see two flare-path lights, one on either side of him. "Well . . . let's get cracking on the run-up."

Hawkins was his engineer, and he took rather longer than usual, testing each engine in turn. Three times he tried the magneto switches on Number Four engine. Then he said reluctantly, "Engines O.K."

For once, Ferris thought it advisable to give the crew the full take-off patter which the training section had rammed into him. He turned to the first officer, "Keep the control column well forward till we reach 60 knots . . . then I'll pull the nose-wheel off the ground. Stand-by to raise the gear and flaps at my command. In the event of an emergency before 90 knots, stand by to give me full flap. I'll throttle back, and we'll stop—I hope."

Sixty per cent flap was used as extra lift for take-off. The remaining forty per cent provided the air braking action, to slow them down.

Then Ferris said to Hawkins, "I'll move the throttles to forty inches, manifold pressure, and then call 'your throttles.' From your position, you will advance them to fully permissible take-off limits. In the event of an emergency, call it out. If we're on the ground, we'll stop. If we're airborne we'll have rated power."

The first officer went through the Before Take-Off Check. Then Ferris turned to Hawkins, "Engines ready to go?"

Hawkins hesitated. Then he said, "Ready for take-off."

The fog around them had taken on the colour of a wet granite wall. Ferris ran out the landing lights, usually used for night take-offs. Immediately they reflected back full in his face. It suddenly reminded him of the time he was caught in the searchlights over Cologne. He switched them off. "We'll take this stuff neat," he said.

The Tower sent them cleared take-off, cleared to Bermuda at eighteen thousand feet. Then they added the visibility was now nearer a hundred yards. But by that time, Easy Zebra was rolling.

Ferris' fingers could hardly keep up with the throttle levers, they were being moved forward so fast from the engineer's position. Hawkins was obviously in a hurry to get the take-off over.

Runway One-Three was slightly up hill. The Marlborough grunted a little at first. The speed built up slowly. A fragment of the white line was still there, racing under the nose, showing up through the darkness like an indicator. It turned slightly to the left, and Ferris jabbed on left rudder.

At 60 knots, he hauled the nose-wheel off the ground. More positive feeling flowed into the controls. The Marlborough was gradually awakening into life. He let his eyes flicker for a moment on the airspeed—85 knots. Another five seconds and they'd have flying speed. The white line was still dead on the nose, though it was getting harder to follow. It oozed out of the night like toothpaste being squeeezd from a tube at an ever-increasing rate.

The Marlborough bumped into the air off an uneven ridge on the runway. Ferris pulled back slightly on the stick. Wobbling a little, as though it was a hefty child just learning to walk, Easy Zebra left the ground. Gaining confidence as her speed built up, she plunged up into the air. Ferris' eyes left the white line, and concentrated on the air speed and the gyro heading of one-three-zero degrees. He kept the wings level on the artificial horizon.

"Gear up!"

The first officer pulled the lever by his left hand. "Can't get it up," he shouted back.

Ferris called out to Hawkins, "Rated power." It was the maximum amount of continuous power allowed by the makers. Ferris was thinking of the hills at the far end of the runway.

Easy Zebra started to climb, but only at two hundred feet a minute. Ferris said to Parker, "It's the solenoid sticking. Get a pencil and disengage it." There was a small hole above the gear lever, where there was a solenoid which ensured the wheels could not be retracted on the ground. Sometimes it jammed, and would not allow retraction even during flight.

Parker poked a pencil into the hole cautiously.

"For God's sake, hurry up," Ferris yelled at him. "Look at the rate of climb!"

The altimeter showed four hundred feet. The hills went up to two thousand. Slowed up by the immense drag of the wheels, Easy Zebra struggled blindfold into the clammy night.

Then Parker's pencil snapped.

"Hawkins," Ferris shouted, "get that gear up for me. This man's useless!"

Hawkins leapt out of his seat, and fumbled in the hole with a screwdriver. Then he moved the lever up. Ferris heard a click as it engaged. "Thank God for that," he said. "Ground's high below. Got to have a clean aeroplane as soon as I can."

Parker took this to mean he wanted the flaps up, too. He leant over and moved the flap lever to "Up."

"Christ," Ferris howled at Hawkins, "look what he's done now!"

The hydraulic system operating the flaps and gear on the Marlborough, due to the immense pressures required, would only operate one service at a time. If flaps and gear were selected at the same time, the whole system went on strike and would not operate either. Easy Zebra's wheels were still hanging down in the slip-stream.

Ferris edged Easy Zebra round to the left in a steep climbing turn, away from the hills, and rammed the flap lever back into the take-off position. Still the gear didn't come up. But by now they were on a northerly heading, going steadily out over the sea. Slowly their height increased. At two thousand feet, Ferris relaxed his tight hold on the stick. "Now," he said grittily. "Let's start all over again. Select neutral on the undercarriage lever!"

Miserably, Parker did what he was told.

"Now select up!"

The lever clicked. Nothing happened.

"Select down, then," Ferris ordered.

Parker moved it right down. They waited for a minute.

"Now neutral!" Again they waited.

"Now up!"

Ferris watched for the three lights that showed the undercarriage down and locked to go out, one by one. But they still glowed back at him, cheerfully green for safety.

"Won't come up," Parker said unnecessarily.

Ferris kept the Marlborough flying upwards on a westerly course, out into the Atlantic.

"Something's sticking, Skipper," Hawkins said. "And there was a flicker on the pressure gauge. It's reading a hundred pounds less than it should do."

"It's the gauge," Ferris snapped back at him. "Combined

with inefficient operation. Wretched system's so bewildered, can't know its arse from its elbow."

"Or a leak somewhere," Hawkins said. "We'll have to go back, Skipper."

"Oh, for God's sake, Hawkins. Stop preaching at me. Get the gear up instead."

Hawkins obediently moved the lever up and down several times without any effect. Ferris glowered down at him. Now at five thousand feet, Easy Zebra was still crawling along with her gear and flaps down. He knew what Hawkins was thinking. The visibility at the Azores was unthinkable for landing. There was only a range let down there. Ever since Leeming had that small fire a couple of months ago around some of the pipelines of the system, the very mention of the words *hydraulic fluid* was enough to make some of these engineers turn pale and start advising the captain to get back on the ground again.

"You're not thinking of going all the way to Bermuda with the gear down, Skipper?" Hawkins asked. "We'd run out of fuel before we got to the island."

Ferris retorted irritably, "Stop asking silly questions, Hawkins. *And get that gear up!*"

"It won't come up, Captain." Just to show him, Hawkins moved the lever up again. And nothing happened. "We'll have to go back to the Azores. Except–"

"Except what, *Mister* Hawkins?" Ferris was furious now.

"Except we can't get in. The visibility . . . So I suppose we'll have to trail all the way back to Lisbon." There was a sardonic reproach in the engineer's voice that infuriated Ferris even further.

"Have you got the impression that *you* are the captain of this aircraft?" Ferris asked him with a heavy politeness.

Hawkins shrugged his shoulders. "This is an emergency. I was only suggesting–"

"Well, keep your damn silly suggestions to yourself. And

get out of my way!" He turned to Parker. "Take over. *Please* take care not to dive us all into the sea." Ferris climbed out of his seat and knelt on the floor by the undercarriage lever. He put it fully down. The pressure gauge flickered slightly. He paused for two minutes. Then he selected neutral, and one by one turned off the hydraulic pumps on the four engines.

"No use," Hawkins said. "Won't come up. The gauge–" Ferris took no notice of him. He put the pumps on again, and then selected up. He glared defiantly at the little green lights.

The two at the side, for the main wheels, flickered and went out. Then the one in the middle snuffed out, too.

Slowly and deliberately, Ferris said, "Undercarriage up."

Hawkins said stubbornly, "Still something odd." After all, the man had to say something.

"All it needed," Ferris said, as he climbed back into his seat, "was a little considerate and efficient operation. Now, get the flaps up, and let's get cracking to Bermuda!"

Eleven hours later, while they taxied to the ramp at Kindley Field, Hawkins said to the captain, "This hydraulic system, sir. I'm still not satisfied with it."

"Works all right now. No trouble getting the wheels down."

"I'd prefer to get the ground engineers to check through the whole system."

"That'll take hours! Mean a long delay."

"The hydraulic tank is down a bit. Might well be a leak on the pressure supply to the gear selector."

"You know as well as I do, Hawkins, that these tanks nearly always have to be topped up. Hydraulic fluid's lost in the system. The accumulator bladders are often distended."

"I still don't like it, sir," Hawkins said.

As soon as he got out of the aircraft the engineer had a

word about it with the Bermuda maintenance staff. There was nearly half a mile of hydraulic pipelines in the Marlborough, often in inaccessible places. They were not enthusiastic. Especially when they heard of the muddle on take-off at Santa Ana. "All the same, if Captain Ferris insists . . ." they said.

Hawkins went back to Ferris. "There may be some weakness in the system," he said. "Works all right now, but it might show up again any time later. These hydraulic pipelines are subject to terrific pressures . . . bound to weaken them. I think one's cracked a bit. Probably a tiny leak."

"Well, what's a hydraulic leak, anyway?" Ferris asked. "You've had a lot in your time. So have I. You're only telling me all this because it's the latest fashion."

Hawkins said, "You know how pushed the company are for aircraft these days, sir. This one'll be turned round quickly at Panama, after the usual two hour check. And the way things are, as soon as they've given it a sniff over at London again, it'll be out on a special. I'd feel happier—"

Ferris had always found aircrew engineers the biggest old women in the business. They were always shaking their heads over something or other. At one time, they were perfectly certain that the main spars were all cracked. At another, they were sure the master-rods on the engines were all fragmentating. Since Leeming's fire, they had been reminding themselves that the flash point of hydraulic fluid was ten degrees centigrade less than the boiling point of water.

"What would make you feel happier, Mr. Hawkins?" Ferris asked evenly.

"If the pipelines were thoroughly checked. This aircraft is still unmodified."

"What do the ground engineers say?"

"Well . . . they don't want the aircraft here any longer

than they can help. That's natural. Especially as it seems O.K. now. But if you insist . . ."

"And if I insist and they find nothing whatever the matter?"

The engineer shrugged his shoulders. "Then I'll be wrong."

Ferris sniffed contemptuously. *"Again,"* he said.

Michael Leeming said to Melanie, "Well, anyway, I got back on schedule."

"What's so wonderful about that?"

He looked at her uncertainly. "Kelston called a night-stop in the Azores. Weather was a bit off."

"But you've still only got five days' stand-off."

He sighed. "It's all these specials, Melanie. Surely you see that?" He was dog-tired. Coming straight off the long haul from Bermuda into an argument was a bit too much. To make things easier, he helped himself to another shot of whisky.

She shrugged her shoulders. "Hardly seems any point in keeping house at all. Just for a few days a month. Might just as well stay with my mother while you're out. And we'll go to an hotel when you're home. Be cheaper. And much less work for me."

"Things'll get better," he said vaguely. "They'll have to train some more captains now." His eyes pleaded with her. "Don't let's quarrel, Melanie. Not on my first night home. Let's at least have five cheerful days!"

"Let's," she retorted immediately. "And that goes for you more than me."

Ten hours behind Leeming, Kelston touched down at London Airport. When he'd cleared customs and his paper work, he went along to the Operations Room as usual. They told him there that Mr. Veitch wanted to see him. Even though it was nine o'clock at night, the line manager was still working.

Kelston said, as soon as he entered the line manager's office, "I suppose it's that night-stop again. I put in a full report."

Veitch had made arrangements to have all Easy Uncle's reports sent straight to him, the minute the aircraft was on the ramp. He held Kelston's Voyage Report in his hands. On the desk just below it was a report from Dudley, condemning Kelston's action in no uncertain terms, bringing the attention of the line management that this was the *second* unofficial night-stop Kelston had called in less than a month, that it had cost a great deal of money, wasted valuable aircraft time. He finished up with an unctuous comparison with Leeming and Ferris.

Veitch looked both reports over for the third time. Then he said coldly, "It strikes me as very odd, Captain Kelston, that out of three pilots flying identical aircraft, two go and one stays."

"It was the weather. In the circumstances, I didn't think it an advisable operation."

"But Captain Ferris and Captain Leeming accomplished it perfectly safely."

"As it happened—yes."

"Are you insinuating that they took a risk in going?"

Kelston said, "Flying isn't an exact science. I won't criticize anyone else's decisions. But I reserve the right to make my own."

He said nothing about take-off limits or the Book. Nor had he mentioned them in his Voyage Report. That might mean trouble for Ferris and Leeming. Kelston kept faith with the usual close brotherhood of pilots against the management. To him, it was just a purely professional difference of opinion—and nothing more.

But Mr. Veitch was not a pilot. He was an able administrator, used to employing his cross-checking system to find out the truth. And this system gave him a completely different slant on the whole question. "Captain Kelston," he said. "Since we took out the Azores' night-stop a month ago, you have had occasion to put it back twice. First for crew-fatigue. Now for weather. No other pilot on the line has done it once. Wouldn't you call it rather a coincidence?"

Kelston shrugged his shoulders. "You can call it what you like."

Veitch felt the time had come, unpleasant though it might be, to bring Kelston's notice to the fact that the management were perfectly well aware of the woman in the Azores. He looked Kelston squarely between the eyes, and said slowly, "I happen to know all about—" He paused, searching his mind for exactly the right word. "It."

For a moment, Kelston appeared puzzled. Then he said, "I suppose you mean—Karena."

"I don't know what the young woman's name is," Veitch said heavily, "but I know only too well of her existence in the Azores."

Kelston's grey eyes suddenly blazed with anger. "Which you think would bias—"

"Naturally." Veitch remained quite cool. He had found out at last to his own satisfaction that Kelston was nothing but a purposeful scaremonger, hankering to get back to an illicit little game he was playing in Ponta Delgada.

With exasperated fury, Kelston turned on him. "Then you don't trust me as a captain on the line?"

"Not altogether—no."

"And you don't trust anything I tell you?"

"Not if it's anything to do with the Azores' night-stop." Veitch had already decided that in the circumstances, the honest truth was the best policy.

Kelston said, "In that case, there's no point talking any further." He got up, and was moving slowly to the door when Veitch called to him. "One thing, Captain Kelston, I feel I shall have to tell you. Unscheduled night-stops are an expensive luxury. Your aircraft was needed here for a special service. Since you are so much against the removal of the Santa Ana night-stop on account of crew-fatigue, perhaps you might like to be transferred to the India route of the company, where the legs are much shorter? And where there is no Santa Ana to call a night-stop at."

Kelston closed the door behind him without replying, but Veitch was perfectly certain that the pilot realized what the hint implied. He would be very surprised if Kelston called a delay—other than mechanical, of course—anywhere along the route for many months to come.

Three days later, on the Monday morning that Kelston was scheduled out on another special service to Panama, Ferris' Voyage Report on his Azores-Bermuda leg made an appearance on Mr. Veitch's desk. The line manager had arrived, as usual these days, early in the morning, at much the same time as Kelston reported for duty at the Operations Room. He could, if he had wanted to, have had a word with the pilot before he took off. But he saw no need.

For the first thing he did that day was to read Ferris' report. There were three pages of it, written in the pilot's scrawling handwriting—all concerned with some ham sandwiches that catering in Santa Ana had provided for the crew's light refreshments on board, and which Ferris proceeded to prove conclusively were utterly unfit for human consumption.

Only a couple of hundred yards from the office where Mr. Veitch was reading Ferris' Voyage Report, Kelston was checking in at the Meteorological Office. The weather to Madrid, apart from the usual winter morning mist over England, looked reasonable. A few isolated thunderclouds. Nothing more. He walked over to the crew rest room. Cockcroft put down the newspaper he was reading and said, "Morning, sir."

Kelston looked at the breezy smile on the first officer's face. "We haven't flown together before, have we?"

"No, Captain. Cockcroft's the name."

They shook hands. Kelston said a trifle grimly, "You're new."

It wasn't a question, but Cockcroft took it as one. "Oh, no sir. Done three round trips. Two with Captain Ferris. One with Captain Leeming. Now . . . I've just come back from a spot of leave."

Kelston worked out in his mind that the man must have nearly two hundred route hours behind him anyway.

"Had a command of my own before I joined this racket."

Kelston did not seem impressed. He glanced at the notice-board to see the names of the operating crew the roster had selected for him. Bates was the navigator, Draper the radio officer, Cluny was the engineer. Not a bad lot, all in all.

Bates came in from collecting his mail and said cheerfully, "Good morning, Captain Kelston."

"Working you hard, aren't they, Mr. Bates? Saw you in the Azores last Thursday night."

Bates sighed. "It's these specials. Never seem to have five minutes at home these days."

"Seen Cluny?"

"He's out at the aircraft, sir," Cockcroft put in. "She's parked on the tarmac now."

"Which one have we got this time?"

"Easy Zebra, sir."

Kelston grunted. "Well . . . in that case, I think I'll stroll over and have a word with him."

He walked over the wet grey concrete towards the Marlborough. She stood between an Astroliner and a Pan-American DC-6. Her silver sides glistened with dampness. He could hear someone moving around inside her. He walked up the main steps, through the empty passenger cabin.

"That you, Mr. Cluny?"

There was a shuffling sound, and the crew door opened. "Yes, sir. Cluny."

Kelston followed him to the flight deck. "Done all your checks?"

"Haven't dipped the tanks yet, sir. Finished everything else."

"This is an unmodified aircraft."

"I know, sir." Cluny hesitated. "I've already checked the hydraulic pipelines. That is, as far as I can, sir."

"Which isn't far."

"No, sir," Cluny said regretfully. "You know what it is. And all the holds are full of freight. There's one piece that's enormous. Part of a ship."

"Where is it?"

"Forward baggage compartment, sir."

"Anything in the maintenance book about hydraulic trouble?"

"Nothing at all. She seems to have been running well. She was late in, yesterday. But that was because she did a shuttle to New York and back as well."

"When did she get in?"

"Ten hours ago, sir. They've given her the normal sixty hour check."

Kelston said again, "Nothing at all in the book about hydraulic trouble? You're sure of that?"

"Nothing, Skipper."

The pilot thought for a minute, stroking his chin with his hands. "Oh, well," he said wearily, "I suppose it's all right."

He heard the door clanging open in the rear cabin, and then footsteps. The rest of the crew were coming aboard.

Dead on the company's schedule of nine o'clock in the morning, Easy Zebra lifted her forty-seven souls on board off Runway Two-Eight Left at London Airport, and turned her blunt nose southwards towards Madrid.

Book Seven

The Beginning of the North-West Quadrant

January 10-March 16

1

At the top of the climb, Kelston said to Cockcroft, "You take over now. Don't put in the auto-pilot." He was trying to make up his mind on the capabilities of this bouncy, self-confident man beside him. Confidence combined with very little experience he distrusted above all other characteristics in a pilot. Flying was a great leveller. A man soon discovered what a midget he was compared to the immense, unexpected powers that hid in the sky.

One thing he found out as soon as Easy Zebra slid into a bank of cirrus-stratus. Mr. Cockcroft's instrument flying was not nearly as good as it should have been. Now that he couldn't see the horizon, the first officer was overcorrecting badly. With increasing irritation, Kelston saw him wander, first ten degrees to port, and then, when he noticed it, turn the Marlborough too far to starboard. Easy Zebra climbed and dived within a mean of seven hundred feet of her allotted altitude. Bates whispered to Draper, "This man's going flat out to make all the passengers sick."

Kelston said to the second pilot, "Here . . . let her fly herself. You're struggling too much. Just correct when she goes off course."

"This cloud's a bit rough, sir."

Kelston grunted. "Not half as rough as your instrument flying."

Cockcroft said reproachfully, "I don't get much practice, of course, sir."

"Ferris and Leeming let you fly?"

"Well . . . the automatic pilot was in most of the time, sir. I wouldn't take it out without the captain's orders."

"I see," Kelston said. Already he could see a pretty hard trip ahead of him. This man needed watching.

Then on take-off out of Madrid, as Easy Zebra touched 85 knots, he saw the first officer's enthusiastic fingers twist round the undercarriage lever, presumably anxious to show the captain how good he was at raising the gear.

Kelston half-turned to him. "Not yet," he said.

Immediately Cockcroft pulled the lever up. The next words he had been expecting to hear were "Gear up." As soon as he saw Kelston open his mouth, he had acted.

Easy Zebra was still below proper flying speed. Kelston pulled back hard on the stick. Mushing badly, in a half-stalled attitude, the Marlborough hung in the air, a couple of feet from the ground, as her wheels retracted into the inboard engine nacelles. Keeping take-off power on, Kelston waited for the speed to build up, all the time hauling the nose up to prevent her sinking onto the concrete runway and smashing herself to pieces. When the air-speed indicator at last showed 120 knots, he eased the aircraft level, and she started to climb away normally. Then he turned to Cockcroft. He spoke quietly, so the rest of the crew wouldn't hear, but his eyes were blazing. "What the hell did you do that for?"

"I was expecting you to say . . ."

"You don't expect anything in this business. For God's sake—*listen* to an order."

"I'm sorry, sir." Cockcroft was inclined to be self-righteous. After all, they had got off without scratching anything. In his own mind, therefore, he had seen no particular danger.

Kelston said no more to him. But as the trip progressed, through Lisbon and on to the Azores, he saw that Cockcroft did the flying without the help of George, the automatic pilot. The man had to get experience some way.

"When you're feeling tired," he said, "then you can put George in. You need the practice. On this trip you're going to get it."

As Easy Zebra flew on towards São Miguel, Kelston kept his eyes on every movement the first officer made. He took over on the circuit at Santa Ana and gently brought the Marlborough down, past the Rabo de Peixe Hill, touching down smoothly a hundred yards beyond the green threshold lights of Runway One-Three.

While he was taxiing up to the ramp, Kelston opened his side window and looked out beyond the parked aircraft to the terminal building. Just in the glow of the main door, Karena was standing quite still, the neon lights firing and glittering on her black hair, her face in the shadow of the night outside.

Dudley had checked on the route weather. It was a perfect starlit night over Santa Ana. The winds to Bermuda were reasonable, only 20 knots against them at eighteen thousand feet. So the trip would be quite a short one—just over eleven hours. And Bermuda was forecasting ceiling and visibility unlimited. Unless there was something mechanically wrong with the aircraft, there was no earthly reason this time, he thought with satisfaction, for Kelston to call a delay.

Kelston gave him a brief good evening as he passed. Dudley asked Cluny eagerly, "Aircraft serviceable?"

Cluny said, "Seems all right."

"Good," Dudley said. "Should be able to get off on schedule."

As soon as she saw him, Karena started to run towards Kelston. There was so little time. Putting his arms round her, he kissed her and said with a grin, "Back quickly, anyway."

Then side by side, they walked through the terminal building. She waited while he checked with the weather.

"Forecast's fine," he said to Bates. "Will you get on with the flight plan? I'll be back just before departure to sign up."

"Sure," Bates said. "That's all right."

While the aircraft was refuelled, Kelston and Karena walked up and down on the deserted road that led to Ponta Delgada. Against a sky just one shade lighter, the jagged peaks of the Serra de Agua made a solid black block to the south-east of the airfield. High above the mountains, the stars seemed to give back a weak reflection of the lights of the flare path, the arc lamps on the ramp, the bright square patches of the terminal's windows. Dudley looked out from his office, watching the two of them on the far side of the road, moving away until they merged with the night, and then turning and coming back, more distinct every step, till they were once more touched by the surplus light that overflowed from the building and spilled in long yellow stains on the darkness outside. He heard the murmuring of their voices. They were walking very slowly. For a little while longer, he kept his eyes on them. Then he looked at his watch. Going out from the back entrance as they approached, he called, "Captain Kelston?"

They came up to him. Kelston said, "Everything ready?"

Ignoring the girl, Dudley said, "Flight plan's ready to sign, sir. I'll have the passengers on board in just under the five minutes."

The two of them walked inside. Bates had brought the flight plan out of the Operations Room. Kelston signed it and turned to Karena, "Well . . . time's nearly up."

"Take care of yourself, Mark."

"Of course."

"You're not too tired?"

He said lightly, "This one's a gravy ride. There's not much wind, and the weather's good."

She looked at him in silence. Then she whispered, "You'll come back soon?"

"In eleven days and two hours," he said, "I'll be back."

The passengers started to converge on Easy Zebra in twos and threes, sauntering, taking their time, alternately shepherded and hustled by Dudley. Kelston and Karena stood a few yards from the crew steps at the front of the aircraft.

"Been short and sweet," he said.

"Wonderfully sweet." She held him close to her, just for a moment hiding her face away from him. Then abruptly she looked up. "Eleven days and two hours. A short time like that will soon go." She tried to smile. Putting up her face to be kissed, she said, "Till then."

"Till then, Karena."

Her fingers, holding his hand, seemed locked round it. The few minutes that she was allowed with him were all but spent. This time, it seemed harder than ever to let him go. She felt the warmth of his flesh in hers, the steady beating of his blood. Very gently, his fingers detached themselves, and he started to walk away from her.

When a few steps separated them she called out, "Mark," and he stopped and turned.

"Yes, Karena?" He had come back to her. She felt that all she had to do was to put her arm between him and the aircraft, barring his way.

"Mark–" She stopped and looked beyond him. Suddenly she saw that the outline of the mountains seemed nearer, as though they were moving down on the two of them. She shivered in the sharp January wind. All her instincts, well trained to sense the tightening strangle hold of circumstances, urged her to say to him, "Don't go." But around her, people were hurrying about their business of an ordinary aircraft departure. Many events had combined to ensure that this parting was nothing but inevitable routine. So that in the end she said the words everyone says to a pilot going away. "Have a good trip, Mark."

He smiled and kissed her again before once more walking

away from her. He climbed the crew steps one by one to become a character in the mechanical play that was being acted around them. Just before he entered the aircraft, he turned and waved down to her.

She stood there, watching the dozen men round Easy Zebra move like robots under the brilliant lights. She could still see Mark, sitting by the open cockpit window, but already she felt cut off from him. The steps were wheeled away from the aircraft. All her doors clanged shut and fast. The long silver cylinder of the Marlborough stood isolated, a separate world of its own, as her two starboard engines leapt into life.

She saw Mark lean out of the window. He pointed to the port engines and put his thumb up, making signs from his world to theirs. The man with the fire extinguisher moved nearer. Everyone else moved away. Number Two's propeller creaked and turned like an old-fashioned windmill, and then raced powerfully round in a burst of speed. A minute later, Number One followed. Now all four were turning, again came the signs. Mark crossed his hands to and fro as though finally cutting all contact with the ground. Obeying his signal, men dived under the shadowy wing and pulled away the chocks. Well in front of the nose, the station engineer waved two torches and beckoned Easy Zebra towards him.

The Marlborough moved. The brakes gently squealed on her wheels. Karena caught a last shadowy glimpse of Mark's face before the great tail swung round in a huge puff of smoke from the idling engines. With her portholes blazing like little round suns all down the length of her fuselage, Easy Zebra rolled slowly forward to add her lights to the cold shimmer of the stars and the twin parallel glare of the flare-path drawn across the night.

Close beside Karena, Dudley stood outside to watch Kelston take off. Together, they heard the run-up. One after another, each engine roared out into the darkness. Then the station manager saw with relief that the aircraft was moving forward. The run-up must have been satisfactory. They were not returning to the ramp—that headache which he so much hated.

The landing lights came on under the wings of the aircraft, shining out like little horizontal searchlights. Then the tremendous noise of the engines at take-off power shook and rattled the windows of the terminal. As Easy Zebra climbed up into the night, Dudley looked at his watch. The time was 22:17 Greenwich Mean Time. Kelston had been ten minutes late off the chocks. The station manager sighed. It would mean making out a late departure report.

For a few minutes more, the aircraft's red and green navigation lights were visible moving higher in the western sky. Gradually, the noise of her engines disappeared. The whole of the airfield seemed suddenly still. Dudley, somehow held by the presence of the girl, kept watch on the Marlborough till it disappeared into the night.

The girl reached the terminal building just after him. He held the glass door open for her. "Thank you," she said as she passed him. With a feeling of shocked surprise at such an exhibition in so public a place, Dudley noticed that her eyes were streaming with tears.

Gomez, the Empire Airways Operations officer on duty that night, was locally employed from Ponta Delgada. Already he had set out a clean white chart on the table to plot Easy Zebra's progress from the Azores to Bermuda. He noted down neatly: "Airborne 22:17. Fuel on board 24,310 pounds. Flight time 11 hours 1 minute. Endurance 13 hours and 36 minutes."

The teleprinter beside him clacked out a message. He filled in the beginning of the Marlborough's track across the Atlantic. Kelston had reported at the top of the climb at 23:02.

He had only the one aircraft to watch over that night.

In between the times that Bates' careful position reports came through, he read a Lisbon newspaper that had come in with Easy Zebra that night.

Things were very quiet. Regularly, one by one, the position reports came in. After three hours the aircraft was reporting at 37 degrees 31 north, 36-15 west. The wind was south-west at 31 knots. Cloud—only a trace of stratus below them at six thousand feet.

The little pencil line was drawing further from Santa Ana. Gomez noticed she had gained four minutes on flight plan. The winds were less strong than forecast.

The teleprinter clacked again. This time it was a message from London. The normal Tuesday schedule would leave on time. Captain 42. Gomez looked it up in the company's signals regulations. Number 42 was Captain Leeming. He chalked up the flight on the notice-board.

The time passed very slowly. Outside, it was still a perfectly clear night over the airfield. Gomez went next door to have a chat with his opposite number in World-Wide Airways, now plotting an aircraft coming from Bermuda. They talked about their jobs and about their salaries. Gomez said, "Quiet night for me. Mine will soon be transferring to Bermuda control."

He heard the teleprinter going again in his office. Going back, he plotted another of Bates' positions. 36-03 north, 43-11 west. The wind was still from the south-west, but its speed was up to 60 knots. Easy Zebra had fallen a few minutes behind flight plan.

Then for the next two hours, the teleprinter did not move. No message from the Marlborough. Gomez was well aware of the difficulties of radio communication. Sometimes aircraft were out of touch for hours at a time. All the same, he phoned the radio station to find out whether they had any message. None, they said.

Wearily now, his eyes half-closed, he slumped in his chair,

occasionally reading the paper, now and again smoking a black tobacco Portuguese cigarette. At five o'clock, there was still no message. But Easy Zebra would have transferred to Bermuda control by now, in any case. It would be their responsibility. His pencilled line, stretching out on the white paper, abruptly stopped at 43 west, not quite halfway to Bermuda. His eyes glazed over, and his head fell on his chest.

He was awakened by the rattle of the teleprinter. It was Bermuda: a request for Easy Zebra's position. He telephoned the radio station the last position he had, now three and a half hours old. Twenty minutes later, Bermuda came back to say that although they had no communication with Easy Zebra, radio conditions had been reported bad over the Atlantic.

Just as dawn broke over the island, bringing up out of the darkness the clear greens and browns of São Miguel, he had breakfast in the deserted restaurant. He was taking his time over coffee when the passengers from the World-Wide Bermuda flight swarmed in, chattering loudly, from the coldness of the air outside.

Back in the office, there was another message from Bermuda. Had Santa Ana any communication with Easy Zebra? They had tried New York, Boston, Gander. No one had heard anything.

It was 7:45 now. The Marlborough should be nearing her destination. It was odd they hadn't been able to raise her. A little anxious doubt crept into Gomez' mind. But then, maybe she'd fallen a bit behind. The winds on the last fix were stronger than forecast. He phoned the radio station to say "nothing more heard."

When his relief came in, Gomez explained and apologized for the unfinished pencil line on the chart. Bermuda had not come back. Presumably they were in contact with the aircraft now. All the same, he stayed. Used to bad radio communication, he was nevertheless conscientious. He suggested to his relief that they initiate a signal asking Bermuda for Easy Zebra's position.

A reply was a long time coming. Bermuda sent: "No communication. Request confirmation of Easy Zebra's estimate Bermuda is 9:18." The message was sent at 9:19.

"Queer," Gomez said. He was really worried now. After they had sent the confirmation, the minutes dragged by and the teleprinter did not stir.

Dudley was just coming in to check on the day's operations, when the next message came through. Bermuda sent: "Still no communication. Am initiating Air-Sea Rescue operations."

The station manager went white when he saw it. The sudden shock of walking into this kept him standing there, apparently unable to make a move to counter this new and terrifying gambit with which life had attacked him. It was Gomez who phoned through to Control to start Air-Sea Rescue operations from the Azores end of the route.

By one o'clock that afternoon, Bermuda still reported no contact. Easy Zebra's petrol must now be considered consumed. There was no alternative landing ground where she could possibly have come down. Four Fortresses with lifeboats slung under their bellies had taken off from Bermuda. From Lagens, six more aircraft were airborne and were now searching the Atlantic along the Marlborough's track. An aircraft carrier, hearing the emergency broadcast, cruised south towards latitude 36 north. Five merchantmen altered course towards the area. Halfway between the Azores and Bermuda, Weather-Ship Easy stopped her endless patrol in small circles and started to speed through the water at her maximum 18 knots towards the last known position. The whole vast effort of humanity was now being immediately focused on Easy Zebra and her forty-seven souls on board.

When Leeming arrived on the normal Tuesday service, eight hours later, they were still searching. At Madrid, they had told him some garbled story of Easy Zebra being "very late" arriving in Bermuda. Like a slow snowball, he accumulated more information at Lisbon. They were not sure, they said, but they had heard something about an aircraft being reported missing on the Azores-Bermuda leg. It could possibly be Easy Zebra. No signal of her arrival had yet been sent. Then he stepped out of Easy Fox at Santa Ana to find the whole station in a complete panic.

Dudley met him, rubbing his hands together as though he was wringing them. "Can't understand it," he said over and over again, as they walked to the Operations Room. "Everything was perfectly all right here. Perfectly all right. It's terrible, terrible."

He poured the whole story out to Leeming, while the flight plan was being made out by the navigator. Dudley punctuated his words every now and again by ringing up the radio station. "Anything heard? Anything seen?" he would ask. But there was always nothing. Leeming said, "Who were the crew?"

He looked down at the names the station manager gave him, picturing them in his mind individually, each one coming up with a sharp sad clarity—Mark Kelston, Cockcroft, Bates, Draper, the engineer Cluny. The steward and stewardess he had not known.

"And the passengers?" he asked.

"Forty, Captain," Dudley said.

"Would have to be nearly a full load. Makes you feel so . . ." Hopelessly, he stared at Dudley. "You're sure you're doing everything?" he said with an odd harshness in his voice.

"All we can do. Fortresses from Lagens and Bermuda. Ships. An aircraft carrier—"

Leeming said, "Well, anyway . . . there's another aircraft here that can help."

"Which one, Captain?"

"Easy Fox. Our own." Leeming turned to his navigator. "Make the flight plan out at sea level. We'll search for them on the way to Bermuda. We're going along their track. Should see something." The thought of actually helping seemed to brace him, galvanize him into a new activity. "We've got to do everything in our power to find them."

"If there's anything there to find," Dudley said sombrely. He was smoking one cigarette after another now. He said to Leeming, "I can't see it's got anything to do with *this* station, Captain Leeming. They can't blame *this* station." Already he was thinking of the inevitable inquiry. There were bound to be questions. And Kelston had had rather a lot to do with the Azores lately.

Leeming asked, "The aircraft was perfectly serviceable when it left here?"

"Perfectly."

"The electrical wiring hadn't been modified. Same aircraft in which I had my fire."

"But that was months ago, Captain!"

Leeming sat on the desk, staring down at the floor. "I know . . . I was just thinking, remembering."

They all sat together in a depressed silence. The navigator went on busily making his calculations. Leeming was just saying for the second time, "We've damned well got to help them somehow," when the teleprinter started clacking out again. Dudley went over to the machine and looked with weary eyes at the words it had printed. The ink was still wet. There was a slight smudge on the last full stop.

It was a very short message. Outside the sender, the time of origin and the address to all stations on the line, there were only four words. It just said: "All Marlboroughs grounded indefinitely."

At long last, Mark Kelston had succeeded in getting Mr. Veitch to act.

Next day, unshaven and with black rings round his eyes, Dudley went up to the Carreras Hotel to see Leeming. He brought with him the yesterday evening newspaper that a World-Wide Aircraft had brought him from England. The huge headlines about Easy Zebra had sunk him even further into a vacillating, useless depression.

The pilot asked him, "Still nothing?"

"Nothing." With a feeble attempt at indignation, Dudley produced the papers. "But look at these, Captain!"

The British press had spread itself. It was a slack season, and they had plenty of space available. Some enterprising reporter had found out about the fire in Easy Zebra two months before. Kelston and the *Santa Lucinda* came up again. Some of them even drew comparisons with the Gibraltar disappearance, over two years before.

Leeming read them. Then he said ruefully, "Certainly splashed it."

"Might make the inquiry a bit . . . tricky," Dudley pointed out.

Leeming said, "Whatever are you getting yourself into a state for? They can't blame you. Or me, for that matter."

Dudley seemed unconvinced. "Captain Kelston," he said, shaking his head. "He had some . . . queer ideas."

"You mean the girl?"

"Mostly the girl. He saw her just before he took off."

Leeming had forgotten about Karena. He hesitated. "I suppose someone should tell her."

Dudley looked at the pilot hopefully. "I was thinking . . . one of the reasons I came up in fact . . . you know her, Captain Leeming."

Leeming said indignantly, "I don't."

"But I saw you talking to her. Only three weeks ago. At

least she's spoken to you. I know her by sight, of course. That's all."

"So you thought I'd go and tell her!"

Dudley said vaguely, "Might make it easier for her."

Leeming saw that the manager was in such a state of panic, he could bring no comfort to anyone. "Anyway," he said, "there's still hope."

"Oh yes." Dudley's voice was unconvinced. "Still a chance. They're continuing the search. You could tell her that. Give her something to hang on to."

In the end, Leeming agreed to do it. He thought about it over his lunch. It was going to be difficult to do well. Gloomily, he picked at his food, while the crew talked in subdued tones among themselves.

"Wonder how long we'll be here, Captain?" the stewardess asked him. She was a girl called Penelope Richards and had been on the line for years. She tried without much success to keep the nervous edge out of her words.

"Till they find out something, I suppose," he answered. "We'll probably fly back to England empty."

An hour after lunch, he went down to the Shipping Office where he knew Karena worked. He was shown up to see a man called Olivarez, presumably her boss. The pilot said to the grey-haired Portuguese, "My name's Leeming. A Captain in Empire Airways."

Olivarez got up from his desk and shook hands.

"Yes, Captain?"

"You have a girl working for you, Karena?"

"Yes."

"I wonder if I could see her?" Leeming's voice was strained and thin.

"She hasn't been in this morning."

Leeming looked surprised. "When did you see her last, then?"

"Yesterday morning. She went up to the radio station

yesterday morning. On an errand for me. Some messages I wanted sent to three of my ships." Then Olivarez noticed the worried anxiety on Leeming's face. "Why . . . is anything wrong?"

Leeming said shortly, "One of our aircraft is missing. Captain Kelston was on board. I suppose you knew she was his . . . friend."

Olivarez' eyes filled with sudden sadness. For a minute, they took no notice of the pilot sitting in front of them. He said something in Portuguese. Then, in English, he added, "Yes, I knew."

"There's still hope, of course. But I think she should be told at once."

"Naturally." Olivarez stared unhappily out of the window.

"I believe you knew Kelston?"

"It was he who saved my ship for me. He was a most gallant man."

"He had his troubles," Leeming said. "Not that he wasn't a nice sort of chap."

"Poor Karena." Olivarez unashamedly wiped his eyes. "They were so happy together. She has had more than her fair share of grief already in her life."

"H-m—well, she has caused her share of trouble, too."

"I do not know what you mean."

"I was thinking about Kelston. He had a wife, you know. And a child."

"I knew," Olivarez said in an almost matter-of-fact tone. "It was unfortunate."

"That affair of his made many people unhappy."

Olivarez smiled sadly. "When you've lived as long as I have, you'll know there's only one happiness. Your own."

"That's pure selfishness," Leeming retorted.

"Some day," the shipowner went on, "you will at last admit we are all selfish. Each in our own way. It is a necessary part of life. If you can't find happiness first in your own heart, it doesn't matter how much you busy yourself finding it for other people. You are still ear-marked for the damnation that awaits all who had the chance—and remained unfulfilled."

"I'll stick to what I've been taught," Leeming said. "And I'll take the consequences."

"There will be no question of that, my friend. The consequences will take *you.* Time is private to each individual. It belongs to you only. And you are responsible for the way it is spent."

Leeming kept his lips tightly compressed. Neither said anything for a long time. Then Olivarez asked, "Tell me, what time do you think something happened to the aircraft?"

"The last message was just before three in the morning. But they might have gone on flying for hours after that."

"All these rescue aircraft and ships. How much hope do you think there is?"

"Very little."

"Almost none?"

Leeming hesitated. "Now . . . I would say just about none."

Olivarez got up from his seat and stared out at the deserted harbour.

Leeming said again, "I think she should be told. Perhaps it would be better if you . . ."

"Yes," the shipowner said impatiently. "She must be told gently. We will go to her room. And I will tell her. I am thankful that she is a person with courage and faith. She would know, of course," he said softly. "She would know if he was dead."

"I think that's most . . ." Leeming was saying, when Olivarez cut him short. "She is not an ordinary woman. They were in love together. I could tell it, almost from the moment they first saw each other. In this office. Three months ago."

Leeming said, "I spoke to her once. For nearly half an hour. She didn't seem particularly out of the ordinary."

"And I have known her for five years." The shipowner kept his face close to the glass of the window, gazing at the light from the office glittering on the dark water outside. "He would come down into the sea?"

"Yes, the sea."

"This same Atlantic that washes these rocky shores," Olivarez said slowly. "But, no, Karena would never do that."

Olivarez was right. The next morning Karena was in the office when he arrived.

"My dear!" he said. "My dear!"

"It's all right," she said quietly. "There is still hope. For me there will always be hope."

2

The three men sitting at the far end of the committee room inclined closely towards each other. For a moment, only the tops of their heads were visible to the thirty-six others sitting in front of them. A black sleek shiny one on the left, Sir Ronald Percival's bald one in the middle and Captain Graveney's shabby grey scrub on the other side. Then the black one, belonging to Group Captain Knight, inspector of accidents, drew away from the others. He asked Ferris, "You still haven't answered the question. Let's put it to you again. Why didn't you get the ground engineers to check along Easy Zebra's hydraulic pipelines at Bermuda?"

The inquiry was going badly.

Already it had been established from the engineering log books that there had been a fire along the hydraulic pipelines of G-AHEZ three months previously. The company had considered it a million to one chance, and due to the operational demands on the route, had authorized modification only as each aircraft had come up for a Check Four. Engineer Officer Hawkins had given a straightforward account of their difficulties, raising the undercarriage on take-off out of the Azores. The loaders had given evidence of the correct trim of the aircraft, and had admitted the presence of a bulky piece of machinery in the forward baggage compartment. Leeming sat gloomily next to Mr. Veitch. As he had expected, he had flown Easy Fox back to London empty, after the Santa Ana engineers had given her a thorough looking over. Due to the outcry in the newspapers, and a question that had been asked in the House of Commons, a preliminary inquiry of everyone remotely connected with Easy Zebra had been called. Those with any relevant evidence had now been summoned to this committee room. Engineers, meteorological officers, operations personnel, aircrew, Mr. Veitch and one station manager, Dudley, were all there waiting in varying degrees of apprehension for their turn to supply a piece to the mysterious jig-saw of Easy Zebra's disappearance.

Ferris said, "The system was working perfectly satisfactorily on landing. There seemed no point. On a complicated piece of machinery like an aircraft, things go wrong sometimes for no apparent reason. And then rectify themselves. And in this case, the system had been badly handled by the first officer."

The man on the right asked, "But in view of the history of this aircraft, wouldn't it have been prudent to do as Mr. Hawkins requested?" Captain Graveney was the senior pilot of a large charter company, now acting as pilot assessor to the court.

"If we worried about every little thing that wasn't quite right, we'd never get off the ground."

"All the same, in this case—"

Ferris interrupted him. "There is no evidence that there *was* a hydraulic fire on board Easy Zebra."

Sir Ronald, who was the Queen's councillor conducting the inquiry said mildly, "We are not saying that there was. As I have explained before, the whole idea of the inquiry is that we feel that some small shred of one person's evidence might bring to light some forgotten, but important, trifle in the mind of another. I think that's all we want to ask you. Thank you, Captain Ferris."

As the court proceeded throughout that afternoon, gradually the tension mounted. When the technical experts were cross-examined, the whole court room seemed to hold its breath, as though expecting them at any moment to agree that all the evidence pointed to a second fire on the hydraulic system of Easy Zebra, this time with fatal results.

But each of the experts was careful to avoid being entangled in the extraordinary chain of coincidences that Knight produced for his inspection. Many aircraft, they said, had hydraulic leaks which had no significance whatever. The fact that Ferris' undercarriage wouldn't come up for so long could be due to dirt in the system, which was eventually dislodged, a sticking relief valve—everyone of them had a different theory, but all their replies were unanimous in that no weakness sufficient to cause a disaster had been brought to light in Easy Zebra's hydraulic system.

Knight said, "Such faults would, of course, produce extra strain on the pipelines?"

They admitted it was possible. Knight went on, "Then it is a matter of opinion whether the system was faulty or not?"

They agreed that it could be looked on in that light.

"But considering the history of the aircraft, wouldn't it

have been prudent to have the system checked over at Bermuda?"

That, too, was a matter of opinion with them. "At least," Knight asked, "something should have been put down in the technical log?"

They pointed out that it appeared to be working perfectly satisfactorily. It gave no more trouble round the route. Try as he would, Knight could not get a definite answer out of them.

In the end, rather wearily, Knight switched onto the other technicalities of the aircraft. The power plants had not given trouble. There was no admissible evidence that the Marlborough was anything else except fully serviceable when she left the Azores.

After the taut excitement while the engineers were being questioned, the court turned almost with relief to the unworried certainty of the meteorological officers. A number of aircraft had been flying on the route at the same time as Easy Zebra. There was nothing out of the ordinary with the weather situation: a weak warm front, halfway across the Atlantic, giving widespread high cloud but very little icing. The assessors questioned them only perfunctorily. At six o'clock, the investigation into the weather and the aircraft state was concluded. Sir Ronald closed the proceedings for the day with the words: "Tomorrow, gentlemen, we will examine the qualifications of the crew."

The next day was wet and windy. Rain lashed in intermittent bursts against the diamond-shaped glass panes in the windows. Inside, it was stuffy and too warm. A lifeless gloom had settled on the room as Sir Ronald and the two assessors entered. There seemed a lack of energy, a reluctance to get started, to go any further with an incident that no longer anyone could do anything about. Knight poured out a glass of water and drank it. Papers rustled and feet tapped nervously on the bare wooden floor.

Then Captain Sanderson, the training officer, was called. He gave a brief résumé of Kelston's capabilities as a pilot, and a report on his last check flight, two months ago.

"He was a reliable pilot?" Knight asked him, with an apparent utter lack of concern.

"Well above average."

There followed details of the crew's careers. It was conclusively proved that they all had satisfactory experience and operational competence, until the name of Mr. Cockcroft was raised.

All Knight said was, "Bit inexperienced, wasn't he?" He still seemed very offhand.

Taking his cue from the assessor, Sanderson casually shrugged his shoulders. "With aviation expanding the way it is, it's impossible to get highly experienced first officers. The company is forced to employ pilots with a few hundred hours' flying. As far as we know, he was adequate at his job."

As though for the record, Knight continued, "But there are no six-monthly checks on first officers, like there are with captains?"

"No. There is no need. After their training, we rely on the Confidential Reports of the captains they fly with along the route. If a man is unsatisfactory, he is either brought back to the school for more instruction, or he is dismissed. Mr. Cockcroft had completed three round trips to Panama without adverse comment."

There was a short pause. Knight leant back in his chair, and pushed his hands deep into his pockets. Then he said in a quiet, toneless voice, "The court would like to see the reports on those trips. You have them with you, of course?"

The whole court room went dead quiet. Sanderson looked at Knight in surprise. The friendly atmosphere between them had vanished. When at last he answered, he seemed to be picking his way carefully through a verbal minefield,

"No report on Mr. Cockcroft was ever received in my office, as far as I can remember."

Knight's face wrinkled up into a puzzled frown. "As far as you can *remember,* Captain Sanderson? Surely, now this very serious accident has occurred, you've done a most thorough check through all your files?"

Sanderson said hastily, "Of course."

"What you really meant was that you are certain that no report on Mr. Cockcroft ever came through to you?"

Sanderson sat saying nothing. Suddenly, Knight's face turned bright crimson, as though his pent-up irritation had flooded all over it. His huge hands came out of his pockets, stretched over the table, and slapped down hard on the smooth polished wood. "Answer me!"

"Yes." The word was hardly audible.

"I wish—" Knight's voice was once more quiet, rather tired. "I wish people would say what they meant *first time.* It would make our job that much easier."

By no outward indication was there a sign that Knight's two loud words had altered the atmosphere of the court. Everything was quite calm again now. But the quietness was uneasy, tense, expectant.

Sir Ronald's soft voice sounded loud in the silence. "That seems odd, Captain Sanderson. You rely on these Confidential Reports. But none in this case ever got back to you."

Sanderson said stiffly, "Captain Leeming flew with Mr. Cockcroft last. I am sure he will be able to satisfy you on Mr. Cockcroft's competence."

In the circumstances, it was the only thing he could say, but he had prepared the pitch badly. The stage was already set as a battlefield, when Knight's bland, "Well, we'd better have a word with Captain Leeming then," summoned Michael Leeming to the stand. When he had sat down on the chair in front of them, he looked at the three men with large solemn eyes. Knight subsided into silence, biding his time. It was Graveney who asked him, "Why didn't you put in a report about Mr. Cockcroft?"

"I didn't think it was necessary. Quite often reports *aren't* sent in. No report obviously means that he was neither exceptionally good nor exceptionally bad."

"Then he was perfectly satisfactory?"

Just for a moment, Leeming hesitated. The sharp eyes of Captain Graveney noticed the pilot's doubt and pounced on it. "Did any incident occur that might have led you to believe he wasn't efficient?"

"He was inexperienced."

Graveney said impatiently, "We know that. Did he do anything wrong?"

Into the little pause, Group Captain Knight pointed out, "You are under oath, Captain Leeming."

Leeming sat there, studying the assessors' faces. He knew he could expect no mercy from Graveney. Unlike the professional close ranks of the doctors, pilots were nearly always the most scathing and definite in their condemnation of a technical error by one of their own kind, once a serious accident was involved. Then Knight appeared to be in a dangerous mood. With an effort, he explained his slowness to answer as, "I'm just trying to remember." He addressed the words to Sir Ronald Percival.

"Well, take your time," Graveney said quite kindly.

Leeming debated the matter in his own mind. All three of them were watching him now. He could feel Knight's eyes go right through him. He looked down at the floor, thinking it all out. But he knew he had to say something. In the end, unhappily and briefly, he told the court about nearly landing in the main street of Kingston.

In its own way, it produced the sensation that the court had been waiting for. Loud whispering broke out, and then died down to a still, expectant hush. It was as though everyone had been sitting there, watching a number of people walk across a tight-rope high in the sky. And now at last, one of them had fallen.

Graveney said, "Now you've managed to remember it . . . why on earth didn't you report him?"

"Everyone makes mistakes. He was inexperienced. I wanted to give him a second chance."

Now, Group Captain Knight came out of his corner. Snorting like a big black bull, he said, "So you hand him over to the company and to other captains as being perfectly competent to look after the lives of up to fifty souls? Is there anything else you can remember about him?"

Leeming hung his head. "He was inclined to be over-confident."

"And still you didn't think it necessary to put a report in?" Graveney asked.

The two pilot assessors, Knight and Graveney, went raging on at him, tearing to pieces anything he said. Finally, Leeming suggested miserably that Ferris had flown with Cockcroft. Twice. So Ferris was called to help him.

Not that he was any use. As item by item, the two of them were cross-examined on Cockcroft's flying ability, they only succeeded in proving that he was not competent to operate as second in command of a large passenger-carrying aircraft.

"Yet neither of you saw fit to let the company know that it was employing such an inefficient officer?" Graveney demanded.

With a touch of the old bravado, Ferris remarked, "I never write Confidential Reports, anyway. I prefer to tell 'em to their face."

"I think, Captain Ferris," Knight said slowly, "I think we shall have to trouble you to *write* them in the future."

In the end, it was Sir Ronald who cut short this heavily polite, one-sided discussion between the four pilots. "I think your point's taken, Graveney . . . Knight. We have all the information we want about Mr. Cockcroft."

Ferris and Leeming were allowed to go back to their seats in the hushed court. Leeming felt people looking at him in a new, contemptuous way. He was filled with the shame of being publicly asked questions that cast doubts on his professional integrity. Then, no sooner had he sat down beside Mr. Veitch than Sir Ronald said, "That finishes the inquiry into the crew's competence. Next is the fatigue angle you brought up, Knight. I'm afraid we'll have to ask Captain Leeming to come up again."

It was some time before he could be made to understand that his testimony was required once more. He had been lost in a daze of anger, thinking furiously that in any case this court was no more than a sop to appease the conscience of the public, that his humiliation was necessary so that others could hold their heads high. He got up at last and walked out again to the front with set tight lips and burning cheeks.

Sir Ronald asked him the questions this time. "It was your suggestion that the Azores night-stop come out?" He said the words quite sympathetically. Purposely, he seemed to be keeping Graveney and Knight away from him.

"It was in the company's own interests."

"Quite. But if the pilots had disagreed, obviously it would have stayed. Twenty-two hours seems a long time to remain actively alert on duty. Would you explain to me—a complete layman in such things—why you came to the conclusion it could safely be done?"

"Other companies do longer."

Sir Ronald smiled rather wistfully. "Not an answer, I'm afraid, Captain Leeming. Each company is responsible for its own mode of operation. Especially when an accident has occurred."

Leeming said defensively, "I'm not the line manager."

This reply seemed to disappoint Sir Ronald even further. "No . . . but Mr. Veitch is not a pilot. He is justified, I feel, in taking seriously the technical advice of one of his senior captains."

Leeming plunged into the whole question of crew-fatigue. He explained the undoubted second and third winds that a pilot experiences after long hours of flying, that in many cases he flies better when he is tired. Twice, he appealed to Graveney to support him. But Graveney was sitting at the side of the table that is never wrong. All he said both times was, "It all depends on the individual."

Knight sallied out with a blustering, "What I can't understand is that in America, and also in the R.A.F., there are most careful regulations governing the amount of hours on duty a pilot can do on transport flights. Even lorry drivers in this country have rigid legislation to safeguard them against being too tired for their job. But British airline pilots even go and ask—"

Sir Ronald interrupted him with a patient, "Quite, Group Captain Knight, quite. I had to tell Captain Leeming that comparisons were not allowed. We, on our part, must keep to our own rules. Now, Captain Leeming, please go on."

There was not much more to say. The pilot went through some of his own experiences. All Sir Ronald said when he had finished was, "I think there's no doubt about the fact that such long hours on duty can be done. Even regularly. But if an emergency arose, of whatever kind, a tired man's reactions are *bound* to be slower. Just when quick, efficient action is most needed." He peered down at the notes he had made. "Anyway, that's all, thank you, Captain Leeming."

Leeming was conscious that those mild-sounding words represented a sharp, unanswerable reproof. The court room seemed suddenly lined with hostile, curious faces. He kept his eyes on the floor all the way back to his seat. Dudley replaced him in the chair in front of the desk.

"Now, Mr. Dudley," Sir Ronald asked. "You are the station manager in the Azores?"

"Yes, sir." Dudley looked white-faced and anxious.

"You used to have a night-stop there?"

"The management took it out some months ago."

"Yes, yes. We know that. But after that time, Captain Kelston called for a rest there. Once for crew-fatigue. And once for weather. We have the reports you sent to Mr. Veitch on both those occasions."

Sir Ronald looked across at him, as though expecting him to say something. But Dudley had his mouth tight shut.

"Now you express your opinion," Sir Ronald went on, "in no uncertain terms that you considered the night-stops were unnecessary. And yet, we have had ample evidence that the first officers were inexperienced. As Captain Kelston says in his own report on the first incident, they apparently needed watching, which would put extra strain on the captain of the aircraft. And as for the second time—"

Dudley said swiftly, "Two Captains took off in the same weather."

Sir Ronald's mild voice suddenly sounded sharp as a sword, "But you did not put the weather conditions prevalent at the time in your report! We have them here. Three hundred yards' visibility. Well under the limits laid down by the company. And yet you give the very strong impression that Captain Kelston acted wrongly. Would you tell the court why you disagreed with him?"

But all Dudley could do was to mumble indistinctly about the other pilots, Ferris and Leeming. So for the third time, both of them were called out, and asked their reasons for taking off under company limits. Ferris did the answering for both of them. "Line Standing Orders," he said, "is just a guide. Not a rigid legal document. Both take-offs were accomplished perfectly safely."

"But you had trouble yourself, Captain Ferris?" Knight suggested smoothly. "With your undercarriage."

"I managed to put it right."

"Quite, Captain Ferris." Knight seemed to be emphasizing each word purposely. "You managed to put it right."

Leeming whispered bitterly to Ferris, when they were once more back in their seats, "You'd think we were responsible for the whole damned thing!" He was aware that this below-limit business represented his third public rebuke that day. Nothing definite was said. It was all covertly implied. *Somebody* had to get the blame for Easy Zebra's disappearance, and the court was in a conspiracy together to see how much of it they could pile onto his plate.

He sat there glowering at Sir Ronald and his two assessors for the rest of the afternoon. Amongst the majority of the people in the committee room, the tension had eased. There were ample signs now which way the wind was blowing. Away from the engineers, away from the meteorological officers, away from the loaders, all snug behind some impregnable protection, it was heading towards that unsheltered corner of the room where the line manager sat with Dudley and his senior pilots. Mr. Veitch was the last witness called. The plump figure, covered in a dark blue lounge suit, raised itself off the chair, and walked over to the three men at the far end of the room. With the head now bent heavily downwards, the odd little hour-glass looked as though it had snapped at the thin join between the two circles. The skin on the round face was ashen and strained. The sand seemed to have run out of it for ever.

Sir Ronald asked him, "You manage the six thousand mile route to Panama?"

"Yes."

"You rely on reports that are sent in to you. As we have seen, many of them are misleading. Some are nonexistent." Sir Ronald looked at the little man opposite him with obvious sympathy.

Mr. Veitch did not say anything. His whole attitude as he sat there implied that he alone was to blame, if it was decided that the company had been at fault. In a queer, misshapen way, Mr. Veitch put up a brave, rather moving front to the whole disaster. Unlike any of the others, as the questions proceeded, he made no effort to shift the responsibility away into somebody else's lap. These people were under him. Their mistakes were his.

It was suggested to him that he had been misled by reports, that he had attempted to control a business thousands of miles long from the far end, that he had been forced to rely on other people. All he said was, "That's my job."

"Did all the pilots agree to the night-stop being taken out?" Knight asked.

"Captain Kelston objected. On the grounds of crew-fatigue. And the need to inspect the aircraft at an approximate halfway mark."

"There was, after all, only one." They were making his excuses for him now.

"He also categorically advised me that all the aircraft should be modified together. Even though it meant grounding the fleet." Far from accepting gratefully their obvious leads, Veitch seemed even anxious to show how far he had been wrong.

"That would have been expensive," Sir Ronald said.

But Veitch seemed not to hear him. As though in some blind fit of penance, he went on. "He warned me about the first officer situation. And yet I told him that if he continued his unauthorized night-stops in the Azores, I would have him transferred to another route. I cannot get it out of my head that had I not done so, he might well have called a delay in the Azores that night."

Sir Ronald said gently, "We don't know what happened really, Mr. Veitch. There are indications that there might have been a fire again, caused by a short igniting hydraulic fluid. But there are only indications. There is nothing served by blaming yourself."

The line manager said wearily, "It was either the aircraft—or the crew. One or the other. Months ago, Kelston advised me to look after both of them. He reminded me of the Gibraltar crash. For some now unknown reason, I chose to disbelieve him."

There was never a word said of Karena and Kelston, and their relationship together in the Azores. In the code of society that these men observed, such affairs of the dead were beyond blame, beyond even talking about any more. By four o'clock, the court had decided it had collected all the evidence it was likely to get, and there was a brief interval before Sir Ronald's final summing up.

The Queen's councillor had tea with the two assessors in a private office. While the other two talked, Sir Ronald was unusually silent. He was thinking about this unknown pilot, Kelston, who had apparently foreseen months before the recommendations to the company he was about to advise. He might not know much about aircraft, but law had taught him a good deal about human nature. There was obviously some reason behind Veitch's repeated ignoring of Kelston's suggestions. He had realized that Dudley must have had some difference of opinion with the dead captain to send in such unfounded reports. In much the same way, there would undoubtedly be found some cause behind Leeming's failure to send in a report about an incompetent officer, his suggestion that the Azores' night-stop could come out, even his taking off from Santa Ana in weather conditions under company limits.

He sighed. It was difficult to know where to stop in such inquiries. If they were pushed to their final conclusions, the proceedings would last for years, involving many thousands of people, maybe, in fact, the whole of society itself, in an effort to establish the psychological reasons behind such actions. And they would be no further preventing another accident, or bringing to life the forty-seven souls on board Easy Zebra.

Then Sir Ronald turned to Graveney and Knight and discussed the summing up with them. It did not take long to reach a decision on the course it should take. There remained, in any case, the final published report, which would not be completed for another month.

But even though it was in many ways a formality, his summing up was careful and cautious. He said, "When an aircraft disappears completely, there is usually no evidence as to exactly what happened. This time, we have at least certain pointers as to the possible causes of the accident.

"We can say with certainty that it was either a failure on the aircraft's part, or a fault by the crew. Or possibly a combination of both. Certainly, the weather in the area has been proved to be not even a contributory cause.

"A similar aircraft disappeared on the same route over two years ago. For what reason nobody ever found out. Then a short time ago, a series of hydraulic leaks developed in the Marlboroughs culminating in a fire on board the very aircraft that disappeared. I am assured by the technicians that a short in the electrical system, combined with a hydraulic leak near the same position, is a most unusual circumstance, a million to one chance. Nevertheless, in view of the fact that hydraulic fluid was so inflammable, the company decided to modify the wiring away from the pipelines that ran throughout the fuselage. This was an expensive and lengthy operation, and they planned to have it done (since on the surface there appeared no urgency) as each aircraft went into the hangar for a complete overhaul. As it happened, Easy Zebra was not due for a Check Four, and remained unmodified. Now, if there was a fire in exactly the same position as before, it would account for no radio signals being sent by the aircraft, since both batteries supplying the power to all the electrical equipment would be quite useless.

"But we cannot say with any degree of certainty that this happened. All we can do is to suggest that it is a theory that fits the facts. There still remains no direct evidence of the actual cause of the accident. These pointers I mentioned may be a series of coincidences. Or they may not be. It is unlikely that we shall ever know.

"Now as far as the crew is concerned: Captain Kelston was a highly competent pilot. The rest of his crew were perfectly satisfactory, with the exception of the first officer. It is this court's opinion that Mr. Cockcroft was *not* competent to act as second in command of Easy Zebra. By a series of regrettable omissions, his incompetence was not brought to the attention of the company. This man might possibly have done something wrong. Certainly in an emergency, it would appear he would be nothing but a liability. Even in the best conditions, Captain Kelston would have to watch him, an extra duty that would contribute to his own fatigue.

"And then we come to this question: the fact that the crew were expected to work for nearly twenty-four hours on end. Even with a rest compartment, it would appear to be too much of a strain. If there was an emergency—and we obviously presume there was—I cannot help feeling that the crew would have acted more slowly than usual. At the very time when speed was essential for safety." He paused, and sat there thinking. Wistfully, he was turning over in his mind much the same idea that was haunting Mr. Veitch: that the fate of Easy Zebra might have been very different, if circumstances had not combined against Kelston calling a night-stop in the Azores. The court room in front of him was unbearably still. It was as though the facts painted a picture on thin air that everyone could see plainly, and yet it was made of nothing and could not be described.

The rain clattered against the windows, and drenched the grey, leafless trees in the square below. For a few silent seconds, those in the court room remembered the death of an aeroplane. And then, with a purposeful, matter-of-fact briskness, Sir Ronald recalled them back once more to a world that must go on living, whatever the cost.

Then he went on briskly, "It might have been the aircraft. It might have been the first officer. Or it might have been plain fatigue, combined with either one, or both of them. A lot of might-have-beens. In the end, we are left with a series of half-clues that end abruptly just at the moment they might be leading us to the cause of the accident. The real reason must still be considered a mystery.

"All the same, although there is no evidence that can be categorically accepted by the court, a number of practices have come to light which it is our duty to recommend that the company immediately overhaul.

"First, the system of Voyage Reports and Crew Reports in our opinion should be thoroughly tightened up, for the purpose of providing the company with an accurate picture of exactly what *is* happening on the route they operate.

"Secondly, we can see no point in calling Line Standing *Orders,* if they are open to interpretation by the pilots to whom they apply.

"Thirdly, we feel that first officers as well as captains should be given six-monthly checks on their competence.

"And last, nearly a day on duty flying an aircraft must be considered far too long. I believe the Marlboroughs are being overhauled, before a new Certificate of Airworthiness is granted to them again. When they are once more back in operation, we must insist on the Azores night-stop being reinstated."

Sir Ronald concluded with a few words on Kelston. There could be no doubt, he said, of his ability and farsightedness. He alone seemed to be able to see that things were snowballing, one on top of the other. He brought the attention of the management to the very facts that had come out in this inquiry. For some unknown reason, he was ignored.

"It's not the intention of this court," he went on, "to lay the blame of the disaster at anyone's door. Under the circumstances, that would be unfair. Mr. Veitch has a difficult job to do. Each in his own way, so have the others whose evidence we have heard. All the same, one cannot help getting the impression that Mr. Veitch would have acted on Captain Kelston's advice earlier, had he not been misled by a number of no doubt well-intentioned people who misrepresented the facts. Or who did not represent them at all."

For a moment, his eyes gazed severely at the little knot of individuals around Mr. Veitch. Ferris, Dudley, Leeming, Featherstone. Ferris looked straight back at him. Dudley was studying the floor. Leeming was considering indignantly the injustice of the innuendoes to which he had been subjected throughout the two-day session of the court. Featherstone appeared not to have heard him.

Sir Ronald had completed the inquiry now. He put the notes he had made back in his briefcase. He stood up, as a signal that everything was over.

As he passed through the door, Ferris whispered what was intended as a word of sympathetic comfort to those men besides himself on whom Sir Ronald's look had fallen: "No names . . . no pack drill."

3

Despite Ferris' comfortable reassurances to the contrary, the inquiry started off a chain of immediate and self-generating consequences. The fact that its recommendations had been immediately put into force did not prevent the newspapers from competing with each other in caustic comments. And the invisible ashes of Easy Zebra might be ghostly and cold, but they nevertheless provided a new supply of gunpowder for a number of Members of Parliament who had combined in pointing a large-calibre political cannon in the direction of the chairman of British Empire Airways.

It followed that a number of changes of the guard and a general tightening up of the defences had to be made. With the usual understanding sympathy in such cases, the line manager was replaced (not without misgivings on the part of the company that he would feel too restless chained behind a desk) by an experienced airline captain called Cotterell. It was felt on the credit side that, being a pilot, he would be more successful in interpreting the individualistic approach to life of his own kind. Mr. Veitch was swallowed up in some anonymous office, high up in the company's huge headquarters. Dudley was quickly transferred to the pool of station managers, a kind of no-man's land which provided temporary substitutes for places where the incumbent was away on duty or on leave. Featherstone lost the flight captaincy to a hard-bitten hunk of new blood from the North Atlantic. And Ferris and Leeming both received simultaneous letters, advising them that Line Standing Orders were now to be regarded not as a guide book but as a gospel, and disciplinary action would be taken against anyone who disobeyed them.

Mark Kelston was the only person who came out at all well in that inquiry. The company, as they always did, saw that his wife and his dependents were well provided for. Veronica received six times his basic salary—about nine thousand pounds—and added to Mark's own insurances of another six thousand, she was in a far better position financially than she ever had been before. She had said to her friends, "I won't pretend that it wouldn't have been a far greater shock to me if"—and a very long pause—"it hadn't happened." All the same, she wore black. She was still wearing it some weeks later, when she opened the front door at teatime and said to her fashion designer friend, "Why, this time, Ivor, you're even early!"

Back on the six thousand mile Mid-Atlantic route, there had also been changes. The grounding of the Marlboroughs for a month, while they awaited their new Certificate of Airworthiness, lost the company the Panama contract. The night-stop in the Azores was reintroduced. And the aircraft were carrying less passengers than ever before.

Nearly everything was a little further back than it had been four months ago. The counterclockwise winds had completed their furious full circle round the quiet heart of the storm. But there in the centre, Michael Leeming discovered, everything had remained oddly unharmed and undisturbed.

He had reached the captain's room in the Carreras Hotel, when he next went out on service, with a feeling of immense thankfulness. At last he felt the sense of peace and privacy he had so much longed for. His mind was now dizzy with its own troubles. Melanie had been so distant that it had been a relief to get away from Fairoaks. The inquiry still haunted his mind. And on the end of his crew list was once again the name of Miss Libby Challoner.

The quiet of the Captain's Room was oppressive. The heavy furniture brooded over him. The comforting, familiar noises of the hotel came, muted by the thick walls and the closed windows, as though from a long way away.

He walked out impatiently, along the corridor and out into the lights and the movement and the noise of the street below. He was carried along on the dark tide of men and women out for the evening promenade. The harsh street lamps hurt his eyes. He was jostled by anonymous arms and shoulders, and vaguely comforted by it.

A murky lighted window on the quayside drew him in by the glimpse of many faces and the sound of voices. He found himself a small table and ordered wine. The air was thick with the smoke and the smell of food and tarry overalls. A ceaseless deluge of human voices filled his ears.

Staring down into his wine, he was aware of a voice, softer and yet more insistent than the others. He looked up into a round pink face, gentle and concerned, fringed by tufts of white hair.

"Captain Leeming?"

He knew who it was. But because something in that face was like all that he had left behind in the Captain's Room, he said blankly, "I . . . I . . . don't think I . . ."

"I am Olivarez." The shipowner put out his hand. "You remember the time Easy Zebra was missing?"

"Of course." Michael Leeming got up and took his hand. "Won't you sit down with me? Wine? Or . . ."

"A glass of sherry, perhaps." Olivarez settled himself slowly into the chair opposite Leeming. Very gently, sipping the sherry the waiter had brought over for him, he looked across at the younger man's face. "So the nightstop is back after all?"

"After all."

There was a long pause. Then at last Olivarez said, "I knew him well. Captain Kelston. He saved my ship for me."

"And the girl?" Leeming asked. "Is she still here?"

"Still here, Captain. Still working for me." Olivarez paused. "But she is not the same. She is a different Karena."

Leeming looked into his wine-glass. Conscious of the overpowering sense of his own troubles, he yet made the conventional effort of sympathy. "Couldn't expect her to be, I suppose. The shock . . ."

Olivarez interrupted him. "You misunderstand me, Captain."

"She is upset, I suppose. But she'll get over it. With time . . . grief goes."

He spoke as though he was an oracle of truth and wisdom.

With much more sharpness in his voice, Olivarez said, "If that is true, then it has already happened. For this is not grief. Nowadays, it is as though she had found her peace. There is a serenity about her that you could almost call happiness."

Leeming said bitterly, "After all he gave up, his loss in the end meant little to her."

"To her, he is not lost."

The words, coming out above the babel of Portuguese

around them had a quiet dignity of their own. Olivarez went on, "Last week her visa for England was granted. I asked her if she would go." He paused.

"Well," Leeming said, "*will* she?"

Olivarez shook his head. "She said she would wait. She wouldn't go until Mark came . . ."

"You're not trying to tell me she still thinks he's alive?"

"That is what she believes. To see her belief is to be convinced yourself. It is as though . . . all the time . . . he is with her even now."

Leeming said shortly, "She doesn't know the Atlantic!"

Olivarez' eyes suddenly blazed. "And you, my friend, don't know love!" Then, moved by pity for the face across the table, he added more gently, "The power of love. The miracles it can work. Its everlasting quality."

"They had," Leeming said, "when all their meetings were added together, ten days with each other. That's all."

As though he had not heard him, Olivarez continued, "The timelessness of love."

"*Ten days!* And you talk to me about miracles and eternity!"

His voice, high and excited, echoed round the little room. The sailors stopped talking to glance curiously across at them, the Portuguese shipowner and the Englishman, sitting together in the sudden silence.

Unaware of them all, Olivarez went on, "Sometimes, I myself believe he will come back. Sometimes," his voice became a whisper, "that he already has." He looked at Leeming with a swift clarity. "But whatever happens, it is something that you cannot destroy. And of one thing I am certain. Never again will Karena be alone. As she has been so often. As so many people are now. And as you and me, my friend, will always be."

THE END